TEMPORALLY DEACTIVATED

TEMPORALLY DEACTIVATED

Edited by

David B. Coe
&
Joshua Palmatier

Zombies Need Brains LLC
www.zombiesneedbrains.com

Interior Design (ebook): April Steenburgh
Interior Design (print): ZNB Design
Cover Design by ZNB Design
Cover Art "Temporally Deactivated" by Justin Adams

ZNB Book Collectors #14

Kickstarter Edition Printing, June 2019
First Printing, July 2019

Print ISBN-10: 1940709245
Print ISBN-13: 978-1940709246

Ebook ISBN-10: 1940709253
Ebook ISBN-13: 978-1940709253

Printed in the U.S.A.

COPYRIGHTS

Table of Contents

Introduction by David B. Coe   1

"Keeper of the Light" by Ken Altabef   3

"The Eyes of Odin" by Alex Gideon   26

"All the Time in the World"   48
by Stephen Leigh

"The Other Walker" by D.B. Jackson   70

"My Dark Knight" by Faith Hunter   92

"Eye of the Needle" by C.S. Friedman   119

"Tempus Erratum" by Emily Randall   133

"Missy the Were-Pomeranian vs. the   153
Lord of Time" by Gini Koch

"The Mirror Trap" by Misty Massey   173

"Love and the Improper Unicorn"   183
by Rhondi Salsitz

"Schrödinger's Fractal"   205
by Edmund R. Schubert

"Clockwork Corsair" by R.K. Nickel   223

"Compassionate Retry"   240
by Marie DesJardin

"Neurons Lost and Found"   265
by Christine Lucas

About the Authors   276

About the Editors   281

Acknowledgments   283

SIGNATURE PAGE

David B. Coe, editor:

_____

Joshua Palmatier, editor:

_____

Ken Altabef:

_____

Alex Gideon:

_____

Stephen Leigh:

_____

D.B. Jackson:

_____

Faith Hunter:

_____

C.S. Friedman:

_____

Emily Randall:

_____

Gini Koch:

_____

Misty Massey:

_____

Rhondi Salsitz:

_____

Edmund R. Schubert:

_____

R.K. Nickel:

_____

Marie DesJardin:

_____

Christine Lucas:

_____

Justin Adams, artist:

_____

INTRODUCTION

David B. Coe

In 2015, I was fortunate enough to be an anchor author in a Zombies Need Brains anthology edited by Joshua Palmatier and Patricia Bray. The anthology had a wonderful origin story: Joshua had been in an airport and spotted a pay phone bearing a sign that read, "Temporally Out of Order." Not "*Temporarily* Out of Order," but "*Temporally*."

And a themed anthology was born.

Last year, when I received a phishing email that tried to steal my private information by threatening me with the "temporal deactivation" of my bank account, my first thought was to suggest that Joshua put together another "Temporal" project, a follow-up to the first. As it turned out, Joshua had received the same email, and was struck with the same idea. Before I knew it, we had agreed to co-edit the anthology.

This is my first foray into editing, and I have been helped immeasurably by my collaboration with Joshua. His expertise, his insights, his eye for narrative and character and pacing, and, most of all, his infinite patience with a newbie editor still trying to figure out how all of this works, have made this first project both a joy and an education.

The process has been made that much easier by the amazing authors who have contributed to the collection. We have stories of whimsy and of gut-wrenching drama. We have epic fantasy, urban fantasy, science fiction, steampunk, and stories that defy easy classification. I guarantee you, though, that every one of them plays with some interpretation of "Temporal Deactivation," and every one of them will keep you riveted.

So sit back, dive in, and enjoy!

KEEPER OF THE LIGHT

Ken Altabef

On a small island off Cape Cod, at the eastern approach to the Nantucket Sound, stands an ancient lighthouse. A perfect sphere surrounds the isle and its causeway, stretching a mile and a half in every direction. To the scientifically-minded, it's an interesting anomaly, an opaque bubble impenetrable to all known matter. For the more romantically inclined, rumor has it there is a man inside that lighthouse, and each and every day that man saves the world.

* * *

It was the beginning of the day, the end of the day, the end of the year, the end of the world. Denis McCullen glowered at the swirling black mass, so close now it filled a quarter of the sky. Even after so many years it still made his skin crawl. Billowing and swirling above, the thick oily cloud writhed as menacingly as if it were alive. Perhaps it was. They didn't know. Perhaps it was nothing more than a shadow, and yet death was in it. The death of the world.

Denis struggled with the lens, careful of the rough edges where salt air had corroded the iron. The fifth-order Fresnel, which threw a concentrated amber beam twenty miles across the channel, was not easy to move. The layered glass, shaped roughly like a beehive, hadn't sat properly in the swivel since a shoddy replacement two years earlier.

Two years, he snickered to himself. Two hundred years? Never matter. He gripped the lens. The timing of this need not be precise, but he liked to get it over with as soon as possible. With a practiced heave, he swung the beam up, away from Nantucket Sound and into the sky.

He recalled the first time he'd done it, so many days ago, years ago. The desperation, the fear. The cloud had come from someplace across the heavens at the tail end of 1910, just a few months after the passing of Halley's Comet. The hysteria surrounding the Comet, whose tail brushed the atmosphere amid widespread proclamations of doom and disaster, was as nothing compared to the panic caused by the cloud. The American Astronomical Society with its giant 60-inch glass and mirror eye at Mt. Wilson had tracked the thing as it cut a swath across known space, negating everything it touched, boiling away the atmosphere, carving a hole through the sky. The experts who studied such things—the movements of the planets, the alignment of the stars—scratched their heads, leaving everyone else to throw up their hands in hopeless surrender.

The religiously inclined loudly proclaimed that the cloud represented the wrath of an angry God, holy vengeance given form, a specter of judgment and immolation. As to how the people of the Earth had offended, making them deserving of such a fate, Denis held with the more traditionalist notions among his fellow Catholics. Modern society had meddled in things never meant for man, harnessing electricity and recklessly rattling the ether with radio waves. Whatever the cause, the clerics found themselves in solid agreement with the scientists on one point alone: there was no doubt what would happen when that cloud hit.

Death was on the wing and all the world held its breath in concert, helpless to halt its coming. Denis had been as terrified as anyone, staring up as that dark eye approached, knowing he had only a few hours left to live. And more than scared, he had been angry. After a lifetime of loneliness and a bitter, wandering existence he'd finally found happiness, finally a measure of peace in this place, with this woman. The thing in the sky would rip it all away.

The impenetrable black of it offended him, the inevitable crawl of it infuriated him. And in his rage, in a gesture of futile passion, Denis McCullen turned the lens of the lighthouse against it. An embittered stab of protest, nothing more. He had never expected what happened next, and to this day still did not understand it. When he cast his pathetic little light at the immense darkness, the darkness gave way.

When Denis signed on as keeper of the lighthouse at Arrow Point he'd been unaware of its long and shadowed history. Local fishermen were quick to fill in the gaps, pointing out ancient ruins amidst the breakers, all but wiped away by time and the sea, unknowable structures now reduced to a scattering of standing stones embedded in the beach. The mark of early man was on them, etched into the grim granite long before western civilization ever broached the northern continent. An ancient watchtower had preceded the lighthouse, built at a crossing of the ley lines, at a time when man still respected the mystical power of the Earth.

Turning the light skyward, shining it against the black cloud in an act of defiance that posited no chance of success, Denis McCullen saved the world. How could anyone guess that a protective reaction from the very Earth itself, a polarized energy as natural as the tides, would flow along the ancient ley lines, focused by the great lens?

As Denis swung the beam up toward the cloud, now as then, a bolt of earth energy coursed up along the iron struts of the tower and shot through the lens, shattering the jeweled surface into a million fragments as it surged to meet the black cloud. Denis had witnessed this same miracle every day for a hundred years, but found it no less amazing each time. A few shards bounced back into the lighthouse tower. Denis was ready for them without having to think about it, turning away to protect his face. He didn't cover his eyes because he wanted to watch. Denis saw the cloud begin to recede, pushed away by the force of the blast. But this time, the cloud wasn't what he wanted to look at.

This time, fear and rage forgotten, thoughts of solemn duty put on hold, he was more interested in the snow. The view across the Sound from the lamp room was spectacular all year round, but never so much as when a light snow dusted down to meet the sea and kiss the beach with frost. It rarely snowed this early in the winter, and in his tenure at Arrow Point he'd witnessed this miraculous sight only once before.

It was a gentle snow but thick, slowly wafting down. And as he watched, the flakes stopped in mid-air, held still for a second, then two, frozen in place, and then began to drift lazily upward, swirling back the way they had come. For a precious minute, it was snowing upward.

Denis stood amazed, grinning like a child.

Kaela called his name and he turned, smiling. "Did you see?" he asked, pointing at the sky. "The snow?"

She shook her head; she'd been climbing the stairs during that frozen moment, coming to tell him that his breakfast was ready. She smiled back at him, waif-like, drinking in his delight, a light filigree of snow frosting her raven hair, her cheeks flushed pink by winter's icy tickle. She wore a sheepskin coat against the chill and the wool at her cuff roughed his skin as she took his hand.

Her hand had cooled with the December air but, clasped in his, it was also warm because she loved him.

"You're beautiful," he said.

* * *

Quite often after breakfast she would sing to him on the watch deck. Kaela knew an impressive catalogue of folk songs from Cyprus and the Sporades, learned on silver-bright mornings in her mother's arms, a treasured slice of her childhood that she carried always with her. She sang as winter reversed into fall outside their windows and the dead oaks sprouted withered leaves of crimson and ochre and yellow.

As Kaela's vocals filled the air with spirited melody, Denis clapped along, providing his own off-beat accompaniment. She sang the *Galatiad*, the song of the secret lovers Galatea and Acis, who carried on their affair beneath the watchful cruelty of the Cyclops Polyphemus, the two eventually transforming into a river, flowing together. It was one of Kaela's favorites and Denis wondered if she saw in it a charmed reflection of their own lives, with her father cast in the role of the Cyclops. As she moved along the circular watch deck, Kaela seemed a perfect gypsy, hair billowing freely on the autumn breeze, a blue and white summer dress fluttering this way and that, carefree and laughing. She couldn't keep perfect pitch, but her audience of one never seemed to mind and she danced on with wild abandon, covering her mistakes with an extra flurry of the hem of her dress or wave of her arms.

She loved the mornings most of all, especially the way the early sunlight played against the striking landscape below. The open-air watch deck offered a glorious panoramic view of the island. Of course, to appreciate the beauty, one had to first ignore the ugly black cloud receding against the featureless gray bubble of the sky.

As the seasons played out backwards, the woods blazed with fall color, stands of silver maple erupted in yellows and reds, and the thicket of scrub oak circling the lake painted itself rusty brown, gold, and purple. The autumn colors burst forth from the bare branches like fireworks, a living pageant of color. Kaela danced across the catwalk, waving a red bandana, with that rouged and gilded foliage as backdrop, until the leaves all turned a uniform green and Kaela fell, exhausted, into Denis' arms, the bandana set loose across the Sound.

The best time for a swim, they had learned, was shortly after noon when early fall turned to late summer. And the best place for a swim was the lake on the south of the island. Nantucket Bay was far too choppy. Good for splashing and frolicking, but when they wanted quiet time, or if they wanted to see the sky, it was always the lake.

At first, they'd been able to see through the bubble. Denis knew a thing or two about naked-eye astronomy as taught aboard ships, and he marked Orion's movements against the night sky. There was no doubt about it. Time was passing normally for those outside the bubble, while its two occupants lived each day as a year in reverse, the black cloud retreating into the sky. But time could stretch backward only so far until, like an elastic band, it shot forward again, resetting itself at the end of each day.

The stars were gone now. After perhaps twenty years or so, they could no longer see the other side. With repeated resets the surface of the bubble, marred slightly with each backward turn of the clock, became increasingly worn like a phonograph recording played too many times—such scuffing eventually faded their sky to a sheet of opaque gray.

But at the lake they still had the reflection of sky on water. When the summer wind was still, the surface lay a luminous blue feathered with white. By mid-day the black cloud had diminished to a coin equal in size to the rippling oval of the sun, a dark twin sharing the sky. They stared at the sky in the lake for quite some time before breaking the surface with their bodies and churning the heavens with their rollicking and splashing. The water was warm in the late summer and they had the sunshine if not the sun itself, warm on their skin. Denis tied a rope to a convenient overhanging branch and Kaela perfected swinging dives into the limpid pool. Denis dove for treasure in the murky depths. Of course, he found none, save the woman in his arms.

The lake was their own private oasis, complete with a perfect stretch of beach. They often lay naked on the sand, Denis making a study of the patterns in the drops of water drying on his wife's smooth, flawless skin.

"How long has it been?" she would ask.

"Hard to keep track, living a year every day. A hundred years or two hundred?"

"Oh, we could stay this way a thousand years, two thousand. Our own world. Every day a perfect day." She sat up, knocking all the little pearls of water loose and ruining his game. "Everyone in the world gone, and only us, starting each day over. Forever."

Denis nodded in solid agreement. Wildflowers sprung up beside the water, coaxed by the honeyed sunlight. The only thing missing from the perfect scene was birdsong. Starlings used to make their nests in the pines, flitting above them, but over time they'd all dared across the barrier and were gone. None had drifted in to replace them. So many things had been lost to them. They didn't have moving pictures, the world's fair, a radio or telephone, high fashion, Isadora Duncan, or a friend in the world. They didn't need the world. They had the stream, the pools, April showers, sunny days. They had laughter. They had each other.

Denis regretted none of it. He could do without the world which had served him up nothing but bitterness and thankless toil, savage beatings at the hands of raving quartermasters, two fingers lost to frigid North Atlantic swells, nights in friendless seaboard towns and scornful looks from those who considered themselves his betters, but he quavered when he thought of all that Kaela had lost. He'd given up nothing, but she had forsaken everything: wealth, status, family. All for him.

At thirty-five, Denis had felt a little childish hiding from her father's wrath at Arrow Point, but life had taught him the futility of opposing the rich and powerful. Giorgio Itasca was a self-made millionaire, a self-made shipping magnate, a self-made pompous ass. The vainglorious might fight someone like him, but they could not win. Denis was without a cent, a third-class crewman on a cargo freighter, but firm in the conviction that there were some things in life far more important than money. He first glimpsed Kaela from the deck of the *Phaedra* when she was eighteen, walking beside her father along the pier. He returned a year later, took a job as a construction hand on Itasca's Cypriot villa annex, and managed a chance meeting. The odds were against him, but he had a poetic heart and she read the blazing devotion in his eyes. The age difference was inconsequential, but the gap in social status was impossible. So they did what they wanted, what they desperately needed, and they ran. A year later they were married on this very island by a Nantucket priest sworn to secrecy, with Denis' brother George and his wife Greta the only witnesses.

"Are you content, Denny?" she asked.

"More than content. As happy as I have ever been, and more than I ever imagined possible."

She rolled on top of him, her dark eyes glistening, her delicate lips gently parted. As her weight settled against his hips, he pulled her toward him, burying his face in the forest of her night-black hair. She pulled back again, her tender smile hovering just above his own. He had given up wondering what she saw in him; her contented, amused gaze answered eloquently enough, obviating the need for bothersome particulars. It was enough to know that she was satisfied. She feathered him with kisses, her lips brushing velvet against his neck and chest. They made love in slow languorous movements, each so fully acquainted with the preferences and desires of the other, Denis burying his face in the hollow of her neck, inhaling her quickening breath, smelling of bayberries and coriander. He measured her expression as she flushed from excitement to release. Her hair, wild after their lovemaking, fluttered against his cheeks, tickling his lips.

He closed his eyes.

A moment later, he was startled awake by what seemed a desperate, piercing cry. A flash of cold sweat, as if he'd just experienced the recoil. But it was August, the middle of the day. It could not have been the recoil.

Kaela lay still. He watched her face, disconcerted in sleep, as if she were disturbed by some dark dream.

The only discomfort in their lives was the recoil, when time lurched forward again in the early morning, pulling them roughly out of sleep, twisting their stomachs violently inside out. Sometimes Kaela, who had a weak constitution, gagged or vomited as Denis got up, pulled on a wool sweater and ascended the tower stair to his waiting business with the dark cloud.

It took them a few days to understand the bizarre circumstance that had ensnared them. The first day, after watching the lens blow itself apart, Denis rejoined the others in the lighthouse. His brother George and his wife were visiting, and they had decided to spend the day together, in quiet pursuits, even if it be their last.

Denis told them what had happened in the lamp room, the fateful blast of light, the reprieve accorded to the world by his unwitting hand. During their picnic lunch by the lake, they watched the writhing inkblot move back up the sky. A miracle!

That night, the recoil stirred them all out of sleep for the first time as if some ghostly hand had seized their innards and wrung them inside out. An intense sensation of dread led Denis unerringly to the tower window. Again the cloud was there. Close. As close as it had been the day before. He rushed to the lens, which he found no longer shattered but whole and unbroken. He did not hesitate. He redirected the beam and the events of the previous day played out again. The lens erupted, releasing the white-hot discharge from the bowels of the earth, forcing the slow retreat of Death in the sky.

To their amazement, the food they'd consumed the day before was still in the pantry, the containers unopened. The gift of fresh eggs George had brought from Boston sat yet again atop the counter, made to reappear by the invisible hand of some unseen magician's trick. Their clothes were not where they had left them, but where they had previously been. The chest of drawers George and Denis had been building in the sitting room was again disassembled and awaiting their tender care. As explanation for these wondrous happenings, they had not a single reasonable theory among them. During the next day, amid a repeat of bizarre weather which took them again from winter through fall to summer, they discovered the bubble, a barely noticeable haze arcing up and around the island like filigrees of frost lacing a windowpane. And in the wee hours of the morning, came again the recoil.

Theirs was a universe in and of itself; the bubble preserved the world around it while remaining wholly apart. Time was irrelevant and if magic existed anywhere in the world, it was with them. As each day reset itself, Kaela remained forever nineteen years old, perpetually young and beautiful, and in love. Denis would do anything to preserve their life together. Almost anything.

As they lay on the beach, Denis pulled up a handful of sand, weighing the grains in his palm as they rushed to slip through his grasp, drawn inevitably back down. He flung it away. The image upset him. What was sand anyway, but fractured shards of rock and shell? He had answered her question of his contentment too quickly, the answer not quite a lie because it was so close to being the truth. He could have lived this way forever and been happy for it, except for the one thing. One tiny little thing. They dared not speak of it lest it shatter the spell, but unspoken or not, he could bear it no longer.

Denis blew gently against Kaela's eyelids. Her eyes fluttered open.

"You fell asleep," he said.

"I was having a dream of Time." She shook her head, casting aside sleep's last cloying tendrils. "You were there. We were caught up in a flow of quicksilver. I've always thought of Time as a river flowing steadily downstream, but there are eddies in any river, this one a circular pool of mercury. We let it take us, round and round—"

"A calliope ride…"

"Mmmm. That puts us back just where we started. Is that so bad?"

"Not at all, in the right company," he said. "If it were just the two of us…"

Her face deadened as if he had just dared to call a ghost by name, and she stood for a moment, silent. She picked up her dress, angrily shaking out the sand and hugging it to her chest. "What happens if you try to scoop quicksilver up?" she asked, angrily. "Try to hold it in your hands? What happens then?"

"I don't know."

Her unanswered question seemed to walk silently beside them as they went looking for mid-summer wildflowers, huckleberry and peppermint, in the meadow to the west. A series of flat, radiant stones glittered amid the abundant green, forming a natural walkway through the narrow glade. As he looked down, one lone tear spattered against one such stone.

* * *

That evening, as the summer cooled toward spring, they enjoyed an outdoor supper. They dined most often in the field just below the tower, on the promenade by the sea which they had nicknamed Mermaid Avenue. Kaela was a fine cook and she worked wonders with their dried stores, fixing meals so delicious they could almost forget they were eating the same food every night.

Often, after dinner, he would tell her romantic stories while she sat on his lap, eyes closed, smiling. He devised epic sagas to her immense delight, featuring his hot-tempered ancestor Bloody Bill McCullen, a daring swashbuckler who had a disgruntled but basically good-hearted kelpie as a first mate and a mermaid for a wife.

After dinner, Kaela wandered away. She'd always been fond of solitary walks on the beach at sunset. It took him a long while to catch on, a delay he attributed to men being much thicker than women, and even longer to make up his mind to talk to her about it. But now it had to be done. He followed after her, leaving the picnic things where they lay. A delicate silver tray, the lone carryover from her former life, the wooden bowls, the dented, mismatched cutlery and frayed linen. There was no need to carry any of it back to the tower. In time, it would all find its own way home.

Denis watched as Kaela bent to pick up a flat piece of shale and carried it to a bed of marigolds in the shade beneath a stand of wilt-pine. She probably used the same stone each time, he thought. She knows just where to find that flat stone, just how to set it up. Such a practiced look on her face. How many times?

One day Denis had set about building a rowboat so that they might spend an afternoon drifting lazily on the lake. He spent an entire day in a heroic effort to make a seaworthy craft, using wood from the cabinetry he and George could never finish assembling. The second coat of pitch had barely dried in time for a sunset cruise. Of course, the next day it was gone.

They could not make their mark here. They could change nothing, build nothing that would withstand the recoil. Their existence was entirely wraithlike, insubstantial.

How many times had she laid that flat stone?

Was this marker for the child they had just conceived, he wondered, or in memoriam of the one from yesterday, lost in the recoil? Or the one before that? Erased. Like so many of their children.

Denis strode toward her. A low pine branch switched against his bare arm, stinging a thin red welt across his skin as he crossed the thicket. He came up behind his wife as she knelt among the marigolds.

"How do you know?" he asked. "We only made love this afternoon."

"A woman just knows."

"Does it happen every day?"

"Only sometimes," she sighed.

"Today?"

"Yes." She turned to look up at him, still kneeling by the flowers, eyes glittering with sorrow. The sky was, as ever, a featureless gray, but the lake burned scarlet as daylight rapidly dwindled away, casting her sadness in shadow.

"We can't go on like this," he said. "You know that."

She began to sob and turned away as hopelessness poured out of her eyes. They were so happy together. She had hoped never to speak of this.

"He–"

"–or she–" Kaela interjected.

"–deserves a chance," he said.

"No matter the cost?"

For a moment he thought he might not have the strength to answer. His gaze trailed away, settling upon the little slab of shale, the nameless marker. How great must the sacrifice be, how many pregnancies erased?

"You can't put up another one of those markers," he said, "Not another one. How few hours would it stand? Just until the early morning, when the recoil puts it back." He knocked the marker down. "Not this time. Not one more. You know I'm right."

"You need me here with you," she said.

"Yes. But now I need you to go."

They knew it was possible to leave, because George and Greta had gone. On the second day, George decided to row to the mainland and return as soon as he learned anything.

They watched him don his straw hat with comically exaggerated determination and tread along the causeway to pass effortlessly through the bubble. Hours later he did return, but could only stand outside, unable to traverse the barrier, pressing his hands against its surface. No way back in, he stood soundlessly battering against it. Greta hesitated not a bit. She ran down the causeway, plunging herself out after him. Denis and Kaela watched as their friends embraced on the other side. George signaled for them to follow, but Denis held back. They didn't dare leave. They still had the death cloud to contend with, and Denis was convinced the lighthouse beam was the key factor. If no one remained to shine the light…

After a while George and Greta shrugged, blew them kisses, and waved good-bye.

* * *

"Don't turn around," he whispered.

Don't turn around. They had already said good-bye a hundred times. He'd wiped away her tears with his hands, his shoulder, his face; and she had wiped his. Now she stood before the bubble, far out along the causeway, facing the uncertain future. She seemed small, doll-like, as if she'd already left him. He felt old, as if all two hundred years had suddenly crashed in upon him like a tide at the beach, as if being perpetually thirty-five was a fantasy made of delicate glass, which must now end.

Kaela paused before the bubble, that opaque cataract, that evil eye through which they could no longer see. And he could tell that she was trembling, probably weeping, but he would not wipe away the tears now. Not this time. Not ever again. Please don't turn around, Kaela. Step through. Resolution wanes in these final moments. You must be strong.

"What do you think it's like," she had asked him, between tears, earlier that day, "out there after so many years? What kind of world?"

"I'll bet it's just the same. People don't change," he replied in a faltering voice. "Taller buildings and faster horsecars, I'd imagine. You'll be fine." Truth be told, he was not so sure. She'd been raised in wealth and privilege, swathed in fine French silks and primrose lace, all of which she cast away in favor of his company. Nineteen years old, and alone, she returned to the world with nothing. Nothing but a whispered prayer, his undying devotion, and an intense hope for what she carried inside her womb. As far as he was concerned, this was the bravest thing anyone had ever done. How much easier to stay with him? How much easier for them both. And yet, impossible.

One more step and she'd be gone. He watched, shivering, trembling in horror, but he could not regret the decision they had made. She stepped through slowly, sinking face-first into a sea of milk, and vanished, leaving not so much as a ripple behind. Did she linger on the other side, he wondered, did she turn, calling his name, and beat her fists against the barrier? He had no way to know. So he chose to imagine her striding confidently down the causeway, stepping out of one life and into another. Denis took consolation in this: she would never be alone.

* * *

Alone.

Alone, he had good reason for getting up in the morning but not for much else. Each day the recoil woke him from cold dreams, almost a blessing, its wrenching pain practically welcome if such a thing were conceivable, its rough touch his only companion.

Each day, each year, he mounted the slick steps of the tower to perform his duty. In the past, repelling the cloud had been an act of self-interest as he began each new day with nothing in mind except to spend the day with her. But now it was merely a duty, a responsibility that rested not on the shoulders of a cleric or a wizard or some great man of science, but had fallen upon him, a common seaman, a lighthouse keeper. Death loomed again. And again. With nobody to prevent it except the man alone in the bubble. He stood for hours on the causeway, within a hair's breadth of the barrier. In darkly melancholic moments he was tempted to step through, consigning the world to oblivion. But he would never do that. He would forever hold the line.

He turned the lens each day, setting light against the seething darkness. There was only enough fuel in the lamp for a week, but because of the recoil it would last forever.

He gave no more thought to Bloody Bill McCullen or mermaids or kelpies. What use fanciful tales if there was no one to share them with, no eager grin, no anticipatory raised eyebrows, no questing eyes. No appreciative smile.

He studied the featureless gray of the bubble with a fevered intensity, sometimes imagining he saw a crack here or there, or a frantic shadow assaulting the other side. The quiet was unnerving, the solitude complete. All the animals and birds had drifted out through the barrier and none could enter to replace them. The erratic weather had killed off all the junebugs, crickets, and caterpillars.

He spent a lot of time among the rocky crags near the ocean. He avoided the lake—its cheery reflection irritated him now. Memories of the happy life they had lived lapped cruelly at the beach. He took long walks on the shore, but only at night.

Time passed, the days blurring into each other as the years raced by, running like weak soup, eroding canyons down his cheeks.

And one day, as the last man on earth dozed dejectedly on his pallet, there came a knock on the door.

Denis thought he'd imagined it, as he had imagined so many sounds in the night of late. But it came again. A determined rapping at the door. Good Lord, he thought, I've passed in my sleep, I've forgotten to shift the beam, the end has come. He turned over and closed his eyes, pressing his face against the bedding. If it be the Grim Reaper at his door, he damn well wasn't going to answer.

The door creaked open. After all, there was no lock.

A figure stood framed in the doorway. Tall, broad at the shoulder, the man seemed dressed for adventure—hiking boots, khaki pants, a denim shirt with the sleeves rolled halfway back, a strange long-billed cap on his head. The hat, which Denis found as ridiculous as a jester's belled foolscap, was emblazoned with the face of a leering buccaneer and a logo which read: Pittsburgh Pirates. The stranger wore a pleasant grin that bore close resemblance to brother George, but there was Kaela in his face as well and Denis knew who he was even before the stranger said, "Father?"

Of course he was father, not Dad. There was a difference. Dad was someone who took you for walks in the woods and to boxing exhibitions, who taught you to fish, or how to handle a rifle. Dad was someone who gave you piggyback rides at the cost of his sacroiliac. What do you call someone who gave you life and nothing else? You call him father.

"This isn't possible," muttered Denis. An instant later, a hopeful glow flashed behind his eyes, "The barrier?"

The man in the doorway shook his head. "It still stands, I'm afraid. May I come in?"

Denis waved him in and as soon as he was within arm's reach, hugged him close. He held on for quite a while, not even a little embarrassed by the tears streaming down his face. Then, seized by a sudden horror, he pushed his son roughly away so he could ask, "Your mother?"

"She's fine." The young man, several inches taller than Denis, gazed down at him with undisguised adoration. Denis had so many questions to ask he hardly knew where to start. How was she really? Did she blame him for sending her away? Had she gone on with her life? Remarried? It had been a long time. He wouldn't blame her. From this myriad of questions, Denis stumblingly chose, settling by chance upon the one perfect question whose answer spoke to all of them. He asked his son's name, which turned out to be Dennis McCullen.

Denis felt suddenly stronger than he had in years, and hungry. He bade his son sit down at table while he drizzled water over a crusty slab of ship's biscuit and laid out salted pork, rice, and warm beer.

"How did you live?" he asked.

"Mother had an inheritance. No legal claim to it after all that time, under the bizarre circumstances, but that didn't mean the Itasca family wouldn't recognize her. After a simple DNA test—I'm sorry—that's a medical test, a way they have to see what family you come from. We were well provided for."

Denis nodded. It was better than he'd dared hope. His misgivings about the type of reception a young pregnant woman might receive alone in the world was a heavy burden now lifted.

"You said the barrier still stands...?"

"Yes, it goes a mile and a half in every direction, even skyward. They have to keep the air traffic away from it—"

"Air traffic?" asked Denis, breaking off a piece of the ship's biscuit but not yet willing to suspend conversation long enough for chewing.

"Flying machines. Jets. Helicopters. And some idiot tried to climb the dome once—"

Denis waved him off. All that could wait. "Not yet, not yet. I need to know how you got in."

"It's sort of difficult to explain in a way that you'd understand. Having been conceived in this place, moving backwards through time, my atoms have a reverse temporal signature—a slightly irregular spin. That makes me just a little bit different than most folks. Not so you'd notice standing next to me on the bus, but on some level, I have a kind of negative polarity relative to the barrier.

"You see, the barrier itself—the entire bubble—is constantly moving backward in time, and that's why it can't be breached from the other side. Not unless somebody invents time travel I guess. But, like I said, I'm different. The barrier is still one-way, but for me it's the reverse. The same way that you can leave but never return, I could get in but I can never pass out again."

"You can't leave?" said Denis, his tone the sharp rebuke of a father shocked by the foolish behavior of his child.

"No, I can't. And no one else can get in either. Not that they'd want to. Few people even believe this place exists anymore."

"Why not? Don't people remember the panic of 1910?" asked Denis, incredulous. "The end of the world?"

The younger man cleared his throat. "Well, kind of…a lot of time has gone by. The whole thing is generally regarded as sort of a myth now. Not many people think it actually happened, that it's just part of the mystique of the null-bubble. A made-up story."

"But the cloud. The cloud. I thought by now, with all these marvels of which you speak, I thought they would have figured out what it is, how to get rid of it. Surely—"

"You don't understand, Father," said Dennis. "The cloud is trapped inside the bubble. They have no way to access it."

They sat in silence for a moment, as Denis tried to take the measure of the man who sat across from him. Thankfully, he had removed the ridiculous cap. The young man's attitude seemed much too cavalier, even a bit sappy, all smiles and barely-concealed excitement, but that could very well be explained by a meeting with his long-lost father. Did he know what he'd gotten himself into? Did he really understand the curse he'd undertaken by coming here?

"How old are you, son?"

"Twenty-eight."

"So young! I wanted you to have a life—"

"But I did! Father, I've walked under the sea, surrounded by the living rainbow of the Great Barrier Reef. I've been to Japan and Australia. I climbed the Great Pyramid at Gizeh and stood nose-to-nose with the Sphinx. I was married for five years to the most wonderful woman on Earth. From the comfort of my living room, while snacking on pizza, I watched a team of men set foot upon the planet Mars."

Denis' jaw gaped. He wanted to hear every fantastical detail but it would all have to wait. More pressing business first.

"If you can't leave, at least we'll be together," Denis added. "It won't be so bad. You'll see."

The younger man slapped his hand on the flat of the table. "That's not what I want," he said firmly. "For her."

The words rang out through the lighthouse like a pair of gunshots. The smile was gone, his face flushed a healthy shade of Irish.

"What?" Denis saw determination in his son's eyes, the firm resolution of a man, not a boy. He liked what he saw.

"She's been waiting a long time, Father."

"If you're twenty-eight," said Denis, "Kaela would be, what, forty-eight?"

"Yes. Forty-nine tomorrow. And she ages a year each day that passes here. So, you'll have to hurry. You'll leave first thing in the morning, just as soon as you show me what to do with the lens."

"Forty-nine…" Denis tried to imagine Kaela's face aged with the years. He found he could see her clearly, her knowing smile, her wild beauty mellowed by time but not tamed.

His mind swam with the possibilities. He was still only thirty-five. A reprieve from this personal purgatory would be a gift beyond imagining but by passing through that milky doorway he would be consigning his son to oblivion. How could he leave Dennis alone in this place? And how could he not, with Kaela waiting on the other side? "Do you know what you're saying? Do you understand—"

"I know all about this place, and all about you," said Dennis. "Mom made sure of that."

"I meant for you to live your life and be happy," said Denis, "not to trade places with me. Not to take on my burden."

"Why not? You took on ours, you took on the whole world's burden." Once again Denis saw a new side to this strange man at his table, a wisdom and maturity which his pleasant demeanor had conveniently hidden. There's so much I don't know about you, thought Denis. And if I do go, only one night to know my son. Such little time.

"And besides, I *was* happy," added the son. "For a time. I was married for five blissful years. My wife died, Dad. She died. You didn't cause the cancer that took her from me. It just happened. So you see, I had my chance. I had my happiness but it's gone. And don't you dare tell me there'll come another, or I'll belt you one, father or no."

Denis scooped some curried rice into his mouth to cover the beginnings of a coy smile. He was saddened by his son's loss, no doubt, but couldn't help an incredible swell of pride just then. Kaela had done so well with their boy. How hard that must have been, without him there to help.

"I left some gear down at the end of the causeway," said his son. "I'll go and pick it up."

"How did you know you'd get through?"

"I didn't. I just had a hunch. We're terrific ones for hunches, us McCullens."

Denis smiled at that. He had no choice but to agree. "All right, let's us two have a walk."

It was mid-summer on the island. Denis squinted against the shouting sunlight as if he'd been asleep for years. The pair strolled along Mermaid Avenue. "What was that you said about flying machines?"

Dennis began regaling his father with the wonders and technology of his time, but cut himself short. "That's not what I want to tell you about. You'll learn all about those things soon enough, even take a ride in one I'll wager. Let me tell you about Olivia."

"Who?"

"My wife."

"Tell me."

If Denis had any doubts about the fitness of his son for the task ahead, the items at the end of the causeway dispelled them all. There was no need to wonder if his son was the right choice to be the world's guardian, to keep this lighthouse in perpetuity, to stand alone, the last bastion against the dark. What had he brought with him? Not scientific equipment with a goal toward analysis and finding a way out, but a boxboard full of paints and a canvas. One single canvas. He knew what he was doing.

* * *

The best time for painting, he found, was late in the afternoon when summer began its fizzle into late spring. He set up shop in the long grass below the lighthouse tower where the meadow afforded rich, unobstructed sunlight. With slow and precise care he applied details to the painting, often spending hours on the highlights of her hair. He still hadn't gotten it right, the expression of wistfulness about the eye, the playful turn of her lips. But there was plenty of time. In the 1890's Claude Monet painted the facade of the Rouen cathedral seventeen times, in varying shades of daylight, until he got it right. Each one a masterpiece.

In the forty years since he'd met his father, Dennis thought often of his parents. They were likely gone now. He could only wonder what changes were going on in the world he protected, what new technological marvels were being developed in think tanks and laboratories and home offices. He believed that eventually they would find a way through the barrier. If not, he was content. As far as he was concerned he'd taken his chances, played his cards. He had already died long ago, holding Olivia's hand in a hospital room in Philadelphia. All the rest was just an extra moment, one beat of the heart, no time at all. Perhaps it would not be forever. No way to know. He would be here, still painting. Her face.

THE EYES OF ODIN

Alex Gideon

I stepped onto the Branch of Midgard the way a drunk steps into the night. Shaky. Woozy. About to vomit. Certain I didn't want to be here. As soon as the tachyonic shift ended, I turned and hurled all over the nearest wall.

When Laplace Corp first implanted the Eye of Odin, they told me I'd feel some slight discomfort when I walked between branches of time. The lab coats must have been through some shit to have the confidence to say that. Each walk felt like running on the bottom of the ocean. Except someone had replaced the water with broken glass and dirty needles and had set the whole fucking floor on fire.

When I finally stopped puking, I took in my surroundings. A dirty alley. Which narrowed my possible location down to any-goddamn-where in spacetime. This was a Midgard Branch though, which meant Homo Sapiens. Good. A lot easier to blend in here than among the tiny red bastards of the Helheim Branches. From the smell of piss and the depressing architecture, I imagined myself somewhere in the twentieth or twenty-first century by this Branch's reckoning.

Atlanta, Georgia. The United States of America. Year 2018 AD, said a voice in my head I didn't recognize. I hated when my agent changed. I liked building a rapport. It made the job easier.

"E.R.T.A., dress me in something standard, circa Midgard, 2018." A ping sounded in my head and my skin crawled as my Ergonomic Recombinating Tactical Armor reformed itself. A damned useful bit of tech. Thousands of preloaded outfits and nothing existed on the lower branches that could destroy it. I'd never get used to the sensation, though.

E.R.T.A. settled on a plain t-shirt, jeans, and tennis shoes. Comfortable and economic. I reached up and touched the comm in my temple. "How far to Nareena's tachyonic disturbance, new guy?"

Just a couple of city blocks. Almost a straight line. Turn around. At the end of the alley, I saw several skyscrapers. At least, what passed for them on this branch. *Now start walking.*

I smiled as I did just that. I liked this one. I touched my comm again. "What's your name?"

Eat a dick.

"Sounds foreign. I like it."

Heard you were funny. I'm Ereth. Glad I got the chance to work with the legendary *Kahlan Kade.* The agent chuckled as I stepped from the alley into the horde of people on the streets. I winced at the sarcasm.

Stop.

A command to my suit. The sudden halt bounced my brain around in my skull. "What the fuck, newbie?"

Don't what-the-fuck me. You were about to walk into traffic. Even your E.R.T.A. wouldn't have saved you.

I watched the wheeled metal contraptions zip by. "Are the transports of this time not equipped with pedestrian braking systems?"

Just brakes. And you've got to rely on the drivers to hit them in time.

"Fuck."

Exactly. This is a primitive branch. Be careful. There's a light on the other side of the street. You can cross when you see the little man appear on it.

I waited for the light and when it turned, I hurried across with the crowd. I didn't trust those transport operators to heed the traffic laws. I turned my attention to the people around me. No projected displays around their heads. Instead, almost all of them had their eyes fixed on strange rectangular devices. I couldn't make anything out on the tiny screens. Perhaps the point of the size. In any case, I found it all strange.

I crossed a couple more streets before Ereth guided me toward another alley. *The closest tachyonic signature is down there. I'll let you know when you're close.*

"Roger."

I activated my Eye of Odin. The tachyonic sight overlapped my own and I stopped dead. Great swaths of pitch black stretched across the fabric of time. They looked like slash marks, all dark and menacing, like a portal to hell. They extended across the damp wall of the alley, over the top of an overflowing trash receptacle, and down on the other side. I reached toward it, and my hand passed through the darkness like it was an evening shadow.

Oh yeah. Nareena was here.

We leave behind small tears when we walk between branches, but this was different. Something had disturbed the time stream, but I had no idea how. Not for the first time, I wished I had both eyes. I could jump between branches and see the flow of time up until my present, but without the other Eye I couldn't see the flow ahead or move along the branch at will. It made time travel a guessing game and put me perpetually following in Nareena's wake.

You're on top of it.

"I know. These aren't time-walk scars."

No. Loki is still on this branch, and she didn't enter here.

I hated when they used that codename. She was still a person, dammit. I kept the thought to myself and said, "Then what the hell is this?"

That's what you need to find out.

I followed the dark slash around the receptacle and stopped in my tracks. A man sat against the dirty wall, out of sight of the main street. Elderly, obviously. White hair and wrinkled all to hell. A cursory scan with my Eye showed no vitals. Body temperature too low. Dead. No visible cause of death. Like this man just decided to sit down and die.

"I've got a body."

Loki's doing?

"Most likely."

I knelt next to the man. Something seemed off. His clothes maybe. They looked more like the younger crowd I'd seen on the streets. "E.R.T.A., gloves." Material crept down to my hands. A second later I wore a pair of white medical gloves.

I found no bruising, cuts, or injuries on the man. No signs of struggle. Nothing to reveal a COD. I pricked the man's finger and blood welled slowly to the surface. He hadn't been dead long. I ran my finger through the drop of blood and said, "E.R.T.A., run toxicology."

My head buzzed and a tinny voice read off a list of foreign substances found. All common enough. Nothing to cause this man to keel over. In fact, from the results I'd think him younger than he looked. Perhaps...

"E.R.T.A., estimate of age?"

Age at time of death: twenty-five years.

Twenty-five? Not possible. I patted the man's pockets until I found a wallet and the ID inside. Jared Andrews. Born, September 9th, year 1993 AD. Twenty-five-years-old. *How the hell?* I glanced up at the dark slash through time.

"Ereth, can an Eye of Odin affect space-time outside of its user in an isolated area?"

In theory. The Eyes give their wearers full control over space-time. But we didn't get much chance to use them before Loki stole one.

"Which means you don't know fuck all about them, huh?"

Not really.

"Shit. Well, I think Nareena used hers to kill. This body I found belongs to a man in his twenties. He looks eighty. No discernible cause of death. This man died of old age."

Again, in theory Loki could speed the passage of time in an isolated system. If so, that makes her even more dangerous. Rerouting branches of time is bad enough, but now —

"Now she's committing murder."

I heard a metallic click, then something hard pressed just behind my ear.

"It's weird to talk about yourself in the third person, asshole." A man's voice. The object behind my ear dug in harder. "Hands behind your back, dickbag."

I moved without thinking. One hand up, wrapped around the weapon at my skull. I turned. Drove the other fist into the man's stomach. He recoiled. I tossed the useless weapon aside. A clatter of metal across the dirty pavement. I'd interrupted his breath with my first blow and I placed another to the man's chest. Then his throat. The man lost his breath entirely. His hands went to his throat. I snapped a kick to his temple. His head whipped to the side. He collapsed into a heap in the filth.

The sound of a discharged weapon ripped through the alley. Something slammed into my side. Pain blossomed across my ribs and I crumpled against the wall. Without E.R.T.A. I'd probably be dead. Fighting to breathe, I tried to get up. My shooter ran toward me and kicked me under the chin. My teeth clacked together and I landed hard on my back.

"I don't know how you're alive but move and I'll put the next between your fucking eyes." The man planted a foot in my chest. His weapon trained on my face.

Just do what he says, Ereth said in my ear. *He's law enforcement on this branch. So was the man you just dropped.*

Through a haze of pain, I glanced over at the guy beside me. Same uniform as the one standing over me. *Shit.* Fighting to stay conscious, I placed my hands out to either side and managed to gasp, "Officer, I promise this isn't what it looks like."

"Yeah? That's what they all say. You have the right to remain silent. Fucking use it."

* * *

Hours later, I sat handcuffed to an incredibly uncomfortable chair. Across from me, Detective Tamika Jones rubbed her temples in exasperation. Unlike the officers who brought me in, she didn't wear a uniform. On my time-line, all law enforcement had a regular uniform, regardless of position. I felt like I was being interrogated by a CEO rather than a detective.

"Let me get this straight." In the last hour I'd begun to hate that phrase. "You're from the future? Some decorated military man. And you were 'sent,'" she made air quotations with her fingers, "to find a man named Loki—"

"Woman." She looked up then, and I saw in her eyes just how crazy she thought me. "Codenamed Loki. Her real name is Nareena."

"Right. Nareena. Lapel Corp. sent you—"

"Laplace Corp."

"Whatever." She thumped the table with her finger. "They tracked this woman to this time and you came here to bring her back. And it's this Loki who killed the geezer in the alley?"

"Yeah."

Detective Jones burst out laughing.

"Jesus Christ, you're one loony ass toon, you know that?" She wiped at her eyes. "It's a good story. And damned convincing. Now let me tell *you* a story." She rested her elbows on the table and leaned toward me.

"We found his wallet on you, so you'd already robbed Andrews. But you still needed more. The geezer seemed like an easy target. You dragged him into the alley and killed him. Roberts caught you in the act and you beat the living shit out of him trying to get away. You didn't see his partner with him and your ass got caught. Then you made up this bogus story to make us think you're crazy so the courts will let you off easy." Her voice dropped to a hiss. "But that's where you fucked up. Because I'm going to make sure you fry, fucker. And the worst part? That man didn't have anything on him."

I'd had enough. I leaned toward the detective and let my own voice drop. "I appreciate your commitment to duty, Detective. But the wallet you have in evidence belongs to the man on the table in your morgue. Jared Andrews. Dead of old age at twenty-five. And your officer put his gun to my head first. For all I knew, he meant to mug me."

"You expect me to believe that old dude is only twenty-five?" She gave a condescending laugh. "Seventy-five maybe. Now tell me you killed him and make this whole thing easy."

I sighed and rubbed my eyes, the chain of my handcuffs clinking against the table. Ereth's voice sounded in my ear. *This is pointless. While you sit here and argue with her we've had two more tachyonic disturbances.*

This isn't pointless, I responded, using the psionic link function of my comm. I hated doing it since it took so much focus, but I didn't need the detective thinking me any crazier. I felt a twinge of pain between my eyes. *If I get the local law enforcement on my side, I might stop her this time. I've chased her for months now, and if I don't catch her soon, there'll be no going back for her.*

Ereth sighed. *There's already no going back. Hurry. I don't like Loki out there without someone on her ass.*

I looked up at the detective and smiled. She narrowed her eyes. "It's obvious we're not getting anywhere like this. So here's what's going to happen." I glanced up at the primitive camera looking down on us. "E.R.T.A., put that camera on a loop." A tiny ping sounded in my head. "Good. Sleeves please." Another ping and the sleeves of my t-shirt crept down to full arm-length.

"What in the fuck?" The Detective scrambled out of her chair.

"As I said. From the future. E.R.T.A., get rid of these handcuffs for me."

I felt a sort of vibration around my wrists. The metal of the cuffs glowed red, then melted onto the table. Detective Jones' eyes had opened so wide I expected her eyelids to rip apart. I stood and she scrambled for her gun. I blinked and my Eye of Odin activated. Time ground to a halt and that pain behind the implanted Eye deepened. I ignored it and walked to the Detective. I took her gun from the holster at her side and moved back to my place on the other side of the table. I let time flow again and cleared my throat.

"Looking for this?" I pointed to her gun on the table in front of me. "Sit down, Detective."

She ran instead.

I stepped outside of time long enough to get between the detective and the door. I blinked and time returned to normal. That twinge blossomed into a dull ache. Jones crashed into me. I'd never seen anyone so confused. I navigated her back to her seat, and retook my own.

"How the fuck did you move that fast?"

I chuckled.

"I didn't. I just stopped time."

"Yeah. Sure. Why the fuck not?"

I slid her weapon across the table. She put her hand on it and left it there. "Now that I have your attention, we're going to sit here quietly until your medical examiner finishes their autopsy. When they tell you he is in fact Jared Andrews, I'm going to help you find the woman who killed him. Because she's got this technology too and you're ill-equipped to handle her. Think you can do that?"

"I don't think I have much of a choice."

"Perceptive." I activated my Eye. Time halted. Agony filled my head. I staggered to my feet.

You're overdoing it.

"I know. Shut up. I need her."

Just don't put yourself out of commission.

I stumbled behind Jones and steadied myself on her chair, trying hard to ignore the pain. I needed just one more push to get her on my side. I let time flow again and said, "You don't have a choice in the matter at all."

The detective leaped from her seat and scrambled around the table. She slammed her back into the wall, her gun trained on me. A quick scan with my Eye told me her heart rate had sky-rocketed. Endorphins and adrenaline dumped. Fight or flight. The reaction I'd hoped for. "Jesus fucking wept," she panted, lowering her gun and clutching at her chest. "I got it. You've got crazy future superpowers."

"And the woman we're both after does too. We need each other." I held Jones' eye. If I hadn't convinced her, it would all go to shit here. After several moments Jones nodded and I had to fight down my sigh of relief.

You got lucky, you know that.

Story of my life, kid.

"If this chick can do the same shit, you're right. But that's a big if. I'll wait to hear what our ME says. If you're wrong, then I'm tossing your ass in holding and throwing away the key."

I smirked. The detective didn't stay rattled long. A knock sounded at the door.

"Come in," Jones yelled, never taking her eyes off me. The door opened and a mousy man in glasses bustled inside.

"I'm sorry to interrupt—" he stopped when he saw the two of us. His eyes darted to Jones. Down to her gun. Then to me. I winked at him and he took a step back. "Is everything—"

"We're fine, Fen. What do you have for me?"

He glanced at me again. "If you'd step outside—"

"Kahlan isn't our killer. He's an Interpol agent. Or so he says. Confirm it for us."

I raised an eyebrow at her and she grimaced. She'd just lied for me. I was touched.

You heard her, newbie. Forge some documents for me.

Coming right up, boss. Want me to put a bow on it?

I snorted a laugh, earning me a look from both. Fen bustled in and spread his files on the interrogation table. I picked up a photo of the old man on the table, his torso spread wide. "As far as I can tell, Mr. Andrews wasn't murdered, that's the—"

"Wait," Jones said, cutting him off. "Did you just say Mr. Andrews?"

"I did. That's the odd thing," Fen said, annoyed. He pushed his glasses back up. "The wallet you found on the suspect...ah..." He glanced at me and I waved a hand at him.

"I'd have thought it was me, too."

He nodded and continued. "I found the vic's prints in the system. The man on my table is the twenty-five-year-old Jared Andrews. Dead of old age."

Jones looked up at me, shock painted across her face in big, bold, crappy graffiti letters. I gave her my best I-fucking-told-you smile and she scowled. To Fen she said, "That's some weird shit, but what does it mean for us?"

"Well, normally we'd call it a medical mystery. Someone other than me would poke and prod at him, stealing all the glory. And we'd all get back to our lives."

"I hear a 'but' in there," I said, crossing my arms. Fen shrugged at me.

"Like I said, we'd normally do that. Except we brought in another body just like Mr. Andrews, so we're calling this a serial murder case."

"Yup. She's dead as hell," Jones said, setting the sheet back in place on the autopsy table. I scanned the body and a thousand processes I didn't understand scrawled across my vision.

Subject name Mia Takanashi, a mechanical voice said in my head after a few moments. *Deceased. Age thirty-two. Cause of death, undetermined.*

"Do you have a COD?" I asked Fen. He shook his head.

"No clue. They found her in a bathroom in a Marta Station, so I expected gunshot or stabbing. But she just died. At thirty-two." He wandered off toward the offices, muttering to himself.

Hey newbie, can you search the records on our two vics and see if there is some reason why Nareena might have targeted them? I'd used the Eye too much and transmitting the message hurt.

Can do, boss. I heard the sarcastic salute.

"What do you think?" Jones said once Fen disappeared into a back office.

"Definitely Nareena's work. That woman was murdered."

Jones gestured for me to follow and we left the morgue.

"How?"

I tapped at my Eye. "Because she's got one of these. An Eye of Odin. Together the Eyes let their user see all of spacetime. See *and* control it. I've got the left one, and she's got the right."

"I still don't see how some glass eye can let someone commit murder." She opened a door and let me pass through into the interior staircase.

"Spacetime is made up of particles called tachyons," I said as we ascended toward the station above. "Like most particles they can have different charges; positive, negative, and neutral. My Eye is negatively charged, so while I'm on a time-line, I can see everything from that moment back. Nareena's eye has a positive charge, so she sees the future. We can also affect time as well, like when I stopped it before.

I think Nareena uses her Eye to positively charge her victim's tachyons. She's aging them to death."

Jones blanched at that.

"Fuck. It's got to be a bitch to age that fast. But why kill people?"

"I don't know." We passed through the station. A few heads turned, but I flashed my recently generated credentials and they went back to ignoring us. "My entire organization has tried to figure that out since she first stole her Eye. We think she's trying to reshape the future. Trickier than you might think. But I've chased her all over spacetime and she's never killed before."

We'd made it outside and she led me over to her vehicle. My turn to blanch. Getting in one of those primitive death traps again didn't appeal to me.

"I'd rather not." I backed up a bit. Jones laughed.

"What's the matter? Scared of cars?"

"I had my fill when your officers manhandled me into the back of one of these hunks of metal."

"I'm a good driver. I promise. Now quit being a pussy and get in the fucking car."

She opened her door and slid inside. I grimaced again, but got in. I was pleasantly surprised by the quality of the interior. A nice faux-leather covered the soft seats, and a gentle circulation of cold air fought the oppressive heat outside. I settled into the seat, and the detective smirked at me.

"See, not that bad. Buckle up." She pushed a stick on the guiding wheel and the car lurched into motion. It took me a moment to realize she meant the safety restraint. She grinned at me again as I struggled to get it into the receptacle and said, "Now, what do you mean reshaping the future is tricky?"

"I'll show you. E.R.T.A. project 'Yggdrasil,' flipped." I held out a hand and an image appeared in my palm. It showed a kind of spindly tree, with a single line at the bottom as a trunk which split off into hundreds of branches.

"You probably think of time like this. A tree. Branching off into a thousand different outcomes. In my era, we discovered this theory was incorrect." I flipped my hand over, and the image flipped with it. "Time does look like a tree, but like this. Upside down. Converging together into one line. The final line. The ultimate culmination of spacetime. That's where I'm from. We call this Valhalla."

"So why does that make changing the future hard?"

"Because once on the Valhalla line, nothing can be changed going forward."

I saw the understanding dawn in Jones' eyes and she said, "Unless you change the lines leading up to it."

"Exactly. Nareena stole one of the Eyes, and she's bounced around, changing the lines to try and make a new Valhalla."

"How?"

"These points where the lines converge," I enlarged the image to show the gap between two lines, and their combined line above. "We call them Schrödinger's Points."

"Like the dude with the cat in the box?"

"Exactly. When two parallel lines have opposing events. Say, a man is shot here," I pointed at one line, then the other, "and here he isn't shot. Both of those lines end at that moment. Spacetime decides the outcome, and creates a new line that's a merger of the two going forward. She's changing these events to eliminate Schrödinger's Points. Doing so makes new lines. I'm sure these deaths are leading to the change of another Point, I just don't know how."

"Then let's stop the bitch before she fucks up my time anymore," she said as I let the image die. I winced at the coldness of her words. "Where do we start?"

"Take me to this Marta Station where they found Ms. Takanashi's body. If Nareena killed her there, maybe I can figure out what her next move is."

We've got a problem. I jumped at Ereth's voice. Jones shot me a look, but I waved her off. *Those two dead? They were part of a startup company. Communications based. That startup grows to become the basis of our own communications matrix here in Valhalla. Which means—*

"She's trying to shut down our intra-time communications. I won't be able to phone home anymore." And if Nareena succeeded, I was fucked.

* * *

Ereth sent me a list of names, each involved in this "startup," as he called it. It swam before me in the overlaid sight from my Eye. Over a hundred long, and with the red lines through the first two names it looked like a hit list. An odd musical tone sounded and Jones pulled one of those square slabs from her pocket. She put her finger on a green circle and slid it across the screen, then put the slab to her ear.

"Jones here. What have you got?" she said to the slab. A communication device. Fascinating. I found the look on her face less fascinating. Something had happened. "I'm on the way. Send me the address."

She pulled the slab from her ear and fiddled with the screen. While driving. I didn't like that combination of activities. "What's happened?"

"They've brought in three more bodies. Just like the two we've seen already."

"Fuck. Do we have names?"

She rattled them off from her slab and I watched red lines slash through each in turn in my oversight. Fucking hell, Loki moved fast. Way too fast. We couldn't chase each of them separately. "Ereth, who's the head of this thing?"

Aarav Agarwal. He's an Indian programmer with a specialty in communications. He's only been in Atlanta for a few weeks in your time. And according to this, he moved there to start this venture.

"Can you send me his address for the current time?"

Coming to you, boss.

"Who are you talking to?" Jones said as a seemingly meaningless series of numbers and words flashed across my oversight.

"I'm speaking with an agent from my own time. He just sent me an address we need to head to." I rattled it off and she input it into her slab.

"Okay, I got it, but what's so important about this place?"

"The man at that address is going to die."

Jones' eyes widened.

"Alright, shit. You don't have to tell me twice." She stomped her foot onto a pedal on the floor of the transport. Her car lurched forward even faster, and I gripped the handle on my door. Hopefully Jones didn't kill *me* first.

She took us into a crappy neighborhood with dilapidated cars. Many of the tiny houses had broken roofs and porches. I'd seen images of the poverty of this time, but witnessing it first hand was jarring.

Lots of people walked the streets, and Jones' sleek black transport drew attention. Not good. I didn't want innocents getting caught in the crossfire. We pulled into a driveway behind a car with a back end so rusted, I couldn't believe it hadn't fallen off.

"Are you sure this is the place?" Jones killed the power to her transport. With a thought, I slid into tachyonic sight. Abnormally positive tachyons surrounded the house. Not good.

"I'm sure. The tachyonic signature is unmistakable."

"Then let's get this shit over with." She flung open her door and climbed out. I followed as she started toward the house, gun held in front of her in an obvious combat position. I placed a hand on her shoulder to stop her. "Nareena is dangerous. And she has more control over her Eye than I do. But I need to talk to her."

"She's dropped five bodies in my city," she said, her eyes hard. "She gives me a reason, and I'm going to put a bullet between the bitch's eyes."

"I understand." Together, we started across the yard toward the front of the house. We took position on either side of the door. I held up a hand with three fingers and started counting down. When I got to one, we both moved. I swung out and planted my foot into the door at the handle. It crumbled in at my kick. We raced inside, each of us covering one side of the tiny house. We didn't have to go far.

"Hi, Kahlan. It's been a long time."

Nareena stood in the middle of a living room cleaner than I expected. She stood behind a man gagged and tied to a rickety chair. Aarav Agarwal. His eyes bulged when he saw us, and he strained against the ropes, screaming against his gag. Nareena twined her fingers into his hair and dragged his head back. She held a knife to his throat and he whimpered, tears streaming down his face.

"Drop the knife and put your hands behind your head," Jones said, her gun trained on Loki.

"Wait." I stepped in front of the Detective and pushed her gun down. "Let me talk to her."

"Don't fuck with me, Kahlan."

"She's my wife."

That stopped Jones cold. She squinted at me, hesitation etched across her face. Finally, she lowered her gun and took a step back. "You've got five minutes. I'm bringing her in after that."

She's your wife? Ereth said in shock. I ignored him and shut down my comm link. I didn't need Laplace Corp interfering here.

"That's all I need." I gave her a smile and turned. My throat tightened. Nareena wore her curls loose and her doe brown eyes complimented her dark skin perfectly. She wore an E.R.T.A. as well, hers a close fitting, midnight black armor. She'd not moved an inch, even with Jones out for her blood. I saw something in her. Something hard I'd never seen before. She'd changed and I had no idea why. I felt like I didn't know her anymore.

"Stop this, Nareena. Just let him go and come with me." I took a step toward her and held out a hand.

"I can't. I'm sorry, love. You haven't seen what I've seen." She took a deep breath and I saw something I didn't expect. Fear. No. Not fear. Deeper than that. Horror. Whatever she had glimpsed was so unimaginably horrible, she'd resorted to murder. She'd always been my sweet researcher, so different from the soldiers I spent my time with on the battlefield. She was my light. But the woman standing in front of me now was a warrior as well. "What I'm doing may seem extreme. But it's necessary. You of all people should understand that."

She pressed her knife into Aarav's throat. A line of red trickled across his skin.

"Nareena—"

Jones stepped in front of me, cutting me off, her gun trained on Nareena again. "Drop the knife. I won't tell you again." She glanced over her shoulder at me. "Sorry, but I can't let her kill another."

Hot panic shot through my chest. I couldn't make Jones back down again without a fight. I didn't see Nareena dropping the knife either. Jones was going to shoot her. I couldn't let that happen. "Nareena. Please. Just do what she says."

"I can't." She gave me a sad smile and I saw the muscles in her shoulder move.

"Don't do it!"

The report of Jones' gun tore through the room.

I screamed, activating my Eye. Time halted. Silence fell. *Did I make it? Dear God, let me have made it.* Fire enveloped the tip of Jones' gun barrel. Her eyes were set. Intent upon the kill.

"A close call." Nareena's voice. Relief flooded through me. The bullet Jones had fired hung just before her face. "Thank you."

"Why aren't you stopped like the others?" She was alive, so now I needed to buy time. I sent E.R.T.A. a silent command.

"The Eyes can't affect each other." Nareena removed the knife from Aarav's throat. Another relief.

"Then I'll have to stop you myself." With a flick of my wrist, I hurled the tachyonic destabilizer at her face. I struck her just above her own Eye and spread to cover it.

"What is this?" She tugged at the destabilizer.

"Something they developed after you stole the Eye. It cuts off its power." I stalked across the room. "Now you can't time-walk out of here. I'm sorry Nareena. I'm bringing you back."

I needed to immobilize her before she ran. I grabbed her hand and wrenched the knife from it. I swung low. Driving my fist toward her gut. She twisted away. My fist met only open air.

She kicked me in the face.

A snap kick. More power behind it than I'd expected. It spun me to the side. I lost my grip on her. She kicked me again. I lost my footing and went down. She aimed a third kick at my head. I rolled, feeling the wind as her foot sped by my face. I lost concentration and time hiccupped. *Shit. Keep it together.* Head ringing like a bell, I scrambled to my feet. Where the fuck did she learn to fight like this?

She'd put Aarav between us. I staggered just a bit, but I stayed upright. I wiped at my mouth and cursed when I saw blood. I didn't want to hurt her, but if she fought me like this, I wouldn't have a choice. I had to bring her back to Valhalla. I met her gaze and I saw the challenge there. She'd fight until the end. Just what had she seen?

I rushed her again and she flipped Aarav up at me. He halted in midair when she lost contact with him. I dodged around him. She followed. Her fist rocketed towards my face. I blocked it. Sent my elbow for her temple. Her turn to block. Her fist for my gut. Downward block, then a chop to her throat. Another block. We traded blows for several seconds before she slipped. My fist sailed through her defense and connected with her jaw. Her head snapped to the side. I tried to end it then, but she ducked my next blow and came up behind me. She planted a foot in my back and I nearly fell again. I lurched forward and only just managed to stay upright.

"You actually hit me." She rubbed her jaw.

"I'm taking you back to Valhalla, willing or not."

She chuckled at that, the sound melancholic.

"I wish you'd help me, you know. You have no idea what's coming." I heard the plea, and it almost broke me. Goddamn it, she was still my wife. I loved her more than anything. But I couldn't let her leave a trail of bodies behind. I think she saw that in my face because she said, "But you're not going to. I'm sorry, Kahlan."

A blur of motion. Something flew at my face. I raised my arms to protect myself and something bit deep into my forearm. A disrupter blade made to bypass E.R.T.A. armor. Buried in my arm. I grabbed the handle to pull it free. Nareena was on me. She drove her palm into the handle. The blade sliced deeper into my flesh. Pain lanced up my arm into my shoulder. I cried out. She struck my throat. It closed. I gasped for a breath that wouldn't come. Then she planted one last kick into my temple.

I hit the ground. Hard. Barely clinging to consciousness. Time sputtered again. Then resumed its flow. My connection to the Eye ended. Aarav crashed to the floor and screamed in pain. I tried to get to my feet again, but I couldn't see straight. Jones yelled my name and rushed to my side. The sudden noise made my head explode.

"Thank you for playing your part, Detective," Nareena said from somewhere in front of me.

"What do you mean?" Jones said, wrapping her arm around me and helping me to my feet. My vision cleared a bit and I saw Nareena gesture to Aarav. A crimson pool spread around him.

"I needed him to die, but you had to do it. And you did splendidly."

"You moved him into position," I rasped at her. She'd planned all of this. She knew I'd bring Jones. "You played us both to make sure Jones' weapon killed him."

"It was the only way."

"Why?" I said harshly, the strain hurting my throat. "Why kill all these people?"

"You're about to see."

The world started to change. A flicker across my vision at first. Then everything went out of focus. Twisting and distorting. I felt Jones' hand on my arm. "What's happening?" Her voice sounded a thousand miles away.

"I don't know." I tried to take a step, but I was so disoriented I couldn't move. Then everything went black. The feel of Jones' hand disappeared.

Pain erupted through my being.

I cried out, but I didn't have a mouth. Or lungs. I was outside of time. Goddamn it. God fucking damn it. Nareena had won. She'd rerouted the line. I couldn't stop her. She stood right in front of me and I couldn't fucking stop her.

Newbie, are you there? I concentrated to reestablish the psionic connection. Nothing. Just as we'd feared, rerouting that line had shut down our cross-spacetime communication. *Fuck!* I needed to get back to the lab and regroup. I focused my Eye, looking for the tachyonic beacon set up to help me find the Valhalla line. After a few moments it pinged in my consciousness and I walked.

I had glass bones when I stepped onto Valhalla. I stumbled and a pair of hands caught me. Their touch set my skin on fire. I'd used the Eye too much.

"Hey there, boss. I thought we lost you." I recognized this voice. Ereth was younger than I'd expected, and he looked at me from under a shock of crimson hair. Natural. Rare on Valhalla. "Fuck, you've got a knife in your arm."

"Don't worry about that. How bad is it?"

His face fell.

"Let me show you." He helped me limp over to the bank of holo-screens on the other side of the command center. "When the line collapsed, we didn't know what had happened to you. She didn't actually change much, but we lost all contact, and we couldn't find your tachyonic signature anywhere in spacetime."

"Nareena?"

Ereth shook his head. "We can't find Loki's signature either. But you survived, so she probably did too."

"I put the destabilizer on her. She didn't have access to her Eye."

"Oh, fuck."

Grief washed through me. She couldn't use her power, so when she kicked us into spacetime, she had no protection. None of us knew what that could do to a person. Most likely it ripped her to shreds. Her existence scattered across time. I took a ragged breath, fighting back tears. I couldn't grieve now.

"Show me what she did to Yggdrasil."

Ereth seemed to want to say more, but he stopped when he saw my face. He settled into the chair and brought up the holo-screens. Yggdrasil appeared before me. The World Tree. All of time in a single image.

"You were on a Midgardian Branch here." He highlighted a strangely empty portion of the tree.

"I don't see anything."

"Because there's nothing there anymore." He circled the entire area to bring the emptiness into full view. "Whatever she changed by killing the people she did, it didn't just affect how that line flowed into the Schrödinger's Point."

My breath caught in my throat. I leaned forward, trying to wrap my brain around what I saw. Up until now, she'd rerouted lines. Changing the shape of branches to change the fate of Valhalla. But not this time. This time she'd deactivated the entire branch. All that history. All those worlds. All those *people*. Gone forever.

"Oh god, Nareena," I whispered in horror. "What have you done?"

ALL THE TIME IN THE WORLD

Stephen Leigh

The first guest on the *Damon Anderson Show*, Tom Lewis—lead singer in the currently-popular pop band *Oxymoron*—leaned toward the host. "You never know what kind of shit your audience is thinking, not that I really give a fuck…"

Up in the control booth, Mark Evert looked up, wide-eyed, from the comic book spread out on his desk. He pressed the button on his headphones, switching from live input to the delayed feed from the file server. At "…never know what…" he hit the button on the broadcast delay unit—affectionately called the 'dump box'—long enough for the pre-set seven second delay to delete the offending profanities.

"Oops. Sorry…I guess I shouldn't say that on a live show," Lewis continued. "Anyway, you don't know what the hell your audience is thinking…"

"Asshole," Sophia Watt, the program director down on the set floor, commented into the staff headphones. "You covered that, Mark?"

"No problem, boss. All gone," he said into the mic of his headset. He loved the sound of Sophia's low voice in his ear. For that matter, he liked pretty much everything about Sophia—the discreet tattoo of an owl on her wrist, her night-black hair that went so well with her dark Mediterranean complexion, her deep brown eyes with gold flecks in the pupils. In person, he tended to stutter when he talked to her; it was easier over the headset. Still, she was always friendly with him, and he even imagined he might ask her out after work to see if the attraction was mutual. *One day. Soon.*

"What an asshole," Sophia repeated. He loved it when she cursed; she did it so rarely and she always sounded a little hesitant. "That was deliberate—you should see his agent grinning in the wings. Ten bucks says he'll drop another F-bomb or three, or worse."

"I'm not taking that bet. I don't make enough as it is."

Sophia didn't directly comment. "Everybody, be alert up there. Mark, put away that comic book for now—I know you have it open on your desk. This joker's on for another five and a half minutes. He may decide to show the audience his junk, the way this interview's gone so far. We may have to cut the live feed entirely, visual and audio."

Mark had to use the dump box for additional profanities and blatantly sexual innuendos a half dozen more times before they cut to commercials prior to the next guest. From the control booth window overlooking the show's set, Mark saw Sophia put her hands together on a mocking slow clap as Lewis left the stage, though the live audience mostly ignored the flashing APPLAUSE lights. Even Damon Anderson himself, whose television smile seemed surgically implanted, scowled at Lewis' back as he departed. "Hey!" Anderson called out to the singer as he left the stage. "You'll never be invited back, you crappy one-hit wonder." Lewis flipped him the bird without looking back. The audience booed.

After the show, Sophia came up to the control booth with her headset dangling around her neck. She waved to the staff before tossing it onto her tiny desk in the corner. Mark smiled at her.

"Well, we won't have to worry about that idiot again," she said, smiling back. "He certainly kept you busy tonight. Good work. Y'know, if you paid less attention to that garbage you read and more to the actual work, I'd be happy to give you more responsibility—that would bump your pay grade."

"Thanks, boss. But when I sell my big fantasy novel I expect to leave all this excitement behind. In the meantime, me and the ol' dump box are good friends." Mark put his hand on the metal top of the dump box in its snarl of wires, intending to stroke it like he might his cat. As his fingers made contact, he had just enough time to feel a tingling before a flash of blue-white light exploded in front of him, fading into darkness.

* * *

Voices called his name, softly at first, then more insistently. Mark forced his eyes to open and found Sophia blocking his view of the control booth's ceiling. He decided he didn't mind that at all. He even tried to smile at her, unsuccessfully, thinking he could do without the faces of the booth crew crowded behind hers. They all looked strangely concerned. Mark blinked.

He started to sit up but Sophia pressed him back down. "Please don't move. The EMTs are on the way."

"Who?" Mark asked. "What happened?" His voice sounded weak and strange.

"Some kind of short circuit in the broadcast delay unit. You got tossed back pretty hard. You hit your head on the floor and were totally out."

Mark felt the back of his head; yes, there was a knot at the back of his skull. But when he looked at his hand he didn't see any blood. "I think I'm fine. Someone help me up."

Sophia took one hand, one of the crew took another. He tried to stand on his own but his knees were wobbly. Together they helped him to his chair. The room spun around him momentarily but he decided not to mention that. "That's it," Sophia said. "You're not standing up again until the EMTs get here and check you over. I'll be surprised if you don't have a concussion."

Mark nodded. That was fine; honestly, he wasn't sure he *could* stand. He felt the knot again. "Ow. That fucking hurts." He gave a bitter chuckle at the profanity. "I guess no one should to try to dump that right now. The stupid dump box is biting me back for the workout I just gave it."

Sophia managed a weak grin. "You might be right. Now let me find something for that knot on your head until the EMTs show up…"

* * *

After checking his pupils and asking him several questions, the EMTs declared he had a mild concussion. They gave him some Tylenol and a coldpak for his head. Mark refused their offer to take him to the ER; the EMTs shrugged at that and told him that he should get to an ER if he experienced blurred vision or dizziness and that it would be good for him to have someone with him tonight. He told them he would; he didn't mention that it would be his cat.

Sophia wouldn't let him take the usual subway and bus back to his New Jersey apartment. Instead, she drove him to his apartment. "You're sure that you have someone coming over to stay with you?" she asked as he walked to the couch and sat down.

"Yeah. My friend Ed said he'd spend the night. He'll be over in half an hour or less."

"You're sure you're going to be all right?"

"I'm fine, Sophia. My head's a little sore, that's all. If you'd like to stay to check on me, though, I could call Ed and tell him I have someone else."

She gave him an uncertain smile at the invitation and Mark cursed himself for making the remark. *That was over the line…*

"Sorry." At least she didn't sound pissed off. "I really need to get back to my place. Look, you take tomorrow off and rest, okay? We can handle things at the studio without you for one day."

"If you say so."

"I say so," she said firmly. She touched his shoulder, her finger pressing lightly. "Keep using that coldpak. And if you have any issues, have your friend take you right to the ER, okay?"

Mark nodded.

"Good. I'll be going, then. Take care of yourself, Mark."

He nodded again and watched her leave. His orange-and-white cat, Finnigan, jumped up to cuddle on his lap, purring as Mark gave him scritches around his collar, jingling the ID tag.

Mark checked his email on his laptop—there was another rejection for one of his stories. Mark sighed and tuned the TV to CNN, putting the volume to a low whisper. Shuffling into the bathroom, he filled a glass with water and grabbed a bottle of Tylenol, setting them both on the couch's coffee table near the remote.

Mark continued to give Finnigan attention on his lap but, as usual, the cat eventually decided he'd had enough. He leaped onto the coffee table, bumping into the water glass. Mark saw the glass starting to tip. "Stop!" he shouted. "Damn it, cat!" His exclamation fell in a muffled, strange silence. Finnigan was motionless on the table, front paws lifted to make the leap down to the floor; the water glass remained tilted, water just beginning to slosh over the lip equally motionless. Mark stared at the tableau for a moment, automatically counting the seconds in his head as he always did when he pressed the dump button. *One thousand one, one thousand two, one thousand three…* The room in front of him might as well have been a painting. Even the TV screen was frozen, with Wolf Blitzer's mouth open in mid-pontification. *One thousand four...*

Mark reached out—*one thousand five*—and caught the glass, sliding it slightly backward so that it was directly under the overflow spill—*one thousand six*—and settled the glass on its coaster—*one thousand seven.*

The world lurched into motion again: Finnigan completed his leap to the floor and stalked off, tail lashing; Wolf Blitzer droned on again; the water fell back into the glass, sloshing side to side.

Mark gaped at the glass. He took his hand from the glass as if it had just burned him. Finnigan stalked out of the room into the bathroom, where Mark kept the litter box. *Seven seconds. I yelled and everything stopped for seven seconds. Just like correcting a mistake with the dump box.*

He looked at his hands, remembering the shock of contact with the dump box back at the studio. Mark gazed around the room. The TV's remote control was on the coffee table within reach. He grabbed it, hefted it once in his hand, and tossed it toward the ceiling. Pointing at it with his finger, he intoned "Stop!"

The control paused at the apogee of its ascent, motionless in the air. Wolf Blitzer paused again, the television scene freezing. Mark counted the seconds: *one thousand one, one thousand two, one thousand three...* At *one thousand seven* he held his hand under the remote, expecting it to fall. It didn't. He kept counting in his head. *One thousand twelve, one thousand thirteen, one thousand fourteen...* and the remote fell into his hand. He fumbled the catch; the remote hit the couch cushions and bounced once. Wolf Blitzer was again ranting about nothing.

Mark stared at the remote, then at the glass of water on the coffee table. *Did I imagine all this? Am I so concussed that I'm seeing things?* Then: *Oh my God, I freaking stopped time for seven seconds, then fourteen seconds...Or am I just a concussed person who's probably imagining all this? This has to be because of what happened with the dump box. The seven second sequences... what else could it be?*

Mark picked up the remote. He tossed it up again, again shouting "Stop!" at the height. Everything went silent and still around him, the remote hanging in mid-air like the bone in the ape segment of Kubrick's *2001: A Space Odyssey*. He began counting, pushing himself off the couch at the same time. At *one thousand fourteen*, the remote still hadn't moved. He kept counting. *Fourteen and seven is twenty-one,* he thought, but at *one thousand twenty-one* nothing happened.

*...one thousand twenty-eight...*The remote suddenly fell; the images on the TV began to move; the remote hit the cushions again.

Okay. Twenty-eight seconds: so the duration of the time stoppage has doubled with every use...Will it last fifty-six seconds next?

Mark leaned over and picked up the remote again. He walked to the window, still holding the remote. Holding it a foot above the carpet, he dropped it, immediately saying "Stop!"

Silence. No movement. Counting in his head, he moved the blinds aside and looked out over the street below. The cars had halted in their lanes; people were frozen in mid-walk on the sidewalks, and in the sky he saw the unmoving lights of a jetliner taking off from Newark.

So the time-stop effect extended outside his apartment. Had the whole world stopped everywhere? Mark shook his head; the concept seemed impossible.

He was still at the window when, fifty-six seconds later, the remote control hit the carpet and the world snapped back into motion once more. Cars honked and passed on the streets; a jet whined overhead, people moved in the streets.

I'm like some weird superhero with a minor power. 'The Fantastic Dump Box?'—no, absolutely not! 'Pause?' 'Stopwatch?' Yeah, I like that. Stopwatch. Why, I can see the costume now...

Then: *Stop it, Mark. You're no superhero.*

He considered trying the experiment again, but he remembered the old logic question of whether you'd take $1,000,000 all at once or accept a penny doubled every day for the next 30 days. The second option sounded terrifically stupid until you did the math and realized that at the end of 30 days you'd have received over five million dollars.

If the original seven second time stoppage doubled every time he used the power, the duration would quickly become hours, then days, then months, then years.

No. He had to think about this. Maybe it *was* a concussion illusion and would be gone tomorrow. And if it wasn't... well, he had time then to find out.

Mark picked up the remote and changed the channel to Netflix. He turned on an ancient *Star Trek: The Next Generation* episode, deciding that it was about all he could handle at the moment. As the theme music rose and Patrick Stewart intoned "Space, the final frontier..." over a backdrop of astronomical images, Mark lay back and allowed his mind to go where it wished—which, it turned out, was to sleep.

* * *

Mark awoke the next morning still on the couch and with the TV still on, playing yet another episode of ST:TNG— one of his favorites, "The Measure Of A Man," with Picard defending Data as a sentient being. Finnigan lay across his legs, and his head no longer throbbed, the coldpak now at room temperature. The glass of water was still on the coffee table, and so was the remote control. The details of last evening slowly came back to him like a phantom dream. *Was any of that real? Or was it just the concussion?*

Groaning, Mark lifted himself to a sitting position, rubbing his head and grimacing. He touched the still-tender knot. He looked at the remote control and shook his head. The call of his bladder was overwhelming; he padded into the bathroom. Afterward, he splashed water on his face, staring at his rumpled bed hair.

"There's only one way to know," he told his reflection. "If time's really doubling with every use, that's a problem, but twice 56 seconds is only one minute and 52 seconds. That's worth another experiment, isn't it? I gotta know for sure."

His reflection didn't answer, just stared back at him sleepily. Mark rubbed his eyes and went back into the living room. He fished his smartphone from his pocket and pulled up the stopwatch app. He held it in his left hand with his thumb over the start button and picked up the remote control again, holding it over the couch cushions as he let go. "Stop!" he said and pressed the start button at the same time, thinking he was going to feel extremely foolish if nothing happened at all.

But the remote control froze halfway to the couch, as did Captain Picard in mid-speech; from the corner of the couch, Finnigan stared like a statue at the formerly-descending remote. The world went silent around him. He glanced at the stopwatch; it was still counting the seconds—so evidently anything he was holding when he stopped time was unaffected; that was good to know. Mark sat on the other end of the couch, waiting and staring at the seconds ticking by on his phone.

At one minute and 52 seconds precisely, the remote control finished its descent and Finnigan pounced on it. Picard's melodious voice returned. "Holy fuck," Mark whispered softly. Visions of himself as a costumed superhero flashed through his mind: *Stopwatch, who can stop Time itself…Ah, the possibilities…*

Mark brought up the calculator function on his phone and found a piece of paper and the stub of pencil. He started writing: 1) 7 seconds, 2) 14 seconds, 3) 28 seconds, 4) 56 seconds, 5) 112 seconds…and so on. It was more laborious a project than he thought. By the tenth time he used the power, the stoppage time would be already nearly an hour; by #20 it was over 42 days. He stopped at #24, which was 1 year, 314 days, 15 hours, 10 minutes, and 56 seconds.

The Great and Powerful Stopwatch might be able to stop time, but having to wait nearly two years before things start up again? That's a long time to be alone in an unmoving world. How long can someone maintain their sanity with no one else to interact with?

No. This required more thought.

* * *

His phone's ring tone—the theme for *Black Panther*—interrupted his reverie before Mark could formulate any kind of answer. He looked at the phone: SOPHIA WATT. Mark grabbed the phone and swiped his finger over the *Answer* bar. "Hey, Sophia! How's it going?"

"Mark—good to hear you sounding so up." The tone of her voice made Mark grin. "I was about to ask you the same thing. You feeling okay? No problems last night?"

Mark decided that discovering he was able to stop time didn't qualify as a 'problem,' exactly. In fact, some interesting thoughts were already sluicing through his mind. "Nope. As a matter of fact, I feel much better this morning. Terrific, in fact."

"That's good." Again, the obvious relief in Sophia's voice made Mark smile. *Maybe I have a chance after all.* "But you should still take the day off and pay attention to how you're feeling. I'll figure on you being in here tomorrow. By the way, I've told Support they need to come in today to check over the file servers and make sure we get a new broadcast delay unit. I don't want anyone else getting shocked."

At the announcement, a strange but undeniable jealousy surged through Mark. *I don't want anyone else getting the ability to stop time. There can be only one Stopwatch…* "Sounds like a great idea to me," Mark told her. *Yes, swap out the unit and no one else could get the ability I have.* "I'll see you tomorrow, then. Looking forward to it, actually."

"Great. See you tomorrow." With that, Sophia hung up. Mark leaned back on the couch cushions, ruffling Finnigan's neck around his collar. He looked again at the paper with the timing figures. "Y'know what, Finnigan? Given the limitations, I think I have a much better idea than being a superhero. It'll just take a little planning on my part. Now let me just grab that remote again..."

* * *

At noon, Mark parked in a company lot on Parsipanny Road across the street from the Chase Bank. He stepped out of the car and took his phone out of his pocket. He glanced first at the note he'd put on his phone giving the duration for each time stop. This would be the ninth—he'd used the remote for #6 through 8 to give him enough time: *29 minutes and 52 seconds. Should be about right.* He opened the clock function on his phone, pulled up the Timer function, and entered the duration. He put his thumb over the Start button, looking at the traffic on the road.

"Stop!" he proclaimed to the world, pushing the button on his phone's screen at the same time.

Silence descended around him, the sound of cars and tires on pavement vanishing as the cars and trucks there went still. A few birds hung motionless in the sky; the wind no longer ruffled his hair. A group of four people leaving the building nearest him halted mid-step and mid-conversation.

"Like *The Day the Earth Stood Still*, only the people have stopped too," he whispered. "Too bad I don't have Klaatu along." His voice seemed to fall dead, like he was speaking in a soundproofed studio.

Mark wove his way across the street between the stopped cars. He examined the faces behind the windshields: frozen in attentive stares; with mouths open singing along to the radio; looking curiously at the driver in the car next to them; carelessly turning to speak to the passengers in the car. He walked across the bank's lot, only the sound of his own footsteps accompanying him. He pulled a pair of gardening gloves from the *Trader Joe* cloth shopping bag he carried and slipped them on before he reached the door—being held open by an exiting customer. He slid past the matronly woman, who looked like someone's kindly grandmother, patting her on the cheek as he passed—*so touching someone doesn't release them from the time stoppage. Good to know.*

He opened the second door, then went into the bank: three tellers, each with a customer, a line of two waiting, and a manager sitting in his glass-walled office. Mark easily vaulted the locked half-door to the back of the teller cages and started walking down the line, taking five twenties from the first teller's hands—*won't she be surprised when time starts up again!*—then snatching all the cash from her open drawer. The bills went into the shopping bag. The other two tellers had their cash drawers closed, so Mark took the opportunity to find their keys and unlock them, taking the paper money there.

He looked at his phone: fifteen minutes gone, fourteen minutes left—well, make it ten to be sure he got across the street before the world started moving again. He went to the bank vault: closed and locked. He considered seeing if he could find the manager's keys, but decided it wasn't worth the risk.

"Have a nice day!" he announced to everyone and left the bank, the shopping bag swinging heavily alongside him. He gave Grandma a kiss on the cheek as he passed her, taking two twenties from the shopping bag and putting them in her purse. He walked quickly across the street and to his car.

He was grinning like the Cheshire Cat as he watched the timer count down the last few minutes, thinking of how confused everyone was going to be: money gone and security cameras showing nothing at all. One moment, all the cash was there; the next instant, *poof.* Gone. No robber entering the building, no strange car in the parking lot to investigate. The world's best magic trick.

It's a hell of a lot easier to be a thief than a superhero, and a lot more profitable. He grinned even more widely, glancing down at the shopping bag and the cash there.

The timer pinged. The world slammed into motion again, the noise blaring through his car windows. He started his car and pulled out of the parking lot.

As he passed the bank, he thought he heard alarms going off, but it may just have been his imagination.

* * *

Back at the apartment, he counted his haul: "$9,327," he told Finnigan, who seemed unimpressed with the money but liked the cloth bag, "though I gave Grandma forty bucks. Hardly a fortune, but not bad for half an hour, I guess. And heck, it's not even noon yet. Though the next time, I'll have nearly an hour to wait..."

He left the money on the coffee table and dumped Finnigan out of the bag. "I'll be back later. Take care of the cash, would you? And don't you dare pee on it."

Finnigan just stared.

Mark went out to the car. Realistically, he only had maybe five more times that he could stop time before the duration went into days rather than hours. He needed to find a way to get bigger hauls of cash if he were going to make this work. Banks, he was starting to realize, don't have much cash laying around. There had to be better and easier places to find lots of cash: restaurants? big department stores? He figured he'd drive around and think on this...

As he pressed the key to unlock the car, a loud, annoying burst of static speared through his head, agonizing enough that he dropped the key and slapped his hands to his ears, though it did nothing to allay the shrieking. The static went away in a few seconds. He shook his head as he retrieved the keys. *What the fuck was that?*

He started to get into the car, then stopped. *Sophia said she was going to have the dump box array replaced today. Could that have been the cause? What if...?*

He didn't allow himself to finish the thought. He glanced at the car's clock: 12:03. The *Damon Anderson Show* started at 4:00 — that made sense; Sophia needed to have the array replaced and checked out before the show. Mark thought he'd drive into Manhattan and find out if the dump array had been replaced and at what time. And if so, he'd also find out what that might mean as far as his new ability was concerned. Worst case scenario: if he could no longer stop time, he was nine thousand dollars richer. He could live with that. A decent bonus payment.

In Manhattan, as he approached the studio, he noticed a Brinks armored truck pulled over near Rockefeller Center. Two armed guards were at the back, one just opening the doors. Mark found it too much of a temptation. He drove several feet past the Brink's truck, then: "Stop!" He wasn't certain anything would happen.

But it did, as it had every time before. There was the odd silence, like he'd suddenly enclosed his head in the world's best noise-cancelling headphones, as the Manhattan street went motionless around him. *I should have nearly an hour this time.* Taking out his phone, he set the timer for 55 minutes, started it, and left the car. He strode purposefully back toward the Brink's truck, walking around the guard whose hand was on the butt of his pistol, then the guard who'd opened the door.

Jackpot! He knew it as soon as he peered inside. Bags of money were stacked there. Thousands, probably hundreds of thousands. Maybe even half a million or more. He hauled bags back to his car, opening the trunk and sliding them in. It took him nearly forty minutes to get it all and he was sweating and out of breath when he was finally back in his car. The timer said he still had five minutes left. He buckled his seat belt and put his hands on the wheel, saluting his image in the rearview mirror. *When things start moving again, I'll just move along with them. Any security cameras will see my car as having already driven past the Brink's trunk when the money's suddenly gone. They'll never have a reason to suspect me, even if they do see my car. Never.*

The timer went off. Mark readied himself to move with the traffic, waiting for the world to start again like a streaming movie taken off pause.

It didn't. At first he thought he must have mis-set the timer. Things would start up again in another minute. Two at the most.

Fifteen minutes later, the world remained dead and still around him.

* * *

After sitting in his car for almost two hours, Mark made the decision to leave again. It wasn't entirely altruistic: he had to pee. He was only four blocks from the studio…The dump box array was there and he was certain that somehow that was the key to everything that had happened.

Getting in the building wasn't hard, but of course none of the elevators were running and the studio was on the 8th floor. He hit the restroom in the lobby—luckily not all the urinals were in use—then went to the stairs. The climb seemed interminable and his thighs were burning by the end. He sat on the last landing to catch his breath, then pushed the door open.

The studio was ensnared in the usual pre-show chaos. Mark made his way to the control booth overlooking the studio floor. He saw Sophia immediately, her headset already on, her finger pointing toward the bank of video screens. Her mouth was slightly open, as if she were about to speak. Mark went over to her, walking once around her and staring as if examining a statue in the art museum. He reached out to touch her cheek: it was warm and he snatched his hand back. "Do you know I'm here, Sophia? Can you hear me at all?"

He leaned in toward her. "What could it hurt?" he mused aloud. He pressed his lips against her open mouth, but it was like kissing the back of his hand and he felt immediately guilty.

He sighed and stepped back. "Sorry, Sophia. That wasn't fair."

He moved across the control room to his own seat; someone was sitting there he didn't recognize—probably a sound engineer from another show subbing in for him. But he noticed immediately that the dump box was new. The old one wasn't anywhere in sight.

"Damn..." he muttered.

* * *

Mark spent the next several hours looking for the old dump box, prowling through areas of the studio building that he'd never seen before, and finally giving up. He felt like he was walking through some odd museum from one static diorama to the next: Engineering; Writers Room; Executive Suite; IT Support; Guest Waiting Rooms; the studios of other shows; the backstage corridors.

The world remained frozen in place around him, time seemingly eternally stopped. Panic slowly rose within him: his mind racing, his heart slamming against the cage of his ribs as if trying to escape, his breath too fast and shallow. He felt as if there were no oxygen in the air and the very walls were pressing in against him.

He stumbled down the stairs and back outside into the sunlight. He walked like a drunken man down the sidewalk, weaving between the people frozen in mid-step on the crowded sidewalk until he found his car again. He took out his key, his hand trembling, then shoved the key back in his pocket: even if the car might start, there was no way he could maneuver through the time-stopped gridlock of the street.

His gaze fell on the tableau of a courier just stepping away from his bike half a block away, stooping down with his bike lock in hand. Mark ran there and got on the bike. The pedals moved and the rear wheel turned in response; he gave a sigh of relief and the feeling of panic started to subside. He could no longer hear his heartbeat throbbing in his temples.

Okay. I can get back home if I want; it's probably thirty miles, but I can take all the time I need. If I have to stop and sleep, so what? Pop into a hotel and sleep on the couch in the lounge. If I get hungry, I'll just go into a convenience store or restaurant somewhere and make myself a meal...

He rode the bike back to his car. He unloaded the money bags, placing them one by one back in the Brinks truck—it wouldn't do if time suddenly started up once more with him gone, his car blocking 5th Avenue traffic, and all that stolen cash stuffed inside. He patted the armed guard on the shoulder when he was finished. "See? No harm, no foul."

Back on the bike, he returned to the studio building in eternal afternoon sunshine. It took another few hours, but he finally found the old broadcast delay unit, sitting in a pile of other discarded studio equipment in the basement. Mark grabbed it and took it back up to the studio. He disconnected the new broadcast delay unit and plugged in the old familiar one. He didn't know what he expected to happen: maybe a repeat of that terrible static he'd heard, maybe for time to immediately start up again.

Nothing at all happened. Mark sat in the studio for another hour with Sophia and his motionless peers, hoping that maybe with the old dump box plugged back in, time would start as it should according to the schedule he'd put together.

It didn't. After another half hour, feeling hungry and starting to panic again, Mark unplugged the old delay unit, plugged the new one back in, put the dump box under his arm, and left the building.

Back on the street, he put the dump box in the carrier of the borrowed bike and began cycling off toward the Hudson River, riding down the middle of the street between the still and silent cars and the statues of pedestrians on the sidewalks.

* * *

He returned home what he thought might be two days later, though the battery on his smartphone had died so he couldn't be certain how much time had passed. Surrounded by silence, surrounded by people who might as well be dead, surrounded by a never-changing day, he found the apartment was, unsurprisingly, exactly as he'd left it. He stroked the fur of an unresponsive Finnigan as he passed the cat, curled up on a corner of the couch.

"Hey, Finnigan." He'd found himself talking to the frozen people around him on his journey home, as if one of them might finally stir and answer. Petting Finnigan was like stroking a stuffed cat. There was no answering purr or lifting of his rump.

Mark plugged in the dump box, caressing its top panel as he had when he'd first felt the shock and been knocked out. He'd happily accept the pain if it also happened to start time up once more, or at least restore things to where they'd been. But there was no response at all.

He sat on his couch, stroking Finnigan for the little comfort that gave him.

What if this lasts forever? If so, I've effectively killed everyone in the world. Or worse, killed everyone and everything in the entire universe. All their dreams, all their potential accomplishments, all their futures gone, and it's my fault. I've caused the end of all time and all existence: my fault. I'm the creator of the frozen universe, where the stars themselves no longer hurtle through space. My fault. And I...I have to somehow live with that. Alone. Forever alone. How long can I stand this solitary confinement of my own doing? How long before I simply go stark raving mad?

He pounded his hands against his head, guilt and fear and dread inundating his thoughts in a tsunami of self-loathing.

Or...Maybe it's just me. Maybe I've been looking at this backwards and the world and everything and everybody in it is actually just fine and still moving forward as it always has—I've simply been tossed outside the time stream. Could there be a portal back into time? How can I find it?

I don't know.

There has to be a way to solve this. There has to be...

He waited, staring at the dump box and praying to a god he didn't believe in for time to start up again. But it didn't.

Not that day.

Not the next.

Not during the next week...

...or the next month...

...or the next year...

...or...

* * *

"...make sure that the first guest—"

Sophia found herself suddenly standing in the midst of flowers that appeared in an instant from absolutely nowhere as she talked to the control room staff. At least a dozen vases were arrayed around her as if she were a shrine, the flowers all fresh. The control room smelled like a funeral parlor. "Jesus!" Her feet scattered blossoms and knocked over vases as she stepped back and away. "What the hell...?"

The other people in the booth stared at her and the colorful, fragrant mess, seeming as puzzled and shocked as her. "Which one of you did this?" she asked. "I mean, great trick and all, but..."

She was answered by a series of shrugs, open mouths, and shaking heads. No one would admit to it, even when she questioned the rest of crew down on the stage floor. Damon Anderson himself would only shake his head. "Honest, Sophia. I had nothing to do with it. Maybe you have a secret lover who wants to impress you."

"A secret lover? Yeah, just what I need. What I *want* is someone to clean this up so I can get your show ready," she answered.

It took an hour and a quartet of the janitorial staff to put the control room back in some semblance of order.

Everyone rushed to get everything together, especially with the substitute sound engineer for Mark, who wasn't used to doing live shows and was obviously nervous. Sophia eventually left the control booth to go down to the stage floor and start the show.

The segments went well enough; after they were off the air, Sophia went up to the control booth for a debrief with the staff and to prepare them for tomorrow's guests. No one was yet admitting to having played the prank with the flowers, not that she could figure out how it had been done. Shaking her head, Sophia went back to the stage floor to supervise the stage crew putting away equipment and resetting the studio.

She was exhausted—and still pissed with whomever had brought in the bouquets. She hoped things would be back to normal tomorrow.

"Excuse me. You're Sophia Watt?"

Sophia turned at the inquiry. She squinted, not recognizing the man approaching her from the aisle between the empty audience seats. "I am. And you're…"

"Detective Captain Harris, Parsippany PD." He flashed a badge in her direction. "Do you know a Mark Evert?"

"Mark? Of course…" She stopped as a shiver passed through her. She put the back of her hand to her mouth. "My God, has something happened to Mark?"

"Why don't you sit down, Ms. Watt?"

Suddenly, her breath was stuck in her throat. Sophia nodded. Her hands shook as she lowered herself into a director's chair near the stage left camera. "I don't understand…"

"I'm afraid I have to inform you that that Mr. Evert is deceased," Harris said. His voice held a professionally-aloof sympathy.

"Dead? Mark? How?" she managed to grate out. She felt bile rising in her throat, hot and burning. She swallowed hard.

"Suicide, I'm afraid. It appears he took his own life. Can you tell me, was he despondent? Did he own a gun?"

Sophia shook her head, bewildered and confused by the questions. None of that sounded like Mark. She repeated the unbelievable words. "Despondent? A gun? Mark… Mark is always upbeat, sometimes too much so, and I remember him once saying that he'd never own a gun. I'm sorry, Detective Harris, but are you *sure* we're talking about the same person? None of this sounds like the Mark I know. I talked to him just this morning and he said—" her voice broke and she stopped to compose herself "—he said he was looking forward to being here tomorrow after his accident yesterday."

"His accident?"

She closed her mouth, biting at her lower lip. Harris wrote in a notebook as Sophia told him about what had happened with the broadcast delay unit and how she'd taken Mark home afterward. She saw him frown.

"And after you dropped him off, you went home?"

Sophia nodded. "I have a roommate. She can tell you when I got home."

"I'm sure she can. If you don't mind my asking, was Mr. Evert more than just a co-worker to you?"

Sophia felt her face grow hot. "Not in *that* way, no, he isn't. Wasn't. I'm his boss, but I do think of him as friend. Look, I talked to him—" she pulled up her phone log and turned the screen so Harris could see "—at 9:08 this morning to tell him to stay home. See?"

Harris nodded and jotted something else in his notebook. "Then I suppose that's all I need from you at this point. If I need more for some reason, I'll be in touch—but it's pretty obvious what happened. I'm sorry for the loss of your friend, and sorry you had to hear it this way."

Harris started walking back up the aisle toward the exit doors. Sophia stared at the man's back, not moving from her chair—not certain she *could* move. It felt so impossible that

Mark could be dead, that he could have committed suicide. Just this morning she'd talked to him, and less than twelve hours later… Her throat closed on a sob.

As Harris reached the studio doors, he stopped and turned around. "Actually, I have another question. How *old* was Mr. Evert?"

Sophia swallowed heavily. "You'd have to ask HR to know exactly, but I'd say around 25, maybe a few years older at the most."

"He was 26, according to the driver's license in his wallet," Harris answered, "but I swear he looked to be easily in his late 40s. Strange. Anyway, sorry to have bothered you, Ms. Watt, and again, sorry for your loss."

Sophia stared in the detective's direction as Harris opened the studio door and went through. The sound of the door's closing reverberated in the studio.

The echo seemed to go on forever.

THE OTHER WALKER

D.B. Jackson

It promised to be a difficult Walk. Not impossible, but taxing. Four turns and several days. Eiani had gone farther, had given more of her life in service to the queen, and she would again. This particular journey would be neither the hardest nor the easiest. Still there would be a cost. For Walkers, there was always a cost.

"We were poorly served," the queen said, as Eiani knelt before her, head bowed in obeisance. "Ever we try to rule with wisdom and a generous hand, but when our ministers offer poor advice and prove themselves short-sighted... Well, how are we to overcome such limitations? We cannot be expected to do all, to see all, to anticipate all. Even our mind is not so nimble as that."

"Yes, Your Majesty."

Silence. Had she allowed a hint of irony to underlay the words? She didn't dare look up, not even to gauge the queen's expression.

In truth, this *was* Her Majesty's fault. *Of course* it was her fault. Eiani had been privy to the discussions leading up to

Therla's decision. The queen received good advice and bad. She listened to sound reasoning and drivel. As ever. In this instance, again, she chose poorly.

Which meant that Eiani would have to Walk back and convince Her Majesty to correct the error. Four turns and six days. Plus the return to this time. Over eight turns in all—more than half a year. Not much in the context of a life, but they were her turns, her days. It was her life. *She*—not the queen—would age those turns, those days. All because Therla hadn't the sense of a stick.

"Rise, Walker."

Eiani stood, eyeing the queen, searching her wizened face for signs of anger. Seeing none, she let out a breath she hadn't known she held. Notwithstanding Therla's lack of intellect, a mere word from the woman, spoken in a moment of pique, could condemn Eiani to the queen's dungeon. Or the executioner's block.

"You will go back," Her Majesty said. "You will instruct me not to sign the treaty, and not to make concessions of any sort in the Sea of Gales. Understood?"

"Of course, Your Majesty." No one *instructed* the queen to do anything, least of all a court Walker with less than two year's tenure in the royal palace. But Eiani understood well enough what needed to be done.

"Good." Therla waved her away with one hand and pulled her shawl more tightly around her bony shoulders with the other. "Off with you then."

Eiani bowed low and backed toward the door. She could have straightened and turned for all the queen appeared to care, but she didn't dare.

Once Eiani had exited the queen's hall, she made her way back to her quarters in the old ward of the palace.

Travelers of any sort—Spanner, Crosser, or Walker—plied their trade in solitude whenever possible. None of their magickally Bound devices, including the golden chronofor

Eiani required for her Walks through time, worked if the user wore a stitch of clothing, or even a piece of jewelry.

She locked her door, undressed, and, shivering in the cold chamber, adjusted the chronofor. Four turns, six days, zero bells. She hesitated. She could not expect to remember where she had been at this time of day so long ago, nor could she recall what sort of day it had been. Hot, most likely. The planting turns in Vleros had been brutally hot, but no one here had remarked on the weather. It seemed blazing sun, torpid, sweltering air, and brief downpours that brought no relief were normal for the isle during Kheraya's latter turns.

In those warm days, though, she had spent most mornings walking the palace grounds or, on a few occasions, practicing her sword work with the captain of the guard and her probationers. Over so much time, the chronofor could only be so precise, but she could at least aim to arrive mid-morning and minimize the risk of encountering herself in the past. She set the chronofor for three additional bells.

Eiani took a long breath, bracing herself for the journey. At last, eyes closed, muscles tensed, she thumbed the release on her chronofor and waited to be pulled into the torment of the between.

Nothing.

After a tencount, she glanced down at the three faces of the chronofor, making certain she hadn't made some foolish error with her settings. Four turns, six days, three bells. Just as she intended. She pressed the central stem again.

And remained where and when she was.

She pushed the stem a third time, and a fourth. Still, it did not activate.

Barely a ha'turn had passed since last she used her chronofor. It had worked perfectly then, taking her to exactly the time she sought and back again. And it hadn't been out of her possession since. Still, it couldn't hurt to have Houna inspect the device.

Eiani dressed and left her quarters. The Binder's workshop sat at the end of an adjacent corridor. Eiani knocked and, at an answer from within, opened the door. Houna sat at her workbench, hunched over a device Eiani couldn't see. A faint nimbus of magick surrounded her, glowing like starlight in the dim chamber. She glanced toward the door and beckoned Eiani inside.

"Give me a moment," she said, and turned her attention back to the object in front of her.

Eiani shut the door quietly and began to wander the chamber, her gaze returning repeatedly to Houna. The Binder wore a pair of round spectacles perched at the end of her nose, her pale eyes wide and fixed on what Eiani could now see was a sextant. She kept her ebon hair short, tucked behind her ears. The ghost of a dimple creased her cheek as she pressed her lips in concentration—the same dimple that appeared when she smiled.

Eiani looked away, perused the apertures and sextants on Houna's shelves. A fire crackled in the hearth and she lingered before it, warming her hands. She had found few friends during her brief tenure in the palace, none more dear to her than the Binder. Which was why she had been reluctant at first to seek something deeper in their relationship.

After another spirecount or two, Houna straightened and removed the spectacles. The magickal glow around her faded. She took a long breath and stretched, much the way she did upon waking. Much the way she had in the silver of that very morning, when they woke together, before Houna stole back to her chamber.

"Sorry," she said, swiveling on her stool to face Eiani. "Mevin dropped his sextant during his last Span—I honestly don't know how he did it. But he knocked the arc completely out of alignment. I've been trying to repair it all day."

"Should I come back another time?"

Houna smiled, and it was like every candle in the chamber bloomed in flame. "No. What can I do for you?"

Eiani drew her chronofor from within her robe. "This doesn't seem to be working."

A frown furrowed the Binder's brow. She took the chronofor, her fingers brushing Eiani's palm. "Since when?"

Eiani lifted a shoulder. "Just now, as far as I know."

Houna turned back to her workbench and plucked a small, flat-edged tool from a rack. The glimmer of magick reappeared and she tinkered with the device.

After a few moments, the radiance vanished and she gave a soft "hmmm."

"Is there something wrong with it?"

"No, it seems fine." Houna inspected it again, front and back. "This is the setting you wanted? Four, six, and three?"

"Yes."

"And you were...you didn't forget to remove some article of clothing?"

Eiani's face warmed, and Houna's cheeks pinked slightly as well.

"I checked everything twice, including...myself."

Houna exchanged the tool she had been using for a smaller one. The glow rekindled. She opened the back of the chronofor, reclaimed the spectacles, and tinkered with the innards of the device. After another spirecount, she closed the back and handed the chronofor back to Eiani.

"I tightened a spring, and checked the connection of another. But those were small adjustments. I saw nothing that would keep it from working."

"All right," Eiani said, perplexed now. "Thank you." They kissed, their lips barely brushing before both of them glanced toward the door. Therla didn't tolerate romances among those who served in her court. Eiani turned, intending to leave.

"You didn't try anything unusual?" Houna asked, stopping her.

"Unusual in what way?"

Houna shrugged. "You're the Walker. I'm looking for reasons beyond the device."

Eiani returned the chronofor to her pocket. "This would have been a routine Walk, and I did everything the way I usually do."

The Binder's eyes narrowed. "There's one possibility that occurs to me. It's a little alarming, really."

Eiani watched her, waiting.

"I've heard other Binders say that in any given time, only one iteration of a chronofor can work. And always, that's the most recent one."

"I don't follow," Eiani said.

"I'm not surprised. Walkers and your devices—you can be quite confounding." A smile flickered. "We've assumed that yours is the only instance of this chronofor in our time, that it's unique. But if you have Walked back to this time from some point in the future—if there are two of you here, and each of you carries that chronofor—only the most recent to arrive will work. That's the theory anyway."

Eiani almost said that there couldn't be another her in this time, but she swallowed the protest, knowing how foolish it would sound. Who knew what Therla would ask of her tomorrow, or a ha'turn from now? Of course there could be another Eiani here.

"You need to be careful," Houna said, head canted slightly, concern wrinkling her forehead again. "You don't want to meet yourself."

"The other me will be careful for both of us." She spoke without thinking, and immediately knew the words for truth. "That's what Walkers do."

"Probably Therla sent this other you back. Again. Future-you will tell the queen what she needs to hear and return to your rightful time. And then you'll be able to Walk back and do Therla's bidding in this time."

Confounding. That was the word all right.

"I wonder if I'll even need to Walk. Maybe the future me is rendering this Walk unnecessary."

"You should ask the queen."

Eiani answered with a wry smile. "No, I shouldn't. That would be the surest way to meet myself."

Houna paled. "You're right. I hadn't thought of that."

"As I say, this is what Walkers do." She crossed to the door. "Thank you, Houna. This has been a most illuminating conversation."

"My pleasure. Come see me again."

They shared a smile that made Eiani's heart dance. She left and retreated to her chamber.

Over the next several bells, she tried repeatedly to Walk back the four and six to which she had set her device, resetting the bells dial every so often to make certain she arrived in the morning, if the device worked.

It didn't.

She joined the queen and the other ministers for the evening meal, and after, returned again to her chamber to make more attempts. To no avail. She didn't give up until close to midnight, when, frustrated and weary, she climbed into bed and tried to sleep, wishing Houna was there with her.

Questions and fears kept her awake. Why would she return to this time and linger here for so long? Had she been hurt or fallen prey to someone, or some group, who wished to prevent her from accomplishing whatever task had brought her here? Or had Houna been wrong about what kept her from being able to Walk? What if the problem was with her and not her chronofor? She had never heard of a Walker losing her ability to journey through time, but that didn't mean it couldn't happen.

At length, exhaustion overmastered her concerns and she slipped into an uneasy slumber. She awoke to the cold of early morning and an insistent knock upon her door. Her fire had gone out as she slept. She didn't wish to leave the comfort of her bed.

"Yes," she said, her voice rough. "A moment." She threw a robe around her shoulders, crossed to the door, and unlocked it.

A uniformed guard stood before her. He glanced at her hair, barely suppressed a grin. She tried to rake a hand through the tangle, but her fingers caught.

"The queen demands your presence," the man said.

Eiani nodded, attempted to blink herself awake. "How soon?"

"A quarter bell ago. You're a sound sleeper."

Damn. "All right. Please tell her I'll be along shortly."

"I'm to wait and escort you."

Of course. "Very well."

She shut the door, splashed frigid water on her face, worked a brush through her hair enough that she could pile it in a neat bun, and dressed in a ministerial robe. It took her five spirecounts at the most, yet she begrudged every instant. The queen was not known for her patience.

She and the guard navigated corridors and outside walkways to the queen's hall, both of them walking at a brisk pace. Not a word passed between them. Eiani knew why she had been summoned, but she had no idea what to tell the queen when Therla asked why she had yet to Walk back.

When they reached the hall, the soldier opened the door, but then stepped aside rather than lead Eiani within.

Coward.

She entered alone, bowed low just inside the door.

"At last," the queen said, more waspish than usual. "We sent for you bells ago."

Much more than a bell ago, the queen would have been abed herself.

"Forgive me, Your Majesty. How may I serve you?"

Therla waved her forward, the gesture sharp with exasperation. "We thought we ordered you to Walk for us yesterday," she said, as Eiani strode toward the throne. "Did we not make our wishes clear?"

"You were quite clear, Your Majesty."

"And yet, we have no memory of you coming back to us. We have no memory of hearing the warnings we ourself composed. Why is this?"

"I have been—"

"Have you Walked back as we demanded?"

"Not yet, Your Majesty."

"So you have failed us."

Eiani's cheeks burned. "It's not—"

"We can only assume you have some excuse. We don't wish to hear it. Either Walk, as we command, or leave our court. We have no time or patience for green Walkers who prove themselves incapable of serving us in the manner to which we are accustomed. You will Walk now, or you will be banished."

"My chronofor doesn't work!"

Therla glowered.

"Your Majesty," Eiani added, dipping into another bow. She gulped for air, her heart racing.

"The device you use. The one *we* gave you."

"Yes, Your Majesty." She straightened.

"You have spoken with the Binder?"

"I have, Your Majesty."

"And?"

"There appears to be nothing wrong with the device. Or rather, nothing that she can repair."

Therla frowned, puzzlement and disapproval warring for supremacy in her expression. "We do not understand. Does your device work, or doesn't it?"

"It won't work; I'm stuck in this time. But Binder Yain can find nothing wrong with the chronofor."

"Then the problem is you."

Eiani heard in this an unintended echo of what Houna said to her the day before. "That is possible, Your Majesty."

"When did you last try to Walk?"

She faltered ever so briefly. "Last night, Your Majesty."

"You will try again now."

"Of course, Your Majesty." She bowed, started to back toward the door.

"Where are you going?"

"To my chamber, Your Majesty. In order to Walk—"

"Yes, yes, we know. We don't care. You will do this here, now, before us, so that we can see and judge for ourself what the problem might be."

Eiani wanted to ask the queen what she knew of Walking and what she thought she could glean from watching Eiani's attempt. She wanted to ask if she might, for the sake of her own pride, retreat behind a dressing screen for a modicum of privacy. She did neither.

"Yes, Your Majesty," she muttered, her face aflame with her humiliation. She snaked a hand into the pocket of her robe. And found nothing.

Her chronofor, she realized, rested on the small standing desk in her chamber. In her haste to follow the guard this morning, she had forgotten to retrieve it.

She remained in her obeisance, eyes squeezed shut. If she survived this morning, it would be a miracle. "Forgive me, Your Majesty, but my chronofor is in my chamber. I...I hurried here and—"

"Hurried?"

Eiani looked up in time to see the queen arch an eyebrow. "We hardly think so."

"I know just where it is, Your Majesty."

"Go then. Bring it back here. You will Walk from this hall, as we watch."

"Your Majesty," Eiani said.

She backed away and, upon reaching the doorway, spun and rushed to her chamber. She flung open the door and strode to the desk. The chronofor rested precisely where she had left it. She grabbed it, whirled again. And halted, having glimpsed from the corner of her eye…something.

A small piece of parchment lay at her feet. Had it been hidden beneath the device? She stooped to pick it up, her entire body trembling.

"We must speak before you Walk back. Tell no one. Go to the Crow."

The tiny words were scrawled in her own slanted hand.

Therla waited for her. Of course, until she convinced this other version of herself to return to her own time, she wouldn't be able to Walk at all. And if she eventually Traveled back four turns and six days to do as the queen asked, she might avoid this morning's confrontation with Therla entirely, in which case any act of defiance now would amount to nothing. She feared the queen, but she trusted herself. What choice did she have?

The *Silver Crow* was a tavern in Yenda, only a short walk from the castle gate. She could be there in less than a quarter bell, as long as she wasn't spotted in the corridors or stopped by the gate guards. She changed out of her ministerial robes and into a plain beige gown and matching cape, clothes that wouldn't stand out in the city.

Eiani walked to the door, but paused there to glance about the chamber. The other her—the one from some different time—had been here not long ago. They might have missed each other by mere moments. A shiver went through her, and she recalled once more the warnings she had heard again and again since her childhood:

Do not meet yourself in the past. Walkers who do have been known to go insane.

Surely, the Eiani from the future had considered this, had thought of some way to mitigate the danger. Again, she had to trust herself—a version of herself she didn't yet know.

She left the chamber, walked silently through the corridors to a stairwell, and descended to the nearest ward.

She left the castle by way of the south gate, which was used less frequently than the east. By now, the queen would be furious. Guards would be scouring the palace for Eiani, and Therla would be ranting about consigning her to the dungeon, or worse.

I hope I know what I'm doing.

She walked swiftly, repeatedly forcing herself to slow, lest she draw attention from others in the lanes. At the door to the *Silver Crow*, she paused to check that she wasn't watched. Then she stepped inside. Pipe smoke and stale ale, bay and cooked fish, baked bread and baviseed—she had spent enough time in this tavern that she could smell the place in her sleep.

Tolly, the barkeep and owner, eyed her from behind the bar, white hair mussed as always, dark eyes troubled.

Eiani stepped to the bar, surveying the great room as she did. The inn was empty save for a pair of old men sitting at a table near the door. They sipped ales and spoke in low tones, taking no notice of her.

"Tolly—"

"She left this," he said, holding out a folded scrap of parchment. "Or you did. Honestly, your kind make me nuts."

She would have preferred that he smile when he said this, but for the moment he looked deadly serious and avoided her gaze. She opened the message.

"Sit at the rear table, back to the door."

This, too, was written in her hand.

"Thank you."

The barkeep dipped his chin, but said nothing. He didn't offer to sell her wine or ale, and she didn't ask. She walked to the back of the bar and sat as the note instructed. For some time she remained alone, but after perhaps a quarter bell, she heard a door open behind her, felt a rush of cold air. Footsteps, light and quick. The scrape of a chair on the old wooden floor.

"I was afraid you wouldn't come."

Her own voice. It sounded strange coming from the mouth of another, rather than from within her own head, but there could be no mistaking it.

"Therla is waiting for me. At this point, I'll be fortunate if she doesn't order my execution. Our execution."

"Clearly she won't. I've Walked back from our future, haven't I?"

Eiani started to twist her neck.

"Don't," the other her said. "I read about this before I Walked. We can interact, but you can't look at me. Our eyes can't meet."

"Insanity."

"Just so."

"But there's no danger otherwise? You're certain?"

"There are no certainties. A hundred paths might lead from this conversation. How can we be certain of anything?"

She settled back in her chair, sobered. Odd that speaking to this other version of herself should made her feel young. "So why have you come?"

"The Walk Therla has ordered you to undertake…"

"Four turns, six days—"

"And three bells. Yes. It would be longer now, if you were to go. You shouldn't."

"You know that's not our choice."

"But it is. You should leave the palace, leave Yenda. Now."

Eiani stiffened, nearly turned again.

"Stop that."

She huffed a sigh, but remained as she was. "How am I supposed to leave the court?"

"You return to the castle, gather what few things we own, and leave. There are always ships coming and going from Vleros. It's just a matter—"

"Why would I go? What possible reason—"

"You know I can't answer."

"Of course you can. You're changing history. That's why you've come: to keep me from doing or saying or seeing something that you've already done or said or seen. So what difference does it make if you tell me exactly what it is you're trying to prevent?"

The other Eiani didn't answer.

"I have to get back to the castle. I have to Walk for Therla."

"As long as I'm here, you can't Walk. And I'll stay as long as I have to."

"Gods! No wonder everyone complains about how stubborn we are!"

Silence met this as well.

"How far back have you come?" Eiani asked, wondering why she hadn't thought to ask sooner.

"I shouldn't tell you that, either."

"I'm leaving." She pushed back from the table, stood.

"If you go back, Houna will die, and we'll suffer in ways you can barely imagine."

She braced a hand on the table.

"Sit down."

Eiani shook her head. "I—I need a cup of wine."

A pause, and then, "Get two."

She plodded to the bar, her legs leaden. A trickle of sweat ran down her temple. Digging into her pocket, she pulled out a trey and set it on the bar.

"Two cups of Miejan red," she said.

Tolly gazed past her to the table.

"You do this a lot? Talk with yourself, I mean. I've heard that your kind can't—"

"The wine, Tolly."

He flicked another glance at the future Eiani before producing two cups and a flask. "Take it," he said. "If the two of you drink it all, we can settle up later."

"Thank you."

Eiani grabbed the flask and the two glasses and started back to her table. She could see the back of the other Eiani's head and a bit of her shoulder. She wore a blue gown, one of Eiani's favorites. For just a moment, her anger flared. Who was this woman to take a gown from her wardrobe? She nearly laughed at herself.

She walked the rest of the way to her chair with her gaze lowered, refusing to chance a second look at the woman. After pouring herself a bit of wine, she held out the second cup. The future her took it. When she passed the flask to the other woman, their fingers touched. Eiani jumped at the tingle that ran through her skin and up her arm.

"What was that?"

"Carelessness," the other Eiani said, her tone hard. "Don't let it happen again."

She sipped her wine, set her cup on the table with a shaking hand. "What happens to Houna?"

The other her didn't answer.

"The more you tell me, the greater the chance that we can find a way to keep Houna alive without giving up our place in Therla's court."

"Do we really care about Therla or her court?"

"I care about having a position somewhere. I care about being labeled a traitor for refusing to follow the queen's commands. So, either tell me what happens, or go back to your own time and allow me to Walk as she instructed."

Eiani drank more wine. Her hand trembled still, but she was pleased that her voice remained steady.

"You would risk Houna?"

"I'd save her, if only you'd tell me what I want to know!"

Silence stretched between them, obstinance and impatience perfectly balanced.

"Fine," Eiani said, spitting the word, determined to leave.

And at the same time, her future self said, "It's Houna's fault."

She went still. "What is?"

"The failure of the treaty. She's why I had to go back, why you have to now."

"I don't understand. How could she—"

"It wasn't a bad treaty—contrary to what we believed, the queen acted wisely enough in pushing for her favored provisions and allowing the Herjeans and Westisle to have their way on others. All the problems that prompted her to send us back were caused by something else. It took me... some time to determine what it was."

What she described over the next several moments was nearly too convoluted for Eiani to follow: a scheme designed to undercut Vleran merchants in the Sea of Gales by sharing with their competitors information about scarcities in Yenda and other Vleran cities. At the same time, it seemed orders for the Queen's navy had found their way to sea bandits who made their home on Westisle. Assaults on Vleran warships had taken a significant toll on the fleet. As the other Walker spoke, Eiani revised again and again her estimate of how far back this version of herself had come, until it neared a year.

When the future Eiani finished her explanation, Eiani asked, "What does this have to do with Houna?"

"Isn't it obvious? They received the information from her. She's a spy."

Eiani let out a dry laugh. "That's ridiculous. Houna's no spy."

No response.

"She's not. She couldn't be."

"I cared for her, too. I miss her every day. I understand how all this must sound, but I'm telling you—"

"Why would she do it? Who is she working for?"

"I don't know. When we worked out what had happened, the queen—well, you can imagine. She had Houna taken by the guard for...for questioning. I never saw her again. From what I've been told, I wouldn't have wanted to see her."

Eiani shuddered. "Maybe Therla was wrong. It wouldn't be the first time."

"She wasn't. We intercepted a courier. He was barely more than a boy and he didn't know much. But he was carrying coin—ten gold rounds—and he was to give it to Houna."

"He could have been lying."

"We had no reason to believe he was."

"*You* could be lying."

"To what end? Think! Put your feelings aside for just a moment and consider what I'm telling you. I've come back to warn you about this, at the cost of considerable time. I'm you. You know I wouldn't have done this if I wasn't certain."

Eiani resisted the impulse to argue further. Of course she knew. It was no small thing spending turns for a Walk, risking insanity by confronting herself, forcing her to defy the queen's orders.

"She did it for gold?" she asked after a pause.

"I never had the chance to ask."

Eiani nodded, though the other her couldn't see. "You said before that we would suffer as well. What did you mean?"

She thought the other Eiani would again refuse to answer, but after a breath, she said, "Some know that Houna was…a friend. I was accused of treason as well."

"But we survive."

"Yes. In time, I convinced Therla's inquisitors of my innocence and I returned to my duties."

"So the cost to us—"

"Torture. The danger of insanity isn't the only reason I don't want you to see me."

She nearly gagged on a half-taken breath. "All right," she managed, after swallowing the bile in her throat. "What is it you want me to do?"

"I've told you. We need to leave this place."

"And go where?"

"Anywhere!"

"That's not good enough. And it doesn't help Houna."

"Of course it does! If we don't Walk back—"

"Therla will discover her betrayal some other way." She paused, barely long enough to inhale. But in that interval, it came to her. "She's the one who has to leave. Not us."

The other Eiani didn't answer immediately. Eventually, she said, "Interesting. You could convince her?"

"Yes. Four turns ago."

"Swear that you'll do this and I'll return to my time."

"I swear it."

"If you fail—"

"I won't. Walk back. I'll do this."

After a tencount, the other Eiani shifted in her seat. Eiani heard her place her cup on the table and push back, her chair scraping again on the wood floor. "I take my leave."

"May the Two guide you back and protect you. Us."

"Blessings upon you as well."

She waited, listening as the other Eiani left the tavern through the rear door. When she was confident the woman was gone, she returned the carafe to Tolly and made her way back to the castle. She went directly to her chamber, removed her gown, and checked the settings on her chronofor. It was still calibrated to send her back four turns and six. She added a day, adjusted the bells setting, hoping she would arrive when the past version of herself was gone from the chamber.

Eiani thumbed the release and was jerked into the between, as if some giant, unseen hand had snatched her out of the present. Colored light flashed all around her. A violent din assailed her—voices, laughter, the clatter of carriage wheels, the patter of rain and the keening of a storm wind, the clanging of palace bells—blending into a discordant clamor that pounded at her head. Noisome smells and vile flavors stung her nostrils and oozed over her tongue. The sensory experience of so many turns and days all compressed into moments of abuse. As the breath she had taken before activating the chronofor spent itself, panic took her. Was this the Walk that would prove too much for her?

She stumbled out of the between, collapsed to her knees, gasped at clean, cool air. A quick glance around the chamber confirmed she was alone, that it was day.

She forced herself up, crossed to the wardrobe on unsteady legs. She put on the blue gown, eased out of the chamber, and followed the corridors to Houna's workshop.

She knocked, entered at Houna's call.

As always, the Binder sat bent over a device, magickal glow around her, dark hair falling over her brow. Eiani's chest tightened at the sight of her. She'd come back to a time before they consummated their relationship. Just before.

Houna is a spy.

The woman glanced her way, smiled. Eiani looked off to the side, started to orbit the chamber.

"You've changed."

Eiani faltered in mid stride. "Changed?"

"Your clothes. You were wearing red before."

She nearly dissembled, but stopped herself. What would be the point?

"No," she said. "I didn't. That was…a different me."

Houna's smile slipped. "How far back?" she asked, her voice hushed.

"I can't say."

The Binder set the device she was holding on the workbench and removed the spectacles from the bridge of her nose. "I see." She swiveled on her stool, crossed her arms. "You came back to speak with me?"

Eiani shook her head. "To save your life."

She paled. "From?"

Eiani halted by the window and stared out toward the sea. She had missed the warmth of the planting turns. "Who do you work for, Houna?"

Weak laughter. "The queen, of course."

"Stop it." Eiani glared her way. "I've come back for you, for both of us. I'm in danger, too. Because of you. I've spent turns to be here. At least have the decency to tell me the truth."

Houna stared, ashen and lovely. At last she straightened, raised her chin slightly. The guileless diffidence Eiani had always found so endearing seemed to fall way, leaving someone harder, older.

"Who do you think?"

Eiani needed all of two heartbeats to consider the question. Vleros had many rivals, but only one true enemy. "Milnos."

Houna's shrug was so casual as to be infuriating.

"You need to leave the castle," Eiani said. "Today. Don't ever come back."

The Binder shook her head. "I can't do that. But you can join me, work with me. I know the king would welcome a Walker to his sphere."

"I serve the queen of Vleros."

"You hate her, just as I do."

"That has nothing—"

"Don't be naïve. You hate her. I'm offering you gold and a chance to work for the side that is destined to prevail."

"You're not listening to me. You're going to be dead in a matter of days. Tortured to death. And I'll be tortured as well. You have to leave now. I'm offering you your life."

"Why would you do this? What am I to you?"

Eiani's cheeks blazed. She glanced to the side. "I think you know."

Houna slid off her bench and sauntered closer. "I want you to tell me," she whispered.

Eiani wasn't aware of drawing her blade. One moment her hand was empty, the next she held her dagger before her, its tip aimed at Houna's heart.

Houna halted. She eyed the steel and then raised her gaze to Eiani's.

"Have you ever killed, Eiani? Have you spilled blood?"

"I was trained in Windhome," she said, knowing it for another evasion. Her hand shook. She couldn't help that. "It doesn't matter if I've killed. I *will* kill you. Pack your things and leave. I intend to inform the queen of your betrayal. I'll give you two bells. After that, your life is forfeit."

"I don't believe you."

"Then you're going to die. I swear it on the Two."

Houna stared for another fivecount. Finally, she nodded. Eiani turned to leave.

"I love you."

Eiani stopped, closed her eyes briefly. "No, you don't. But I could have loved you."

She left the Binder's workshop and returned to her own chamber. A risk, but she didn't know where else to go. She kept her blade in hand; she wasn't sure why.

When two bells had passed, she left the chamber and walked to the Queen's hall. There, she informed Therla that she had been sent back by Her Majesty herself to keep Vleros from entering the Sea of Gales Treaty. Therla wasn't pleased, but a brief explanation of what would come of the agreement convinced her. Eiani said nothing about Houna.

As soon as the queen dismissed her, she hastened back to her chamber, undressed, and Walked forward to her own time.

Upon arriving in her new future, memories came to her— ones she hadn't had before. The day after Therla declined to sign the treaty, she was summoned to the hall and questioned at length by the captain of the queen's guard. What did she know of the Binder's sudden disappearance? Where might Houna have gone? Why would she have left Yenda so abruptly?

Much was made of her friendship with the Binder; many were aware that they spent time together. But in the absence of evidence, the captain—and the queen—had no choice but to believe her when she professed ignorance.

A ha'turn later, Eiani received a terse missive, unsigned, scrawled in a neat hand similar to her own, but different enough to leave little doubt as to who had sent it.

I trust this finds you well. I am safely away, feted as a hero, favored in my chosen court. And so I will say now what I should have said before: Thank you.

If ever you choose to leave your current circumstance, you will be welcomed here, by the king, by the other Travelers and ministers, and by me most of all.

She burned the parchment in her hearth.

The next time she tried to Walk back—only a few days, to warn the queen not to eat fowl that sickened nearly every man and woman in the palace—she had no trouble making the journey. Nor did she struggle with subsequent Walks.

Only her heart remained stuck in time, and she knew of no remedy for that.

MY DARK KNIGHT

Faith Hunter

Author's Note:
This story takes place before the novel *Cold Reign*.

She waved her hand in front of Mama and Daddy's open doorway, pushing a little of her magic into the working. It wasn't what Mama called *elegant* but it *was* strong. They wouldn't wake up or hear her. She sneaked down the short stairs into the den, setting her toes and then her whole foot carefully on each step. Once on the solid icy flooring, she inched forward, past the unlit Christmas tree and the few wrapped presents. Around the reclining sofa.

Mama had left her cell on the table beside Daddy's spot and there wouldn't be a better time to make her call. Even EJ was deeply asl—

"Hey, Sissy."

Angelina made a little squeaking sound and stopped with a jerk. The glare of an extra-bright flashlight hit her in the face. "Turn that off," she whispered. The light went out and Angie blinked against the blindness from the glare. She used a *seeing* working and spotted her baby brother cuddled under a blanket in Daddy's spot. He was a wriggling mass of blue and gold and purple magics, bound with Mama's greens and Daddy's yellows. EJ giggled at her and she frowned at him, trying for Ant Jane's mighty scowl. "You're a son of a witch on a switch." Which was Mama's swear words. And Mama would threaten to spank her if she heard her say that. Mama said witch words had power, Angie's words especially. But EJ was a *paaaaaain*.

Her baby brother giggled.

"How did you know I was up?" she demanded.

"Yous magic was singin'"

"Magic doesn't sing. It sparkles."

"Sings. And the magic from the woods is singin' louder. It hu'ts my ea'us."

Angie moved to the window and looked up the small hill behind the house. The woods were dead-dead, not just winter dead. Mama had killed all the trees and bushes by accident and they were gonna take a long time to regen'ate. Yet, her brother was right. The pale glowing magic that had been in the woods all day was sparkling brighter. Way brighter. It was a big magic, yet Mama and Daddy said nothing was there. For some reason, they couldn't see it and they had refused to listen to her.

She could call Ant Cia and Ant Liz or Gramma to come deal with it. Or she could call Ant Jane. She was undecided.

"It sings like a wolfie and a bird and the bells in the church."

Angie turned to her brother who had joined her at the window, dragging his blanket. They had waked George and KitKit. The Bassett Hound and not-a-familiar-cat joined them at the window. George growled, a deep menacing vibration. KitKit hissed and arched her back. "A wolf?" Angie asked her brother.

He nodded, his head moving hard up and down, his bright red hair catching glints from the working on the hillside "Yup. And a bird and bells."

They had just attended a bell service for Christmas and EJ had loved the bell choir. Now, to him, everything sounded like bells.

Angie said softly, "It shines the color of a were-creature. That might make it an animal." She frowned at the hillside. "A paranormal animal-person Mama can't see, maybe a were-creature, or like Ant Jane." Were-creatures could only be the were-creature that bit them. Ant Jane was a Cherokee skinwalker and she could be any shape she wanted. But it wasn't her.

If Angie called her Witchy Ants for help, and if it was were-magic, they could get bit. Her brother could get bit. He stood beside her, a corner of his blanket in his mouth, his blue eyes staring up at her in the dark. He was kinda stupid but Mama and Daddy liked him so she had to take care of him, him and the new baby on the way.

She dragged her eyes back to the hillside. The magic on the hill didn't move like an animal. It moved in a line and a clump. Daddy would say it moved like chaos. Daddy was big into chaos. The sparkles were witchy, the colors were-creature, but the size of the magic was wrong for a moveable witch ward or glamour and wrong for a were-creature. Mama said it wasn't there at all, so it wasn't witch magic.

She studied her own magic, zinging through her blood, knowing she needed someone close by, someone strong, to deal with the strange not-witch magic. There were only a few she trusted and her magic told her that Ant Jane was too far away. Her Dark Knight, Edmund, was vampire strong and when she thought about him, the magic in her blood got brighter. He was nearby.

She retrieved her Mama's cell, returned to the window, and punched in the security code. She looked through the contact list for Edmund, the vampire she'd sworn a blood oath to. She had wanted him to be her fiancée, but when he swore his blood oath and fealty, he didn't promise to marry her. He swore, "to the Everharts and Truebloods…I shall protect your children and your children's children unto the laying down of my own undeath." He had included her whole family, which was how he became their protector. The mystical bond wasn't what she wanted but it was good enough until she grew up and convinced him to marry her.

She was just about to touch the CALL button when EJ said, "Sissy? Its bells is comin' co'ser to the house. If it's a animal, it can get in the ward."

She found the glow in the dead trees on the hillside. Fear shot through her, a bright sizzle of her own red-gold magic. The line-and-clump magic *was* closer, and brighter. It was directly outside the ward that protected the house and grounds. This wasn't good. The *hedge of thorns* was built to allow Ant Jane to get in. If a Big Bad Ugly had figured that out and had a way to use that one weakness, they were in trouble. She had to make her parents understand. Still holding the phone, she grabbed EJ, his blanket, and the flashlight, and hauled him across the TV room toward her parent's bedroom. The critters followed, KitKit meowing.

She made a fist at the entrance of the bedroom and envisioned the power she had stretched over her parent's sleep. "Wake up," she said. The magic flashed red-gold, a sizzle of light, and rushed back into her, popping like a rubber band and covering her with a copper-pink glow. "Ow! Mama! Daddy!" she shouted.

In the dark, Mama rolled over. "Kids? What are you doing up at this hour?"

And then the ward made a gong, GONG, *GONG!* Daddy sat up, still asleep, one arm waving in the air, his other reaching for his flute. Mama raced clumsily to the window and threw open the drapes, looking up the hill, holding her baby bump. Bright light blasted in. Mama said a very bad word, followed by, "Evan, what *is* that thing?"

Her little brother's hands covered his ears. "It's louder! Bad bells hu'ts my ea'as."

Angie pulled EJ closer, under her arm, standing in the doorway. She heard nothing now that the gonging had stopped, because her magic didn't work that way, but there were the dazzling, angry lights of an attack. "I told you it was out there," she accused her parents as Mama and Daddy poured magic into the wards. The thing on the hill started gonging again, which everyone could hear, louder and louder. It threw lights at the ward. Hammering on it. The ward began to hum and echo, brighter and brighter.

EJ cried in pain. KitKit leaped onto the bed, her eyes on Mama, stalking her across the mattress. George tangled into EJ's blanket, underfoot.

Mama screamed, "I don't see anything!"

"Me, neither," Daddy said. "But the ward is fracturing."

The foreign magic was beating a way through. That shouldn't be possible. If it busted the ward, there would be an explosion. They could all die. Unless they dropped the ward and just let the attackers in.

"Evan!" Mama shouted over the magical noise. Terrified.

"Angie," Daddy yelled. "Make a ward. The strongest one you can. *Now!*"

Angie breathed in hard, shocked. Mama and Daddy didn't know she could do big magic.

"Do it! Use all you got. I know you can," Daddy shouted. He blew a long, piercing note full of magic on his flute, creating a personal ward for Mama. He was red-faced and breathless. Mama was panting.

Using her hands and her power, Angie pulled the bindings off EJ, her parents' confining magic tangling around her, sticking to her fingers. Beneath the bindings, EJ's magic glowed a soft purple with sparkling green lights.

"Ohhh," he said. "That feels good."

Daddy's music filled the room, the notes full of power. The *hedge of thorns* shivered. Mama's magic went black as a cave, so dark it sucked all light out of the air, her Death Magics like a cloud around her. They were wild raw magic and every time she used them she risked losing control and killing them all. Now they had two ways to die.

EJ's eyes got big. "Sissy, I'm sca'aed."

"Me, too." Scared because her ward would protect her and EJ, but it wouldn't stop the thing on the hill or stop Mama from using Death Magics, and the ward Daddy wrapped around Mama was unfamiliar. Daddy stumbled, sweating, his magic sputtering as he started a personal ward for himself. To EJ, Angie said, "I learned how to do this in magic camp." Which wasn't entirely a lie. "You trust me?"

EJ threw his arms around her waist, knocking them to the floor, George under her knees. Angie reached inside and found her magic. She looped and twisted it with EJ's. Carefully, she imagined a circle around them, over them, and under them, like being in the middle of a beach ball. Daddy said to make it strong, so she thought about the *hedge of thorns* and the magic of heaven. Angel magic glowed brighter than any magic anywhere. It was the strongest magic she had ever seen. Maybe she could…Angie reached out and pushed the world aside, just a little. Angel magic glowed out from the other side, blinding bright.

The *bonging* was so loud EJ screamed, his head in her middle. Tears raced down Angie's face, burning. Daddy's magic went louder too, as he snapped a pale yellow ward in place over himself.

Mama's magic went pure black. It hit her new, yellow ward.

KitKit leaped, claws out, cat-screaming, for Mama.

Angie pulled the new magic into hers and said softly, "Safe."

* * *

Edmund Hartley wiped the blood off his sword with a square of chamois. The injured scion bowed and limped off the circle, into the crowd. The silence was absolute,

Mithrans in the stands not breathing, not moving, not even blinking, a sign of respect. Humans in a similar situation would have been applauding and screaming, stamping their feet. Vampires were far more courteous and elegant in their appreciation. His host, Lincoln Shaddock of Clan Shaddock, inclined his head in approval at the demonstration of *La Destreza*, the Mithran form of swordplay.

Addressing the Mithrans in the stands, Edmund said, "The moves, in order." He placed his feet in proper position and lifted his weapon. "Alle—"

His cell phone rang, the emergency tone that very few had.

Edmund snapped his fingers. The assistant scion raced to his side with the cell. Edmund swiped the screen and was about to say, "Yes, Molly," but instantly he knew this wasn't Molly. A prescient fear sang down his spine and through his veins, as if his blood boiled. As if he was being summoned, his bond commanded. "Angelina?"

"My Dark Knight. We have troubles," the little girl said, sounding nearly vampire formal. She took a breath that sounded full of tears. "Come save us. Hurry!" She pulled on the bond between them, a sharp twanging pain.

Edmund tossed his sword to the scion and raced from the sparring chambers with a pop of displaced air. As he passed his host, he murmured, "The Everhart-Trueblood place is under attack. Call the family." Back into the cell, sounding calm even as he sped through the night to his car, he said, "Angelina, are you in danger?"

"No. Because EJ and me is under a strong personal ward. But Mama and Daddy's in their bedroom and they aren't moving." She whispered, "I'm afraid."

Dead? Pray God they aren't dead. He sprinted down the drive to his vehicle, everything to his sides appearing as unmoving blurs. Dread and fear swelled inside him, as strong as the thirst for blood, but when he spoke, his voice was calm. "I'm on the way. Tell me what happened. Tell me what you see." He leaped into his Thunderbird Maserati, the top open to the night's chill. Roared the car to life and hit the gas. The 1957 prototype leaped off the bald mountain and down the drive, Edmund shifting gears through the icy streets toward the Everhart-Trueblood home.

"Our ward was being attacked from the hill in back of the house. Daddy said to make a small *hedge*, as strong as I could, for EJ and me. I started making it. Daddy made one for Mama. Then he started one for himself. Then Mama's magics—" Her words cut off.

Ed had access to intel on all the paranormals in the territory. Molly Everhart's Death Magics were one of many secrets to which he was privy. Carefully, Ed said, "I know about the Death Magics, Angie. It's okay."

She sobbed hard, as if a weight had been taken from her. "Okay. Everything happened at once, Edmund. Mama's Death Magics shot out. Daddy started his ward. I got our *hedge* up and it's really strong. But now everything's stopped, even the glowing thing in back of the house."

"Explain stopped." He took a turn too fast and black ice swept him into a fishtail. Wind blew through the convertible. If fear hadn't taken up residence in his heart, it would have been exhilarating.

"Daddy's glow got dim and the gonging on the ward stopped. Mama's standing at the window with her arms out and her magics stopped like a cloud. KitKit's hanging in the air in the middle of a jump. Daddy fell and his head is bleeding everywhere."

A stray thought presented itself. "How did you know I was close?" he asked. Driving one-handed, Edmund swerved around a truck, hitting seventy on the coiling roads outside of Asheville. Up into the hills that surrounded the city.

"I felt you in my blood."

Shock moved through him. Angelina Everhart-Trueblood should not be able to sense him. She was not a Mithran, not his scion, not…not anything that should permit a mental or mystical connection. Their connection was a bond of fealty, not a bond in the Mithran vampire way, yet he had felt a command through that bond, a *calling*. What had the little girl done with his sworn word?

He swerved around two slower cars and took a turn too fast. Angelina was a double-X-gened witch, having received the witch trait from both her father and her mother. Double-X-genes were rare; he knew of only a half dozen in the Americas. Over the connection, he heard panting. Angie was powerful. And terrified.

"I'm only a few minutes away, Angelina. Tell me about…" his mind went blank for a moment, "…about the dog. Where is he? Will…will he bite me?" he asked, to give her something to focus on.

"No. George is under the *hedge* with us."

"Tell me about him."

"George is my Bassett Hound and Mr. Shaddock gave him to me. I'm teaching him to fetch, but his legs are short and he keeps tripping over his ears. George. Not Mr. Shaddock." Edmund smiled and she kept talking as he negotiated the hills and the snaky roads. He pulled up to the house, braking hard to miss the *hedge* that glowed red over the house and grounds, clearly visible to Mithran eyes. A warning to his kind to stay away. Oddly, it was bright enough that even humans could see it tonight, bright enough to cast a reddish shadow. Faster than human, he slid his weapon from the glove box and leaped from the car, dashing into the shadows, away from the beacon of car lights, leaving them shining to attract a predator's attention, should they not all be "stopped."

As Angie talked his ear off, he studied the witch ward, shining into the night. There were shadow groups in the human government and human military, and many less-than-savory characters from the underbelly of society, who wanted witch children. They were in high demand in the magical slavery market. He had no idea what he could be facing. Fear made his pupils expand fully; his fangs clicked down on their hinges.

He would protect this family.

"I am here, Angie. I'm going to scout the edges of the *hedge*, up the hill. I need to end our call to be silent. I'll call you right back. Is that acceptable?"

"Okay, Edmund. I saw your car lights. Bye."

Edmund turned off his cell and pocketed it. He moved around the side of the property, wishing he had kept a change of shoes in the Maserati. The soles of his Italian leather *La Destreza* shoes were useless for an inaudible reconnoiter. He made his way to the back of the property and saw a shimmer of brighter light there, mostly yellow with striations of blue, purple, red, and hints of green, oddly static looking. Inside the glow were two forms, a man and a woman, both wearing night camouflage. The two were indeed "stopped," like mannequins, as if they were frozen outside of time in a…a temporal distortion.

The woman knelt, facing away from the man, wearing a dual ocular headset, a matte black sniper riffle in her arms, aiming back up the hill. Her hip pressed the man's and the point of contact glowed silver. The man leaned against the *hedge of thorns*, a small device in both hands, pressed against the energies, emitting the prism of light. He wore dark glasses against the glare.

The colored light was odd, wavy, spotty, broken, as if it was no longer moving, but hard, stationary, plasticized. Whatever had stopped the people had stopped light, too, or slowed it to something visible. Edmund thought back to Angie's description of creating her small, strong ward. Was it possible that she had tied it to the outer *hedge* and to her mother's Death Magics? If so, this temporal anomaly could be unstable.

It had been centuries since he felt the cold, but it crawled up his spine on icy feet now.

He sent his senses searching up the hill where the woman was aiming. There was no glow of undeath, no sound or scent of life except for small animals and a distant herd of deer. Yet the magic of death clung to the land and he had an instinctive revulsion to the dregs of power that had depleted the hillside of life. Fear clung there, as if the Death Magics cast by Angie's mother still had the power to drain him.

Retrieving his cell phone, he took dozens of photographs under various filters of the couple and the device they used. He sent them to his military and tech security team, texted the situation, and asked for input.

He had no idea what might happen if he reached into the light or touched the couple who had attacked the ward. Edmund chose a stick from the dead forest and touched it to the rainbow of light. The stick passed through easily. Gently, he slipped it forward, through the stopped magics, to inspect the man's pockets, lifting a lapel, poking at pouches on his military-style pants. All were empty, but a faint silver glow appeared at the point of contact each time the stick touched him. The same glow appeared when he inspected the woman, growing brighter each time. It seemed cautionary and he stepped away, tossing the stick uphill, completing his circuit of the large *hedge of thorns*, back to the car. He turned off the headlights, slid the weapon into the waistband of his dress slacks, strode to the *hedge*, and called Angie on his cell.

When she answered, he said, "Angelina, let down your personal *hedge*, please, and come to the front of the house."

"Ummm. I tried." She sounded mortified. "I can't make it go away."

"We's stuck!" EJ chirped in the background. "And I gotta peepee!"

"Angie, do a *seeing* working and tell me if you detect a thread of your magics tying your small ward to the *hedge of thorns* around your home."

She whispered over the cell connection, "Ohhhh. I tied them together."

The Everhart witches had devised numerous wards based on the original *blood-hedge* of protection. Because few of them had to be recharged, he presumed they were either solar charged or ley line powered, though they never volunteered such information. The outer ward wouldn't simply stop at dawn, wear thin, or die off. It had to be turned off, as if with a switch.

"Edmund, it's worse," she whispered again. "My protection ward has tails. One goes to the back of the house. Somehow, I tied my ward to the magic that was breaking through the *hedge*. And…oh no. It's tangled in mama's Death Magics and to angel magic, too."

"Angel?" The little witch must have created a ley line feedback loop, powering it with even more energy than Angie possessed herself. If it broke, would the children enter the temporal distortion, blow up the house and parents and themselves, or perhaps send time-warped space and Death Magics out like shrapnel?

"Whoot!" Angie shouted, and he jerked the cell away from his head. Vampire ears were not made for the shrill tones produced by a witch child's vocal chords. "I got it! I can't make it go away but I can move it. Me and EJ are scooting to the front door."

"Angelina, wait. Take some pictures of your father and mother and send them to me."

"Okay." He heard clicks, followed by grunting and dragging sounds and the chuffing whine of an unhappy dog. The front door opened and he saw the children through a red-gold ward of energies as they came down the steps and along the drive. The children were beneath a low-lying, moveable ward, the upper dome of which was just high enough to allow them to sit up. "I'm hanging up so I can push," Angie said. The call ended and Edmund studied the photos she had texted. Her parents did appear frozen.

Ed felt the power of more witches as two cars climbed the hill to the house, one a half mile behind the first. The Everhart twins had arrived and another witch followed. The first vehicle stopped, the engine went silent, and the ginger-haired identical Everharts joined him at the *hedge*.

"Oh dear," Cia said quietly, the taste of a *seeing* working on the air as they studied the frozen ward. "I had hoped Shaddock was mistaken about an emergency."

Puffing with exertion, the children reached the *hedge*. "Hey, Ant Liz and Ant Cia," EJ said, waving. Angie straightened her nightclothes and made sure her brother and the dog were wrapped in the blanket they had dragged with them, patting the Bassett Hound and her brother equally.

Liz raked short red hair back from her face and said, "EJ. Angie, is there some reason you called a vampire instead of family?" Her tone was carefully calm, but a defensive scowl lit Angie's face, one so like her mother's that Edmund smiled.

"The attack isn't witch magic," Angie said, her tone unapologetic. "It's animal or something else and I didn't want you to get bit by a werewolf or something."

"Big teefes to eat you with!" EJ said happily.

"Ah," Liz said, still composed. "Next time, please call us, too."

"Yes, Ma'am," Angie said, but she transferred her antagonism to the vehicle parking beside theirs. "Who's that?"

"Melodie?" Cia called in surprise as a dark-haired witch emerged from the car.

"Mama said not to talk to people I don't know."

"Angie," Liz said sharply. "Manners." But Angie's scowl grew worse as the third witch approached.

Melodie said, "I'm sure the child has been through a lot tonight. I'm Melodie Joy Custer-Luckett from the Custer witch clan, Angie. I'm renting a room from your aunt Elizabeth while I finish a course at the university." She added, "I was studying late and saw you rush off, Liz. I'm a paramedic. I thought I should follow."

Angie regarded the three women, her mouth turned down. Edmund prepared himself for what she might say.

Angie's suspicion remained but she said, "It's a pleasure to meet you, Miz Melodie."

She elbowed her brother and he pulled a slobbery finger out of his mouth to say, "Pweasure meet you." And stuck his finger back in his mouth.

"Edmund," the little girl said, her formal tenor returning, "Ant Liz, Ant Cia, Miz Melodie, we must break the ward and save my mama and my daddy. And KitKit."

"Breaking an Everhart ward will be difficult," Melodie said.

Liz and Cia nodded, but Angie's eyes narrowed at Melodie's words. Edmund had come to trust the child's discernment. His senses went on alert.

* * *

There was nothing obviously wrong with her, but Angie didn't like the strange witch being here.

"Sissy, I havta to peepee," EJ whispered. "And I'm hungwy and cold."

"We'll be free soon," Angie said, hoping she wasn't lying. She wrapped George in the blanket, too, to give EJ some heat. George promptly fell asleep, drooling on EJ's leg.

The grownups discussed the "situation," as they called it and looked at the pictures she had sent Edmund. Ant Liz said, "Tell me what happened, Angie Baby, and very carefully, walk me through what you did to make such a strong ward."

"I messed up," she admitted. Angie described what had happened, emphasizing the colors of the magical working and EJ piping in with its sound—a drum beating slowly.

"You twined the magics together," Ant Cia said, her tone worried, one hand smoothing her braid over her shoulder.

"Yes," Angie said. "It's what Mama and Daddy do to our magics when they bind 'em so we can't use 'em."

"And you can see the magics? The energies they use to bind you?" Miz Melodie asked.

"It's why it's so easy to get out. But this is different. Mama and Daddy and KitKit are all frozen."

Ant Liz asked the others, "Could she have triggered a temporal disengagement?"

"Or a temporal deactivation," Cia said.

Which sounded very bad.

Melodie said, "Temporal...You Everharts are an interesting bunch."

"I gotta peepee!" EJ said, holding his private parts. "I gotta peepee noooow!"

"First thing then," Ant Liz said, giving him her usual fond expression, "is to get my favorite nephew out of the protection ward so he can go potty."

Ant Liz never looked at *her* that way. No one ever looked at her that way except Ant Jane. She should have called Ant Jane. "He's your *only* nephew," Angie said crossly. "And I gotta use the bathroom too."

"Alrighty then," Ant Cia said, unwinding a ball of string and starting to trace a protective circle.

EJ muttered, "Hold it. Hold it. Hold it. Hold it. Sissy I gotta go *now*!"

"You'll need three of us. Where do you want me?" Miz Melodie asked Liz.

"North is here," Ant Liz said, taking that position, "so each of you to the side in a triangle pattern." In seconds the witches were sitting and closed the circle, the powers flaring into place with a flash of light.

"Oh my..." Miz Melodie said, staring at the small ward, then up over the *hedge of thorns* that covered the house. "I've never seen anything like this. Do you Everharts do this kind of," her hand made little circles in the air, "working often?"

"No. But there's always a first time," Ant Liz said, sounding grim. "I've never seen one so tangled. Cia, Melodie, can you determine the first step?"

"The strand from the top of the hedge, perhaps?" Cia said. "Except we'd never get to it."

"No. But Angelina can reach her end. Angie," Melodie said, studying the energy patterns. "Do you see the energy strand trailing from the *hedge,* one you twined into your smaller ward?"

She meant the glowing yellow strand. "Yes," Angie said.

Miz Melodie said, "Good girl. Reach up to where it touches the top of your portable circle and, gently, tweak it loose."

She trusted her ants but something felt wrong. Angie frowned and looked at Edmund, who nodded slightly. Scowling, Angie reached up and tapped the top of her ward, plucking at the yellow strand of energy, unweaving it with her fingers, colors and sparks shifting in the air. As she pulled the tail of the thread loose, the *hedge* overhead shivered and shook, throwing a light show of sparks and flickers of color.

* * *

Edmund watched the three witches. The Custer witch kept glancing at him and he wondered why, beyond the general hatred most witches harbored for Mithrans. He smelled nothing leaking from her pores. Betrayal and ambush had a foul scent in humans and witches. However, Angie still frowned at her. "Question," Edmund said mildly, watching Melodie. "If the small ward falls, won't the children be caught in the same temporal displacement as their parents?"

"Angie, stop!" Liz said.

Angie's fingers stopped moving. Carefully, holding as still as a Mithran, she turned wide eyes to her aunts.

For an instant, Melodie's lips flattened. Her pores emitted the sour stink of frustration, hot on the night air. She lowered her head and schooled her expression to concern, but he was Mithran. Even had he not caught the facial expression in the dark, he would not have missed the spike of scent change.

Edmund said, "If Angie peels away the power she is drawing from the *hedge of thorns*, might that also destabilize the entire ward, resulting in a release of energy?"

Cia sucked in a breath of shock. "We could have blown up the entire hillside."

"We'd have been fine under our own circle," Liz said, "but at the very least Ed would have been toast and the kids would have been stuck or killed."

"I gotta peepee! I gotta peepee *now!*"

"Elizabeth," Edmund said. "What would happen if the children simply pushed their small ward through the larger one?"

"We'd have...I don't know. Cia?"

"I gotta peepee!"

"I think...the smaller ward would peel away and the kids would be free?" Cia said. "But–"

"Good. We're coming through," Angie said.

"No!" both twins shouted.

* * *

Angie touched the edge of her protective shield against the outer ward. It stuck. It didn't explode or make a light show or—

"I gotta peepee! I gotta peepee! I gotta *peepee!*" EJ's voice shrilled.

Angie shoved the small shield hard against the larger one. It took both hands, her arms, body, and toes pushing. The edge pressed through and she and EJ and George followed. Nobody died. The small ward did not peel away or explode. It was too strong. Stronger than the house ward. Angie was proud but her ants looked mad. "What?"

"You disobeyed us," Liz said.

"I been studying the wards and how the energies worked. I figured it would be okay."

"*I gotta peepee!*"

Angie pulled on the yellow thread of energies and her small shield made a strange cracking noise, like bubble-wrap popping. It fell in a shower of sparks. EJ jumped upright, his feet tangling in the blanket; he nearly fell. Edmund caught EJ and carried him behind a tree.

"I get to peepee on the tree? Sissy, I get to peepee on a tree!"

Edmund stepped back around the tree looking amused.

Angie brushed off her hands and said, "He is such a paaaaaain."

And that was when Ms. Melodie raised her hands, broke the circle, and shot at Edmund. With a gun.

Several things happened at once. Ed said a bad word and dove back on top of EJ. Ant Liz threw a *wyrd* working at Ms. Melodie. Edmund popped beside George and her, picked them up, and raced behind the tree where EJ was hunkered down, moving so fast her hair flew out in a wave. Edmund looked dangerous, the way Ant Jane looked dangerous. It made her feel better, even as more gunshots rang out from Miz Melodie. Edmund plopped them on the ground, saying, "Angelina. Stay. Behind. The tree."

"Why?" But it suddenly didn't seem important and he was gone anyway. Angelina petted George, who was too lazy to care that they had been hidden in the dark, and then petted EJ, who snuggled up against her muttering sleepily about wanting a hamburger. Thankfully, the blanket was warm and the smell of little boy pee wasn't too terrible. But the sounds were strange and…Angie realized that Edmund had used vampire compulsion on her. Which was *so* not fair. She broke the compulsion and duck-walked around the tree to see better.

* * *

Edmund watched as the twins zapped, tackled, and restrained the now unconscious Melodie with plastic ties they mysteriously had on their persons. Everhart witches never ceased to delight him.

As snowflakes began to float down, Liz asked, "Why would she shoot you?"

Edmund gave a small smile. "Perhaps I was the greater threat. Take me down and then take down the less powerful witches."

Liz gave a very unladylike snort of derision, which he quite liked. "Greater threat? I don't think so. We were prepared, you weren't. And what good would it do to take *us* down?"

"I assume that this particular witch is working with the humans attacking the ward," Edmund said. "There have been tales of black ops government groups and even of private armies kidnapping witches for personal use."

Liz glanced up at Ed as she secured the unconscious witch's ankles. "Fangheads, too. Witches for the power, bloodsuckers for the blood."

A faint sound caught his attention and Edmund whirled. "Movement cresting the hillside. The two back there may have backup."

"Melodie's gunfire alerted them," Liz said. "Damn."

"Keep the children safe," Ed said, and disappeared with a soft pop.

* * *

Liz made a fierce face that Angie had never seen before. It matched Edmund's. "Give no quarter," she shouted.

Angie didn't know why attackers would want quarters. Dollar bills were way better. Her ants grabbed EJ, George, and her, and raced behind their car, before setting up a protective, *warming* working. EJ rolled over and George drooled on EJ's back.

The *warming* working thawed Angie and she lay down, trying to figure out what she had done to freeze time. The stopped energies spiraled up to the high center of the *hedge's* dome like whirls on a multicolored candy cane. She had torn through to the angel place and taken energy from there. Heaven had been bright as the sun, those energies and the utter black of her mother's Death Magics tangled in a messy ball at the *hedge* top. It looked like something KitKit made when she got into Gramma's yarn basket.

Angie sighed. She had really messed up. The problem was the combination of heaven and death. They'd met and entwined when they should have cancelled each other out. A small yellow strand was dangling from the very top of the dome. On the other side of the ball of magics was a lightless strand of death. Right *there*. Not that she could reach either.

The Death Magic strand wiggled slightly and grew just a little. Nothing else moved. Somehow, Angie knew that was bad.

From high on the hillside came the sound of gunfire. Then someone screamed, abruptly cut off. Edmond's fury leaked through their bond before the connection disappeared. Her Dark Knight had the Big Bad Ugly.

* * *

Edmund carefully wiped the blood from his lips and licked the fang-marks from the human's throat. He now knew who the attackers were, how many there were, how well they were armed, and what they wanted. He tucked the enemy's weapons into his pockets, shouldered the man's body, and jogged down the hill, his victim's heart beating fast and arrhythmically from blood loss.

Movement at the Everhart-Trueblood back door caught his eye. Evan, Angie's father, was on his knees, pushing his protective ward down the steps, his eyes wide, his face and beard bloody, shirtless body pale with shock. Angie had said her father was bleeding everywhere and Edmund realized that meant the male witch had not been caught in the temporal dislocation.

"Evan." he said, as he approached the *hedge of thorns*.

"My children?" Evan gasped.

"Safe."

The big man seemed to reshape with relief. Ed dropped his dinner at the *hedge* wall. Evan was huffing when he got there, fresh blood trickling from a nasty head wound, probably concussed. He fell to his backside, breathing heavily, as he pulled on sweats. "Update me."

Edmund told him everything, including how Angie had pushed her ward through the *hedge,* and watched as Evan tried it, successfully ramming his small protective ward through. He dropped the tattered ward and staggered to the glowing protuberance of the *hedge* energies where two humans were frozen in time. "They were...going to kill us."

"Yes."

"I'm not a violent man," Evan said, his face twisting with fury. "But..."

"They will not trouble you again," Edmund said gently. "My military and tech team are analyzing the people and the device. They will be dealt with."

"Good." Mixed scents of self-loathing and satisfaction came from Trueblood, tart and acerbic. "What did he tell you?" Evan gestured toward the human at Ed's feet.

"He is with a group called DTP. Death to Paranormals. Starting with the Everhart/Trueblood family. There are two more warriors and two 'suits' over the hill in a van. We must assume they will be along presently."

Gunfire rang out. Pain seared along Edmund's side and in his right chest.

He fell. The witch dropped too.

* * *

Gunshots. From the hill. Angie broke the *warming* ward and reset it, leaving EJ and George safe and asleep. She scrambled around the car and froze at the sight of Ant Liz and Ant Cia on the ground, twitching beneath an *attack* working that writhed like red snakes. Miz Melodie, struggled to get loose from the straps on her ankles. Angie wasn't good with delicate spells, so she just raised her hands and hit the evil witch with *sleep.* That one she knew real good. Miz Melodie fell over.

She ran to her ants and studied the *attack* working trapping them. It was solid and squiggly at the same time, like jail bars hit with lightning. The electricity made her ants shake. Ant Cia was turning blue. She had been injured once and her lungs were bad. She could die. Angie didn't have long.

She took a deep breath, pinpointed the nearby ley line, and shoved her hands into the *attack*. It punched her like… like something awful. She shook. Bit her tongue and tasted blood. But she directed the *attack* working down into the ley line, draining it. The blackness of night shrunk her vision. It had never happened before, but she was pretty sure she was passing out.

* * *

Edmund sped up the hill and tackled the shooter. The sniper's rifle skittered off the boulders, breaking the scope, firing a final shot into the sky. With a furious, vicious twist, Edmund broke the shooter's neck at C5. His own wounds were painful, though not life threatening. To heal himself he fed, reading the man's thoughts. Verified three others waited on the far side of the hill. He carried the still-breathing human, racing back to heal the witch. But Evan had wrapped himself in a protective ward and had not been shot. Ed dropped to his backside beside the big man, calling Lincoln Shaddock. It was past time to request reinforcements.

* * *

Angie scowled as Daddy said, "We don't have good options, Angie. You, Little Evan, and I will go home with your aunts and we'll try tomorrow—"

"No." She crossed her arms over her chest just like Daddy did when he was putting his foot down. "Mama's Death Magics are growing. They'll kill her and the baby by morning." Daddy looked weird, the way he had when a rattlesnake found its way into the backyard and Angie killed it with a hoe. She had been four. "We have to stop it now."

"None of us knows how, Angie," Daddy said softly.

"I do." She pointed up. "We have to find a way to get up there and unravel the knot of death and heaven." Daddy didn't reply. He just shook his head.

Edmund said he had a 'cusion. Whatever that was. Edmund also said Mr. Shaddock was taking care of the bad guys on the other side of the hill. She didn't want them taken care of, she wanted them dead, but no one asked her.

"The top of the *hedge* is twenty feet above the roofline," Edmund said. He rested his hand on the ward and the frozen *hedge* only buzzed. "The *hedge of thorns* feels slightly warm, with a faint vibration. I can leap and climb to the top, provided the *hedge* is as solid at the top as here."

"Even if you got up there, over the house, in the air," Cia said, her voice rough and hoarse, "even if the *hedge* held your weight and didn't fry you like bacon, you aren't a witch. You can't unravel the working."

"Hell," her twin said, "I don't think *we* could."

"The hedge won't hold more than two hundred pounds," Daddy said.

"I can do it," Angie said.

"No, Angie. You can't," Liz said.

"That isn't happening," Daddy agreed.

"In a moment of panic," Edmund said, "Angelina merged all of these energies. I fear that if this temporal deactivation explodes, time-warped-space and broken Death Magics might destroy the surrounding area. Might perhaps result in worse consequences."

Liz cursed. Daddy looked mad.

Angie said, "Edmund can carry me up the *hedge*. I can pull the threads through and unravel all but the last strands. Then we can slide back down with me holding them. On the ground, I can pull them. The *hedge* and the temporal thing should fall." She tilted her head, watching her family, her red-gold curls sliding to the side.

Edmund said, "You figured that out on your own?"

She sighed. "Somebody hada. It's my fault."

"You didn't do this on purpose, Angie Baby," Cia said. "If your mama hadn't drawn on the Death Magics, they wouldn't have been there to get tangled up in your shield."

"If Mama hadn't used them, then EJ and me woulda watched Mama and Daddy die."

Daddy sucked in a horrified breath.

Edmund said, "As viewed from a military perspective rather than a personal one, Angie is correct. It will take all of us to stop this, and only Angelina can untangle the energies."

Daddy started to argue, but he stopped, staring at Edmund. "You swore to protect my family."

"Even to my true-death. Yes."

Cia said, "Angie needs food and water first." She brought a bottle of water and a banana from her car, along with EJ's blanket. Angie ate and drank and went behind the tree where EJ had peed. When she was done, Edmund held out a hand and Angie placed her small, cold one into his.

* * *

Edmund adjusted Angie on his back, wrapped her arms around his neck, her legs around his waist. "Hang on tightly." She did. It was a good thing Mithrans didn't need to breathe. He stepped back several yards, toed off his ruined shoes, reached for the gift of speed that was part of his nature, and raced at the *hedge*. Displaced air popped. Toes digging into the frozen energies, he sped up the side of the *hedge*. At the top of the massive ward, he stopped and swung Angie off his back, sitting her on the slightly curved dome, the blanket around her.

Wide-eyed, she said, "Can we run like that when I'm not scared and cold?"

He chuckled. "If we succeed, Angelina, I will take you on a full moon run. For now, can you untangle the magics?"

She pressed her fingers against the top of the ward where the energies of the original *hedge* had been drawn up like a balloon and sealed. She pressed through the energies, her tiny fingers weaving, or perhaps unweaving. She mimed pulling a strand up and up and had to stand to continue. He steadied her to keep her from slipping, and still she pulled the invisible energy strand through the small opening she had made. She tossed it and began another.

An hour passed.

He had to restrain himself from looking toward the east. There was no sun protection here and though he would give his life for the Everharts, to burn up in front of Angie might scar her. Undoubtedly, it would be painful for him as well.

Another hour passed and sunrise had begun to tint the sky gray when Angelina sat back from the opening, leaning against his legs in exhaustion. She held her hands in front of her, as if she held reins, and he saw flashes of light and pulses of power in them, though there was nothing tangible to focus on.

"I'm done," she said. "Being an Everhart is hard."

"Why is that?"

"We have to save the world sometimes. Like Ant Jane."

"Ah. That is indeed a heavy burden. Do you have the strands you want?"

"I have two. I can't ride down on your back." She looked up at him and her cheeks dimpled. "You can carry me like a bride!"

"Oh, Angelina."

Her dimples slid into an expression he could only call grief. "We're never gonna get married, are we?"

"It is unlikely," he said gently, helping her to stand.

"I woulda made a beautiful bride."

Edmund choked back a laugh and lifted her into his arms. "Coming down," he shouted, and leaped. His bare feet caught the surface, skidding along the frozen energy like snow-skiing. He dropping to his backside when the angle became too great to maintain balance. They hit the ground in a run.

"Twenty minutes until sunrise," Liz said. "Cutting it close, fanghead."

Ed said to Angie, "Give me one minute to get in back to take out the time-frozen humans. Then I want you to say, 'One, two, *three*,' and yank the strands of magic on three."

He looked up. "Cia and Liz will rush in the moment the magic falls and help your mother. Evan, you'll have to carry Angie to safety. Are you up to it?"

"Yeah. I can do that." But Edmund wasn't certain. He looked as if he'd topple in a slow breeze.

"On three," Ed said again. "I'll hear you."

Angie nodded.

* * *

Angie said, "One, two, *three!*" She jerked the last strands from the time-space deactivation. The *hedge of thorns* shrieked. It fell.

Daddy picked her up and carried her away from the screeching energies and the sparks and the lightning power that burned her skin. He placed her in the front seat of Edmund's car with George and EJ and left her there.

She heard shouting. Heard her mother crying. And then Edmund was back, bloody and fanged, inside with them, raising the convertible roof. His fangs clicked closed and he turned on the engine and the heat. Softly, he said, "You did it, Angelina. I'm proud."

Angie began to shiver. She had fixed the mistake she made. A moment later, Angie threw up. All over Edmund's expensive leather upholstery. And Edmund.

* * *

Edmund sat with Big Evan at the bar of Shaddock's barbecue restaurant. The big witch was aptly named, a mountain of a man who had just finished a mountain of ribs and brisket and side dishes. He wiped his mouth, taking extra pains with the sauce on his beard, and said, "How'd you get Angie to stop wanting to marry you?"

Edmund stopped a smile. Such a union would have been the very worst possibility to a witch father. "She has recognized the implausibility of such a mating. She matured considerably when she accidentally endangered her family with her magics. And those of your wife. She recognizes the responsibility of heritage and family and witch clan. Your daughter is an impressive child."

"She's scary is what she is. How'm I gonna keep her from doing something like this again?"

"You will talk to her."

"Not bind her magics?"

Edmund smiled and drank his beer. It had a hoppy, sharp taste, citrusy and tart. "She sees magical energies without the need for a *seeing* working, making her capable of undoing your magics. She is powerful and that power deserves respect, rather than fear." Ed placed a fifty on the counter. "I am yours to command, Evan Trueblood. Call me. Especially if there's another temporal deactivation. This was…interesting." With Mithran grace, Edmund departed.

EYE OF THE NEEDLE

C.S. Friedman

TIME TOURS INC, the sign said. The bright, bold letters were scrawled high over a video screen that displayed a sequence of historical panoramas. Medieval peasants dancing around a maypole—storm-tossed waves crashing over the bow of a Spanish frigate—toga-clad men and women at a feast—an army of Vikings descending upon a terrified village. Each vignette appeared for ten seconds, then gave way to the next, in seemingly random order. But Christopher McLaren III understood the advertising world well enough to know that there was nothing random about it. An army of psychologists had no doubt been recruited to study every possible sequence of scenes, analyzing the emotions that each inspired, combining them in the way most likely to get a hesitant visitor to open the door.

For McLaren, the vignettes were uninteresting. Insignificant. He deserved better.

He had put on his best Armani suit for this meeting, a silk tie that cost as much as the average American mortgage payment, and shoes hand-stitched by a 90-year-old artisan in the hills of Italy. Let no one mistake him for a budget-conscious rube, whose financial constraints must be catered to. He had set his sights on the kind of prize that only a rich man could win, which meant that he must be recognizably rich.

It was all about advertising.

The door opened at his approach, revealing a sleek reception room. There was a waiting area to one side, with a stack of tablets on the coffee table: something to read while you waited. He would not be asked to wait, of course. When your worth was measured in as many digits as his was, no one asked you to wait.

He walked up to the reception desk. "Christopher McLaren III," he told the red-headed receptionist. A video scene displayed over her head shifted from a Druidic ritual to a baroque ball; was that the Sun King? "I have an appointment."

The redhead smiled. "Of course, Mr. McLaren! Welcome to Time Tours. Mr. Fortier will be your agent. Please come this way."

She led him through a common room with half a dozen cramped desks surrounded by racks of tourist brochures. *Witness History in the Making,* one urged. *Secrets of the Past Revealed!* another proclaimed. After that came a quiet hallway flanked by private offices. Much more appropriate to his station in life. She stopped at a door with the name *Q. Fortier* on it, knocked, then opened it. "Christopher McLaren is here for his appointment, sir."

"Excellent," said the man inside. "Send him in."

Q. Fortier stood as McLaren entered, a polished professional smile on his face. He was middle aged, pale-skinned, partly bald, and neatly but not impressively dressed. Likely a man of modest means, which was good for McLaren's purposes. He was standing behind a desk, so McLaren couldn't see his shoes, which was a pity. You could learn a lot about a man from the condition of his shoes.

"Welcome, Mr. McLaren. I'm Quentin Fortier, and I'll be handling your itinerary. Please, have a seat." He waved toward a chair opposite his own. "Is this your first temporal adventure?"

"It is." The office had no video screens, McLaren noted, but was full of historical artifacts carefully arranged on glass shelves. A Babylonian cuneiform nail, an ivory tusk covered in scrimshaw designs, a number of small yellowed scrolls stacked in a neat pyramid. Some might call the display misleading, as temporal science had not yet advanced to the point where people could bring back souvenirs, but it did give the room an air of significance.

"Time Tours was one of the first travel agencies to take advantage of time travel technology," Fortier told him, "and it remains a leader in the field of temporal tourism. Our equipment is cutting edge and our operators have years of experience, with mandatory recertification at regular intervals. There is no agency that can offer you a better transtemporal experience. Now—" His eyes sparkled "— what jewel of ancient history would you like to witness with your very own eyes? The original Olympics, perhaps? A Shakespearean performance? If you prefer something more primitive we have an outstanding Neolithic package—"

"I would like to attend the Sermon on the Mount," McLaren said.

The smile on the agent's face faltered. "I'm sorry. Do you mean—"

"The one with Jesus. *The Meek shall inherit*, and all that." He paused. "I want to be there. I want to hear that famous speech with my own ears."

For a moment the agent was silent. No doubt he was envisioning the fat commission that was about to walk out the door. "I, uh, regret that we can't offer that event at this time. We do have others—"

"That's the only one I'm interested in."

"We have a few other events involving Jesus." Fortier touched his computer screen a few times to bring up the relevant data. "Mostly he tended toward smaller, more intimate gatherings, and those can't be entered into the system…government regulations…ah, here's one that's just been activated." Leaning closer to the screen, he read aloud: *A fascinating riverside sermon in which various species of fish are presented as models for different types of human behavior.* " He looked up. "Or perhaps you would enjoy an action-oriented event more than a speech in an ancient language—"

"I speak ancient Hebrew, Aramaic, Latin, Greek, and Arabic. If you believe Christ would have preached in some other tongue, then tell me which one, and I'll learn that as well." He leaned forward. "I've been preparing for this trip for a very long time, Mr. Fortier. Since the day time tourism began. Back then, I couldn't afford to be among its pioneers. Since then, I've founded and sold three top-earning companies and spent my every waking minute working to amass the knowledge and resources that this outing would require. Now…here I am. Ready to time travel. And there is only one tour that interests me." He leaned back in his chair, steepling his fingers in front of him. "The question is, what will it cost me?"

Fortier managed to maintain a smile, but his eyes betrayed his frustration. "I'm sorry, but money can't change the science involved. We don't transport your actual body back in time, only your consciousness, and in order to do that we need a host able to receive it. For five minutes you'll override that person's consciousness and view the world through his eyes—see what he sees, feel what he feels. You might even have minimal control over his movements if the connection is strong enough. Sometimes speech is possible.

"What all that means is that for five minutes your host's brain is off-limits to every other time traveler, because *you* are using it." He paused. "Now, imagine that a thousand other time travelers want to view the same event. Five thousand.

Ten thousand. They can't all do that, can they? Every event has a finite number of witnesses, Mr. McLaren, and every witness has a finite amount of time when he's present at that event. That's not even taking into account government regulations that restrict the number of hosts we can claim in any one setting."

"All of which means that hosts are *available*," McLaren pointed out. "You're just not allowed to use them."

"The law is what it is, and we must work within it." The agent spread his hands, a gesture probably meant to placate. "Look, Mr. McLaren, all the available slots at the Sermon on the Mount were filled long ago. It was one of the first events in the system that we had to deactivate. Even if I wanted to send you back to that event, I couldn't. Our machinery simply won't accept the coordinates."

McLaren waved off his objection. "Then find someone who can reactivate it. I don't expect that to be a free service, mind you. I'm prepared to pay whatever additional fees are involved." He paused. "I'm also prepared to offer you a generous gratuity for your assistance."

He sighed heavily. "It's not that I don't *want* to help you—"

"One million dollars."

Fortier's eyes widened. The flow of words ceased.

"The money is waiting right now, ready to be transferred. Help me arrange this tour and it's yours. You could be a millionaire when you wake up tomorrow morning."

For a moment Fortier couldn't seem to find his voice. "Why?" he finally managed. "Why is this one event so important to you?"

McLaren laughed. "Why would I want to hear the speech that is the cornerstone of Western civilization? Why would I want to witness one of the most famous oratory displays that our world has ever known, from Christianity's most revered figure? Why would I want to stand there at that pivotal moment in time, when the fate of our entire world was being decided, and be part of it?" He shook his head, as if the question was too ridiculous to contemplate. "I'll pay whatever it takes, Mr. Fortier. Bribes for technicians, lawyers to help get around government regulations, lobbyists to change those regulations, if necessary...If your current equipment won't take me to this event, then I will buy you new equipment. *Whatever it takes.*" He leaned back again. "Now. Either you can help me do this, or I will go to another agency and make them the same offer. And if they fail me, I will go to another agency and try again. Someone, somewhere along the line, will say yes, and I will make that person rich. While you..." He looked around the room with a sigh. "I suppose this isn't *too* terrible a job to do for the rest of one's life."

Fortier's pale face lost what little color it had. Apparently, the only thing worse than seeing a million dollars walk out the door was seeing it walk into another man's office. "I suppose...there might be a way to do it."

See? Money always wins out in the end. "And that is?"

"If one of the people who originally reserved a slot at that event failed to attend, his reservation would still be available. He could sell it to you instead. "

A triumphant smile spread across McLaren's face. "There! That wasn't so hard, was it?"

"The only problem is, no one failed to attend. The records are quite clear on that point." His brow furrowed in thought. "I suppose that doesn't mean there *couldn't be* someone who failed to attend. History often corrects itself when disruptive changes are attempted, but sometimes a small one can slip under its radar. If I arranged for an agent to meet with a person who attended this sermon, before he actually did so, and if said agent could convince him to keep his reservation open until today...he could sell it to you for a pre-arranged amount."

"I have money enough to pay any price." McLaren said confidently.

"It could be higher than you think," Fortier warned. "I'm sure you're not the only one who's been after one of those reservations. They've probably changed hands repeatedly, the price increasing each time." He sighed. "Scalping tickets to see God perform. I can't believe that would speak well for a soul on Judgment Day."

McLaren reached into his jacket pocket and pulled out a small leather-bound book. "In here is a list of all the assets I'm willing to assign to this project. Anything that is in there, I'll pay as you advise. Plus the million to you, of course, for facilitating this deal." He put the book down in front of the agent.

Fortier stared at it for a long moment, then reached out and picked it up. "You do realize how ironic this request is, right? Given Jesus's teachings about wealth and all."

"Irony is the refuge of the weak," McLaren told him. "I look forward to hearing from you."

* * *

Waiting was hard enough for Christopher McLaren under normal circumstances. Waiting for a deal that had not even been proposed yet (what *was* the proper tense when you were waiting for something to happen in the past?) was agony.

But there was nothing more he could do now. His fate was in the hands of other people, and he could only hope that the bribes he'd paid out and the incentives he'd offered would be sufficient to swing things his way.

On the fireplace mantle of his library was a small, well-worn statue of the Virgin Mary. Years ago it had graced a more modest mantle in his grandmother's home, and every time he saw it now it brought back memories of her reading the words of Jesus to him. She had always stressed the parts that condemned material wealth, as she clearly thought he needed to hear that message. *The men and women who gathered on the Mount to hear Jesus speak were truly blessed. Do you think they rode fancy carriages to get there? Paid merchants, to buy their spot on the grass? Not all the money in the world can buy you that kind of experience, Christopher.*

He had taken it as a personal challenge to prove her wrong.

"Mr. McLaren?"

He turned to see his butler standing in the doorway. "Yes?"

"There's a woman from Temporal Vistas to see you. She's waiting in the reception room."

Temporal Vistas? He'd never done business with that travel agency. Why would one of their people want to talk to him? Unless…was it possible that Fortier had used them to get him a reservation? He could not keep a smile from spreading across his face as he hurried to the reception room to find out. *You see, Grandma? Money can buy anything.*

The woman waiting for him was impeccably dressed in a designer suit, with a Versace handbag tucked under her arm. "Greetings, Mr. McLaren. My name is Sarah Roberts. I'm here to talk to you about your reservation for the Sermon on the Mount."

The smile was twice as broad now. "Please. Have a seat. Can I get you a drink?"

She smiled. "Not necessary. But thank you." She took a tablet out of her handbag and turned on the display. "I've been authorized by my agency to make you an offer." She smiled pleasantly.

"An offer?" Suddenly he was confused. "What kind of offer?"

She read from the tablet. "Mr. Winston Rothingham, CEO of Greenway Industries, is interested in purchasing your reservation. I'm authorized to negotiate on his behalf." She looked at him. "He's prepared to be quite generous."

For a moment he was at a loss for words. Finally, he managed, "I'm sorry, Ms.…."

"Roberts. Sarah Roberts."

"Ms. Roberts. I'm sorry, but I don't understand. You're offering to buy my reservation?"

"Well, technically I'm here to negotiate the terms of purchase with you. The exchange itself wouldn't take place until…" She consulted the tablet. "…September 9th, 2053. You would be obligated to keep the reservation open until then." She offered him the tablet. "A suggested schedule for payment is laid out in the proposed contract."

"But…I don't have a reservation to that event."

"Are you sure?" She took the tablet back and scrolled through a few pages. "The instructions are right here: *Offer terms at 604 5th Avenue, Penthouse Suite, August 22nd.*"

"It's only the 21st," he pointed out.

"Oh." Her eyes grew wide. "*Oh.* I'm so terribly sorry. That's the trouble with transtemporal contracts, you know. Communication can be so glitchy." She turned the tablet off and slid it back into her purse. "Forgive me for taking up your time. I'll see that the offer is rescheduled."

Suddenly the full significance of her visit hit home. Just as he had sent people back in time to negotiate with those who had an open reservation to the event in Galilee, someone from the future was now sending agents back to negotiate with *him.* Which could mean only one thing: he was going to get his booking!

At 2:13 P.M the next day he received official notice from his travel agent: five minutes of host time had been reserved for him at the Sermon on the Mount. He barely had time to open a celebratory bottle of champagne before a temporal agent showed up to try to buy it from him. By 3:30 there was a long line of people outside his front door, each one from a different travel agent from the future, representing a different wealthy client.

Few pleasures in life were sweeter than knowing you had something others wanted. He thoroughly enjoyed saying no.

* * *

Heat: that was the first thing he became aware of. Dry heat, sauna intensity, penetrating every cell of his flesh. Then a blazing light that seared his eyelids, and the world turned scarlet. Given that his body was actually floating in a room-temperature sensory deprivation tank, in total darkness, the sensations were fascinating.

You will be disoriented when you first arrive. There may be some sensory distortion. This is totally normal. The initial adjustment can take as long as half a minute—which will seem like an eternity while it's happening—but just be patient. Focus on the body you are in. Breathe in, breathe out. Things will come into focus soon enough. The clock will not start on your excursion until consciousness transfer is complete.

A vintage Lamborghini roadster. That's what this little excursion was costing him. Also a chalet in the Swiss Alps, a luxury condo in Manhattan, a small private island off the coast of Brazil, and oh yes, ten million dollars. All in all, not a bad deal. McLaren had certainly been prepared to pay more. But it turned out the one man willing to sell his ticket to history wasn't some savvy business mogul fixated upon the value of stock options and board seats. He was just a normal, everyday guy, successful enough to afford an early ticket to a prime event, smart enough to realize that the combination of limited supply and unlimited demand would soon send the value of that ticket through the roof. While other reservations passed from hand to hand, billionaires sending messengers to bribe and negotiate and coerce their way into the temporal queue, he had simply waited patiently for the right offer to come along. It was the vintage Lamborghini that had ultimately tipped the scales in McLaren's favor. Apparently, this guy loved cars.

Lying in the darkness-that-was-not-dark, baking in the heat-that-should-not-be, he reviewed details from his orientation. *Your control over the host body will be minimal. You will be able to initiate small motions, but nothing more; you may or may not be able to speak. Remember that your role is to be that of an observer, not an active participant. Any attempt to alter the flow of history will be detected by our system and is a felony under temporal law.*

Supply and demand: that was the heart of all human commerce. So might there come a day when people traded temporal reservations to prime events like they now traded material goods? Would the price of a 1% share in the Gettysburg Address be treated as a commodity—speculated upon, bid for, listed on the New York Stock Exchange? If so, that would be ironically tragic, for those who had the greatest interest in witnessing such events would be the least likely to do so. A college professor whose entire life had been dedicated to studying the Norman Conquest wouldn't be able to afford a ticket to see the event unfold; devotees of a holy man would not be able to witness his teachings. History would become a playground of the rich and powerful, with scholars and pilgrims left out in the cold.

A twinge of pain suddenly shot up his leg. That was odd. They hadn't warned him to expect any pain. The heat was growing stronger, too, and his skin felt odd, as if his body was coated in something thick and greasy. There was salt on his lips—

And then he was standing in the open air, blinking against the brightness of the sun. The pain in his left leg was searing. Something rough was tucked under one arm, pressed against what felt like open sores. Not exactly the arrival he'd hoped for.

But he was here!

As his eyes adjusted to the brightness, he could make out details of a land baked in heat and crowded with people. Everything seemed oddly fuzzy. The hillside he was standing on was terraced, and he could make out a few distant figures more brightly dressed than the earth-toned crowd surrounding him. Maybe in togas? He squinted, trying to bring the scene into focus. Beyond that, at the peak of the hill, was a single figure. Maybe Jesus? He was too far away—and too fuzzy—for McLaren to tell. As for whatever speech the man was making, the few words that were loud enough for McLaren to hear them were incomprehensible. Jesus might have been speaking Aramaic, but if so, it was a dialect so unlike what McLaren had studied that it might as well have been ancient Assyrian.

The pain in his leg was agonizing now. He managed to look down, and discovered the limb was withered and twisted; the crude crutch under his arm was all that kept him upright. The pain was increasing with each passing moment, and memories associated with it flooded his mind. They had warned him back in the 21st century that something like this might happen.

You will share the physical experience of your host, and perhaps some of his mental experience as well. He will not be banished from the scene, but present in the back of your mind in a sleep-like state, perceiving bits of his surroundings as if in a dream. Fragments of his memories may surface, and will become available to you.

It had all sounded interesting enough back in the 21st century, but when your host had lived for years with agonizing pain, his memories were not going to be pleasant. And when McLaren tried to escape them by shifting his focus back to his current surroundings, he suddenly realized why everything looked so fuzzy. His host was *nearsighted*.

"Fuck!" The expletive escaped his lips before he could stop it. A few people glanced at him, but mostly the crowd didn't seem to notice or care. Only one man turned to look at him. "Could have been worse," he said at last, in English. "They could have assigned you a leper."

Startled, McLaren nearly lost his balance. The homemade crutch stabbed him in his underarm, prompting a fresh wave of pain. He focused on breathing for a moment to steady himself—slowly in, slowly out—then cleared his throat to test how much physical control he had. Then he attempted to speak. "That's not exactly comforting."

The man's shoulders twitched slightly; perhaps he had tried to shrug. "They came in hopes of being healed. It's hard to begrudge 'em that."

"Time travel's a crap shoot," someone on McLaren's other side observed.

A man muttered something in Spanish.

A woman, sotto voce in English, said, "First rule of Broadway: check the location of your seat before purchasing your ticket." Then she chuckled.

"Shhh!" A woman ahead of them all turned back to glare. "Some of us are trying to hear the sermon!"

"Good luck with that," someone else muttered.

People were looking in his direction now, and he could pick out many whose stiff, minimalist movements suggested they were not in full control of their bodies. In fact, the majority seemed to be moving in that manner. Good God, were they *all* time travelers? If so, there were far more tourists at this location than regulations allowed. But then, had he not tried to bribe Fortier to defy those very regulations? He'd even suggested changing the law to suit his convenience. Multiply those efforts a thousandfold, centuries of tourists trying to bribe their way back to this one event, none of them caring how many people had made the attempt before them, or how many would follow. The result would be an event so overloaded with spectators that few locals would even witness it. And that would not only happen here, but at any historical event significant to the human race.

How might the world had been different if more people from the past had actually heard this sermon? Or the Gettysburg Address? Or Martin Luther King, Jr.'s final speech?

The thought was too much for him. The heat was too much. His crippled leg gave way beneath him and he did not have enough motor control to save himself from falling. His head smacked hard into the ground, which made the whole world spin around him. Alien emotions filled his head, crowding out his own thoughts. Pain. Desperation. The exhaustion of a man who had reached the end of his bodily endurance. But other things flowed in the wake of those sensations, feelings that McLaren had no name for, for they were unfamiliar to him. In helpless wonder he observed how they dulled the pain, assuaged the fear, and nourished the exhausted spirit.

Hope.

Faith.

Peace.

On the shores of Galilee he shut his borrowed eyes and let the faith of a crippled stranger sweep him away for his remaining 2.4 minutes. After which time Christopher McLaren III separated from his host, returned to his own world, and wept.

TEMPUS ERRATUM

Emily Randall

Halfway through the scholarship dinner, Rowan O'Carroll could feel their glamourie begin to erode, threatening to reveal their pointed ears and feline eyes to the all-too-human donors surrounding them.

They plastered a false smile on their face and took a deep breath. The main course—a roast beef in a too-rich sauce— had already been served, and the donors had made serious inroads on it. Surely no more than an hour could be left in the meal itself; they had to be able to hold out that long.

Dean Hathaway rose to her feet and the donors quieted. "Thank you all for coming. Sherborne Academy is in your debt." She gestured at the three students scattered amidst the wealthy gentlemen. "As, of course, are our scholarship girls!"

Rowan's smile grew even more forced. Girls, yes…it might have been an accurate description of the other two students at the table, but the word grated against their skin almost as badly as the iron decorations. But Dean Hathaway would not welcome an interruption now, so Rowan kept their mouth shut and fought against the urge to raise a hand to their ear. Glamourie might have hidden its sharp point, but touching it could dispel the already-fading illusion.

And that, in a room full of wealthy donors, would spell disaster. None of them would countenance a Faeblooded student, much less a Faeblooded scholarship student, and Rowan had no desire to return to the slums of Londinium where they'd grown up. Sherborne Academy was their ticket to a better life—they couldn't lose their spot now.

At last the dean sat down, and relief flooded Rowan. But, before they could move, Lord Nightmane, Sherborne's wealthiest donor, speared them with a glance. They shrunk back in their chair. What did he want? Could he see through their glamourie? Surely he could…Alistair Nightmane, the Queen's Scythe, was a pureblooded Fae lord. Their paltry spell must have been little more than a cobweb to him.

As he rose, envy scalded their throat. He, unlike they, had no need to hide the heritage visible in the silken waterfall of sunset hair that reached his waist or the emerald eyes that bore the oblong pupils of a hunting cat. The lords of Faerie were less powerful now, in this age of factories and airships and cold iron, but they still commanded respect and terror in equal measure. The other donors might have feared him, but they would not shun him and risk his wrath, much less the wrath of the Court of Oak and Thorns. One Fae lord could express his displeasure in any number of deadly ways, but if the Court itself chose to intervene…such stories were fodder for nightmare.

Rowan's hands clenched. That same Court would gladly throw Rowan to the Wild Hunt if they found it amusing, for the purebloods regarded their part-human offspring as little better than pets. Pure humans, meanwhile, saw the Faeblooded as abominations—thou shalt not suffer a witch to live—and took their fear of the Fae out on the far-less-powerful Faeblooded. Forget that most Faeblooded held few, if any, of their parents' powers. Humans still treated them as vipers in the cradle.

At the moment, surrounded by powerful men from both species, Rowan wasn't sure which was worse. Only one man held their fate in his hands, though. Would Nightmane be cruel enough to reveal their secret? The Fae did reputedly enjoy such sadistic games…

Servants clad in black and white uniforms delivered dessert and Rowan threw a panicked glance at the clock. Half past eight. Their glamourie felt as fragile as the lace cuffs of the dress they'd been ordered to wear, liable to flake away at any second under Nightmane's scorching gaze. Couldn't the clock move any faster?

An unnerving jolt sent them grasping for the edge of the table, stomach lurching as though they'd just fallen a thousand feet. The clock struck nine. Where had the time gone?

Nightmane's eyes narrowed as he turned to the dean. "If it would not be too much trouble, Dean, I would like to speak with your scholarship students later."

"Anytime," Dean Hathaway replied. "You may use my office, if you wish."

Nightmane inclined his head. "My thanks."

Rowan pushed their plate away. If they threw up, maybe they could be excused from that meeting…

* * *

But Dean Hathaway insisted, and so, a half hour later, Rowan stood just inside the dean's office, facing a man who could have them expelled with a single word if it amused him to do so.

Nightmane smiled graciously. "Rowan O'Carroll, is it?"

When they nodded mutely, his smile widened. "Dean Hathaway tells me you're quite the talented student, especially in the workshops."

With an effort, Rowan forced their arms to remain at their

sides, rather than curling protectively over their chest. "I do my best, sir."

"Good, good." He leaned back against the desk. If not for his careful avoidance of the iron-bound globe that the dean kept on one corner, he might have appeared human, but Rowan could sense the power coiled underneath his skin, and it sent shivers down their spine. Despite his black suit—made of fabric a touch too dark and supple to be man-made—that aura meant he could never be mistaken for a normal man.

He studied them for a long moment, then, to their surprise, chuckled. "Keep up the hard work, then. It is always good to see a student from the old country." He pushed away from the desk. "Do give your dean my regards."

And, with that, he strode out of the office, leaving them alone. They blinked as the heavy oak door swung shut. Why hadn't he said anything about their Fae blood? Was this all part of some cruel scheme to put Rowan off guard before he pounced?

A glitter on the wooden floor disrupted that train of thought. Rowan knelt to see a golden orb, sparkling with jewels, halfway under the dean's desk. Had Nightmane dropped it?

The taste of copper, accompanied by the faintest hint of cinnamon and smoke, filled Rowan's mouth as they picked it up. Thunder rumbled somewhere in the distance as their glamourie shattered around them, but the artifact in their hand consumed their full attention. Shimmering gold, inset with a thousand diamonds in an interlocking pattern of geometric shapes, and hinged, though it bore no latch.

When Rowan ran a finger along the hinges, sparks leapt onto their fingertip as the world spun around them. They hissed and recoiled, only then fully aware of the way their ears extended through their crimson hair. "Shit!" They dropped the ball on the dean's desk and forced themself to breathe deliberately. Achingly slow, the threads of glamourie pulled back around them, hiding feline eyes and dulling the vibrant shade of their hair to human norms.

Once the illusion settled back in place, they picked up the orb and hurried for the door, only to nearly run into the dean as she pulled it open. "Rowan." She frowned in puzzlement. "What are you doing here?"

"Talking to Lord Nightmane?" Rowan dropped their hand to their side.

Dean Hathaway canted her head. "He left over an hour ago, dear. Are you feeling alright?" To Rowan's surprise, she made no mention of the golden orb. "I know the donor dinner can be overwhelming, dear. Why don't you hurry off to bed?"

Time had vanished again. What was going on? Rowan nodded numbly, half wondering if they were going mad, and the dean smiled. "Go on then. Sleep will make everything better."

Rowan nodded again, though they felt no trace of sleepiness. Adrenaline sharpened their senses, filling their veins with lightning. Had Nightmane, or maybe the artifact in their hand, done something to them? Suddenly, the simple sphere felt like a serpent coiled to strike.

But its fangs remained hidden as they made their way back to their dorm room, only to find both of their roommates still awake. Helena, clad in a long white nightgown, sat at her mirror as she brushed out her hair, while Adelia read a romance novel that would have earned her detention for a month had Dean Hathaway seen it. Both spun when Rowan entered.

Adelia leapt up first. "How was it? How were the donors?"

Rowan sank onto their bed. "Ah…"

Helena, Rowan's best friend, smirked. "That bad, huh?" She leaned an arm over her chair. "Wasn't Uncle there?"

Rowan glanced down at the orb, only now wondering why they had taken it from the dean's office. "He was, and I think he left this. Do you know what it is?" Though Nightmane wasn't Helena's uncle by blood, he was her father's business partner, and she often spoke fondly of him.

Before Helena could speak, Adelia plucked it from Rowan's palm. "Oh, that's gorgeous!" She traced one of the diamond circles. "Look! It's some sort of box."

"Adelia, wait, don't…"

A golden sphere of light bloomed around her as she attempted to pry open the orb. Rowan flung out a hand. "Adelia!"

As a wave of weakness washed over Rowan, the light froze.

Adelia, too, froze, face a mixture of puzzlement and dawning terror. The light, which moments before had illuminated her face, now rested in a solid sphere around her forearms. Not a single ray extended beyond its bounds, despite all the laws of physics Rowan knew.

Rowan and Helena exchanged horrified glances. Barely daring to breathe, Rowan touched the light with a fingertip. Then, when nothing reacted, they dared to lay their whole hand on it. As smooth as glass, it held the warmth of flesh under their palm, along with the rigidity of crystal. Adelia's skin, when they carefully touched her shoulder, felt the same.

Rowan threw a panicked look at Helena. "What's going on?"

She peered at the orb in Adelia's frozen hand. "Um…I don't…Should I wire Uncle?"

"No!" What would Nightmane think if he saw this? Best case, he'd restrain his anger long enough for Rowan to make a deal with him, put themself into his debt and hope he let them stay at Sherborne. Worst case…well, expulsion was far from the worst case, but, as Adelia appeared unharmed for now, Rowan didn't want to contemplate anything worse.

They hesitated. What if Adelia was dying, though? A life in the slums or a debt to a Fae lord had to be better than killing a friend. How could they even contemplate being so selfish?

Maybe there was another way. Rowan was Faeblooded, after all, albeit untrained. Maybe they could fix this themself.

Butterflies surged in their stomach. Helena, like the rest of the students, had no idea about Rowan's heritage. But they'd been friends for years, best friends even—maybe she would be willing to overlook Rowan's Fae blood. She didn't seem to fear Nightmane, after all, and she'd accepted Rowan's stammering explanation of their gender without batting an eye…

The taste of cinnamon filled Rowan's mouth as they stepped closer to Adelia. "I'm going to try something."

Before they could think twice, they closed their eyes and lifted their hands, sending tendrils of glamourie to wrap around Adelia. Though invisible to the normal eye, Rowan could sense them probing, questing for any crack in the steely shell that surrounded her. But the thing, whatever it was, appeared impenetrable.

Then something in Rowan slid sideways as one of the glamourie tendrils sank a hair into the shell. Rowan snapped open their eyes, then swore under their breath, for a fragment of Adelia's shoulder had vanished as though it had never existed. Rowan could see the door through the small hole. But no blood seeped down Adelia's nightgown and her expression remained unchanged.

A curse fell from Rowan's lips as they glanced nervously at Helena, who was staring at them with an odd mixture of shock and satisfaction. Rowan didn't need to lift a hand to their now-visibly-pointed ears to know that their own glamourie had failed once again.

"You…you're Faeblooded," Helena breathed.

Rowan nodded and waited for disgust to emerge. However fond Helena was of her uncle, halfbreeds were hardly fit company for a wealthy heiress like Helena.

But Helena, after a long pause, just nodded. "But you don't know what this is."

"No." Rowan gave their friend a shy smile as relief made their knees weak. "Nothing I've seen before, for sure."

"Will it wear off?"

"I hope so?" Rowan's voice shook. "I really, really hope so. But, if not..." They knelt to retrieve their craft chest from beneath their bed, pulling out some of the tools they'd smuggled out of the workshops. Maybe they could figure out a way to remove this, whatever it was.

Quickly, one thing became clear—Adelia's frozen form radiated no energy. And, though she was present in the visible spectrum, both infrared and ultraviolet light passed through her as though she didn't exist. Very, very low electrical currents, on the other hand, flowed around her form as though she was encased in a Faraday cage.

That was puzzling enough, but the hole in her shoulder left Rowan even more confused. Though it made their stomach squirm, they could stick a finger into it, but could feel nothing—no muscle or bone or blood. It was as if Adelia simply didn't exist at that point in space.

Rowan bit their lip, then pulled a silk-wrapped bar of cold iron out of a concealed compartment in the chest. As its emanations stung their fingers, they gritted their teeth and laid the bar against Adelia's arm, right above where the sphere of light cut off.

Light flared. Heat, furious and feral, surged up Rowan's arm, and they yelped as they dropped the bar. Helena gasped. "Rowan!"

Slowly, the sparkles cleared from Rowan's eyes. "I'm okay. I'm okay." Scorched, but alive.

Adelia, though...the part of her arm that had touched the iron was gone without a trace, just like the hole in her shoulder. Still no blood, but Rowan's eyes stung nonetheless. Would all of their efforts to help end like this? How much longer did Adelia have? The bindings around their chest were suddenly too tight. Something deep inside them said that she was unharmed, but could they really trust that wisp of intuition?

Helena laid a comforting hand on their shoulder. "I'll send a telegram to Uncle. He'll know how to fix this."

"What if…" Rowan couldn't complete the sentence.

"He won't be mad," Helena promised, and Rowan snorted.

"You can't know that." He was a Fae lord. Capricious was his middle name.

As Helena hesitated, Rowan sighed. "Just let me try a few more things."

* * *

"Rowan. Rowan!" Rowan lifted their head off of the wooden floor and blinked muzzily, then shot upright as the knocking at the door startled them back into full alertness. As quickly as possible, they yanked the tattered threads of their glamourie back around themselves, while Helena opened the door. "Yes?" She angled her body so the visitor, whoever it was, couldn't see Adelia's frozen body or the sphere of light in the middle of the room.

Mistress Taylor, the governess in charge of the older girls, answered. "You three missed breakfast. Is everything alright?"

A wave of cold washed over Rowan. But Helena, bless her, had an answer ready. "Rowan's not feeling particularly well, I'm afraid, and Adelia's been taking care of them."

"Well, I hope she feels better soon. Remember, you all are expected at services this evening, unless you are too ill to rise from your beds. And, if that's the case, you must let me know immediately so we can summon a doctor."

"I'm sure they…" Helena lightly stressed the correction. "…will be fine." She curtsied. "If that's all, Mistress?"

Mistress Taylor huffed. "Very well."

Tension seeped out of Rowan's shoulders as the governess's shoes clicked away down the hall. "Quick thinking." Their throat tightened as they looked at Adelia, who, despite all their efforts, remained a statue. The strange, solid light remained in place around her hands as well, still violating every law of physics Rowan knew. Since when could light just stop?

Unbidden, equations slipped into their mind. If the energy carried by the light took *this* form, then *that* must be the expected flux through a sphere, which meant that...

"Rowan."

Rowan jolted upright as a wave of dizziness swept over them. "What?" They flushed. "How long..."

"Just a few seconds," Helena reassured them, though Rowan could have sworn it had been far longer than that. More time disappearing...Rowan shook their head, making Helena chuckle. "I know that look of yours."

Rowan's flush deepened. "Sorry." They stooped to pick up their tool chest. "And sorry for falling asleep last night, too." They'd only planned to sit down for a couple minutes, hoping that the world would stop spinning around them...But now it was daytime and Adelia was still frozen. How long before Mistress Taylor or another teacher discovered her condition? How long before Nightmane realized his orb was missing? What if Adelia really was dying and their instincts were lying to them?

Helena wrapped an arm around their shoulders. "Relax, Rowan. Uncle can fix this."

Rowan squared their shoulders. Tempting, so tempting, but... "No. We've got one last thing to try." As Helena lifted an eyebrow, they bit their lip. "Goblin Market."

Helena frowned. "Isn't that dangerous?"

"If you make the wrong bargain, yes. But..." Rowan flipped open their craft chest. "I have artifacts to trade with." And most of them contained no iron, unlike the vast majority of human crafts.

"So how do we get there?" Excitement warred with nervousness in Helena's blue eyes.

Rowan hesitated. "There's a portal in Greenwich Park, but...Helena...you said it yourself, it's dangerous."

Helena pursed her lips. "And it's safer for you?" When Rowan hesitated, she shook her head. "I'm coming and that's final. Besides, I can summon one of Father's steam carriages, and that'll get us there in no time." She rose and propped her hands on her hips. "I'm not letting you go alone."

Gratitude mingled with fear in Rowan's veins. "Are you..."

"Yes, I'm sure," Helena interrupted. "Now, I'm going to go summon that carriage."

As she strode out of the room, expression boding trouble for anyone who tried to stop her, Rowan turned to Adelia. "We'll figure this out," they promised, though they suspected Adelia couldn't hear them. "I swear."

The air shivered around them. A weight descended on their shoulders, wrapping around their throat in an invisible collar, while the taste of lavender filled their mouth. Should they break that promise, Faerie itself would retaliate—but, by making that promise, they had also gained a measure of support from the Fae realms. Should Faerie, in the depths of its unknowable consciousness, be able to help them, it might very well choose to do so now.

* * *

An hour later, Rowan and Helena stood in the middle of Greenwich Park. Though steam carriages rattled by on cobblestone streets scant meters away, the park itself was cool and quiet. Even the ever-present smog of the city was lessened beneath the evergreen arches. Instead, the scent of wildflowers that could never grow in the human world drifted through the air, underlaid by stranger smells that Rowan couldn't identify.

They took a deep breath. "You can still stop here, you know." Goblin Market was dangerous enough for a half-breed like them, according to the tales. For a pure human like Helena...

Helena smirked. "When will you stop arguing with me?" She looped her arm through Rowan's. "So we just step through there?" She nodded at the stone archway in front of them. The air beneath it shimmered faintly, but it bore no other signs of magic—to human eyes, Rowan suspected, it would look like nothing at all.

They nodded. "That's what I read."

Helena laughed. "Then what are we waiting for?"

* * *

The cacophony was the first thing that struck Rowan as they recovered from the disorientation of portal travel. A hundred different voices yelled about a thousand different bargains, all promising delight beyond measure. "Dirical wings, hot off the griddle!" "Fortunes told, veracity guaranteed!" "The finest courtesans of the North, at the low cost of a single dream!"

And the sights! Booth after booth after booth full of wonders—clockwork dragons played in the awning of one, while silks in all the colors of the rainbow spilled from another. Food, drink, games of chance…Rowan even spotted a shop selling lifelike automatons. "Guaranteed to obey your every command to the letter!" according to the proprietor, a scaled lizard-being with vestigial wings rising above its shoulders.

Rowan's heart attempted to soar and sink at the same time, while Helena gawked at everything like a country bumpkin entering the city for the first time. So much to learn here, so much to discover! But how would they ever find what they were looking for in this chaos?

Then a hand snagged Rowan's wrist. "Come with me, dearies. Now."

Rowan jerked away, but the bony fingers just clutched more tightly. The owner of said fingers, a wizened old woman wrapped in layers of beaded shawls, clucked. "Do you want to draw the entire Wild Hunt down on you? Follow me, and quietly."

"No, thank you." Follow a stranger into the depths of the market? Rowan might have been a halfbreed, but they weren't stupid.

The old woman sighed. "I swear to you, I will not harm you, nor let any harm come to you should it be in my power to stop it, for the duration of time you remain with me. Now will you please come?"

Faerie shivered. Once again, Rowan felt the weight of a promise descend on their shoulders, binding them to the stranger. Helena yelped as she felt it as well. "What the… Rowan?" She stepped closer, eyes wide. "What's going on?"

Rowan studied the woman for a long moment. What sort of Fae wore the guise of a human grandmother and bound herself to strangers without hesitation? But that very oath made her trustworthy, at least to some extent, so Rowan nodded. "Very well."

The woman grinned, exposing rotting teeth. "This way, then."

She led Rowan and Helena deep into the market, past innumerable booths selling all manner of curiosities. Plenty of patrons sent them curious looks, but none challenged them; some even called greetings to the old woman. She, for her part, cackled and nodded, but did not slow her stride, urging the two along every time another wonder drew them in.

At last, she stopped in front of a stall draped in violet satin hangings. It bore no sign above its door, just a trio of glittering eight-pointed stars. "Here." She pulled back the hangings. "Enter and be welcome."

Not without trepidation, Rowan and Helena obeyed.

The inside of the shop resembled nothing so much as a charlatan's fortune-telling den in the heart of Londinium. A crystal ball sat in the center of a heavy wooden table surrounded by overstuffed chairs, lit by candles placed in a circle around it. Ornate tapestries hung over the walls, while an equally ornate rug covered the wooden floor.

Then the old woman clapped her hands and the tapestries melted away, revealing massive glass windows that looked out onto a sunny tropical beach. The woman smiled as Helena gasped. "Please, take a seat."

Inside the shop, her voice bore none of the quaver it had held outside. Rowan squinted at her. "Who are you?"

Her grin revealed gleaming white canines with no hint of rot. "Does it matter? I need an Aos Sidhe and you need answers. We can help each other."

Rowan leaned forward. "Aos Sidhe?"

"You, of course, dearie!" Her cackle was far more menacing now that she didn't sound like a grandmother. Then she sobered. "Ah. Of course."

Helena folded her arms across her chest, wonder banished by suspicion. "Of course what?"

"Your friend here doesn't know what they are," the woman replied with a hint of a smile.

"You, wait, what?" Rowan blinked. "What do you mean?"

"You've got Aos Sidhe blood, child. And you've got a problem on your hands."

As much as Rowan was grateful to not be called a girl, 'child' still stung. But they pushed aside their irritation. "I take it that's why you brought us here?"

The woman shrugged. "It's the Goblin Market. All paths cross here."

At least the stories had been right on one thing. But that didn't explain why the woman had sought them out. "Why me?" What did it even mean for them to be Aos Sidhe?

"And how did you know we have a problem?" Helena put in, eyes narrowed.

The old woman waved a hand. "Whatever else I am, I have some small talent with portents and omens."

"But you..." Helena started, then clamped her mouth shut.

"Look like a fraud?" The woman cackled. "Would you rather I look like this?" A fairytale princess clad in a rose-petal gown smiled at them. "Or this?" An eagle-headed warrior, fierce and genderless, materialized. "Or this?" A Fae lord with copper skin now sat across from them.

Helena bit back another gasp. "Point taken." Awe lay beneath her matter-of-fact tone.

The man smirked. "Welcome to Faerie, kid." His voice had deepened, but retained the same cadences as the old woman. "Now, to business."

Rowan took a deep breath, then set their craft chest on the table. "If you've seen why we're here, you know the remedy we need. If you can provide us with it, you can take any one of these." They flipped open the lid.

The Fae man gave the artifacts an incurious glance. "Cute trinkets, but no. I need an Aos Sidhe, kid, not some human knickknack."

Rowan closed the chest and rose. "Then I don't think I can help you." Someone else in the market was bound to be able to help for a reasonable price.

"Sit down, sit down." From under the table, the man retrieved a thick book bound in blue leather with an hourglass stamped into the cover. "You want to know what it means to be Aos Sidhe? Read this, and do it quick. I wasn't joking when I warned you about the Wild Hunt."

A shiver went down Rowan's spine. "What are you talking about?" The Hunt was a nightmare made flesh, one that took particular pleasure in hunting down Faeblooded bastards like Rowan, according to everything they'd read.

"The book will explain it all." He pushed it closer to them. "It even holds the key to your current predicament." He smiled. "Once you've read it cover to cover, return here, and we'll talk about what you owe."

Butterflies surged in their stomach as Rowan shook their head. "I'm not agreeing to an open-ended bargain." Even a child knew that much. But it pained them to say it—what if the book really did hold the key to saving Adelia? Rowan could save her without anyone else's help, without going into debt to Nightmane or revealing their secret to the dean. Wouldn't that be a fair price to pay? They hesitated.

Helena gave their hand a surreptitious pat. "How about this?" She leaned forward. "You're offering us no more than hope, so we'll trade you the same thing. One conversation. No more, no less."

Something glinted in the man's eyes. "And what do I get out of that?"

Helena smiled sweetly. "The chance to make another bargain once Rowan learns whatever you want them to learn. Father always says a happy customer is a repeat customer."

To Rowan's surprise, the man laughed. "You drive a hard bargain, dearie. I'm offering your friend something of tangible value and all you offer me is a chance. I want something more." Amber eyes, fox eyes, glittered. "One favor, comparable in size to the loan of a valuable book. Redeemable when I choose."

"Rowan may choose whether or not to perform any given favor," Helena countered, laying her arms on the table. "And you may not retaliate against them for any refusal, nor ask again for the same favor." She glanced at Rowan. "If that's acceptable."

Rowan threw their friend a smile. "Yes." Still a dangerous deal, but a contained danger…and the reward was more than worth it.

After a moment, the man chuckled. "Very well. It's a deal." He held out a hand.

Rowan, after a moment of surprise, shook it, and he smirked. "Enjoy the book, kid." He turned to Helena. "You sure you don't have any Fae blood?"

Her smile was edged. "I was taught by the best."

* * *

By the time the carriage pulled up to the gates of Sherborne Academy, belching smoke, Rowan had learned more about the Fae world in an hour than they had in the past sixteen years. The Court of Oak and Thorns, the Queen who ruled

it, the different varieties of Fae and their unique powers...
even the theory as to why some Fae resembled humans. But,
more importantly, they'd found a possible key to Adelia's
condition.

Thankfully, Adelia remained right where they'd left her,
with no furious teachers surrounding her. Late afternoon
sunlight poured in through the windows—they still had
time to make it to evening services, if everything went well.

The holes in Adelia's arm and shoulder remained, but
that didn't worry Rowan now. If their theory was correct,
Adelia herself remained unharmed; the holes were merely
illusion. Or, more accurately, a gap in an illusion.

Rowan said as much to Helena, who frowned. "Is this
another one of the weird theories Mistress Donovan likes to
talk about, how none of us are actually here?"

"No. Well, kinda." Rowan laid a hand on Adelia's
shoulder. "Technically, she's not here, but we are."

"So where is she?" Helena gave Rowan an impatient look.

Rowan hesitated. "Well, if my guess is correct...she's still
sometime last night."

Silence descended. After a long moment, Helena lifted an
eyebrow. "Rowan, that's not a place."

"I know. But I think that's where she is, regardless." It all
made sense the way the book had explained it—time was
just another set of dimensions. The Aos Sidhe could, with
proper training, walk those dimensions just as they walked
through the normal physical ones. But, without that training,
their natural abilities had a tendency to act on their own—
as had apparently happened here, when Rowan's untrained
magic had acted to save Adelia from whatever the orb was
about to unleash. That might even explain where all those
missing moments of time had gone...

Rowan let their hand fall away from the illusion that had
taken the place of Adelia. The book had explained that, too—
when something was frozen in time, it dropped out of the
world most people could see. For all intents and purposes, it

ceased to exist. Except that made it very easy to lose things, so the Aos Sidhe magic created illusory copies of them, linked back to the original.

Rowan had to admit, it was an ingenious system. Maybe even one that had saved Adelia's life, despite the panic it had caused. And the possibilities it opened up!

But first, Adelia.

Rowan dropped their craft chest on the bed and closed their eyes. No tools needed for this, just willpower.

When they opened their eyes again, the world glowed with an unearthly silver light. Helena, watching from her bed, was festooned in argent ribbons, which stretched out in every direction. Even the furniture held a ribbon or two.

Adelia's shell, however, was practically a void. A single thread, no wider than a hair, was the only source of illumination, and it ended soon after leaving her skin.

Or did it? Rowan squinted, and it slowly came into focus. A million different Adelias overlapped one another, bound together by that one slender thread.

Carefully, oh-so-carefully, Rowan tugged on it. And, oh-so-slowly, the overlapping Adelias began to move.

Then, with a shudder, they merged.

Helena swore. Adelia screamed. Golden light exploded over all of them, searingly hot, until Helena had the presence of mind to snap the orb shut.

Then silence fell. All three students stared at one another, wide-eyed, until Adelia screamed again. "Who are you?" She glared at Rowan, who realized belatedly that their glamourie had dissolved once again. Though they didn't have the aura of a Fae lord like Nightmane, their Fae blood was all too visible in their ears and eyes. "Rowan? What are you? Get away from me!"

And, before Rowan could say anything, she whirled and ran out the door, dropping Nightmane's golden orb behind her.

"Now, what do we have here?"

Rowan froze. What was Nightmane doing here? Dressed in silver armor, rather than a business suit, his presence sucked the air out of the room. Power hung in a glittering sheath around him and he moved with the boneless grace of a serpent. Rowan shrunk back.

Nightmane smiled urbanely. "Relax, Miss O'Carroll. I'm not going to hurt you."

"Uncle, they aren't a girl," Helena pointed out, in a tone of exasperation.

"My apologies." To Rowan's surprise, he offered them a shallow bow. "My words still stand."

"What in the world is going on here?" Dean Hathaway, face like a thundercloud, stormed down the hallway. "First Miss Nightingale runs into my office babbling about Fae trying to steal her, as though she's living in a children's story, then I find you two…three…" She gave Nightmane a belated curtsey. "My lord, my apologies! You shouldn't be in the girls' dormitories…" Her eyes fell on Rowan. "And Miss O'Carroll! What in the…"

Nightmane offered her a gentle smile. "I know this is all very shocking, my dear. Why don't you come with me, and I'll see if I can explain?" Swift as a stooping hawk, he plucked the orb from the floor. "And I believe this should come with me. It's served its purpose."

While Dean Hathaway gaped like a beached fish, he bowed to Rowan. "We will talk later, I think. Now, let me do you a small favor, hmm, so you can stay at the school?" And, before they could say anything, he retreated, drawing the dean along with him through sheer force of personality.

Rowan collapsed onto their bed the moment he was out of sight. "Well." Nerves and adrenaline made their fingers tremble. "That could have gone better." How was Nightmane going to convince the dean to forget what she had seen? And what was he going to demand from them in return?

Helena sat beside them and slung an arm over their shoulders. "Uncle will fix things, don't worry." She smiled. "I think he likes you."

"That's what I'm afraid of," Rowan murmured. Though, if his favor allowed them to stay at the academy...

"He won't let Dean Hathaway expel you," Helena promised, guessing where Rowan's mind had gone. "And you can trust him."

Rowan leaned against their best friend's shoulder. "I hope so." At this point, they had no choice.

Though, in the future...They glanced at the book lying on their bed. Once they mastered their newfound powers, anything could be possible.

MISSY
THE WERE-POMERANIAN
VS. THE LORD OF TIME

Gini Koch

Beth was excited, more excited than she'd been since last month.

Last month she and her Pomeranian, Missy, had manifested their Superhero Destinies to become an Official Sidekick and an Official Mascot and then had impressed so much that they were immediately promoted to Official Superhero and Official Wonder Dog, complete with an Official Nemesis and New Team of Evil To Combat. It had been a great day.

But today was looking to be even better. Because today she was getting to sit in on a Meeting of Heroes as they discussed the latest Evil Villain who'd come to the Big City.

Mrs. Marconi, aka Wonder Gal, was Beth's mentor and once Mrs. Marconi had promoted her to Superhero Status, she'd also given Beth some truly amazing news.

Beth's family were all Superheroes! Beth had been shocked at first, but then she realized that it made sense. Her grandparents always knew what to do, after all, and the rest of her family always seemed vague about their jobs and such. The logical answer—that they were Superheroes in Hiding—just hadn't occurred to Beth. She'd seen their Secret Identity Disguises all her life and been completely fooled.

But once Beth and Missy proved themselves, Mrs. Marconi forced Beth's family to Admit the Truth, which they did, with varying degrees of enthusiasm. Her grandfather in particular had been less than thrilled, stating plainly that they'd all retired for a reason.

Therefore, all her family as well as Mrs. Marconi were attending the Meeting of Heroes, despite her grandfather mumbling about preferring to watch the Big Game, any Big Game, on TV instead.

It was the start of the three-day full moon cycle as well, meaning Missy would be able to show off her powers. Missy wasn't just any dog—she was a Were-Pomeranian. Sure, this phenomenon probably wasn't working out like the villain who'd created it—Mrs. Marconi's estranged son, Laurence— had planned, but Missy was impressive, nonetheless, and in Were-Form had greatly increased strength and the ability to speak, at least as well as the Great Dane on the Super Team, possibly better.

"No sidekicks," Mr. Fantabulous said the moment Beth entered the room. "And definitely no wannabe mascots."

Beth managed to keep her emotions in check because Heroes Held It In, but the day had gone from potentially the best to potentially the worst ever in what seemed like a second.

"Gerald, I keep on telling you, she's not a sidekick," Mrs. Marconi said. "She's Wonder Girl. Legitimately."

"You can stop selling my niece short any time," Aunt Cil added. "We show the talent young in our family, in case you've forgotten."

Mr. Fantabulous shook his head. "I'm not trying to be dismissive, Cil. But you didn't become Ms. Super until you were in your twenties and Beth isn't even legal age to drive yet. She's too young to be a Hero, despite what you and Helen say to the contrary. She's sidekick age. Period. And her dog?" He patted Missy on her head. "This is an adorable dog, yes, but she can't hold a candle to Rex."

"Rright!" Super Duper Dog woofed, rather smugly if Beth was any judge, while Mr. Fantabulous petted him in a manly way.

Missy sniffed at both of them. Not in the curious way, but in the dismissive way. Beth wanted to sniff at Mr. Fantabulous, too, but knew better than to try it. Her parents would definitely consider that grounding-worthy.

"Excellent," Beth's grandfather said. "We'll just be on our way back home, then. You enjoy destroying the Big City in the name of Righteousness. We're all good here."

"Just a minute, Herman," Mr. Fantabulous said sternly. "Since you and the rest of the Retirees are here, we expect you to provide your Seasoned Input and help us deal with the newest threat."

"What *is* the newest threat?" Beth's mother asked, a trifle nervously.

"Someone who calls himself the Lord of Time," Miss Mist shared. "He claims that he can deactivate and manipulate time."

"Maybe he can," Beth's father said. "Why would you need us to help with this?"

"Really, Roger?" Kid Amazing—who wasn't a kid anymore and was actually older than Beth's father—said. "You have to ask why? You of all people?"

Beth's father shrugged. "Time manipulation is dangerous, yes. But no more or less dangerous than any of the other Evil Villains out there."

"I'd think you and Susan," Master Class said, nodding at Beth's mother, "would be interested in helping most of all.

You lost your parents to a villain like this, didn't you?"

"Yes," Beth's father said, voice tight. "But since you're not willing to listen to Wonder Gal about our daughter and her dog, I find it hard to believe that you'll listen to the rest of us about anything else."

Beth was touched. She knew her family loved her, but for them to Go to Bat for her and Missy in this way was something quite special.

"Look," Mr. Fantabulous said, sounding somewhat conciliatory, "let's discuss your daughter and her dog, and the Lord of Time, while Beth and Missy are not in the room. Just so we can all speak freely."

Her grandfather snorted. "Oh, of course." He took Beth's shoulder and walked her and Missy out of the room. "Bunch of inflated egos in that room," he muttered.

"I'm disappointed, too, Grandpa." Beth hugged him. "Thanks for sticking up for me."

He hugged her back. "Stay ever-vigilant. We're at our most vulnerable right now."

"But we're in Team Super Headquarters! How could anything get anyone here?"

"You'd be surprised. Or maybe you wouldn't. Just stay alert. I'm only okay with Gerald's demands because it leaves someone capable outside of the room. You and Missy keep eyes, ears, and noses vigilant and your powers ever-ready." He patted Missy, who drooled at him. "Huh, the change is coming, I see. Maybe go into the ladies' room until she's her were-self."

Beth nodded, picked Missy up, and went in search of a bathroom, while her grandfather returned to the Meeting of Heroes.

"Do we have time to look around?" Beth asked Missy, who barked softly, which Beth figured meant yes.

So they wandered. Most of this top floor of the tallest skyscraper in the Big City looked like any other office building, though more like office buildings in movies, where the Executive Suite was like a huge penthouse. Mr. Fantabulous had his living quarters here, which were Off Limits, so Beth only looked through them quickly. They were swanky, but she preferred her own home.

There were several bedroom suites for Visiting Heroes, more conference rooms like the one everyone was in, and lots of bathrooms, which Beth approved of, seeing as her mother and grandmother both counted the lack of women's restrooms as proof of a Patriarchal Conspiracy. It was good to know that the Super Team had equality going strong, at least for adults.

There was also a Hall of Heroes which was impressive — statues to every Superhero who'd ever been. Mascots had statues, too. But not, Beth noted, sidekicks.

Sidekicks did have a room, not a Hall, off to the side, kind of an afterthought. Beth verified that the Petit Pied Piper, or Triple P for short, had a statue there, though his had two plaques — one extolling his virtues and one decrying his Fall from Grace. She had to admit that Laurence had been a lot cuter as a sidekick — he wasn't an impressive adult. Maybe it was the evil showing through.

There were several other sidekick statues who had double plaques — a few even had three or four. Clearly, being a sidekick meant you faced a lot of choices in your life and didn't always make the right one.

Laurence had made Missy a Were-Pomeranian, though, so even though he was on Beth's Nemesis List, she couldn't totally hate him. Of course, she and Missy had been drenched in some weird, blue liquid during The Take Down, and Beth was still waiting to see if that was going to alter either one of them in any good ways.

Beth went back to the Hall of Heroes. Interestingly enough, there were some Heroes who had multiple plaques, just as the Sidekicks had. So maybe your Hero made bad choices and you, as their Loyal Sidekick, went with them.

She pondered the Duality of Power as she studied the statues. "Maybe he's right," Beth said with a sigh, as she tried to recognize her Aunt Cil as Ms. Super, without much luck—most of the female superheroes wore wigs, and the masks hid more than you realized. "After all, despite that bath in the mysterious blue liquid Laurence had in his lair, I haven't exhibited any superpowers at all."

Missy licked Beth's hand, then whined. Beth knew the Change was on its way, but since they were alone, she chose to wait for the Change in the Hall.

Sure enough, Missy groaned, whined, and twitched. Then she got a little less cute, somewhat larger, with eyes that looked more feral and intelligent, and with a severe underbite. "Rowr morw dan ood enoouf," Missy said.

Beth picked her up and hugged her. "Thank you. I hope I'm more than good enough. And you're definitely the Wonder Dog. I'll bet that Rex is just jealous that he has competition."

"Ray-re."

"Not maybe, definitely." Beth put Missy down. "I just wish that blue liquid of Laurence's had done something other than make us wet. I was really hoping for superpowers."

They headed back to the big conference room. Beth listened outside the door but heard nothing. She debated whether or not to go in, then decided that Heroes Didn't Hesitate and opened the door.

To find a horrible sight.

Everyone was frozen. It was clear that some had been talking, some eating, some drinking, a couple scratching somewhere, and Rex had been cleaning his Super Unmentionables when whatever had happened happened.

Beth looked around. Her whole family and Mrs. Marconi were frozen, too. Everyone looked shocked, other than her grandfather, who looked like he'd been expecting whatever had happened to happen.

Beth raced around the room. She tried shaking everyone. Nothing. She considered what else she'd seen people do to wake up someone unconscious—since her training in how to wake up people who'd been frozen was slim and related to snow and ice, not a temperature-controlled conference room setting—so she slapped Mr. Fantabulous, just in case that was the right thing to do to pull them out of whatever had happened. She also tossed cold water in his face. Neither worked, but Beth felt virtuous for trying.

Missy, meanwhile, put her nose against everyone, even Rex. A cold, wet snout with some extra drool didn't wake any of them up, either.

"The Lord of Time has been here," Beth told Missy, once they'd tried all they could think of.

Missy ran around the room again, sniffing like made. "Ress, rand he's rill here." Missy turned and trotted off. Beth followed.

They ended up in the Sidekicks Room, of all places. There was a man there, staring at a statue.

He looked totally normal, just like a regular guy in a suit. If he was in here, though, that meant he was either a Superhero—unlikely since he wasn't in the main room—or an Evildoer, or a Super Who'd Turned To Evil. Beth figured that, no matter what, she had to find out. Even if Mr. Fantabulous was right and she was only a Sidekick, she still had a Duty to do what she could to Save The Day.

Beth went over and stared at the statue, too. "Noxious Boy. Interesting choice."

"They said I would never amount to anything," the man said, turning to her. He was definitely older than Beth—maybe college age—but a lot younger than Laurence. Better looking, too, not that this was a high bar to jump over. But he was tall, dark, and handsome and reminded Beth of someone you'd see in a commercial, extolling the virtues of going to the gym or drinking a protein shake, or, after he smiled, getting your teeth whitened. "The good guys and the bad guys both." He put out his hand. "Jack Simack. And you are?"

Beth eyed his hand. "I'm thinking you're Noxious Boy, or you used to be. And I also think that now you're the Lord of Time."

Jack smiled and kept his hand out. "I am. I'm not going to hurt you, or pull you out of time. I just think it's proper manners to be introduced to your adversary or your ally."

Beth gave him a hard look while she pulled up what she knew of Noxious Boy from his trading card and what she'd seen on his plaques. Noxious Boy had been part of the Doom Squad. He'd switched sides when the Wonder Team had beaten his gang and had worked for a while as Notorious Boy. He hadn't earned a trading card as Notorious Boy, meaning he hadn't done anything Truly Worthy. Then he'd sort of faded from view. Whether that meant he'd gone back to The Ways of Evil or not, Beth didn't know.

Jack didn't seem shifty like Laurence had. But that didn't mean anything. Many Perpetrators of Evil looked ordinary and even nice. However, her mother had raised her to be polite. And besides, Missy was in Were form, meaning Beth had real protection. She put her hand out. "I'm Beth."

Jack took her hand, shook it solemnly, and let go. So he hadn't lied, meaning maybe he was actually here to Do Good. "Nice to meet you, Beth. You come from a good family."

"Thanks. How do you know?"

"I recognize the bravery and the bravado."

Flattery was used by both sides, no help with confirmation. Time to Ask a Probing Question. "Okay. Do you come from a good family?"

He smiled and shook his head. "My uncle was Yankton Robins."

"I don't know who that was."

Jack nodded. "I guess you wouldn't, would you? You'd know him as Lord Megaboss."

Beth gasped. "Lord Megaboss was your uncle?" This didn't mean Jack was Truly Evil—many Supers had evil relatives. Mrs. Marconi had Laurence, after all.

Jack seemed pleased by her reaction. "He was. Your family destroyed him."

"He destroyed part of my family."

Jack nodded again. "That's why I'm here. To make amends."

Maybe he was here to help! But then again, it always paid to Ask About the Plan Directly. "By time freezing my family and all the other Supers?"

Jack shrugged. "I didn't say what kind of amends I planned to make."

So he was probably evil. Beth kept herself from sighing but readied herself for an attack. Not that Jack seemed ready to do anything other than hang out and chat. "Why aren't you attacking me?"

"I don't see any reason to. You weren't in the room, meaning you're, at best, a sidekick. I remember what that was like." His expression went hard. "You're never good enough, even though you're usually the one saving the day, many times by being the bait. You're ignored, tossed aside, and belittled, but if you're not there when they need you? Then they complain even more and try to tell you that it's your fault that you're not as good as they are. They say you have no drive and no ambition, or that it's wrong if you *have* drive and ambition. They build themselves up by keeping you down."

"Maybe that's how it works for Evil Villains but that's not how it goes with Supers."

He barked a laugh. "Really? You weren't in the room, Beth. Why was that? I mean, think about it—I'm sure you *wanted* to be in the room, to be included, to be considered an important part of the team. So why weren't you? And don't say because you had to go to the bathroom. I've been here longer than you realize and I know what you were doing, and while you did make a pit stop, the bathroom wasn't your destination. You had no destination. I recognize bored curiosity when I see it. So, why were you wandering around, bored and alone?"

Beth heaved a sigh. "Because no sidekicks were allowed."

"Exactly." He turned back to his statue. "The 'good guys' are no better than the 'bad guys,' you know."

"I don't believe that."

"I'm sure you don't. But the good guys will still keep you out of the room."

"Until you prove yourself."

"Didn't you already do that?" He turned back to her. "You stopped Triple P from enacting a City Domination Plan and his protégé, Conason the Barbarian, is still bitter about it and plotting revenge."

"I'd hoped to save James from the Dark Side," Beth admitted. James Conason had been her best friend until he'd fallen under Laurence's influence and she and he and Missy had had their First Battle. Now James was her First Nemesis. "And that's a terrible Villain Name he's chosen for himself."

"Not everyone's creative and some people can't avoid their destinies. You fought with Wonder Gal, and she was supporting you, and they still call you a sidekick. Why aren't you furious?"

Beth shrugged. "I don't know. Maybe they're right."

Jack gave her a long look. "Do you think they're right? Honestly, I mean."

Beth knew, in her heart of hearts, what she really was. "No."

He nodded. "Didn't think so. Based on what Triple P and his protégé have told me, you were impressive and you have no powers, other than the Powers of Smarts, Spunk, and Spirit. It's why I knew you were more than they were going to allow you to be. You could be called Triple S."

"Gag. I'm Wonder Girl, thank you very much. But I was willing to be Wonder Gal's sidekick. To Learn the Business."

"Only she felt you were ready, because if she hadn't, she wouldn't have brought you here."

"I suppose. Why did you do whatever you did to the Supers?"

Jack looked a little surprised that she was asking. "I'm going to take over the Big City. I'm going to do it without killing anyone or destroying anything or hurting a single soul."

"How do you plan to do that?"

"By keeping all the Superheroes temporally deactivated. I've already done the same with all the Villains."

Beth was impressed. "Really? How?"

"I called a meeting, like the one here, only at League of Evil Headquarters."

"How can you be sure you got all the Villains to show up?"

"I provided a free top of the line buffet and open bar. Trust me, they *all* show up for that. That's how I know what you did with Triple P. His protégé warned me about you."

"Did he?"

"He said you were pretty smart for a girl."

"He's pretty dumb for a boy."

Jack grinned. "I know that meant you surprised him by being smarter and braver than he was."

"Thanks, I think."

"Arre dey ormal?" Missy asked.

Jack looked down in surprise. "You can talk?"

Missy cocked her head at him. "Ress."

"Interesting. Triple P said you were a failed experiment."

"There's nothing failed about Missy," Beth said, scooping her Were-Pomeranian up into her arms. "She's a Wonder Dog. *The* Wonder Dog."

"Well, the Wonder Dog deserves an answer. They seem normal, as normal as the Villain Side gets, at any rate. Why?"

"Missy bit both of them. We were wondering if they were going to turn into were-somethings."

Jack looked thoughtful. "I froze them before the full moon cycle started. So, maybe. It'll be interesting to find out."

"Yes, I'm sure it will be. So, what's your plan?" No matter what, Beth knew that part of her job, as either Sidekick or Superhero, was to coax the villain to Share the Secret Plot.

"I'm just going to leave them there, Villains and Heroes both, temporally deactivated. They won't die, they won't age, they won't know what's going on, and that means they won't interfere. Then I'll go about my business."

"And what business is that?"

"I'm going to become the King of the World."

Beth didn't have to ask how he'd achieve this. She could easily see the benefits of freezing people in time—you walked up to the bank, waited until someone opened the safe, then froze them, took out all the money, walked away, and unfroze them.

But she did have a question. "What do you plan to do, as King of the World?"

"Run things."

"Run them how?"

"The right way."

Beth's history teacher had spent some time discussing how history repeated itself until Lessons Were Learned. Meaning if Jack was controlling time, then he'd never learn any lessons. But she knew better than to argue. She still had Information to Gather. "So, how do you do it? Freeze time, I mean. They said Lord Megaboss could do something like it, but I don't really remember what his power was."

"My uncle could speed up or slow time. So, if he was destroying something, for example, he could destroy it faster, faster than most of the Superheroes could react."

"The Speed Demon was who stopped him, right?"

"Yes, the Fastest Person on the Planet." Jack smiled. "Her speed didn't pass on. While there are some fast superheroes right now, there aren't any fast enough to stop my uncle, let alone me."

"How do *you* do it, I mean?" Beth asked.

"It's a part of who I am. And I do it like this." Jack touched Missy's nose.

Beth gasped. Missy, however, bit Jack's finger.

"OW!" Jack jumped back, holding his hand. "What the hell?"

Beth didn't hesitate. She turned and ran, still holding Missy. Jack ran after them, shouting for them to stop.

She didn't really have a good plan for where to run, so she went back to the conference room where everyone was. Maybe Jack being bitten had broken whatever Time Spell he'd cast.

"Why didn't you time deactivate?" she asked Missy as they neared the room.

"M'immoone?"

Beth considered this as she got inside the conference room and locked the doors. "I wonder if you're immune because you're a Were-Pomeranian."

"Got wet," Missy said, rather clearly. "Ooo goo."

"The Blue Goo? Maybe we're going to get special powers from that blue liquid of Laurence's after all!" Beth looked at her dog. Missy was a little larger than she had been. She was always a bit bigger in were-form, but she was even bigger now. "I think whatever Jack did affected you in some way." She put Missy down on the conference table.

"Hunnngry," Missy growled. She scarfed up all the snacks that were out, and that was a lot of food. And she got bigger still.

Jack pounded on the door. "Let me in!"

"No! You did something weird to my dog!"

"Your dog is weird, that's not my fault."

"I'd kick you for saying that, but I know better than to let you in. I'm not going to let you time freeze me."

"I wasn't going to temporally deactivate you," Jack said. He started slamming against the door. Beth didn't think the locks were going to hold too long.

"Sure you weren't." She ran to the opposite side of the conference table, standing between Miss Mist and Kid Amazing.

"I wasn't. I need a partner. You don't become King of the World without assistance you can trust."

"And you thought you could trust me?" Beth didn't know whether to be flattered or offended. She chose to be both.

The doors burst open. "No locks can hold me," Jack said, rather breathlessly. "I'd better not turn into a were-something."

"Serves you right if you do, trying to hurt Missy."

Missy was still on the table and she turned so she was looking right at Jack. "Still hungrrry."

"You are not to eat people," Beth said sternly. "Not even Heroes Who Have Turned to Evil like Jack has."

"Rry not?"

"Because it's wrong?" Beth wasn't sure this was a solid enough answer. "Missy, you need to be a good dog."

"Ray-be."

Jack stared at Missy. "Uh, Beth? I don't think I could have done this to your dog. I control time, not how a were-creature acts. I could have aged or regressed her, and I could have temporally deactivated her, but I couldn't have done anything to make her like this."

Missy growled. It was a low, feral growl. Beth had never heard her dog growl like this, not even the first time Missy changed.

Jack waved his hands in a variety of ways, all directed at Missy. The only thing this did was make Missy growl longer and louder. He finally motioned to Beth. "Get over here," he said urgently.

"Why?"

"Because I think we need to get away from your were-dog."

"Why would I need to run from Missy?"

"Eat youuuu," Missy growled at Jack. Then turned to Beth. "Goooo!" Missy's eyes looked crazy and Beth was frightened for the first time. Missy stared at her and started to move towards her slowly, growling and drooling.

"Beth," Jack said urgently. "Move!"

Missy leaped and Beth jumped to the side. Missy hit the window, bounced off the glass, landed on her feet, and growled again. "Hunngryyy."

Beth scurried around to the end of the conference table. She grabbed Rex's chair and shoved it at Missy. Missy snorted at her and jumped back onto the table. Beth put herself behind Mr. Fantabulous, ready to shove him at Missy, whatever good that might do.

Missy continued to growl and advance. Then she winked and turned to growl at Jack.

Beth realized that, whatever else was going on, Missy was in Full Wonder Dog Mode and was trying to get Jack to Trust Beth's Motivations. So, Beth inched towards him, pretending to be frightened.

"HUNNNGRRRRYYYYY!" Missy roared. "Eat youuu boaf!" She started to advance on him. Jack flinched, but he kept his hand out towards Beth. Beth was impressed. Jack was scared, but he wanted to protect her. She noted that James had possibly wanted to protect her, but only a little. In terms of Nemesis Rankings, Jack was definitely winning in the Chivalrous category.

While Missy did her best impression of a true werewolf, Beth considered what her dog's plan could be. "Maybe… maybe you should unfreeze the others so, you know, Missy has other people to focus on."

"She's focused on us," Jack said, as Beth was almost within reach.

"Yeah, but maybe that's because she can smell us as alive. She can't smell them when they're deactivated from time. She told me when we found them." This was a blatant lie, but the Side of Good was always allowed to lie to the Side of Evil in situations like this.

Missy's teeth were showing and she was drooling so much that drool was running off the table. Master Class was soaked.

"Good idea," Jack said. He grabbed Beth's hand and pulled her behind him. Then he waved his hands at the room.

The Heroes woke up. Missy roared. "HUUNNGGRRYYY! Eat you ALL!"

"She's gone full werewolf!" Jack shouted as he pulled Beth out of the room. "There's no stopping her!"

The Heroes needed no more encouragement. They ran out of the room, toward the elevators. Rex ran so fast he tripped and skidded into the wall. Beth's father tried to grab her, but Jack pulled her away and out of reach of her family or Mrs. Marconi.

"Go," Beth said, making what she hoped was meaningful eye contact with Mrs. Marconi and Sharing a Clue. "I've got this. She's *my* dog." If she could get the other Heroes out of here, then Jack wouldn't be able to temporally deactivate them again.

"The elevator's not coming," Mr. Fantabulous said. "It's on the first floor and we're on the hundred and fiftieth. It's going to take forever to get here!"

Beth tugged at Jack's hand. "We need to get somewhere safer, away from the others."

He nodded and ran off, heading them for the Hall of Heroes, Missy hot on their heels.

They reached the Hall and Jack closed the doors just before Missy got through. He ran and closed the other side just in time as well.

"Now what?" Beth asked, more to give herself time to come up with another idea than anything else.

"We wait for your dog to get tired or change back."

Missy roared and slammed against the door. Then she roared again but it sounded like she'd run off. More roars, though they sounded farther away, and a lot of screaming from the Heroes. After a few minutes of screaming and roaring the screaming stopped. The roaring didn't.

Missy growled and scratched at that door, then ran around and worked on the other, switching back and forth between them. After a brief time, they could both see her claws and her teeth through either set. There was no sign or sound of the other Heroes.

"*Now* what?" Beth asked, ensuring she sounded frightened. "I think she's eaten the others!" She didn't, not really, but she certainly wanted Jack to think Missy was enjoying an all-you-can-eat Superhero Buffet.

"Now I think...I think it's time to deactivate us both," Jack said as they met in the middle of the Hall.

"Excuse me?"

"You said she couldn't smell the others when they were temporally deactivated. So I'll do that to us and she'll lose interest in us."

"But if you freeze me and yourself, who will unfreeze us?"

Jack grimaced. "The deactivation only lasts twenty-four hours. My original plan was to move the Heroes and Villains to an Impregnable Chamber in the basement of my Lair, where I could just deactivate them every day."

"Where's your Lair? That's a lot of people to move."

He grinned. "The smaller office building right next door to this one. I'm the CEO of Temporal Enterprises. The youngest one ever."

"The cell phone people?"

"Among other things. I took the company over after my uncle died."

"Well, that *is* impressive," Beth admitted. "And your plan seems like it could have worked. And I guess to take over the world you couldn't just stop time for everyone, everywhere, forever."

"True. I want a world that's living and thriving, not one that's all destroyed. I want to be a benevolent ruler." He looked earnest.

"I'm sure you do," Beth said. He probably did. But, as her grandfather always said, anyone who wants to run everything can't, by definition, be a good guy, no matter what he tells himself. "But doing that destroys The Natural Order, doesn't it?"

"Who cares? The Natural Order stinks." Jack took her hand again. "Think of it. The Lord of Time and Wonder Girl, in charge, making things right, keeping the people safe, from Villains *and* Heroes."

"Why me?" Beth asked.

"You're impressive, a better Hero than all the others, and you don't even have superpowers. Plus, you think I was a Hero. You see the best side of me."

"I can't be the only one. Why are you so interested in having me around? I'm not even old enough to drive."

"Not yet," Jack said. "But you will be, sooner than you think."

"Not if you're always freezing me in time."

He shook his head. "You're special, Beth. I can see it, even if most of the Supers can't. One day, you'll understand." He touched her, like he'd touched Missy, on her nose. Beth froze.

Jack kissed her forehead. "I'll see you in twenty-four hours." Then he touched his own nose and he froze.

Beth allowed herself to breathe and blink. She waved her hand in front of Jack's face and slapped him. He stayed frozen. She sighed in relief and opened the Hall doors.

Missy bounded in. "Rro-kay?"

Beth picked her up. "Oof! You're a lot bigger! And yes, I'm okay. Great plan! But I do wonder why I didn't time deactivate."

"Got wet," Missy said meaningfully.

"Oh! You think Laurence's Blue Liquid Goo made us immune to the Lord of Time?"

"Ress. Rand ore." Missy jumped out of Beth's arms and shook herself. She went back to her normal Were-Pomeranian size. "Rry it."

What more could Missy mean and what did she want Beth to try? Beth considered and concentrated on being bigger. "Ow!" Her head had hit the ceiling.

"Well, never let it be said that I'm a man who can't admit when he's wrong," Mr. Fantabulous said, as the Superheroes came into the Hall. "Why didn't you tell us you could grow?"

"I didn't know I could," Beth said as she focused on going back to her normal size. "And maybe it took the Lord of Time to activate the power."

"Speaking of which, what are we going to do with him?" Mrs. Marconi asked.

"Not hurt him," Beth said sternly. "He may be on the Side of Wrong, but he didn't actually hurt anyone."

"Really?" Master Class asked. "Because I'm soaking wet and I smell like dog drool."

"That's the price you pay for doubting Wonder Girl," Mrs. Marconi said. "And Missy, the Were-Pomeranian Wonder Dog."

The Superheroes who weren't part of Beth's family all had the grace to look embarrassed, even Rex. "We're sorry," Miss Mist said. "We won't make that mistake again…Wonder Girl."

Beth decided to Be Gracious in Victory. "Thank you. I'm just glad you all figured out to pretend Missy was eating you."

Her grandfather coughed. "Missy can talk. She told us your plan. We just went along with it. And now we need to put Young Master Lord of Time somewhere inconvenient for him."

"Why don't we put Jack where he planned to put all of you?" Beth explained Jack's Lair Setup in the neighboring building.

Mr. Fantabulous shook his head. "Kids these days. You'd think just amassing wealth would be enough for them, but Villains always prove that theory wrong."

"Now," Beth's grandfather said, "someone's eaten all the food, so since it's going to take a lot of time for all of you to apologize properly to Beth and the rest of us, let's go get some dinner. You're buying, Gerald, so I want steak and lobster."

"Rand raw rickens!" Missy said, as Beth picked her up and they went to the elevator, which had finally arrived to take them Back To The Streets, so Good could keep on fighting Evil in the Big City.

"Will Jack be okay, do you think?" Beth asked, as Kid Amazing and Master Class carried him to the elevators.

"I'm sure he'll recover to try again another day." Mrs. Marconi put her arm around Beth's shoulders. "Another Nemesis, I see. You're really amassing quite a Rogue's Gallery, Wonder Girl."

Beth grinned. "This has definitely been the best day ever."

THE MIRROR TRAP

Misty Massey

Bertie stopped at the door to Lab 472. A paper sign taped to the glass read Closed Until Further Notice, but she could have sworn she'd seen people working in there just yesterday. She pressed the call button on her walkie and waited for Henry to respond.

"What do you need, Bertie?" his voice crackled.

"472 is on my roster for tonight, but there's a sign—"

Henry interrupted her. "Sorry, my bad. They closed it this morning and I forgot to update the roster."

"What were they doing in there?" she asked. Please don't say dissecting animals, she thought. The graduate students didn't leave dead creatures behind at the end of their day, but the smell of formaldehyde lingered and turned her stomach.

"Not sure. Quantum something-or-other. I think it's math, so you know it's weird."

She nodded, even though no one could see her. "Do I clean it?"

"Trash and mop, please. But stay out of the side rooms—security is coming in the morning to clean out Dr Wright's notes and such, so they should have put tape across those doors."

"Thanks," she said, dropping her walkie back into the pocket of her apron and slipping the little earbuds her son had given her for Christmas into her ears. Henry didn't mind if she listened to music while she worked, as long as she answered when he buzzed the walkie. She unlocked the door and opened it, pushing her cart full of supplies inside and reaching back to flip the light switch. The florescent bulbs clicked and hummed to life, bathing the room in greenish light. Three monitors sat next to each other on a long lab table against the far wall, all asleep for the night. Three rolling chairs were pushed neatly into place. A rack of open cabinets hung on the wall above the monitors, full of binders bearing titles that made no sense to Bertie at all. There were two closed doors at opposite ends of the room. One had the expected "no trespassing" tape across it and a black window next to it revealed nothing of the room inside. A strip of tape hung loose from the other door. Several waste baskets underneath the lab table were stuffed full of crumpled junk mail catalogs, empty snack bags, and banana peels. When she'd been promoted to cleaning the science building instead of the dormitory common rooms, Bertie had assumed the trash might somehow be a little more upscale. Not so. Graduate students and professors were just as messy as freshmen.

She busied herself dumping the trash into her cart, then swept. She squirted a shot of Spanosol cleaner onto the floor and was about to squeeze the excess water from her mop and finish the job when she heard someone yelling.

"Yes, I came back, and I don't give a crap that you deactivated my temporal privileges! I need one more week to complete the research. If I have to barricade myself in here to finish, then that's what I'll do, Furman!"

The voice came from the office with the torn tape on its door. Had he been in there the whole time? Bertie took her earbuds out, set the mop down and crossed to the door with broken tape. If someone was still working, she didn't want to wet the floor and end up in trouble for someone else's broken hip. She tapped on the door. "Excuse me?"

The door flew open. A red-faced man in a dingy lab coat stood there, holding a cell phone to his ear. "What?" he barked at her. Before she could answer, he turned away and started yelling into the phone again. "You'll have to power down the whole building to stop me. And what will that do to Baumgartner's turnip blight experiment?" He laughed, an ugly sound coming from him. "That's right, you can't stop me." He hurled the phone across the room and it smashed into pieces against the concrete wall. "So who the hell are you?"

Bertie had worked long enough in the dormitories to know a temper tantrum when she saw one, especially from white men with more money than sense. If one of her boys had acted this way, she'd have turned him over her knee. But she had to tread lightly with this one. Badly as he was behaving, he was still higher on the pecking order than she was and he could have her fired just for looking at him funny. "I'm the custodian," she said. "Sorry to bother you. I came in to mop the floor, but I can leave you alone if you're still working."

He stared at her, squinting curiously as if he'd never seen a woman before, then smiled. "No, no, you can mop. In fact, if you wouldn't mind, I need you to mop the mirror room." He stalked to the closed door, yanked the tape off, and turned the knob.

Henry had specifically told her to stay out of the side rooms, at security's orders. But if she didn't bother anything inside, just mopped the floor and left, maybe she could keep this fool calm. Holding the mop handle in one hand and the cart handle in the other, she steered the cart toward the open door. The man leaned inside and flipped a light switch, then waved her through.

The room was bright as a day on the beach, making the outer lab's fluorescents seem dim in comparison. All four walls were made of mirrors. In every direction, she saw endless lines of herself. A million middle-aged brown-skinned women, wearing blue aprons, khaki pants, and sensible work shoes. She spun in place and all the copies of herself did the same. A wave of dizziness washed over her and she looked up to try and settle herself. The ceiling was mirrored, too. And the floor. Nope, she thought. I can't work in here. She stepped back, intending to run out the door, but as she turned, the man slammed it shut and locked it with an ominous click. A smooth panel of mirror slid into place. Bertie threw herself at it, feeling around for a hinge, an edge, anything that she could pull on to open it back up. "Let me out, you bastard," she yelled.

"Relax." The voice echoed from an unseen speaker somewhere above her. "This won't hurt. And you'll be famous afterward."

"I don't want to be famous. I'm a grandma. I mop floors, for God's sake!" she said. She hated the panic making her words quiver, but she couldn't help it.

A low whine shook her back teeth, making goosebumps rise on her exposed skin. The light surrounding her throbbed and she squeezed her eyes tightly shut. Whatever was going to happen, she didn't want to see it coming. "Protect me, Jesus," she whispered. "Please protect me."

She wasn't sure how long she stood there, praying and holding her eyes closed, but at last she noticed the light wasn't assaulting her eyelids the way it had a moment before. She let one lid slip open and peered around.

The mirrors were gone and now she stood in the middle of an old-fashioned classroom. A huge, dusty blackboard took up one wall. In front of it stood a big, wooden desk. The kind of grade book she recalled from her childhood sat open, with a pencil next to it. A dozen student desks were lined up neatly across the floor. Well, eleven were lined up—one had been bumped sideways by her janitorial cart. To the left of the blackboard was a four-paned door and along the wall were two heavy windows covered by paper roller shades pulled all the way down to the sills. A map of the world hung on the other side, next to an old-fashioned calendar advertising the joys of owning your own encyclopedia. Below it, on a sturdy table, sat an enormous radio, the kind her grandparents had owned. She wondered what she'd hear if she dared to turn it on.

Radio...she had a radio in her pocket! Holding onto her cart with one hand, she reached into her apron pocket with the other, pulling out the radio. She clicked the button several times. Henry hated it when employees did that, so she'd be guaranteed to get his attention. She didn't mind if he yelled at her, as long as he came in to rescue her.

Nothing happened. She pushed the talk button. "Henry! Can you hear me?" She shook the radio and tried again.

"They can't hear you." The voice sounded tinny and she realized it was coming from the huge radio on the table. "Your handheld hasn't been built yet."

"That's nonsense," she said, not quite believing herself.

"You're in 1952," he said, his voice dripping with pride. "I solved time travel."

Bertie rolled her eyes. Time travel, as if. No one could do that, least of all this horrible man. She didn't know much about such things, but she was certain she'd read an article on CNN that said scientists at a much better school than this one had been able to send bitty little particles through time, not people. It was obvious this nutcase had built some sort of funhouse with his mirrors. If she touched the walls, she'd feel smooth glass. She walked over to the window and laid her hand against the shade. Instead of cool glass, paper crackled under her fingers. She yanked her hand back. It wasn't the mirror. She grabbed the string on the bottom edge of the shade, snapping it and letting the shade roll up. Beyond the window, she saw trees and a green lawn. Three girls lounged in the sunshine, their wide skirts spread out to cover their neatly tucked legs from view. Two boys tossed a football back and forth to each other. Out on the street, an enormous sea-foam green sedan with rounded fenders rolled by. Bertie beat her fists against the panes, yelling at the top of her lungs. Maybe the glass was too thick for anyone to hear. She dragged a desk over and climbed up to reach the window lock. She turned it and tried to pull the window up, but it held solid.

"Yeah, that's the problem." That irritating voice again. If she ever got out of this room, she'd knock him into next week with her broom. "You're in 1952, but only in one specific day of it."

Bertie turned toward the radio, stunned. She hadn't even been born until 1958. Her mama would have been barely a teen herself, living in Grandpa's rickety wooden house. The scientist had to be messing with her. But the sedan outside honked its blaring horn and she realized she hadn't seen that kind of car since her grandparents traded their old Buick in 1976. And the students outside the window were all white-skinned. If this truly was 1952, all the brown teenagers would have been across town at Freeman.

"I sent a grad student back yesterday, but he…well, he decided to kill Nixon before he could become president." He chuckled. "Nice idea. Kid never even made it off campus. Ran out in front of a bus. Splat!" He laughed out loud and Bertie winced at his cruelty. What kind of teacher laughed at a student dying?

Now that she was paying attention, she noticed the calendar was open to February 1952. And the world map… she climbed down from the desk to go over and peer at the tiny names on each of the countries. Jugoslavia. The Union of Soviet Socialist Republics. She covered her mouth. East Germany. She'd watched the Berlin wall come down on television years ago. If this was 1952, that fool on the other side of the door had trapped her in a place where she was hardly considered a person at all. Where her son could have ended up dangling from a rope just for catching the wrong white man's notice. How dare he put her, or anyone, in danger like that? She wondered if the poor student had been brown like her, or if the scientist even cared about anyone's life but his own.

"Furman suspended my temporal privileges. He said I was endangering students, wasting money, that my theories were ultimately useless. He claimed he'd shut down the experiment entirely, but he didn't know how. The fool." He chuckled. "I just need to leave a subject in until the day changes. It should deactivate the temporal lock and I'll be back in business."

He seemed to want someone to talk to, or at least, to talk at. Bertie wasn't inclined to give him even that much. She tried the door. Again, no luck. She paced around the room, trying to think, and bumped into the handle of her mop. Maybe she could break the window glass. She pulled her dripping mop out of the water, not even bothering to squeeze it dry, braced her feet, and jabbed the end of the heavy wooden stick at the center of a lower pane. It bounced off, rocking her backward, and the man hissed.

"Don't do that," he said. "You might break the mirrors. You're inside them, in a quantum state. I can't say what might happen if you damage them from in there."

How could she be inside a mirror? How could he see her? She let the mop fall, flattened both hands, and started feeling around.

"Why don't you just take a nap or something? You can't leave until I let you."

The hell she couldn't. The classroom might have been in 1952 but she lived in 2019, and no man could order her around. There had to be a way out. She wanted to go home to her cozy house, the one that belonged to her free and clear. She'd drink a cup of coffee, put her feet up, and maybe call the grandbabies tomorrow when they got home from school. She wanted to see all the tomorrows she was supposed to, the ones her ancestors had fought and bled and died to guarantee her. The last thing she wanted was to be this man's guinea pig. What if he never let her out of here? Would she starve to death? Or would she eventually slow down and come to a halt in here, trapped in a moment for eternity? This was all too much to think about. Something for the mathematicians to noodle over, not for her. And she was determined not to die at the hands of some crazy white man, the way too many of her forebears had done.

She returned to the section of wall where she thought she had entered. It appeared to be sheetrock, painted a boring industrial bluish-green. Swiping her hand across the wall, she couldn't detect any gaps or cracks that might have been the panel, but this had to be where it all began, where the mirror had closed on her, trapping her in its silvered web.

And just like that, it hit her. She let a smile curve the corner of her mouth and walked to her janitor's cart. The mop lay on the floor, but she didn't need it this time. Reaching into the side pocket, she pulled out a pair of heavy rubber gloves and snapped them onto her hands.

"You're going to clean the room?" he asked. "If it makes you feel better. It'll be interesting to see if the cleaning holds."

She picked up the bottle of Spanosol and flicked the stopper off the spout. Aiming it at the space she'd chosen, she shot a spray of the chemical cleaner at the wall and returned the bottle to the cart. Picking up a scrub brush, she set to work cleaning the wall.

"What are you doing?" he asked. For the first time, he'd lost that superior tone. He sounded nervous, and that alone pleased Bertie no end. She scrubbed harder, humming to herself as she did.

"Stop that!" he cried. "You can't get out that way. You'd

need acid to cut through glass. That stuff's not going to do it."

"Not trying to cut through glass," she said at last. "The warning on the bottle says not to use Spanosol on silver. Tears it right up, it does."

"But the silver's behind the glass," he protested.

"So am I."

For a moment, the only sound was the scratching of her brush on the wall, until suddenly, the eerie hum she'd heard before kicked on again. She rubbed harder. Maybe she'd damage the mirrors, and maybe she'd die because of it, but it would be her call, not his.

The light increased around her as she worked. The wooden floor under her feet began to shine and the wall smoothed and cooled under her hand. Before she knew what was happening, the classroom faded away, replaced once again by the infinite reflections of herself. Almost infinite, that was—right in front of her was a gray-black spot the width of her palm, with no silvering left on it. She stared into its dullness, willing that panel to move, to open, to let her out. And it did, sliding quietly open to reveal the door. A gentle click told her the lock was disengaged.

She let her hand drop and leaned forward to turn the knob. The door swung open. Her captor stood in front of a panel, pressing a button over and over. He glanced at her when she stepped through the door and his face fell. "Look what you did! You interrupted the flow!" He started toward her, his hands curled into fists. "I should kill you for that!"

Bertie swung her wet brush, flinging cleaning fluid at his unprotected face. A few drops hit home and he reeled backward, whining and pawing at his eyes.

Time to run, she thought, but before she could move, the hallway door opened and two security guards ran in. She pointed at the scientist. They grabbed his flailing arms and walked him to the open door. He caught sight of her and pointed. "She ruined the mirrors! Arrest her!" but the security guards paid him no attention.

A frazzled looking man approached her. "Mrs Jackson, I'm Dr. Furman, dean of this department. Are you injured? Did he hurt you? I'm so very sorry about this. I knew he was upset, but I had no idea he'd do something like this. The school will make sure any medical bills are covered." He wrung his hands worriedly.

Bertie patted him on the arm. "I'm fine, sir, just fine."

Henry stood next to Furman. "Bertie, they told me this was called an atomic trap made out of quantum mirrors and I can't even guess what that means. How on earth did you figure out a way to escape?"

Bertie stepped back into the mirrored room and took the Spanosol bottle out of her cart. She turned it around to show Henry the front label. "Cuts your cleaning time to nothing at all."

LOVE
AND THE IMPROPER UNICORN

Rhondi Salsitz

Everyone should have Paris on their bucket list, she thought.

It had been on her hunting inventory, anyway.

* * *

"It's the meningioma," said the doctor, a woman. "It's grown markedly since your last MRI, pressing on optic nerves, and causing the more severe headaches and vision changes. It may also affect your memory and ability to focus. The neurosurgeon will probably recommend radiation. The location isn't operable."

"You told me," she responded, "that they were usually benign. That they were like freckles on the brain. That I didn't have to worry. You said all I needed were regular check-ups."

"I'm still telling you not to worry, the tumor is small, but it needs to be treated."

"How soon?"

"Very soon."

"Why?"

And the neurologist held up an exam paper. "This is why."

Marjory stared at the clock face. "I don't understand."

Her doctor tapped the drawing. "Because I told you to number the hours from 12 to 12."

"And?"

"Marjory, you can't tell by looking at it or when you were creating it, but…all the numbers are on one side of the hemisphere. It's a full circle but you could only perceive half the circle."

She remembered leaning off the edge of the exam table to look closer, but she could not discern the problem. "I did it wrong? I broke time?" She flicked a glance to the schoolroom clock by the door.

"You did it wrong. But we're going to fix that."

When she readied to leave the doctor's office, she had a fistful of authorization papers to get another MRI with contrast, the address of the surgeon, and instructions on how to prepare for the testing, and she couldn't remember what else because she'd called a car to take her to her apartment, dropped everything, grabbed her passport and a suitcase, and left.

* * *

New York coffee shops seemed to be too noisy for the intimacy promised by the name, but it didn't bother Peter Richards at all as he leaned close over the small tabletop. "It would be easier to detail my career if you'd come to my apartment to look at my photos and scrapbook."

"I couldn't."

"Of course. I understand." He smiled broadly, showing off good teeth as well as good humor. "But they are studio glossies, I promise. Nothing extraordinary."

She checked her watch. "I really haven't time, this visit. My flight is in four hours, with early check-in time, and so I can't detour."

He looked downhearted and she stretched out a finger to touch his wrist. "I want to thank you for seeing me on such short notice."

"It was wonderful to get your call. Sometimes one wonders if they're missed, actors being what we are, and you let me know I am."

"No one did swashbuckling like you and a few of your friends."

"Thank you." He shook his head in a little disbelief. "Chet is still at it, you know."

"Chet?"

"Chester Malvern. He's in Dublin currently, getting ready to film for HBO on that spin-off for *Game of Thrones*. Says he's perfect for an elder statesman who can use a sword." He shook his head again.

"I can't recall Mr. Malvern at all."

"Oh, but you must! He was the youngest of us all. A redhead."

"No. No, I don't think so."

"Come to my place and look at my photos. I'm just a ten-minute walk away—you won't even have to move your car."

She laughed softly. "With New York parking, that's a real incentive." She crumpled up her napkin. "All right, you've won me over."

Once inside, she asked to use the bathroom. Marjory left the sink water running to cover the slight noise she made rummaging through the medicine cabinet. She didn't find much, but when she opened the vitamin bottle she saw it contained only a dozen or so distinctive blue pills, not the sort of supplement on the label. She shook half of them out and replaced them with pills of her own.

He tapped a photo on the wall as she came into the room. "Here we are. *Zorro Returns*. That's Chet, this is Eddie Woods, and me. Eddie got the big black horse because…" he paused significantly.

"He played Zorro."

"Naturally." He let his arm slip around her shoulders and walked her companionably down the wall, past pictures of senoritas and desert sunsets. "Tom Novaks isn't here because he played one of the enemy, the captain chasing him. That's him over there." He pointed to the dashing leader of half a dozen men in uniform. "He's still a good-looker. Hated horses, though. He's retired and living in Denmark. Copenhagen, somewhere. Loves it."

She snuggled his arm around her a bit tighter. "Perhaps I can stay...just for a while longer."

"Oh? Oh!" Peter winked. "I need to take a vitamin then."

"Take two. I'm told I'm quite vigorous."

He didn't make it far past the bathroom door threshold on his return. The authorities would probably note it as accidental—counterfeit pills cut with fentanyl, another cautionary opiod tale. She let herself out.

* * *

In Dublin, Chet Malvern could not wait to take her out for a spin on his boat, all the while boasting about the script in his possession that he absolutely, positively, could not divulge any details of, no matter what the incentive. He took her out far enough that no one saw her put a knife into his ribcage, tie him to the freed anchor, and drop his body overboard.

From there it was a short jaunt to Denmark and Novaks where she found a chubby old man happily farming chubby old pigs. She was tempted to feed his body to them, but that disturbed even her sensibilities, so she merely left him bleeding out on his kitchen floor. He'd been the only one who saw her begin to make her move and cried out, begging, telling her if she had half a heart, she'd leave him be. Marjory simply answered she'd have to find one first.

That left Paris.

* * *

"This entire room is the heart of Versailles," the guide extolled, spreading wide her arms, "and a Mirror of Time."

She moved somewhat impatiently through the first rooms but when she entered the Hall of Mirrors, it seemed as though the epoch stopped.

Or perhaps, like the instances it mirrored, it had shattered into jagged bits of time itself. Every edge a moment, a breath, an eternity.

Light, reflected a thousand times over, hammered at Marjory's eyes as she stopped in her tracks. The impending migraine narrowed her gaze, yet she could not help but look. She'd come to find something missing in her life. She paused, uncertain that the palace of Versailles could fill that void.

Marjory shaded her brow with her hand, canopied by a multitude of chandeliers above and surrounded by gueridons a-light. Ladies with creamy limbs, some dressed in veils, a few replaced by cupids, they stood nearly as tall as she did, with each holding an exquisite torch beaming down a royal length of room.

"The gueridons," the guide explained, "are replacements for silver statues that had been melted down to finance the war effort of 1689. We cannot imagine how much more grand the originals might have been."

Beneath her tread, the gleaming wooden floor showed wear beyond measure, as had the marble steps outside on the stairs, a tide of visitation eroding upon the shoreline of the palace.

She fell farther and farther behind, most of the seventeen arcaded windows under the mirror-clad arches ahead of her, the gardens outside in full bloom, yet empty. She heard the tour guide faintly say, "Aristocratic re-enactors will be performing tomorrow. It would be a good day to return and see the Versailles and her gardens as they had been in their glory."

Why then, had she come today?

Because she had bolted from a neurologist's office as if her life depended upon flight. And then she had done unspeakable things that should never see the light of day.

The sunshine without and the artificial lamps within dazzled her vision when a slight movement caught the corner of her sight. She looked back to a window near the hall's beginning. A man leaned casually against the window frame, weight balanced on one foot, the other flat upon the wall. He wore blue velvet and had his long hair pulled back and tied at the base of his neck. His coat revealed lace cuffs and an ivory swordsman's shirt. His beauty struck her. He watched the tour pass by with a faintly amused smile tilting one corner of his mouth. One of the actors, undoubtedly, perhaps here for an early rehearsal. She might have recoiled at that thought, but he seemed whimsical and inviting. His presence tugged at her curiosity. No one else seemed to have noticed him; he relaxed so quietly among the angles of mirror and light and time. Always drawn to shadows, she found herself assessing him rather than the splendor of the hall.

And then he caught her watching. The indulgent amusement vanished from his face, replaced by one of surprise. He straightened the cocked leg and took a step towards Marjory. He tossed her an ironic salute. She dipped her chin in answer and his astonishment merged into a brilliant smile. The saber belted at his waist hindered him not in the slightest, nor the delicately heeled slippers he wore or the ribbons at the bottom of his calf-length pants. A damn fine costume. A masquerade crown of a white unicorn head topped him, its flowing mane trailed over his dark and lustrous hair, both catching the sparkle of a morning sun. He looked as if he strode in another world, one that beckoned to her.

She looked back at the tour, to see if she would be missed. Nobody took notice. Impulsively she moved toward him, yet kept an eye on the crowd.

A breath grazed the curve of her ear from behind. "You see me. And fortunate man that I must be, I see you."

"Why wouldn't I?"

"There are a hundred different reasons why you shouldn't."

What language were they speaking? She couldn't name it. She didn't want to. They understood one another and that was enough. "Are you real?"

"Am I? I thought I was. If your opinion differs, does that diminish me?"

"I hope not."

She thought she felt a hand on her shoulder. "What brings you here?"

"A bit of sweet among the bitter." She wanted to face him, but waited. His was the rejection if there was to be one.

"And why would you search out the bitter?" The fingers tightened on her. "Who hurt you?"

"That no longer matters."

"But it does. You seek revenge, I think. It's in my heart to know a bit of yours." The hand moved from her shoulder to her chin and turned her head slightly.

Eyes of caramel brown, nearly amber, regarded her. Hair of bistre caught reflected light from the famed windows and mirrors. He ranged a bit taller than her, with a strong jaw line and lips that curved in an ironic smile. His finely featured face reminded her of a painting. "And when your revenge is finished, what will you do?"

Her resolve flickered. She knew what she had set out to do, but now didn't know if she could finish. "This is the last on my list. I haven't many options. No place to go." His fingers stayed warm on her chin.

He tsked in the way so many French could. "That is foolish."

"Necessary. I do what must be done. And you?"

"If I may suggest a solution?"

His hand slid to the curve of her throat and stayed there in an elegant caress. She blinked before answering, "What?"

"Imagine. I have this," and he gestured at his place at the window. "My head may be bouncing off a guillotine into a basket for all I know, but I am here and now." He leaned forward, holding her, and brought her close to him, so that ivory hat shaded them both from the radiance throughout the Hall, and whispered instructions in her ear.

She looked up at him when he'd finished. "I can do that?"

"If you wish. Magic, like love, is for those who search. A unicorn always seeks love." His one hand stayed at her throat, warm and embracing.

"I'm no virgin."

"Then I am most improper to implore you. But I am, if you wish?"

A heartbeat. "I do wish."

"Then you can." He stepped back in sudden retreat, his warmth gone, his scent withheld, his eyes no longer so close she could see the amber shades of them, his mask cloaking him away from her. She heard a shout from down the length of the gallery and he gave her a gentle push. "But hurry. My foot is in the doorway and it presses to close."

"Madam! Madam, please, join the rest of us. I cannot have you trailing behind." The voice confused her briefly, feminine where she expected masculine. The tour guide charged her, hands fussing in elaborate signals to catch-up and rejoin the group. Marjory found herself standing with her hand pressed to the window and quickly took it back before garnering another scolding as the guide rounded up Marjory like a well-trained herding dog.

When she finally had time, at the end of the long hall, to retreat and find him, he was gone. Disappointed, she continued on, glad only that they had passed through the bedazzling corridor, for its unrelenting shine left her eyes weary and her head throbbing. She trailed the tour group, her thoughts cloaked about what she thought she'd seen and felt. But that was her, wasn't it? She'd always preferred a bit of darkness. On the way out, she bought her last ticket to Versailles.

* * *

Shadows dappled her childhood home and its tiled courtyard. Silhouette figurines enveloped her as she played and then endeavored to imitate them. From the second-floor studios, they struck and engaged, parried and retreated, swords or sabers held at length. Even when small, she knew her father's shape from those of his students. He stood tallest. Moved most assuredly. Clapped his hands in praise and reprimand, his voice echoing after. But try as she would, she could not imitate him as she wished until she picked up the sticks. Gardeners had trimmed, leaving bare branches, and she'd seized them. That's when her silhouette matched his, blending, dancing at one with them, and she lost herself until her mother swept her up in her arms.

"There you are! I've been looking everywhere for you, my angel." Eyes brimming with worry and her apron smelling of laundry soap, her mother gathered her. Amid kisses and a breath or two, she added, "What are you doing with these sticks?"

Marjory squirmed down. "This!" she cried, and whirled away, showing the form she had learned, her small voice punctuating her movements. "En garde! Lunge! Parry and again!"

Her mother became still, one hand placed over her mouth, but she said nothing for long moments, only then put her other hand out in that commanding way mothers do to their children, and Marjory reluctantly complied. Their fingers knit together, her mother bent over. "You must not bother your father while he is working."

Marjory squinted up at the studio. Her mother's hand closed tightly and she sensed the fear and anger in her hold. She nodded and did not fight as her mother pulled her away from the courtyard and into the house. It would not be the last time.

It would, however, be the first time she heard her mother shout at her father when he came in for dinner, wiping his hands dry with a fine, white towel. "You can't let her near the studio while you work!"

"Amelinda, they are students. I must have students, it's my job."

"They are actors." A sound followed, like spitting, as she listened at the wooden door separating adults from her.

"I teach those who are sent to me. It's my work, and keeps us here in this grand house, our home."

"They are predators, all of them, and the men who hire them, worse!"

"You're distraught."

"*Naturalment.* I have been in the offices of such men." Her mother's voice paused. "Come work for my father. He's asked you several times. His import-export business is flourishing. You have language skills and charm…"

"I'm not a salesman. And you're the one who knows all the languages."

"The Olympics is far behind us, and besides, you excel at the sword, not the foil. You cannot go back. Grow up, Monty."

"Never!" A kiss between the two of them sounded and Marjory let out a little breath she'd been holding, realizing the worse of the argument should be over. "I promise to keep my students away from her. As for the blades, that's up to her and her heart. She is my daughter, no?"

She hid herself away then, finding fresh sticks, and a new corner where she could still hear, if not see, her father's instructions. Her mother always seemed to find her and finally she watched silently, as he presented Marjory with a set of practice sabers, to her complete joy. She matched him when she could; stroke for stroke, step by step often still by silhouette and sometimes in the studio itself. She kept it up even as the movie business took them around the world, though often in out-of-the-way places. The courtyard gave way to small, crowded rooms, or sometimes grand parques, or even grubby sound stages where she drew stares she did not like, but she was happiest when they returned home. Yet her mother and father yelled fiercely at one another again in the small hours of the night.

She crouched on the sidewalk on one such night. The moon glowed high in the sky, bright as a street lamp. So bright that she knew immediately when another joined her, though he moved as silently and gracefully as a cat.

He halted and she stayed in her place, both of them listening.

"Another fight," he said.

She did not answer him. The voices grew sharper and louder. Her visitor sat down beside her and drew her onto his lap, offering comfort. She turned her face towards the cradle of his arm, not wanting to hear the quarrel.

He tickled her bare arms gently, stroking, murmuring to her that she was a kitten and he would keep her safe. As she tucked herself closer, his hands fell to her bare legs.

The voices stopped. The back door banged open and then her father and the porch light spilled out onto the sidewalk.

"Eddie, what are you doing here?"

"I came for extra lessons but you've been busy…and is this the little wildcat you've kept hidden from us? I think I have her purring."

She looked up at her father.

"Get away from my daughter!"

"Now, now. She's enjoying herself, and I'm enjoying her."

Fingers slid along her bare legs again, up her thighs.

"I'll kill you."

Her protector surged to his feet, dumping her to the walkway. "It's nothing, Monty…"

"It's never nothing! Get away and stay away. I'm done with you. No more lessons, Eddie. Not ever. Get out!"

"Come on now. You can't do that. My film…"

"Your film can go to hell."

Eddie's tone roughened. "You'll never work in this industry again."

"With men like you in it, I don't want to. Run or I'll geld you like one of those fancy horses you like to ride!"

Her captor did not move. "But she liked it, didn't you, kitten?" Both stared down at her and she crept off the edge of the sidewalk, frightened in a way she didn't comprehend.

A low growl and her father lunged, chasing the other away like a big dog going after a frightened cat. All she could do was watch, not quite understanding.

* * *

They moved from the first, great house with its upstairs studio and tiled courtyard, ponds and grassy lawns. The homes became smaller. The jobs shorter. The arguments sharper. She grew tall enough to match blades with him and he drilled her as fiercely as he did any of his other students, those he could scrape up.

Somewhere along the way she lost her name and became Marjory. Was it when her mother pulled her away from her father one last time? Or before? She could never quite remember. Or perhaps it was when her father was ruined.

She was old enough to understand then, her mother with lips pressed so tightly they cast sharp wrinkles alongside her mouth and deep into her face, circled by reporters with microphones and cameras and shouts. Questions. "Did he ever attack your daughter? Or any of her friends?"

"*Nao*! Never! He would not."

"Did you know about your husband?"

"I know he's a good man! The rest is lies. Now leave us alone. See the attorney, not me. Not us."

Doors shut, and boxes were packed in a hurry, and they left again. Her mother told her not to remember, that what everyone said had happened had not, that the truth would come out one day. They hid in Portugal for a while, with her mother's father.

She never put up the sabers but she took a degree in finance and another in general law and became an actuary, a boring but steady job. Marjory put aside living for existing. She kept her mother safe. She lived safely herself. She endured headaches that seemed unendurable. And then she hit forty. The truth had not come out, so she went digging for it.

* * *

After the Versailles tour, Marjory struck out on her own. She fingered a slip of paper in her pocket to make certain it had not disappeared. The address it held had not come cheaply, nor had the foreign country stamps on her passport, stowed in an inner pocket. She tired of traveling. This last bit of paper should lead her to a final puzzle piece, the culmination of several years back and forth on scant vacations. It listed four names and addresses, but the top three had been crossed out. Only the last one remained.

Turning the corner, she stopped at a small doorway, a slim building bordered by a block of slender dwellings, neither luxurious nor pedestrian in looks. Above the house number, a small badge had been hammered into the stucco: a pair of miniature, crossed swords.

She weighed considerations but, before she had made a decision, an upstairs window flew open.

"You! Move along. Don't stand and stare. *Americains!*"

In fluent Portuguese, Marjory answered that she was not American, but apologized for admiring the doorstep of the great actor Edouard DuBois. She added in somewhat broken French that she worked as a location scout and had been viewing possibilities around Paris neighborhoods for filming.

The window snapped shut and a moment later the first-floor door opened.

"Ah! You're in pictures."

The English was not good, but better than the woman's Portuguese, so Marjory responded. "Yes, and again, my apologies for disturbing you and monsieur DuBois."

"He is not at home today." The woman—his wife? housekeeper? friend?—shrugged. "Perhaps tomorrow or the next day."

"I would not think of bothering him."

"It is no bother! He fears being forgotten, you know?"

"How can he be forgotten? There has never been anyone like him."

Another French shrug. "When one gets the gray hair, one gets forgotten. It is the way of life, hmm?"

"That cannot be." Marjory leaned forward, lowering her voice, as if to tell a secret. "I know the casting director is considering him for a major part in this film I'm doing."

"No!"

"But yes."

"But how?"

"Only someone like DuBois can portray this man, a man of action who has retired, but is encouraged to come forward and be a hero once again." Marjory gestured. "The studio must be talking to his agent, no? Or my director could not make plans."

The woman's expression narrowed. "No doubt." Then, she brightened. "You will come back? Talk to him? Tell him to shake some sense into his agent?"

"Well…"

"You must! He will be delighted to meet you."

"Perhaps. Tomorrow?"

"I will make certain he is back."

"Au revoir then." Marjory stepped back into the narrow street and waved encouragingly. She slipped her hand back into her pocket, again tapping that slip of paper.

She could not explain the sorrow she felt as she left to make her way to her room, the tiny cage of an elevator cranking her upstairs to where she stayed. She fell asleep only to awaken in the middle of the night to the aroma of baking bread. Without knowing if it made her feel better or worse, she closed her eyes again. A day fled by her, so quickly she did not know if it was jet-lag or the clock in her head that lost it.

Morning downstairs brought her to fresh croissants, good tea, marvelous butter, and an exquisite jam for her plate. A newspaper had been left by the previous breakfaster and she swept the pages open, only idly curious. Two headlines vied for her attention: Interpol Tracking Killer in Paris? America to Denmark to France! Next to it, in even more lurid color and font, the main headline: Spain's Lottery Jackpot Hits All-Time High $$$$$. Rioting for tickets!

Marjory smiled fully for the first time in days as she broke open a fresh mini-baguette and reached for the butter knife.

* * *

When she knocked at the DuBois home, the door flung open as if the occupant had been watching her progress down the narrow street.

"You'd said you'd come yesterday!" The woman pulled off her apron and knotted it in one hand, motioning for her to enter.

Marjory tilted her head and spread her hands. "I had work, madam. So sorry. Is the monsieur at home?"

"Oh, yes, and waiting! Would you like some water?"

"That would be perfect. Chilled and flat, if possible."

"Of course, of course. The parlor is up the stairs. I go this way to the kitchen," and her greeter darted off.

She heard movement upstairs, her heart beating a little faster with each deliberate step. Did she have questions she wished answered? Not any longer.

A worn Oriental carpet stretched from the staircase and beckoned around the corner to the open sitting room. Burnished parquet flooring gleamed under the carpet, offset by white apartment walls and an immense ceiling. The room hadn't been updated in a while but held the unmistakable cachet of French rooms in Paris. The man sitting on the taupe couch rose. The room held a fireplace that had been closed off and nearby potted plants cascaded through an open veranda door and onto the balcony. Herbs grew from most of the pots, with a sprinkling of flowers scattered throughout. She did not let the display over the fireplace draw her eye. She must not.

"Mademoiselle! How charming of you to drop by." He'd evolved into a silver fox, she noted, and let his accent coat his words seductively. He spread his hands wide in greeting.

She nodded, hugging her messenger bag closer to her flank. "I am so sorry to intrude."

"Intrude? A fan? Never. Have a seat, please." Edouard took a stance framing the fireplace and mantel adorned with the glory of the Oscar statue and the crossed swords over it. Now she took note. How they were positioned. Fastened. Edged.

She laced her fingers together over one knee. "You're kind."

"My housekeeper mentioned you work in the business."

"A location scout. Nothing grand."

"It takes a team," he said magnanimously.

"Of course it does." She leaned forward. "Are those the same…"

"My blades? Yes. I practice daily, although I don't use those anymore. The real performance came from my heart, my voice, my talent, not my steel. And yet," he sounded a bit nostalgic, "those are always mentioned."

"One can hardly blame the question."

"True." He tossed his head a bit, and the famed curls had gone toward snow white, showing at the roots. "Louise said you mentioned a part."

"Oh, not a part, monsieur. A starring role."

His eyes lit up. "Really."

"Indeed. The co-star has already been cast, not a professional, but the director and producers wanted an innocent, someone fresh…"

"An innocent," Edouard DuBois repeated. He pursed his lips in thought. "Difficult to act with the untrained."

"But you have such a rapport with young women."

"Yes, yes, of course." He scratched his right brow. "How young?"

"Very. Barely ten years of age, but well-behaved. An old soul you might call her."

He sat back on his couch and crossed his legs in a masculine stance. That eyebrow itched again. "My agent has said nothing."

She let herself frown. "I can't speak for the studio, of course. It's not my place. I should have said nothing, really," and she pitched to her feet. "Please don't tell anyone I've come here."

"It could be troublesome for you?"

"Oh, yes, and my dau—" Marjory plunged to a halt.

"Daughter?"

She could feel her face warm as her skin reddened. "I've said too much."

Edouard leaned forward now. "This fresh young actress wouldn't be your daughter, would it?"

Marjory stammered without getting out a coherent word.

"Now I think I understand." He smiled. "You wanted to meet me, intrigue me, and see if you could arrange a package deal. Ah, stage mothers. How little has changed over the years."

"I haven't lied. Not…entirely."

"Of course not. There is a film in the works."

She nodded.

"And it needs a mature star, such as myself, who can act and do some action to anchor it."

Another nod.

"And it requires a young co-star with whom the male lead can bond sympathetically."

She cleared her throat. Louise appeared then with a tray of iced waters, put them down on a small coffee table, and fled. Both of them stayed silent for a moment.

When her footsteps had trailed off downstairs, Edouard said only, "Have you the script?"

"I do."

He put his hand out.

Marjory rose to open her messenger bag, took out the script, and laid it across his palm.

He scanned the first opening scene, then he dropped it carefully on the table. "It opens well."

"It does, doesn't it?" Marjory took a step forward enthusiastically. He put his hand up to halt her in her place.

"Before I proceed any further, before I read this, before I send my agent haring off to present me as interested in the project, I need to know if the girl is any good."

"Of course."

He checked his wrist watch. "Louise leaves at 8 PM. I will have her set out a cold dinner for me, something the child will like. Bring her then and leave her."

Marjory opened her mouth and he wagged a finger. "My terms. No stage mother hanging over to make her nervous. I want an hour. If she is any good, you will have your package deal. I have favors I can call in, and I could use a good project at this stage in my life. Are we agreed?"

Her throat had gone dry. She seized one of the glasses and drained it half dry. "Agreed."

* * *

Summer skies had only begun to sink into sunset hues when she returned to the DuBois home. Sconces downstairs shone muted through the one window and the little pane in the door itself. She checked herself and her guise in the street quickly before stepping through the unlocked door and glancing up the heavily shadowed stairs. Above seemed to glimmer as if only candlelight glowed and Marjory caught the corner of her lip between her teeth for a moment. It was not yet too late.

No. It had always been too late.

She put her foot upon the stair. It creaked as she put her weight upon it, ascending to the next, a murmur of the wood, as though it had the soul she thought she no longer possessed. Another step. Another. A single table lamp augmented the candles as they flickered.

Edouard DuBois met her at the top of the stairway. "I must admit I am not surprised, but disappointed."

"Disappointed that you have no child to defile and it is only me? Or that the end is near?"

"Hardly that. Interpol contacted me several days ago, warned me that I might be visited by someone who seemed intent on doing away with swordsmen actors. I could hardly believe such an odd action. Nor did I expect a woman, whoever you are." His gaze raked her up and down. "I gave them the hour of the rendezvous. They will be here shortly."

The scorn did not surprise her. She feinted right and went left, under his arm, past his flank, darting to the wall over the fireplace, where his famed sabers rested on brackets. She took one down and slid the other his way across the flooring. "Defend yourself!"

When he moved to the blade, she could see that he had indeed stayed in practice, for all the good it would do him, for he'd never been the best of students and the teachers who'd worked with him could not compare to his first instructor. As he hefted his saber, she moved into position and smiled. "I am Inez Montenegro. You killed my father. Prepare to die."

He began to laugh but the sound fell short as he choked a bit. "Montenegro? Monty? Who the devil are you?"

"You called me kitten once."

His eyes gleamed with realization. The tip of his blade circled. "He jumped to conclusions."

"No. He knew you. You and your friends. And now they've all paid but you."

"I had nothing to do with what happened to Monty."

She advanced. "You had everything to do with it! You and Peter Richards and Chester Malvern and Tom Kovaks."

"Chet is dead too?"

Her lip curled. "They haven't found his body yet. They may never. But each of them talked to me first. Begged me to let them go. Told me the truth."

"What happened to Monty was his own fault! He decided to play hero. He should have left us alone. He barged in where he was not wanted."

"How could any decent man have left the four of you to play with children? And you left him in that disgusting nest of yours, staged it to look as though he was the one who—" She shook her head vigorously. Her ears rang a moment. "He'd only gone to rescue a victim, but you trapped him. En garde!"

He sprang forward in attack and she had her hands full for a moment, having forgotten that he was left-handed. It almost undid her. Like her father, she'd learned to lead with either hand, but the momentary lapse unnerved her. She tossed her saber over and noted that her opponent's lips tightened and face paled, ever so slightly. Metal sang as they struck and parried and struck again. They were fairly matched. She kicked aside a sitting table and he leaped over a bench to come at her as she did. She faked a retreat, to let him press his advantage, and he did.

She turned on heel and sliced across his torso. His shirt slit open and crimson stained the edge of her saber. First blood. A shallow cut, nothing substantial, but it scared him. She saw him falter a moment as he put his palm to it and then wipe his hand off on his thigh.

"It's nothing."

"It is only the start."

He forced a thin smile and re-set himself, shuffling aside the oriental carpet where it lapped into the living room.

"You never fenced. I would have heard of you."

"No. I took another path."

"Monty's daughter." He made a noise, half growl, half purr, deep in his throat, meant to irritate her. She barely heard it. "You disappeared, you and your mother."

"Long before he killed himself in prison, yes. But not forgotten. Never forgotten." She began to move, delicately, to her left, to his vulnerable right, since he fought left-handed. She had not quite decided how to end it, but end it she would, and soon. And then, hope she actually had an escape, a successful fade to black. Her head pulsed, pain beginning to come in waves. She narrowed her gaze and focused.

He fell back under an onslaught of thrusts, parrying each aside, but barely, and then he shoved the table lamp over. It shattered on the floor, plunging the room into half-darkness.

He did not remember that she'd learned in shadows. Truth, she reveled in them.

Above the growing harshness of his breathing, she listened for the distinctly European wail of sirens. If he had indeed invited Interpol here, they would be on her heels at any moment. He would have only left enough time to find out if there had genuinely been a girl offered up to him and decide his recourse. She had no time to waste.

She whirled, as his blade whistled by her ear, and she caught him solidly across the bicep, stepped back and plunged the tip of her saber into his thigh as he reeled in reaction. "One. Two." She moved into a two-handed position.

"Three." She sliced, with all the power she could manage.

His head rolled back on his shoulders, throat a-gape.

She dropped her saber and ran to the veranda door, and through, out onto the balcony where she dangled a moment before hitting the small yard in a parkour somersault. Then she, Marjory, ran off. She caught a taxi on the street over, even as official cars whizzed by, small globes on their roofs blinking in official haste.

* * *

Versailles at night, with fireworks beginning to boom and flower in the darkening sky, not a daily occurrence but scheduled for this evening. She joined the crowd, aware that at least two cars had followed her taxi and she was not free. Not yet. She slipped under the braided ropes and went up the front stairs, backwards, as he had told her. Then at the top of the stairs, she turned round counter-clockwise, before heading into the galleries. She kicked her shoes off, carrying them, although the delighted reactions of the crowd and the explosives hid her intrusion.

She ran into the Hall, momentarily stunned by the brilliance, all the lights, still glimmering, still reflected a thousand times over.

He stood, hand held out to her. "Hurry." Blue velvet and silver unicorn splendor, all man and all mythology, caught in a splinter of darkness.

She did, although a voice cried out behind her: "Halt! Put your hands up and freeze!"

She paid no heed and reached. Their skin touched. His fingers closed tightly upon hers as shots rang out. Did she feel their sting? She did not believe so.

His mouth warm at her cheek. "Are you finished?"

"Yes."

"Then welcome." He kissed her most gently, his mask lowering over both their heads and he repeated softly as he drew her in, "We are all only reflections here." He danced her into the shadow of time.

SCHRÖDINGER'S FRACTAL

Edmund R. Schubert

*One of the most bizarre premises of quantum theory
—a premise that has long fascinated
philosophers and physicists alike—
states that by the very act of observing,
the observer changes the observed reality.*

∞*Weizmann Institute of Science*

Jake,

This may seem like an odd place to begin this recording, but odd doesn't begin to describe the circumstances, so please bear with me.

I'm in your hospital room right now, surrounded by a collection of machines, black and silver, molded-plastic and chrome—your ventilator, your heart-pump, your feeding tube: all the sterile, computer-controlled devices needed to keep your failing body alive. People talk about how unpleasant they find the smell of a hospital, how the biting odor of bleach is a poor mask for all the disease and death. But to me it's the beeps and hisses and thrums of the equipment that tighten my throat and sour my stomach. They blend together in my mind to create something absolutely horrifying: an asynchronous, unstoppable clock counting down to your death; a clock I can hear but have no idea how to read.

It's impossible to know how these machines are all connected—which ones function on their own versus which ones are dependent on the one next to them. I used to adore clocks; their inner workings fascinated me. But I have no idea how to deal with the sprawling network of devices your doctors Frankensteined together to keep you alive.

As I sit in your hospital room and record this message, surrounded by these thrumming, hissing machines, you're fifteen years old and in a medically-induced coma. I don't know when you might be well enough to listen to it, but this recording is my insurance policy in case my plan goes horribly awry. You see, I'm about to start jumping into the future. It's the only way I can think to save you.

After each jump, I'll come back to the hospital to update you on my progress. At fifteen years old you're practically a man, so I'm going to talk to you in these recordings like you're an adult instead of a kid. I'm also going to say "when" and not "if" because talking to you like one day you'll wake up again is the most optimistic thing I can think to do.

And in case I don't get my miracle and see you awake again, or if this goes completely sideways and I disappear, there are others I'd like to explain myself to as well, people who I want to understand what happened and why.

Your mother, first and foremost. She deserves that. Rachel, if you're listening to this, I know you had a different idea about how we should handle things, but I had to trust my instincts.

Caitlyn Hughes also needs to know what happened, though for different reasons. Caitlyn knows better than anyone why using a time machine to send a person into the future is both illegal and unethical. Every time I jump into the future, it creates a new timeline, and each timeline is but one subset of a larger fractal; a non-linear geometric pattern that repeats at increasingly smaller scales. Imagine yourself climbing a massive, immortal apple tree that is always growing, each branch a different timeline shooting off in new directions, each producing its own unique fruit. Yes, they're all apples, but they all have distinct shapes and flavors; irregularities and blemishes.

Travelling up and down the tree from limb to limb and branch to branch becomes exponentially more complicated the farther you get from your starting point, and God help you if you're on a branch and it breaks off. Then you're irretrievably lost. That's my greatest fear: disappearing from your life if a fractal branch somehow breaks while I'm still on it.

If that happens, I know Caitlyn will destroy the time machine and make sure something as dangerous as time-travel — something dangerous not just to me but to every person on this planet — never happens again.

And if you think "dangerous to every person on the planet" is hyperbole, let me assure you it's not. Time machines are powered by cosmic strings, one-dimensional left-overs from the big bang. They have length but not width or height. Drawing two of them together creates an object with the density of a black hole, but because they're so slender, I can fling them like a fisherman casting his line in a river. Once I mastered the necessary equations, I could hit any point in the space-time continuum and then travel along the paired strings to get there.

So yes, I'm effectively flinging one-dimensional black holes around the universe. And you know what, Jake? That's the *least* dangerous part of this plan, the part that terrifies me less than any other.

I imagine, however, that you're less interested in the technical mumbo-jumbo and more interested in knowing how we got into this situation. You get that from your mother. She's got a Ph.D. in chemistry, but a Master's degree in curiosity.

There's no good way to tell you this, so let me just say it straight: a few months ago you suffered a massive stroke. No one has any idea why. Fifteen-year-olds aren't supposed to have strokes, but there are a lot of things in life that aren't supposed to happen, yet somehow they do anyway.

Immediately the doctors put you into a medically-induced coma. Said it was the best option to counteract the swelling in your brain. Last week a severe infection set in and your condition worsened. The doctors had told us pentobarbital—the drug they used to put you in the coma—might leave you susceptible to infections, but they also said it was the best choice. Your mother and I were too frantic in those early days to question their expertise.

Right after the infection set in, someone also started screwing with Fortier Industries. They drained a huge percentage of our cash reserves, raiding every division and subsidiary.

When someone screws with my business, they screw with my ability to take care of my family. Your medical care is unbelievably expensive, even for your mother and I, and the only way I saw to save you was to find the person who stole our money.

Naturally when I learned our accounts had been drained, I hired investigators. But your condition has started deteriorating so rapidly that jumping into the future became unavoidable. I can't wait for the investigators. I need answers now.

You might think it would be simpler to fix this by traveling into the past, but that's not an option. If all possible futures branch off like an insane apple tree, the past rages toward the present with the single-mindedness of the Mississippi River during a flood, ripping through everything in its path, sweeping up anyone dropped into it and forcing them back where they came from. If you time-travel into the past, there's only one possible outcome: you get swept right back to where you started—*fast*—queasy from the experience and gasping for air.

So your mother suggested I travel instead into the future. She thought I might be able to find a clue there about who stole our money.

The ironic twist is that when I return to my own timeline after each jump, I won't have any idea what will happen next. My presence in the future guarantees that what happens there will never happen again. Not in my timeline, nor any other timeline.

I'm going to repeat that, because I know it sounds bizarre. But it's true; it's precisely why traveling into the future is so dangerous. *My presence in the future guarantees that whatever happens in that timeline will* never *occur in my own timeline.* It's as if the very act of looking at one branch of that apple tree causes a new branch to sprout, and new fruit to grow. And any fruit that grows on the new branch can't possibly grow on any other branch.

I know; it's a lot to keep straight. Sometimes I wonder if one person is capable of wrapping their head around all of the implications of time travel. One more reason why it's so dangerous.

All I can do is leave this recording for you and hope for the best.

* * *

Jake,

I've actually made a couple of jumps since I last spoke with you. I know I promised to make a recording every time I jump, but I'm not having any luck learning who stole our money. I was too embarrassed to tell you I've been coming back empty-handed. Standing in front of you, having failed you again and again…It's too easy to imagine you opening your eyes and saying, "Come on, dad, is that really the best you can do?"

What makes me especially crazy is that there's no way some random hacker got into all of our accounts *that* fast. Even all of our personal accounts have been hit. No, the person who committed this crime has to be someone close to me, someone I trust. It's a privately-held family business and no one comes on board without my personal approval. Clearly I made a mistake somewhere along the line.

Fortier Industries has been a private company since it was founded back in the 1940s by your great-great-grandfather, Quentin Fortier. He established it when he landed a top-secret contract to supply food and beverages to the U.S. Government. I know it sounds odd — a top-secret contract for food — but it was for the Manhattan Project and everything associated with the Manhattan Project was classified top-secret. During the height of World War Two, strict rationing made coffee worth almost as much on the black market as penicillin. Actually, to the eggheads at Los Alamos, coffee was worth more than uranium, so your great-great-grandpa Quentin — or Q as the eggheads called him — made a killing. He also made friends who opened a back door — literally and metaphorically — to side-deals for tech gadgets the boys at Los Alamos didn't think anyone would miss. To make a long story short, that's how our little family business became the twelfth most valuable company in the world, with subsidiaries producing everything from toothpaste to time machines.

Well, just the one time machine. It turns out that because they're so dangerous, time machines are also worthless. The real money is in toothpaste.

Because it's a family business, I get to hand-select all of my top people. And now one of them has betrayed me. There's no other explanation.

I've already reviewed and re-reviewed all of the logical options: Andrew Bennington, my CFO. He's loyal, but has a greedy side. Joss Regal, my COO. He's the best ops man on the planet, but he clearly has ambitions beyond just operations. I think he'd like my seat at the head of the table. Even Caitlyn Hughes, my CIO, isn't above suspicion. She'll do what's right if she finds out I'm using the time machine, but she's also working on a failing start-up of her own and thinks I don't know how badly it's going.

There are a handful of other possibilities, but to tell you the truth I don't have any solid suspects; just a half-dozen names and a digital black hole that's sucking our bank accounts dry. All I can say with certainty is that the money is gone. I do have corporate stock, but if I start selling that, I run the risk of an outsider—or Joss Regal—taking control of the business. I have to be in control if I'm going to fix this.

One other detail you should know: your mom now comes with me each time I jump. She insisted after my first jump, saying she wanted to be by your side, to spend as much time with your future self as possible. She sits in your hospital room, watching you lay there, unmoving and comatose. I honestly don't understand it, Jake. She could just as easily sit with you in the present. I keep reminding her that she'll never see that version of you again, but she says that's exactly the point.

* * *

Jake,

I didn't leave a recording the last time I jumped. I don't want to confuse or dishearten you, but that version of you died—which turns out to be more complicated than it sounds. I also didn't have any more luck finding the thief than I had during previous visits.

Caitlyn came by your hospital room, though. Scared the crap out of me.

"Rick," she said as she walked into the room. "I thought I'd find you here."

Caitlyn knows about the time-machine—all the C-suite people do—and I nearly panicked, thinking she'd figured out what I was up to. More than any of my other top people, Caitlyn violently opposed messing with time travel.

Well, her and the number two scientist on the project, Thom Chiang. Thom was one of the first people who testified to Congress when they began the process that ultimately outlawed time travel.

Could he be the one behind the attack on my bank accounts? Did he think crippling me financially would somehow prevent me from using the time machine? I closed my eyes for a second and imagined the conversation he and Caitlyn would have if they discovered I'd been using it.

"I don't think he understands the ramifications of what he's doing," Caitlyn would say. At least she would give me the benefit of the doubt.

Thom would reply, "He knows damn well what he's doing. Every time he jumps forward, he creates a new timeline and every new timeline creates a new Jacob. More than ninety-nine percent of those Jacobs are going to die."

Caitlyn would shake her head. "Why would he do that to his own flesh and blood?"

"I don't think he gives a rat's ass. As long as he saves the son who exists in his own timeline, the rest of them are nothing but lab monkeys. You've seen how much he cares about the monkeys down in pharmaceutical."

I opened my eyes and blurted out, "I *do* care! I just don't know what else to do..."

Caitlyn was still entering your hospital room when I had my outburst. She froze, looking confused. I always feel stupid when the words in my head leak out of my mouth and into the real world. But listening to that conversation, even if it was only in my head, was gut-wrenching. I'm mortified to admit it, but until that minute it never occurred to me I could be creating so many versions of you and condemning them all to die. How many times had I jumped? Close to forty, I think. Forty timelines, which means forty Jacobs, doomed because of me. It was bad enough to do that over and over, again and again. But to not even realize it?

"Is there some problem with me visiting my son?" I snapped at Caitlyn, trying to cover up my embarrassment. "What else am I supposed to do?"

Caitlyn put a hand on my forearm and said with surprising sympathy, "Rick, I know Jacob's stroke has been hard on you and Rachel. But I need you back at the office. It took me two months to land this meeting with the Japanese and the video conference is at four o'clock. You have to get back to the boardroom. You have to get your head in the game."

I checked my watch. It was 3:20. She didn't suspect anything was amiss; she was just doing her job—and being a friend. I felt guilty for suspecting her of stealing from me.

There was also a new wrinkle. Now I had to hope that finding out about the meeting with the Japanese wouldn't screw up any potential deal. We'd been trying to team up with the Nakatomi Corporation on a VR project for almost a year and now I'd learned when the meeting was going to take place. When a person from a different time period sees or does things in the future, it can never occur exactly that way again. My only saving grace was that time has a way of keeping two versions of a person from being in the same place on a particular branch of the apple tree. Since my future self would be attending the meeting, and not me, that would limit what I could see and do—limit the damage I could inflict.

On the other hand, Caitlyn, Andrew, Joss, and their executive assistants, would all be at that video conference. That would give me an opportunity to search their offices.

"Give me five minutes and I'll be right there," I said, tapping the face of my watch. "You go make sure the equipment in the boardroom is 100%. I'll be right behind you."

"Five minutes?" she said skeptically.

I held up one hand and spread my fingers. "I promise."

I watched her walk out of your room, knowing she'd probably arrive at corporate headquarters and find "me" waiting in the boardroom and wearing different clothing. She might put down the new clothing to a quick-change before the meeting, but I'd have to pray she didn't say anything to future me about seeing *me* at the hospital. Caitlyn is sharp. If she catches him off guard even for a second, her alarms will go off.

On the other hand, if she realizes she ran into a time-traveling version of me, that won't be the worst possible outcome. The quantum mechanics of insane, immortal apple trees ensures she'll never catch me that way again. There are dozens of other ways she might catch me, but it won't be in this hospital room.

Corporate headquarters is only ten minutes from the hospital. I waited for three minutes, then went and searched Caitlyn's office. I left an hour later, empty-handed and dejected. To be honest, by that point I was hoping to find something that ruled her out. But I'd found no evidence of any kind.

I also had just enough time to search Andrew's office. Didn't have any luck there, either.

I left corporate and returned to the hospital. When I arrived, your mother greeted me in the hallway, which was unusual. That's when I learned that you'd died.

Your mother was *so* excited.

Don't get me wrong, she was torn up, too.

"This is fantastic, Rick," she said through tears that showed no sign of ending. She wrapped her arms around me and mashed her face into my chest. Doctors and nurses and patients walked around us. The doctors and nurses were practiced at ignoring people in the throes of emotional breakdowns, but the patients and their families were unsettled by the display.

Your mother lifted her head from the wet spot she'd left on my blue button-down shirt, snuffled loudly, and said, "Jacob had another stroke. A massive one. It killed him before anyone even knew what happened."

I pushed her away. "What do you mean, no one knew what happened? Someone should have been with him *every goddam minute!*"

"*I* was with him," your mother snapped.

"That's not what I mean and you know it." It makes me insane when she does that, twisting my words, making me look stupid or uncaring.

She stepped back, eyeing me like I was the class dunce. "Don't you understand what this means? I watched him die from a second stroke. Dr. Crane confirmed it. From now on, as long as I'm by his side, he can never have another stroke. This is precisely why I came into the future."

"Look," I said. I hated to be the one to break it to her, but it wasn't that simple. "Your presence by Jake's side doesn't guarantee he won't have another stroke. At best it only guarantees he won't *die* from a stroke." I paused for a moment, my mind racing up and down every possible branch of our insane apple tree, grabbing every possible piece of fruit. "Actually, it only guarantees he won't die from a *massive* stroke *on this day* in the future. Jake could have a massive stroke and *not* die, leaving him worse off. He could have a series of *small* strokes that kill him. He could have a massive stroke *tomorrow*. He could—"

"*Enough!*" your mother shouted. She raised her hands, her fingers locked into claws. For a moment I was sure she was about to attack me with those claws. But instead she stood there, arms extended, frozen in place like something unearthed in Pompeii. Tears ran down her stony face.

"Enough," she repeated, so softly that I could barely hear her. I'm not sure I actually did hear her. I may have just seen her lips move. But I knew what she'd said.

Enough.

I was heartsick. I had just taken something precious from her.

But it didn't change the fundamental truth: she hadn't prevented you from dying. There were too many details, too many things that could still go wrong. She meant well. She just hadn't thought it through. As if anyone really could, with so many moving pieces.

You had died, though, and that was for the best. For all your mother's miscalculations and misunderstandings about visiting the future, she had actually found one scenario where you died when we needed you to.

Anyway, that's what happened the last time I jumped. It's why I'm dawdling here with you now, instead of going home to your mother. It will be a while yet before she cools off.

* * *

Your mom didn't go into the future with me last time, Jake. I think she's done time-jumping. Last time we went, we met your new doctor. Freaked your mother out pretty badly. If I'm being honest, it freaked me out, too. I was unprepared for the universe to throw a piece of fruit at me that was quite that rotten.

We had jumped together, as usual, arriving to find a middle-aged woman checking your chart. Her hair was as white as her crisp lab coat.

"Good morning, I'm Alison Fulford. I'm Jacob's new doctor," she said as we walked into the room. "I'll be taking over for Dr. Crane."

"I don't want anyone replacing Dr. Crane," your mother said snappishly. "He knows Jacob's case intimately. I want him back and I want him back now."

The way your mother said "I want him back now," I wasn't sure if she was referring to Dr. Crane or you, Jake. She misses you so much it sometimes consumes her.

Dr. Fulford inhaled deeply and held it a moment, not meeting anyone's eye. Finally, the air escaped her lungs and brought forth hard words. "We all want him back," she said. "But I'm afraid that's not possible. He's dead."

"What do you mean, dead?" I said. "He's thirty-five. Healthiest man I know."

"He got hit by a truck," replied Dr. Fulford. She turned and left, clearly affected by Dr. Crane's loss.

The minute your new doctor stepped out the door, your mother said, "Dr. Crane came in the room last time I was here, when Jacob died. He was in here for a long time. I talked to him. I interacted with him. This is the universe's way of making sure we don't ever see Dr. Crane again. *We* did this. *We're* responsible!"

"Life is full of risks," I said.

"A risk we created," your mother said in a hissing whisper. "A risk he didn't even know he was taking!"

"The man did his job," I replied. "Lived his life. That's all anyone can do."

It's not that I didn't care he'd died; I simply couldn't afford to waste time and energy feeling bad about it. I finally had a lead on who stole our money. I had digging to do. My CFO Andrew Bennington was looking innocent. But his number two, Micah Alvis? Not so much.

But that business with your doctor didn't sit well with your mother. Not at all. She's opted now to stay behind. Says she needs to remain by your side at all times because her presence in the present will protect you.

I didn't tell her about all the other versions of you we had already created each time we jumped. Figured she had enough on her mind as it was, without adding another moral predicament.

* * *

Jake,

I've been wandering around all day. Just wandering. Trying to figure out what to do, what to say. I don't know who else to talk to, so I've come here to talk to you. You're a good listener.

I can't think of a way to break this to you gently, so I'll say it straight out.

Your mother did it, Jake. All along, it was your mother who'd stolen the money. She "robbed" our company in order to manipulate me, hid the money and then *tricked me* into going to the future—specifically so she could tag along. She wanted to be present for as many problems as possible, thinking she could eliminate them one by one. She thought she could stack the deck in your favor and increase the odds of a miracle. It was a stupid plan with a million holes, but she pulled it off brilliantly.

But that's not the worst of it, not hardly. The worst of it is this: I never would have found out if she hadn't told me, and she only told me because I fucked up. Fucked up so badly it doesn't matter what your mother did. What I did was so much worse.

I'm sorry, buddy, but the last time I jumped forward, I watched you come out of your coma.

I didn't mean to. I don't even know why I went to see you. I guess because your mother had stopped visiting. Somehow the thought of ignoring you, even in the future, felt wrong. Five minutes, that's all I was going to spend. I'd be in and out in five minutes.

But this last jump, just as I appeared, you started coughing. It was the first time you'd moved since you were put into the coma. Doctor Fulford and her crew rushed in. The future version of your mother was there too, because the present version wasn't around to displace her. And before I realized what a disaster it would be if I stayed, I got caught up in the excitement as the doctors successfully brought you back into the world, alive and out of danger.

I was hugging your mother, crying with joy, when one of the nurses—crying every bit as much as your mother and me—said that it was a miracle, a true-blue, one-in-a-million miracle. Said how blessed she felt to be present for such a miraculous event.

That's when it hit me: the third time she said the word "miracle."

I'd fucked up. I should have gotten the hell out of there the minute it looked remotely possible you might recover.

That cough could have been a one-time event. It could have been a lot of things, but the longer I stayed, the more of a disaster I made it.

Traveling into the future and then trying to go home again is like drifting down the Mississippi and then thinking that you can swim back upstream again through the *exact same* waters. But you can't; those waters have already passed by. And the new waters that come behind it bring a whole new collection of logs and frogs and boats and fish. And apples.

It's the same river, yet a totally new and different one at the same time.

All of which amounts to this: I took your one-in-a-million miracle and I annihilated it. I set your miracle on fire and watched the ashes sink into the swirling, muddy waters of the Mississippi. I poisoned every branch of the entire apple tree and every apple it would ever bear. Pick whatever metaphor makes you happy; it amounts to the same thing. After all my stress about the different versions of you I'd created—after all my anxiety about all the versions of you that would go off on their own timeline to die—I had landed in the middle of the single alternative that was worse.

The version of your mother standing next to me in that hospital room was *ecstatic*.

How was I supposed to go back to the present and tell *that* version of your mother—the one I lived with—what had happened in the future? What I had seen and done?

What I had *un*done?

* * *

I'm a coward, Jake. My first instinct after your future self woke from the coma was to hide. I kept imagining all the different versions of the conversations I'd end up having with your mother.

I saw myself saying, "I never would have gone into the future if you hadn't manipulated me. Why didn't you tell me your plan from the beginning?"

"I did tell you," she would reply. "You brushed me off

like so much dandruff. Said my Ph.D. was in chemistry, not physics. Said I should stick to topics where I knew what I was talking about."

"Oh, like your presence in Jake's future represented any less of a hazard than mine," I'd say.

And just like that, we'd be off to the races, fighting.

Clearly that wouldn't work.

Maybe I'd try, "If you had gotten out of there right after Jake died, Dr. Crane might still be alive. Then this whole scenario would have played out differently."

She'd come back with, "You never would have seen him recover if you had remained focused on finding the thief and stayed out of his hospital room like you *told me* you were going to."

"*You* were the thief," I'd shout. Of course that would go as badly as you'd imagine.

On and on it went, me running conversation after conversation through my mind until finally I'd run out of excuses, tested all of my defensive snipes, and spun all of my sideways half-truths.

Even though the arguments were hypothetical, Jake, there was no escaping the pain I'd inflicted. In the end I only had one option: tell your mother the unvarnished truth.

With so many versions of reality to work with, who would have ever thought *that's* where this would end up.

* * *

Jake,

If everything goes according to plan, this will be my final message for you. I know it seems abrupt, but your mother and I talked all night and we think we have a solution to your dilemma.

This recording will be different in one important way: the version of you that it's intended for—a specific, future version of you—I will never see again. Neither will your mother. But your mother and I believe it's the only way. We need to know there's at least one Jacob Fortier out there who might survive. One Jake who at least has a chance.

Do you remember what I said about time machines being powered by cosmic strings, and how I can combine them and fling them through space-time? Well once I deliver this final recording—the only way you'll know what we've done—I'm going to head back to my own timeline. During the return trip I'll sever one of the cosmic strings. Cutting one of the two strings should break this time-fractal off at its base, separating it from the larger pattern and creating an independent new time-line.

I think the one remaining cosmic string will be enough to bring me back to my own time, but if not, so be it; it's a chance I'm willing to take—to give *you* a chance. I owe you that.

If my plan works, your mother and I will never know how this story ends. We'll have spun you off, on your own, into the unknown and unknowable. We'll have set you free from our prying eyes and hands and sent you to a place where anything is still possible.

There are people in this world who've won the lottery twice; it does happen. It just can't happen on this tree anymore. As far as your future with us is concerned, I've irrevocably poisoned this tree. Your only chance now is to go someplace new and start over fresh.

It's our hope that by cleanly breaking off this single branch, it might set down new roots and become a beautiful tree in its own right. To bear better fruit for you.

If you ever wake up—if you ever recover and hear this message—think of us. We'll certainly be thinking of you.

We wish you the best, Jake. Whatever your future holds.

With quantum entanglement,
certain particles remain connected
in a way that actions performed on one particle
still affect the other, even if
they're separated by great distances.
The phenomenon so agitated Albert Einstein
that he called it "spooky action at a distance."

CLOCKWORK CORSAIR

R.K. Nickel

Roth clutched the steel bars of his cell, holding tight to maintain his balance as the ship swayed. Even airships as expensive as *The Feathered Portent* weren't immune to the winds and clearly, wherever in the skies they were, a storm was brewing.

Beside him, a prisoner retched. The smell of bile mingled with that of piss and the pervasive damp of cloud-fog. Roth did his best to avoid breathing through his nose, but the pursuit was hopeless. Like most of Roth's pursuits.

How long had he been at this? Years. A lifetime, it felt like, though he was still on the fresher side of forty. The fact was, Roth was tired. The kind of tired that ached down his left leg, that cracked in his neck whenever he got out of bed—the kind of tired that nagged at him, telling him life would be so much easier if he simply...let go.

But he would not let go. No matter how much he wanted to. He would hold on, dammit.

She deserved that much at least.

Click. The large ion-chipped clock embedded in the wall chimed the end of the early-evening shift. With that, Roth flickered the two steel bars in front of him and they disappeared.

More accurately, they ceased to be a part of the time stream. At least momentarily.

Roth darted through the gap where just an eyeblink before had stood oppressive steel, doing his best to ignore the pain in his arm where his bracer pierced his skin. Another hopeless pursuit.

Too slow. A guard appeared in the doorway above the stairs, expression quickly morphing from shock to anger to that deadly sense of duty that painted the faces of all the Sovereign's men. Mindless. Soulless. Bent and broken and forged to follow orders.

Roth focused and a thin rapier appeared in the air before him. He grabbed hold of it as the guard drew a short sword and attacked. Roth deflected the guard's blow with ease—years of piracy had their merits—and smiled to see shock paint the guard's face again so soon. Clearly the man hadn't expected a starving slave to know his way around combat.

"I—" sputtered the guard. He never got the chance to finish his sentence. Roth clasped the man's shoulder with his right hand and the guard disappeared.

Roth stepped to where the guard had stood, extended his rapier, then hummed a tune to pass the time, his scratch-throated shanty set to the roaring accompaniment of shouts and shrieks from the still-caged prisoners, who either cheered him on or demanded explanation for what they'd seen. He ignored them, as he'd ignored so many before. Roth's focus was singular. It had to be.

Finally, the guard flickered back into the time stream. Roth knew the fear he saw in the man's eyes. He'd felt it himself time and time again—the dread call of the neverending—but before the guard had time to process what he'd felt, he let out a lightning-crack scream and pawed at the rapier extending from his chest. Suffice to say, a rapier-sized chunk of flesh now existed somewhere in null-time.

The guard took one last desperate swing with his sword, but Roth caught the blade on the steel plate that guarded his palm and flickered the sword into nothingness.

To his credit, the guard managed to gurgle a final bit of defiance, locking eyes with Roth as life left him. "Do you know who you're stealing from?"

Roth shrugged.

"You're dead," said the guard. "You're storming dead. This isn't some merchant caravan." Blood flecked from the guard's lips, spattering across Roth's face. "This is a Sovereign transport."

Roth pulled the blade from the guard's chest. "I'm well aware."

As the guard collapsed, Roth reached out his right hand. He took a moment to marvel at the metal wires that wove in and out of his arm, blood flowing visibly through the bracer. Helped with the intimidation. One second. Two. Then the guard's sword flickered back into existence, and Roth closed his fist around it.

"What about us?" shouted a prisoner, rags soaked in sweat, face barely recognizable beneath the layers of grime. His life would be one of torture and labor and death.

"I'm not here for you," said Roth.

He was here for her.

Roth headed above-decks, dodging guards as he ran—scamper to the lower gun deck, hurl the guard's sword into a sailor's belly, flicker a Sovereign's man, climb to the upper gun deck, flicker the door, main deck—alarum, mayhem, the wooden planks slippery from the cloud-fog condensing all around him, cut down that guard, flicker the axe, dodge a pistol shot, rapier, neck, climb the rail, the plank, out to the edge, then—

Roth leapt and plummeted through the clouds.

As far as Roth knew, he was the only person in the Stormlands who possessed a riftless ion stone. Well, two riftless ion stones to be exact. The Sovereign held the rest, secreted away in his underground workshop, his recters toiling endlessly to design new apparatuses. Each year, the Sovereign lashed out with some powerful new technology and each year his already-suffocating grip on the Stormlands grew that much tighter.

But Roth had been royal once, until suddenly he wasn't, and though he'd been a mere child at the time, he managed to escape with two stones. His parents shoved them in his pockets, stuck him on a horse, and told him to ride. Even from leagues away, he'd seen the flames of their estate licking the sky.

He had spent his youth tinkering with the stones, investigating how they shaped reality, searching out the few remaining independent recters, and finally, finally, he'd invented the bracer.

Touch something with his right hand and he could remove it from time, usually just for a few seconds. The longer he was forced to alter reality, or the more objects he flickered at once, the more strain the clockwork put on his body.

The rapier had been trickier, but eventually, he'd been able to craft the bracer's opposite: a sword that existed outside of time, only appearing when Roth focused it into being. Every few steps, he'd flicker it imperceptibly and release it back into null-time, keeping it close.

She'd been the one responsible for his breakthrough: a recter, working in secret, far from the Sovereign's vigilant gaze. Together, they'd toiled. Together, they'd tinkered. Together, they'd dreamed. Together, they fell.

Roth fell. Fell through clouds, through cold, past lightning, there in the skies, crystals of ice cutting into his flesh, cold working under his skin, thunder rolling ear-splittingly through his mind, until finally, Roth spotted the flagship below him, sailing through the rain-gray storm.

The Sovereign's Blade, the ship was called. The unassailability of three redundant airpods, whispers of a thousand cannons, large enough to house five hundred men. The ship was more floating city than transport vessel. It was his true target.

Roth plummeted, adjusting his body so the airstream aimed him toward the ship's stern—faster, faster. Images passed through his mind: splattering on the deck, snapped up in the jaws of a stormdragon, or, worst of all, missing the ship entirely and falling, falling until finally he plunged into the black acid sea. But just before he crashed into the deck, transmuting from pirate to pulp, Roth touched his hand to his chest and focused.

For the barest of moments, Roth ceased to be, flickered from the time stream. But even the barest of moments, existing out there, somewhere, beyond time, lasted an eternity. An eye blink. An eon. The experience could not be comprehended by mortal minds, for thought, Roth knew, was simply another form of lightning, and lightning, fast as it was, took time to strike.

When Roth reappeared, a marrow-deep tearing sensation appeared with him, burning a fire through his skull as his mind worked to readjust itself to reality. He gritted his teeth as he sprang into being and dropped the last span to the deck, gravity taking hold as if he'd simply jumped from atop a barstool.

Feeling the solid wood beneath his boots, Roth let out a sigh, then sagged, fighting to stay upright. Too much energy.

Too long, he'd done this. Too long, he'd searched. But the heart was here. It had to be. He could still save her.

* * *

"Name yourself," shouted Captain Ari as the ornate door disappeared and Roth stepped through. The Captain pulled a blunderbuss from the sash at her chest, her long black hair rippling.

"Hello, Captain," said Roth, taking in the lavish quarters. Chests, maps, a telescope. None of it important.

"My guards are dead, I assume."

"Aye."

"I will not hesitate to end your life, interloper. I hope that is clear."

"I'm sure you'll try," said Roth. He could nearly taste the disinterest on his tongue. Danger didn't affect him the way it used to. "Where's the heart?"

She scowled. "I don't know what—"

"Please, Captain. I came a long way to be here. Got captured. Starved. All to get close to this ship. I've killed. A lot. Gone weeks without seeing another living soul. Can we dispense with all of this..." Roth waved his rapier in a shrugging gesture "...dishonesty? I have my sources. The heart is aboard this ship. And I'm going to steal it."

"I can't let you do that. My apologies." The Captain fired her gun.

As she pulled the trigger, Roth threw his hand forward and focused, rapidly flickering the air in front of his palm in and out of time. The bullet struck the fluctuating draft, disappeared, reappeared, and dropped to the floor. Stopping a bullet with his palm never ceased to impress.

Sure enough, the Captain scowled, which, as reactions to this particular stunt went, was about the calmest Roth had ever seen. Roth inclined his head ever so slightly. Well played, Captain.

"Tell me why," the Captain said as she dropped the blunderbuss, then pulled another from her sash.

"Does it matter?"

"The Sovereign paid dearly to acquire the heart. Immortal life, as clockwork replaces his body piece by piece. I'd say the stakes are high." She fired again and again Roth flickered the bullet.

His breath grew fast. Sweat dripped down his brow, stinging his eyes. His head pounded. Air was so much less tangible, so much harder to focus on. But he'd fought all his life. He could fight now.

The round ball of lead clinked against the ground.

"A neat trick," said the Captain.

Roth rubbed his temple. He'd chewed the last of the urgen root ages ago. Months of pain without relief. Was it really too much to ask? A warm fire. A cat. His wife.

"Please," Roth heard the plea in his voice, "I don't want anyone else to die. I mean, to be perfectly honest, I don't really care much one way or another, but it sounds like a lot of effort."

The Captain hesitated, then sighed. "I must deliver it."

"Or the Sovereign will have your head. Blah blah blah." Roth bent his knees, adjusting his center of balance. He doubted there'd be much of a fight, but he might as well prepare.

"Who sent you?"

"No one sent me, dammit. Can we just get this over with? I'm wet, and bloody, and sort of peckish." As long as he joked, he wouldn't think about how close he finally was.

"Does the Sovereign suspect something?" When Roth only sighed, she continued. "Does the Uprising not trust me? I must know."

"Uprising?" Roth took a breath, catching himself. "You know what, I'm not going to ask. Doesn't matter." Roth struck. The Captain parried, blades ringing in the quiet cabin.

Then the Captain's blade glowed blue and electricity lanced along its edge, passing into his rapier. Luckily, the moment the first sparks touched Roth's hand, he reacted on instinct, releasing the blade back into null-time, electric charge with it.

Unarmed. He hated being unarmed. But if he could just get her to step where the blade would appear—

The Captain's sword burst into flames, tongues of fire licking toward Roth as if propelled by great winds.

"The hell?"

"I designed it myself." The Captain lunged, forcing Roth to stumble backward. "You're the first man who's seen him in all his fury. Luckily…" she swung and Roth rolled. Her blade bit into an alcohol cabinet, which caught fire. "I doubt you'll be able to tell anyone what he can do."

She extended an arm toward the cabinet and Roth saw for the first time her bracer, wires weaving in and out of her flesh, red tubes pumping. She clenched her fist and the fire went out, leaping somehow into the bracer, whose copper scintillated as it caught the flame.

Of all the people who might be guarding the heart, he had to face off against a recter whose ingenuity matched his own.

Roth danced behind the Captain's desk, though calling his staggering movements a dance was probably generous. His failing knee. His aching back. How had he gotten so old so young?

She trailed him — just what he wanted — and the pair wove a slow circle.

"I designed mine too," said Roth, holding up his arm.

The Captain drew closer. "I look forward to taking it apart piece by piece."

"Always wanted to meet one of the Sovereign's recters. Bought with coin or blood, I wonder?"

The Captain growled. Actually growled. Guess he'd struck a nerve.

"You don't know anything about me." She extended her hand and the flames trapped within poured out. Roth got his palm up just in time, flickering each ripple of fire as it came, then dodging back to where he'd lost the rapier. He called it forth, clasping it in his left hand as it appeared, and the pair squared off once again.

"I haven't had to break a sweat in a long time," the Captain said, cracking her neck.

"Must be nice. I'm always sweaty." Their blades met once more. Fires burned. Electricity lanced. Roth dodged and flickered, but always the Captain wriggled just out of reach, avoiding his free hand. He flickered floorboards out of time, but she adroitly sidestepped the sudden gaps. He flickered her desk, a letter opener, anything—he knew how many heartbeats they'd be missing—but she kept perfect track of the objects' locations and never passed through the space where they'd reappear.

Strike. Parry. "You know, pirate," said the Captain between breaths, "we could use a man like you."

"I know how this speech goes. Save your breath."

"Not the Sovereign," said the Captain. "Listen." She stepped back and lowered her sword.

"I'd rather not." He could press the advantage, but as long as she was talking, he was catching his breath. And as the older of the two, he sure as hell could use a moment.

"I think I have the measure of you."

"Do you now?"

"You're a mean bastard. I like it. Moreover, I'm one of the best recters in the Sovereign's employee. Not a boast. It's simply true. Your clockwork is at least as inventive as mine. It's refreshing." She brushed sweat-matted hair from her face. "I need the heart."

"Not going to ha—"

"I need the heart because the Sovereign rarely, if ever, deigns to meet with us. There's almost nothing left of him. His arms have turned to gears, his legs pneumatics. Intricate lenses fill the sockets where once he saw with eyes of flesh and blood. His brain rests in a skull of indestructible ion-stone alloy. Soon, he will be unkillable. Cut off a limb and he simply attaches a new one. Strike his neck and your sword shatters. Not to mention he can see you coming from beyond his walls, can sense your heartbeat, can hear your breath. A single ruler, endlessly replaced piece by piece, eternally upgraded. I can't allow it."

Roth scowled. The Captain of *The Sovereign's Blade*. She'd simply met an opponent who struck fear into her and this was another storming tactic. "What're you playing at?"

"You asked me to dispense with the dishonesty." Roth thought he sensed a resonant weariness in her then. "I aim to strike him down." A tactic. That was all it was. A tactic. "Deliver the heart, get close, and end him. While he can still be ended."

"Why tell me?"

"Because I'd rather not keep fighting you. And because I suddenly wasn't sure I'd win."

Roth lowered his rapier a hair. "Sounds like a suicide mission."

"Yes. It does."

"Don't know about you, Captain, but I kind of like the whole living thing."

"I'm..." the Captain trailed off, a faraway look in her eye "...tired. Tired of the death, the divide, the rich preying on the poor." She knotted her fingers in her hair, a clearly subconscious motion. "The idea that I might be able to change something—it's the only thing that keeps me going."

Was everyone and their mother so beaten down? Roth had assumed he was worse than most, but he'd never bothered to find out. Guess you had to actually interact with people to have a chance at understanding them.

The Captain grabbed a bottle of wine from a short table beside her and took a rather liberal quaff. "We can get back to it, if all you're here for is the treasure. Is that it? You wish to be a rich man? Whore your way through the Stormlands, drink until you don't feel anything anymore? Seems to be the way with pirates."

She took another long swallow, wiped her arm across her lips, then hurled the bottle at Roth, leaping forward as her blade ignited. Roth flickered the bottle away and met her blade.

"Who invents a bracer like yours just to steal?" She hammered at him—heavy, furious strokes. "How can someone with that sort of mind be content simply to live?"

More sweat dripped into Roth's eyes. The heat of the fire singed the hairs on his arm. "No matter who you end up killing along the way." He backpedaled. "No matter how many people it harms." She scored a hit across Roth's side—a blazing sting of steel, but the flames cauterized the wound even as Roth turned away. Dammit. He was slowing down. She paused, seeming to consider him. "Leave the bracer with me and I'll let you go."

Roth clutched at his side. He hadn't taken a wound like that in ages. "I can't."

"What could possibly be so import—"

Roth feinted, then landed a solid kick, knocking the Captain back. "My wife. It's my wife. She's dying."

"So there is more to you after all."

"I can still save her."

"I sympathize. My lover died in the third desolation war. There's nothing like loss to guide a person's path. But how many men's wives will die if the Sovereign continues to reign? How many husbands? How many will be sold as slaves? How can one life measure up to all that?"

"Because I love her."

"Are you sure she'll survive?"

"I don't know. But I have to try."

"How long has she been injured?"

"Stop with the questions!" Roth shouted. She was getting to him. He hated her for it.

"How long?"

"A decade. Nearly a decade." The water in his eyes was nothing more than sweat. He blinked it away.

"You've been searching for all that time? How is that even possible?"

Roth thought he'd been tired before, but now he could hardly stand. The weight of it all. The years spent worrying, caring for nothing else, caring for no one else, having no one else. A man shouldn't be so singular. Maybe he really would've been better off whoring his way through the

Stormlands. Ha. Some pirate he was. He hated when people made sense.

"Listen—"

A huge man burst into the room. Clad in spiked armor from head to toe, he nearly blocked out the light filtering through the door. The ion-chipped blue glow of his plate-mail cast an eerie haze over the room.

The Captain spoke. "Lieutenant?"

"Captain." The man's voice rumbled with a basso disdain.

"You're just in time. You see—"

"What sort of reward ya think I'll get when the Sovereign finds out about your treachery?" the brute continued, ignoring her. "Maybe he'll let me be the one that guts ya."

The Captain sighed, turning her blade toward the man. "I suppose I'll have to pretend there was a mutiny."

"No need to pretend, m'lady. Boys!"

With that, a half-dozen guards stepped up behind the man, each armed with an ion-chipped scourblade.

Why did everything have to get so complicated? The Captain never should've been as strong a fighter as she was. Roth had dealt with the sentries. He'd done everything perfectly. The heart should be in his hands. He should have his wife back already. He deserved it, dammit. He'd come too far.

The Lieutenant drew his sword, a bastard of a blade. "Try not to kill her, would ya? Sovereign'll wanna pull the truth from her pretty little teeth."

Search for the heart while they fight? He'd never find it in time. The Captain didn't stand a chance against seven men, even quick as she was. Let them kill her and take his chances with the survivors? It came down to one thing, really.

She was a good storming person.

Roth stepped up beside her. She nodded to him. He nodded back. Why couldn't Roth be a real pirate for once? Too soft. He'd always been too soft.

The Lieutenant strode forward. "I don't know who this is, but I really couldn't give two shits." He came at them. Roth caught the first strike with his rapier. The sting of the impact jittered through his entire arm, turning it nearly numb. Damn, this Lieutenant was a strong bastard.

Roth reached out. A few more inches and he'd be able to flicker the man.

The Captain's blade lit up with electricity and she swung it into the Lieutenant's side. Even better. Plate-mail might be good at stopping a blade, but it was conductive as hell. As the lightning surged through him, the Lieutenant let out an inhuman shriek and fell to the ground.

For a moment, the battle paused and everyone watched as the Lieutenant writhed and wailed and clawed at himself. Roth had seen a gutter dog snatch up a possum once and the shrill, squealing howls it made as the canine's teeth cracked its bones were not dissimilar.

It seemed almost as if the guards might break from the horror of it, but before the winds of battle changed, the Lieutenant managed to slap his fist against a section of his armor and the plate-mail fell away from him. Clearly, recters had found a way to create plate that sprung together and apart at a touch. Time saver.

"Skies above," muttered Roth when he saw the man. The cloth beneath the plate must have kept him from being electrocuted, but it hadn't stopped the heat. Every inch of the man's skin oozed with roiling red-and-black blisters. His face looked like oily meat barely sturdy enough to stick to the spit before it was carved and served.

"What're you looking at me for?" the man slurred, a piece of his lip falling to the ground as he spoke. "Kill the bitch!"

The fight began anew.

Roth and the Captain had learned the way of one another. A gout of flame from the Captain's sword burned a hole in a guard's chest. Roth parried a blow, then grabbed his attacker's arm, flickering him from time. The Captain kicked the wine table to where the guard had stood.

Roth slid his rapier across the ribs of one of the men and the Captain finished him. The previous guard flickered back into being and screamed. Only bits and pieces of his legs had returned. The wine table prevented the rest.

Bullets flew. Bullets fell. Fire and sparks and blood and blade. Then the Lieutenant stood, massive sword wobbling through the air. Roth caught it, flickered it, grabbed the huge, bloody mess of a man in an embrace, and pulled him close. The blade reappeared, point extending from somewhere in the man's belly up through his left shoulder. A mercy, really. Roth doubted if the man would've survived.

When Roth let go, he saw that the rest of the guards were dead. A few fires blazed throughout the room, but the Captain calmly called them to her bracer, one by one.

"Sorry about your quarters," said Roth.

The Captain looked around, then laughed. "Makes the mutiny story rather easy to believe. Not that it matters much." She took a seat behind her smoldering desk. "So, what now?"

It had felt good to fight beside someone. Roth could almost feel his old self, somewhere deep beneath his skin. Had the Captain's electric blade sparked something in him? Had a dormant part of himself been ignited by her fire? No. Merely adrenaline. The thrill of a good fight. But when had Roth last thrilled at a fight? Each swing of his sword these last years had felt more like the lurch of a pick. Chipping away relentlessly at a quarry, all alone, hoping that with enough blows, he might find the precious rock within. But his hands had grown blistered from the effort. Perhaps the Captain was right. Could he really let so many die? The Sovereign had killed his family, for storm's sake. The Sovereign had ruined his life. The Sovereign's men had—

Roth caught movement from the corner of his eye. The Lieutenant, twitching in the throes of death, a fallen blunderbuss in one hand, finger on the trigger. The man squeezed.

Roth leapt in front of the Captain, focusing, flickering the air as the explosion from the gunpowder rang in his ears. Concentrate. Palm out. Breathe. A hot flash ignited inside him. It couldn't be.

Blood poured from his chest. He hadn't been ready. Hadn't been fast enough. He'd been too tired. So tired. So very tired. His knees buckled and he watched through hazing eyes as the Captain drove her blade through her Lieutenant's neck, then rushed to Roth's side.

Roth coughed, and then suddenly his wife knelt before him. Blood leaked from a matching wound in her chest.

"Molly," whispered Roth. This wasn't supposed to happen.

"Roth," she said, and the emotion in her voice nearly broke him. "Roth, it's okay."

He tried to focus. Tried to flicker her again, but he didn't have the strength. He'd set the bracers to flicker her in and out of time with every step he took so that she'd be forever by his side, so that she'd stay alive. Each step, she lived but an infinitesimal moment. To him, a decade. To her, a minute. She was as beautiful as he remembered.

"No no no. You can't. You'll die," he sputtered.

"It's okay. I died all those years ago, plum. It's just taken a little longer for the last goodbye, that's all."

"There's still time." He nearly fell over, but he caught himself with a hand.

"You have to let me go. For me and for you." Her eyes fluttered. The flow of blood from her wound slowed. The damn Sovereign soldiers. They'd shot her. They'd shot her for making clockwork outside the chains of the Sovereign's workshop. They'd shot her for thinking on her own, for refusing to be a slave. Roth had killed them, but the soldiers' blood had done little to replace hers.

"My life is over, Roth. I loved it. I'm so lucky that even a small part of it was spent with you. But yours doesn't have to be over as well. Let go and make it worth it. Live, plum. Live for me."

"Molly, no. I can't. This whole time, I've—"

"You've driven yourself half-mad, I know. I've been there. Beside you every step of the way. Please, plum. I'm ready." She closed her eyes.

He crawled, screaming in pain. In anger. In hate. In love. Crawled through their pooling, co-mingled blood and placed a hand on her shoulder. His bracer hand. He felt her skin beneath his fingertips. Growing cold.

Roth focused.

He ignored the sting in his chest. Ignored the weariness that ached through the whole of him. He fought against the searing heat in his nerves, against the cold that worked its way up from his fingers. He focused.

And let her go.

"I love you," he said, tears dripping onto her face.

She didn't respond. Would never respond.

Perhaps he would see her before long. He'd never believed in much, but maybe now was a good time to start.

From somewhere in the haze of his understanding, Roth heard movement. Rustling. The opening of a chest, perhaps.

"Oh no you don't." A woman's voice. His wife? He looked down. No. Poor Molly. Poor, sweet Molly. At least this way, maybe the Sovereign wouldn't kill any other innocent people who were simply trying to live their lives. With that, Roth left the world of the living behind.

* * *

The crack of thunder. The creak of a wooden ship. Humming? And, of course, the distinct reek of piss. Not what Roth had imagined the afterlife would smell like.

"Feeling better?"

Roth opened his eyes. A wooden ceiling. He tried to sit up, but his body had other plans.

"Easy." He turned his head. Still in the Captain's quarters. What? "I'm glad you're awake," she said.

"I don't understand."

The Captain nodded solemnly toward his chest. He craned his neck. A massive, angry scar ran down his ribs and, emanating from within his chest, he could just make out a faint purple glow. He closed his eyes, took in a breath, and listened. The *tick tick tick* of clockwork.

Suddenly enraged, he turned to the Captain. "She's dead. Don't you understand? That's all I had. And now this? Why would you do this to me? What about your plan?" He wanted to rail further, but a coughing fit stopped him.

"The way I see it," said the Captain, "I owed you. A life for a life." She stepped forward and placed a hand on his shoulder. "The bullet was meant for me."

"Think I don't storming know that? It was supposed to mean something. At least if you'd killed the Sovereign, ended all the needless suffering, it would have meant something, but now..." He didn't want to think about it.

"I met a man recently," began the Captain, "who got me to thinking. What if there were another way to get to our nigh-immortal leader? What if it didn't have to be a suicide mission at all? What if, instead, someone could cause all the gates and locks and failsafes and countermeasures to simply, oh, I don't know, disappear? As if removed from time." She looked at him, a smile on her lips. "That'd give me a fighting chance, wouldn't you say? That is, if you're ready to take on something new?"

Something new. Roth mulled it over.

Despite the pain in his chest—and the pain below that, deeper, a pain he knew he'd never fully heal from—Roth extended his hand. As the Captain shook it, Roth felt a lightness he hadn't felt in years.

COMPASSIONATE RETRY

Marie DesJardin

Theo gave Brianna a kiss before dropping into his armchair. Straightening his tie, he cued his morning messages to scroll through the internal display on his implant. "Freeze."

A message from the Justice Department, marked OFFICIAL. Theo focused on the header, which expanded into glowing letters that overlaid his normal vision.

Dear Mr. Williams: You are hereby informed that the vehicular incident resulting in death that you witnessed last month (see Attachment) is scheduled for a COMPASSIONATE RETRY. To minimize disruptions to your personal history, timeline reset will commence within 24 hours. If you have any questions, contact the participant priority hotline immediately (below). Your receipt of this message has been automatically logged. Thank you.

Theo broke into a sweat.

"Baby?" Brianna uncurled from the neighboring armchair. "What is it?"

Theo could only stare, the words *disruptions to your personal history* burning into his eyes.

Brianna padded over on stockinged feet and squeezed onto the chair beside him. Her warmth and softness were cruel reminders of what he stood to lose. Unable to speak, he shunted the message to the living-room screen.

Brianna read it and gasped. "Theo!"

"I know."

"I thought they were supposed to do this kind of thing within a few days."

Theo dismissed his internal display so he could see her clearly. Brianna's brown eyes pierced his soul. "Babe, even if they'd done it the very next day, it wouldn't have made any difference. Not to us."

Brianna pressed her face against his neck. Theo felt her anguish. "So, they're going to reset us. If that girl avoids the accident this time…"

"I know." Theo pulled her close. "You and I would never have met."

* * *

Only six weeks ago, Theo's world consisted of the forty-some people who shared his office space. He arrived early, worked alone, left on time—often to continue coding at home. Theo enjoyed his work, but his life was empty. He felt it every time he sat behind the glowing screen of his computer, as the ticking of keys marked the hours passing by.

Until that day. Theo had been taking his before-lunch walk, as he did every day when the weather was good. As he followed the pedestrian path eastward, screams broke out across the street.

Through the traffic, Theo saw a white car in the westbound lane ram the curb. As pedestrians fled, a solitary bicyclist tumbled through the air, his bright-green jacket vivid against the trees. He looked unconscious, or dead. Theo didn't see him land; the white car blocked his view. But he heard the thump and the horrified cries of the bystanders.

Rattled, Theo crossed at the nearest intersection and joined the packed circle waiting to give their reports. Never good with crowds, he tried to block out the weeping of the first-hand witnesses. Even so, he was shaking by the time the investigator reached him.

"Name?" she asked.

"Theodore Williams."

She scanned his ID chip, then glanced at his personal readout on her display. She turned the notepad so it could record his image and voice. "All right, Mr. Williams, where were you?"

He pointed. "South side, going east."

"Did you see the driver?"

"No." Theo avoided looking at the driver. Peripherally he could see her, young and blond, drooping against the side of her dented vehicle and tearfully appealing to the police.

"What did you see?"

"The car was already in the bike lane. I saw the cyclist in the air…" He couldn't finish.

"Is that all?"

Theo nodded, feeling sick.

"All right, Mr. Williams, we'll contact you if we need your testimony." She stopped recording, then her voice softened. "Mr. Williams, many people find an incident of this kind distressing. We're hosting a Witness Assistance program at the station tonight. It's a safe space where you can share your reaction to today's events. I strongly recommend that you attend."

Theo balked. "I don't do well in groups."

"Then just come to listen. Believe me, Mr. Williams. These groups have helped a lot of people."

"What time?"

"Seven o'clock. I suspect you'll see a lot of these people there tonight."

"Thanks." Theo turned away from the agitated crowd, eager to lose himself in the calming reiteration of code.

* * *

Time travel was big business, needing big energy. Almost as soon as its parameters were defined, a global agency coalesced to exploit it, its primary goal to alleviate past disasters. Predictably, a popular movement arose arguing that, if time travel could improve life for hundreds or millions, why shouldn't it improve the life of dozens—or even just one?

Thus was born the Compassionate Retry, the ability to truly give someone a second chance. The immense energies of a global time vortex were too expensive to fire up for such a limited purpose, but some bright bulb figured out how to harness the whorls of time displacement that were thrown off as a byproduct of the main effect. The energy could be bottled temporarily to pinpoint, like a tornado, a change to targeted lives.

Whether those lives wanted to be changed or not, Theo reflected.

After reading the official notice, Theo called the CR participant hotline. He knew they had his file when he was forced to endure a series of tunes from his preferred channel before an actual human came on the line.

"Yes, Mr. Williams. How can I help you?"

"This compassionate retry…why did it take so long to be authorized?"

"The driver claimed that the self-drive on her car failed. A number of technical experts examined it, but were unable to confirm her assertion."

Theo blinked. "She lied?"

"The results were inconclusive. She does have a record of self-harm, but no signs of aggression toward others."

"Why would they grant her a retry?"

"It was the victim's family who made the request. Given that the offender is a young woman with no criminal history, and considering the tragedy left the victim's family without a father, the committee voted to approve a retry."

"I see."

"Mr. Williams, you won't personally be aware of any changes to your timeline. You'll simply return to the moment of the reset and your life will go forward normally from there."

"But that's what I don't want."

"I beg your pardon?"

"I don't want my life to proceed as it would have. I didn't like the life I had before."

She paused. "Mr. Williams, whatever changes you've made to improve your life, you'll almost certainly make those changes again, in the new timeline."

"I can't. You see, I went to a Witness Assistance program the night of the incident. I met someone there. We clicked. She...she's the person I've been searching for all these years, ma'am. Now that we've met, I can't imagine living without her."

The pause lengthened. "What would you suggest we do, Mr. Williams? Deny the reset?"

"Well..." That's what Theo wanted. It was the only sure way to keep his life intact.

"Without a reset, the victim's wife and children will have to manage without their husband and father. The driver will be forever haunted by her role in this tragedy. Everyone else who was traumatized by the event, including yourself and your new partner, will continue to be traumatized. Is that the scenario you'd prefer?"

Theo's mouth was dry. "I just want to live the life I have now."

"At least you have a life to live."

"A shallow one." Hating himself for his weakness, Theo ended the call.

* * *

Dinner that evening was a subdued affair. Brianna had taken steps to make it special: white tablecloth, crystal wine glasses, candles, cracked crab. They sat close to each other, their hands meeting repeatedly throughout the meal. Afterwards, they made unhurried love in Theo's bed, holding each other fiercely. Theo ended in a misery of tears that eclipsed all words.

They shuffled through the next morning, pulling on work attire. Brianna's every familiar action hurt his heart. Even fragile and exhausted, she exuded such grace. Grace that was about to pass out of Theo's life forever.

Brianna turned to him at last. Her eyes were moist. "What if we just stayed home? If the reset saw us together, might it…I don't know. Keep us together somehow?"

"I don't think so, babe. We'll just…disappear." Theo shuddered. "I don't think I could bear it, waiting for you to evaporate from my arms."

Brianna hugged him tightly. "I love you, baby. I love you forever."

She kissed his cheek, then turned abruptly. Catching up her purse, she paused on the threshold. "Goodbye, my love. I don't even have the comfort of saying that I'll never forget you." Brianna's face crumpled and she dashed outside.

The sound of the closing door reverberated through the still house. Theo hitched a breath. *This is your life now, again. Get used to it.*

He tapped his temple to switch on the implanted phone. He was immediately glad he'd turned it off last night, because a list of missed calls scrolled past his eyes. Curiously, all of them had ID withheld. He jumped when a new call popped over the saved list. Another ID withheld.

Theo set his jaw. If this was a telemarketer, they were going to get an earful. But it just might be the hotline calling back. He fixed his gaze on the notification to answer.

"Mr. Theodore Williams?" said the implant in his ear.

"Yes?"

"Mr. Williams, I've been trying to reach you all night."

"Who's calling?" he asked glacially.

"My name is Pete Shroff. I know that doesn't mean much to you, but I run a company called NDO."

"Never heard of it."

"Don't hang up, Mr. Williams! I got your name from the CR hotline."

Theo froze. "What do they want?" For a wild moment, he thought he might be granted a reprieve.

"*They* don't want anything. I'm what you might call an alternative service."

Theo's skin prickled. "What alternative?"

"I've been looking into your compassionate retry case. Apart from the principals, only two people's lives appear to have been significantly altered as a result of the incident: you, and Miss Brianna Lewis."

Theo's pulse throbbed in his ears. "I'm listening."

"NDO means 'No Do-Overs.' Sometimes life throws you a bone and sometimes you get a kick in the teeth. I help people to choose the bone."

"How?"

"Meet me in twenty minutes behind Christopher's Café. You know it?"

"Yeah." It was down the street from his office, beyond the accident site.

"We have only three hours before the reset. We need to make this fast."

"I'll be there."

* * *

Theo had never been inside the café, but he knew the place from his daily walks. He was grateful that he had a self-drive car. In his distracted state, he might well have caused another "incident" during the short drive there.

When the car tried to park itself out front, Theo took control and steered for the back. A man slightly older than Theo loitered next to a parked car. Theo pulled in beside him and shut down. When he stepped out, the man gestured to a small grove of trees.

"Mr. Williams? Over here."

Apprehensively, Theo followed.

Beneath the leafy shade, the man extended his hand. "Pete Shroff."

Theo tentatively shook.

"Sorry about the precautions, but we're out of view of any cameras back here. I have to ask you not to record this meeting, or speak of it to anyone else—including Miss Lewis."

"You said you had an alternative."

"No Do-Overs," Pete stated. "That's how life used to be. You took the good with the bad, whatever life dealt out. Compassionate Retry changes that."

"I know, but...I'd always thought that was a good thing. I mean, someone makes a mistake—starts a fire, causes an accident. Isn't it fair to give them another chance?"

"Except everybody *doesn't* get a second chance, only those approved few. I listened in on your call yesterday. After a solitary life, you finally found your soul mate. How fair is it for you to lose her?"

Theo couldn't respond.

"That's the flaw in the system," Pete went on. "The relationship you have today is the true timeline. Why should you have to give that up in favor of somebody else?"

"The dead guy has a family."

"Lots of people have families. Does that make your needs any less valid? Besides, a reset isn't a guarantee. For all we know, the guy they mean to save could get run over again tomorrow. For centuries, everyone in the world had to accept their fate as it happened. Why start making exceptions now?"

"What's your alternative?"

"I've figured out a way to piggyback onto the CR signal. When they trigger a reset for the driver, I can snag a field for *you* that has the same characteristics as the primary. In other words, both fields are temporally deactivated."

"Meaning what?"

"Meaning that you preserve your memory of the incident after the reset. That's how the driver knows she caused a death. How else can she take steps to avoid it, right?"

"Ri-ight."

"Same thing for you. When I bind onto the CR signal, your current knowledge travels back energetically and merges with the energy field of the former you. That's how the primaries travel, also."

"And then?"

"Then you can do anything you want, based on your current knowledge—such as keeping the present timeline intact."

Theo paused. "You mean, let the accident happen."

"That's one possibility. Or, you can pursue Brianna in some other way, now that you know she exists. In any case, you have the opportunity to adjust your actions."

"What do you get out of it?"

"The knowledge that one more person isn't getting screwed." Pete's smile twitched. "They gave this reset once to a bus driver. Drove off a mountain with a busload of people. They brought him back to that point, but you know what? The conditions were still bad."

Theo was riveted. "What happened?"

"He kept the bus on the road, but he took out a car trying to do it. My brother-in-law." Pete looked away. "No reset for him. They put you as close to the event as possible to minimize anomalies. The committee decided that the chances to improve the scenario were poor, so they let the reset stand."

Theo was moved. "I'm sorry."

Pete shrugged. "What can you do? It's their show. But I decided, then and there, that I'd find a way to make it fairer for everybody. I found some like-minded innovators and we came up with this hack. Now I can offer people the reset I never got. If you're game, I can send you back this morning, no strings attached. You play out the scenario, however it unfolds. If you like the result, make a donation to my foundation. You can find NDO online. Transfer whatever amount you think is fair."

Theo narrowed his eyes. "Is this a scam?"

"How can it be? I'm asking for nothing up front. Check me out at your leisure after the reset. You'll find that enough people appreciate what I do to keep me in business."

"How many people have you sent back?"

"That's confidential. But I can assure you that the procedure is safe. All my hitchhikers came through just fine."

"Of those hitchhikers…how many chose to let the original scenario play out?"

Pete hesitated. "A few. A person's choices are up to the individual. I'm just a reformer who found a weakness in the system. I tap the CR hotline and look for people who will be victimized by a 'compassionate' reset, like you, and give them a call."

"Brianna is also affected. Why approach me and not her?"

"The vivacious Miss Lewis has many friends. If she declined my offer…Let's just say I prefer to fly under the radar."

Theo fell silent. He felt the minutes slipping by, like the breeze brushing his skin and stirring the overhanging leaves. "All right. I'm in."

Pete smiled. "Follow me."

Their destination turned out to be one of those storage places. The windowless shed was musty, exuding a whiff of gasoline. Naked lights illuminated the stark interior. The machine stood in the center of the floor, looking like an electrical accident waiting to happen. Theo surveyed the conglomeration of straps and dials skeptically.

"Don't let the setup fool you," Pete said. "I keep everything portable, to ship it where needed. You got any electronics on you?"

Theo proffered his wrist. "ID chip—"

"External, I mean. The field can corrupt it."

Theo shook his head.

"All righty, then." Pete gestured toward the seat. "It's your move."

Theo took a breath and stepped forward.

* * *

He was at work. Theo was always at work. But his screen was wrong. It was showing a routine that he was certain he'd delivered about…

Six weeks ago.

Memory seeped back, like ink into cheesecloth. Pete had done it. The hardest part of the whole operation had been for Theo to sit in that jury-rigged chair, maintaining the "integrity of the bubble" while waiting for the official CR signal to kick off. Then, with no seeming transition, Theo was here. Just that quick, it was again the day of the "incident."

Panicked, Theo checked the time. He usually started his walk now. But to be in a position to intercede, he'd have to change his route from the south side to the north. That meant he'd have to battle the noon traffic. If he arrived even a moment too late, he'd miss his chance.

Theo bolted for the door. No one remarked upon his hasty exit; no one in his previous life had cared.

Theo barreled into the street. The normal lunchtime mob had collected at the nearest light. He plunged into the throng and worked his way to the front. There he fidgeted, biting his lips until the bikes, cars, and trams eventually halted in their respective lanes. The light turned. He dashed across the street, dodging other pedestrians, and sprinted eastward down the path.

As he ran, he wondered what the driver would do. She, like him, would recall the previous event. If her self-drive had malfunctioned, all she had to do was turn it off and manually stick to her lane. She'd avoid the accident and the victim would live.

Theo wasn't as certain of what *he* would do. To restore the past, he'd have to watch for the car, step into the bike lane just in front of the cyclist, and hope the man would swerve into traffic. But that would make *Theo* the cause of the accident. Worse, it wouldn't even be an accident anymore, because he would have intentionally murdered someone for his own gain.

"I look for people who will be victimized by a 'compassionate' reset," Pete had said. How many of his clients had justified their actions by rationalizing that the victim would have died anyway? That kind of self-serving behavior upended the whole intent of a compassionate retry.

Theo slowed; he was nearing the scene. Here, along this stretch. He remembered those trees...

There was Brianna.

Of course she was there. In the original timeline, she and a group of friends were headed for the deli near Christopher's Café. Theo had learned that they often lunched there, while he'd been walking alone.

Theo caught his breath. Brianna was so beautiful. Not like a model, but through her infectious charm. The sunlight burnished her hair with golden highlights. Her smile gleamed as she laughed. Now that he'd meet her, it seemed impossible that he could have missed her before. Her radiance should have drawn him, even from across the street.

His stomach clenched. Beyond Brianna, a solitary cyclist rode in a gap between clusters of bikes. He wore bright green gear that matched his bike and a black-visored helmet. The victim. Ray Lin, thirty-four-year-old father of three. Architect. Guitar player. Blithely repeating the ride that had marked the last moments of his existence.

Behind him was the car. Theo picked out the white flicker from the onrushing stream. Driver Lisa Romano, age twenty-three. High school dropout, part-time telemarketer. Adrift in life, but now solidly in her lane. Theo's heart hammered as the pair came on.

Suddenly he knew that, no matter what other hitchhikers might do, he could never push an innocent man into traffic. Not for Brianna, not for anyone. What kind of person would he be, if he could do that?

Motionless, Theo watched Ray approach, in sole possession of that span of lane—the man with a life worth living. He smiled at him sadly. *You lucky SOB.*

Suddenly, the white car angled into the bike lane. Even through the tinted windscreen, Theo saw the driver's face. Her expression was grim, her eyes open as she bore down on the cyclist.

In a flash, her plan became clear. This spot marked the farthest point between the traffic cameras, which were focused on the intersections. From that distance, they wouldn't be able to see through the tinted glass to determine whether her auto-drive was on or off. Since it had worked the first time, Lisa clearly intended to use that advantage again.

Focused as he was, Theo reacted instantly. He stepped into the lane and caught Ray's elbow, hurling him onto the footpath. As the car crunched over the abandoned bike, Theo tumbled over the oncoming hood. He rolled to his feet as the car rammed the curb. Pedestrians scattered when Lisa revved the engine, the wheels struggling to mount the tall curb.

Theo gaped. This was no accident. For whatever reason, malevolence or insanity, Lisa was deliberately trying to kill someone! Apparently, Ray was just the poor slob who'd happened to be in the wrong place both times.

The crumpled bike lay at his feet. Theo swept it up and swung it in an arc, full into the passenger-side window. The glass burst into thousands of rounded beads.

He saw the drive panel clearly through the shattered window. The self-drive was off. The creep had turned it *off* so she could kill someone. He reached in and slapped the control. The self-drive light turned green. The car, sensing itself off the road, instantly shut down.

Theo collapsed against the window frame, even as Lisa bolted out of her door, screaming toward the ring of startled witnesses, "The self-drive failed! It failed!"

Theo ignored her. The on-board computer would show what had happened. And this time, there'd be Theo's word to back it up. No retry in *this* timeline. His whole body trembled with nerves.

He jumped when someone touched his shoulder. "Are you all right?"

Theo turned to meet Ray Lin's eyes. He'd removed his helmet, but the green suit was unmistakable. Ray was a short man with an athletic build, as befitted an avid cyclist. He gave Theo a wobbly smile. "I think you saved my life."

Theo had seen pictures of the victim posed with his family, but it was a whole other deal to meet the man in the flesh, to hear his soft voice and feel the warmth of his hand. Gratitude was palpable in his eyes, a very light brown that caught the light. Like Brianna's hair.

Brianna. Theo scanned the crowd quickly. She wasn't there.

Craning his neck, he spotted a halo of soft brown hair down near the intersection. Apparently, the noise of a bike getting crunched and a car hitting the curb hadn't been enough to attract Brianna's attention. This time there'd been no horrified screams, no body twisting through the air. She and her friends, already past the impact site, had merely walked on.

Theo looked back. The driver was busy insisting to the crowd that her self-drive had failed. The girl had issues. Well, his testimony would ensure that they'd finally be addressed. At least Theo did *that* much good, in this new reality.

Ray said, "Man, you are one quick-thinker. How can I ever repay you?"

Theo's weary gaze fell across the broken bike. "Live. Just live your life."

* * *

Theo clasped a cold beer in his darkened living room, dully watching the news. It seemed the traffic cams had captured enough of his little stunt to make a newsworthy video.

The sequence started with Theo standing motionless, looking east as Brianna and her friends walked out of frame. The next moment Ray appeared, followed by the white car.

Theo watched himself step into the street, hurl Ray onto the pedestrian path, and dive over the hood to escape. He made a face. His actions did look impressive; he doubted he could duplicate them intentionally. One unexpected result of his intervention was that, with the window shattered, the cameras were able to pick up the fact that her self-drive was off. In this timeline, there wasn't even a question of the driver's guilt.

He snorted over the reporters' commentary. *Guardian angel*, one remarked. *Hero*, they all kept saying. He took another swig. Hero, right.

Theo had been acutely self-conscious when he'd answered the investigators' questions. Some of the witnesses had noticed him running beforehand, and Theo knew that *somebody* would have it on video. So he invented a story about being late for his regular walk, and then ran until he was distracted by an unusual bird. They seemed to buy it.

But those questions had taken time. When the investigators finally let Theo go, he hurried toward the deli. Forty minutes had elapsed. Would Brianna still be there?

He was nearing the front door when she stepped out. Brianna's head was down, but her smile lingered from some remark. Theo was spellbound; he couldn't remember seeing her so carefree. They'd met as wounded souls, haunted by what they'd seen, driven toward mutual comfort. This

Brianna had avoided that ugliness. Thanks to the reset, her life was unscarred.

She looked up and their eyes met. How strange, to see no recognition there. No welcome, just…blank, as she would look at any stranger.

Theo realized he was staring. He cleared his throat. "Hi."

"Hi."

Her three friends collected behind her, puzzled. The deli door closed.

Theo was no good at this; he'd never been any good at this. "I saw you at the accident site."

"Accident?" Brianna looked confused. "Oh, the car hitting the curb. I saw that someone had fallen, but he got up right away. Was anyone hurt?"

"Not this…No." He swallowed. "Some girl turned off her self-drive."

Brianna rolled her eyes. "Idiot."

Theo stood rigid, pulse pounding. The old Brianna he could have talked to. Now, the silence grew awkward.

The woman behind Brianna murmured something and she nodded. "Well," Brianna said to Theo, "thanks for letting me know. I've got to get back to work."

"Me, too."

Brianna narrowed her eyes. Theo knew he was acting strangely, but he couldn't help himself. Her presence drew him like a flame.

The woman took Brianna's arm. "Come on, Bree." She said pointedly to Theo, "Have a nice day."

The group walked off. Theo watched them go. He knew he shouldn't stare, but Brianna's pull was too strong. He steeled himself for the inevitable separation.

The same woman looked back. This time she outright glared. She pulled Brianna closer, and the group quickened their pace.

Sweating, Theo ducked into the deli. He leaned against

the cool plastic wall, drawing long breaths, feeling his world dissolve.

"Can I help you?"

He jumped to see a pretty girl with a menu smiling at him. Theo straightened. "I don't think so. Thanks, anyway."

He walked slowly back to his office, retracing his normal route. No one greeted him when he walked in the door; no one remarked on his absence. Hollowly, he sat before his computer screen, which still displayed the code he'd written six weeks ago.

Reset. This was his life again. Blinking, he leaned forward to input the same old sequence, knowing that he'd get the same result.

* * *

Subjectively, Brianna had moved in only two weeks ago. This morning, the day after the reset, Theo felt estranged from his own home. His stuff was back where it had always been. Now, he saw it with fresh eyes. Had everything always been so bare, so ugly? He missed Brianna's exotic vases, her colorful mosaic over the sofa. He missed her perfume lingering on the air. He missed *her*...

Theo's eyes were blurry when he emerged from his car near the office. Bikes whizzed by on the street. Today, Ray Lin would be among them. It was a misty, gray day, but at least it was a day. Last time around, Ray hadn't had this one.

Normally Theo was the first one in, but today he heard footsteps moving around as he plodded up the stairs to the top floor. He turned left and stopped.

A gang of grinning coworkers had assembled under a hand-lettered banner reading, "Theo = Hero." Each letter of the message was printed in a different bright color. Seeing him, everyone burst into applause.

"Way to go, man!" "Theo, the hero!" "You *rock*, boyfriend!"

For a moment, Theo really didn't know what they were talking about. Then it came to him: the news. Someone must have seen that hyped-up report and arranged this little surprise for him. He shriveled inside from the undeserved praise.

His team leader, Jaya, stepped forward, presenting a gold statuette. "It's all we could find on short notice."

Theo took it from her. It was a child's basketball trophy, the player extended to make a shot. "That's you," Jaya said, "pulling that guy to safety."

Everyone applauded again, their goodwill patent on their faces. Theo felt less able than usual to rise to the occasion. Wishing himself anywhere else, he mumbled, "Thanks."

Used to his shyness, no one took offense. The group dispersed, smiling people patting him on the back and wishing him well as they drifted away.

Jaya poked his shoulder. "Lunch is on me. Just tell me where and when."

Theo nodded, desperate to escape. He made a beeline for his cubicle and stopped just inside, feeling ill. In a day, he'd gone from potential murderer to hero. Considering Brianna's rejection, the only scenario he'd wanted in this timeline seemed to be the one he wasn't going to get.

A fellow programmer slapped his shoulder as he passed. "Good going, buddy."

Theo started. "Thanks."

He moved farther into the safety of his cubicle. He deposited the trophy on a shelf where he wouldn't readily see it and fretted. He'd been too depressed yesterday to activate his implant; he didn't have the presence of mind to cope with the dual vision. Now, he desperately needed a distraction. Theo tapped his temple and watched the display scroll before his eyes.

As usual, it began with the day's headlines. Figures; it chose to lead with the accident, probably because he was name-checked. Flicking it aside with a glance, he focused on his regular activity list. Dullness was what he was after. There was his daily caloric expenditure, exercise minutes, work log—

And seven saved calls.

Theo hadn't saved any calls before he'd met Brianna. How…?

Registering his fixed gaze, the implant opened the list. Theo felt gut-punched. Those were Brianna's calls, saved under a gorgeous profile picture. He'd kept them for no other reason than to play them occasionally when he sat at his desk, just to hear her voice. They said nothing in particular, just "Meet me for lunch!" or "Let's try the New Impressionists art show. It could be fun." He'd expected the messages to be reset along with everything else. But, here they were.

Theo frowned. The Compassionate Retry people deliberately restricted the information they transmitted on a reset to minimize changes to the timeline. So the saved messages must be due to Pete's setup. Theo remembered his query: "You got any electronics on you?"

Pete had been looking for external devices. But Theo was a geek, an early adopter. Brain implants were still uncommon. Perhaps Pete's temporally deactivated "bubble" had shielded the implant along with the rest of Theo's body.

Troubled, Theo scrolled farther down. *1 new recording*.

Theo frowned as his mind quested back, ages ago, to yesterday morning. He'd stood in the dappled shade while a stranger said, "I have to ask you not to record this meeting…"

Record this. Theo had programmed those words into his implant back when he first got it, intending it as a precaution against tricky situations. "Can I record this?" he'd ask Jaya, or whoever. Whether the person said yes or no, the device was activated, logging the conversation in case an issue came back to bite him. Theo had never used it, but the function was still ready, waiting.

Now Theo's stare activated the recording. Pete's words came into his ear: "…record this meeting, or speak of it to anyone else—including Miss Lewis."

The implant had done a good job compensating for the breeze; the words were perfectly clear.

"Transfer whatever amount you think is fair."

Theo pondered. Pete had said NDO was well-funded. Clearly *some* people liked how their alternative future had turned out. But Pete was, by his own confession, a "reformer." Focused on his cause, he might have missed the potential abuses of his hack.

Suppose someone else discovered the implant trick. That person could persuade Pete to let him hitchhike on a CR he wasn't even related to and take back whatever knowledge he wanted to exploit. In fact, the person wouldn't even need an implant. He could simply memorize key information and then apply it to make a killing in the stock market or wherever. For all Theo knew, Pete might already have a relationship with any number of people who did just this. The hitchhikers would make out like bandits, and NDO would have its donations—a win-win.

Theo set his jaw. That's not what a compassionate retry was for. It was about giving people a second chance. Through mental disease or a twisted plea for help, Lisa had blown her second shot. But an unscrupulous hitchhiker could create far more damage than a CR was intended to correct. The Compassionate Retry people should be warned.

Whatever Pete might have known, Theo owed him for the reset. He left him a brief message through NDO's contact page, warning him, before dialing the hotline number, still stored in his implant.

This time he got regular music on hold. Theo smiled. The system didn't know him. In this timeline, Lisa Romano's case had never even come up for consideration. With any luck, she was talking to a shrink right now.

The same counselor, or her twin sister, answered. "Hello, who's calling, please?" She sounded puzzled, as well she might. How many people happened upon the participant priority line by accident?

"Hi, there. I wanted to let you know that your hotline is bugged."

"I'm sorry, sir. I don't see your name—"

"Don't worry about it. What's important is that someone is monitoring this line. Are you recording?"

"Yes, sir. All our calls are recorded."

"Good. Here's what's been going on."

* * *

By day three, Theo had become reconciled to his solitary state. Still, he had an advantage over most people in his situation: he knew the identity of the person who could share his future. Having known happiness once, Theo wasn't going to blow *his* second chance by not seeking it again.

As a first step, Theo intended to shift his regular walk to coincide with Brianna's. Her lunch group would see him around and eventually might decide that he was just a normal person, not a stalker. He could then figure out how to approach Brianna romantically.

Focused on his plan, Theo stepped out the front door around noon. He crossed the busy street, then ambled down the strip he was coming to know well. Glittering flecks of metal in the bike lane, residue from Ray's crushed bike, marked the eventful spot. At least Lisa hadn't crushed Ray this time. For the first time, Theo felt satisfaction over his part in that.

"Hey, asshole."

Theo whirled. Pete Shroff leaned against the wall of the pedestrian path, simmering with antipathy.

Theo felt a twinge of guilt. The guy *had* tried to help him. If Pete now wanted to knock Theo's block off, so be it. He slipped between groups of walkers to join him. "I guess the CR people fixed the tap in their hotline."

"Yeah, your call yesterday was the last I'll ever hear." Pete glared, arms crossed. "Why'd you do it?"

"To prevent any of your hitchhikers from unscrupulously manipulating the timeline."

"Why would they? They've had their reset."

Pete looked so confused, Theo thought, *He's never considered the abuse angle.* Pete was only trying to right wrongs. The realization made Theo sad, despite his relief over foiling any number of potential crimes. He asked, "Were you able to save the equipment?"

"Yeah, much good it will do me. Without the hotline tap, I don't know which reset is coming up or who to contact. Thanks for ruining my life."

"I'm sorry. I thought your setup had a danger you didn't appreciate."

Pete's disgust let Theo know he wasn't getting through. "Never mind. The important thing is, you were right. There *are* no do-overs. There's only *do.* I did something different the second time around, but it didn't change anything *back.* Now, I can only go forward, same as you."

"Yeah, with no way to correct any CR injustices."

"One of the hazards of messing with the time-space continuum, I guess."

"Drop dead." Pete pushed off the wall and walked briskly through the crowd. A little regretfully, Theo watched him go.

A call from the street distracted him. "Theodore Williams!"

Theo turned to see a cyclist pull up to the pedestrian path. No one he recognized. The rider's suit was a dizzy array of stripes, his bright-yellow bike decorated with orange flames that matched his helmet. The rider flipped up the visor and grinned.

Delight overcame remorse. "Ray!"

Ray stepped onto the footpath. Off the bike, he looked even more outrageous, like some colorful human bug telegraphing its lethality.

Theo ventured, "New suit?"

"Yeah. I wanted to go for maximum visibility. What do you think?"

The stripes actually sparkled. "You achieved it."

"Thanks. My wife isn't too crazy about the look, but considering what happened, she couldn't say no." Ray nodded at the curb, bruised with skid marks. "You checking out the crash site?"

Theo supposed it was obvious. "Yeah."

"I did that yesterday. I picked up the last few bits of my poor crushed Goblin. That's for Green Goblin—you know? The cartoon character?"

Theo shook his head.

"Anyway, I think I got it all. The kids are keeping the pieces for souvenirs, if you can believe it. Besides, I didn't want anyone to get a flat tire."

Theo looked him over. Small and trim as he was, Ray commanded the space through sheer dynamism. Already, he was putting the incident behind him, moving on.

This, Theo thought suddenly. This was what the compassionate retry people were after. A life that deserved to go on, did. Whatever came afterward, the reset was worth it.

Ray said, "We didn't get a chance to talk much the other day."

Theo shrugged. "No problem."

"No, really. You could have been hit. I thought the least I could do was invite you to our regular Saturday bash. It's just an informal backyard barbecue. I have about twenty friends and relatives who'd love to shake your hand."

"I…"

"Look at it this way: my kids are asking so many questions about 'Mr. Williams,' you'd be doing me a favor by dropping by. Bring anyone you'd like. We cook enough for a swim team."

Theo dithered. He didn't deserve to be idolized by some poor, impressionable kids. On the contrary, he felt that any acknowledgement placed him in a false position.

Ray shrugged in humorous acceptance. "Well, I'll send you an invite anyway." Looking past Theo's shoulder, he smirked. "Although, I completely understand if you're busy." He remounted his bike. "Take it easy, amigo!"

With a swish and blur of color, Ray was gone, merging easily into the bike traffic. Theo smiled and turned to find Brianna watching him.

He froze.

Brianna's previous suspicion was gone. She merely looked thoughtful, maybe a little puzzled. "Hi," she said.

"Hi."

Today, even more than at the diner, Brianna looked… good. Collected. The strength that he'd always sensed in her was on full display. It showed in the way she held his gaze, how her head tilted on her elegant neck.

"I saw you on the news," she said.

"Oh." Theo winced. One of his trademark witty rejoinders.

"Why didn't you tell me at the deli that you'd just saved a guy's life?" She glanced down the bike path. "That was him just now, wasn't it? The guy?"

Theo wanted to disappear. "Yeah, that was him."

"I'm glad you saved him."

"Thanks." Theo's mouth was dry. Her next response mattered. "Did you come up to me just now because you think I'm a hero?"

"No. I came up to you because you think you aren't."

"Oh." Theo's heart raced.

"I think almost anyone else would have mentioned it." Brianna's eyes twinkled. "Anyway, I wanted to thank you for being so brave. That's all."

"You want to go to the art show next week?" Theo blurted.

Brianna looked surprised. "Which one?"

"The New Impressionists. I thought…it might be fun."

Brianna's smile grew. "I was thinking about that. Thanks, I'd like to."

The distance between them hadn't changed, but now it was easier. There was a bridge.

"Are you headed to the deli? I'll walk you," Theo offered.

"Sure. I'll buy you lunch. I've heard that food helps loosen up you bashful types."

"Maybe, but *I'm* buying the lunch."

"Have it your way. Hero."

"Theo," he corrected.

"Brianna," she said.

Theo's heart sang. He owed it to everyone that Pete could no longer help not to waste this opportunity. This was his reset, and Theo would treasure every moment.

NEURONS LOST AND FOUND

Christine Lucas

Faster, old fart. No shinies today? No blinkies? Move your bones! The youngins have already picked these parts clean. You do want some chow today, don't you?

There. Over there, old cow. Beneath that rubble. Remember that landslide? Years ago? Before the Dudes came? One of them flying cars got caught there. Go on, sniff it. There's the stench, that little tease. Oil. Gasoline. Yes, there's an old car under that, old like you, and rusty, its guts full of shinies and blinkies and cogs and wires and springs. Not too deep for your claws.

Missus Scar itches. Stop scratching. Look what you done now. Bloody fingers. Bloody face. Leave Missus Scar alone. Enough brain rolled out your thick head already. Keep poking, lose more. Then be like them turnips. Sing to Missus Scar, put scratch to sleep. There. Better now.

Them youngins still around. They know Rosie's nose for shinies. They hanker your chow again. There. Behind thorn bushes—thieving, hungry eyes. Let Mister Stick say hello. That will show them.

Yes, that's right, little brats. Run, before Mister Stick comes for you!

Tummy rumbles. Again. Only Dudes have chow, these days. They have gruel and apples and water that doesn't stink. But Dudes want blinkies and shinies for food.

* * *

Youngins gone now. Dig, then, old fart. See? See how Mister Stick helps? A clank. Another clank and Mister Stick's job's done. Claw your way in, now. It's still light. But not for long. Leave Missus Scar alone. Not with those dirty hands. *Dig.* Find those blinkies while it's still safe out here.

There you go. Pick and pluck and cut out and fill your sack with dead car's parts. Happy tummy tonight.

Faster, now! Kick dirt over your find. Hide dead car. Many days of chow here. More days than your fingers and your toes. Be smart.

Even in dark, them old feet know their way back. Their way home. Once-home. Before war. Before death. Before aching tummy. Now, Dude-home.

There the fences. There the well. There Dude-guards for well. Water worth more than chow now. More than Dudes. More than once-home, once-garden. More than Rosie. But Dudes won't hurt Rosie. They said so. They *promised*. Rosie brings them shinies and blinkies.

And there the fire. Dudes all around. More than your fingers, more than your toes. Them bellies don't ache. Watch your step. There, you've done it again, old fart! They laugh now. Come on, you know it's funny. An old cow biting the dirt? So fucking funny. So you'll stay there, now? Perhaps you should. Let them have their picks from your shinies. And let them crows eat granny meat tomorrow.

Perhaps sleep is best. Long sleep. Last sleep. This way, you'll see Old Dude again. *Your* Dude. Family. Once-family. No-family now. Heart aches. Tummy aches. Heart can wait—for the One. Tummy won't wait.

So get up. Come on. Fix your clothes. You're around proper people now. And, for heaven's sake, woman! Hide your valuables! The pouch around your neck, woman! Those are *yours*. Button up your shirt. No Dude wants to see granny's tits. Your blinkies safe in there.

All set now. Go on. Earn your chow.

One step, two steps closer. Too many Dudes tonight. Where from?

Is One-dude with them? Which one? Head hurts. Missus Scar itches. Think you'll know him, half-witted hag?

Blinkies will know.

Missus Scar will know. And she'll scream.

Oh, enough nonsense. Your once is gone. *All gone.* Not you. You walked on. Still do. And drag bag after bag to Scar-dude. There he is. Drunk. His girl on his lap. Straw-chick. Skinny. Yellow hair. Always hungry. Always on Scar-dude's knees. Girl's got to eat. Old farts need chow too. So move.

"And who's that?" Another Dude. New Dude. Red beard, better clothes. Big knife. Not the One.

"Ah, that's Old Rosie. She was here when we found this place. She thought she'd fight us off with her walking stick." He laughs, cracks his knuckles. "We taught her a good lesson. But she proved ... stubborn. And useful." Scar-dude's picks his nose with shit-fingers. Waves you on. "This half-witted hag can track down all sorts of stuff: car parts, electronics, medical equipment, even cans of food at times." He scratches head. How rude. His poor lice. "I don't know how she does it. We feed her scraps and get good things in return." He chuckles.

Choke, shit-souled bastard. Mister Stick would love to come and play with that ugly head. Soon.

Scar-dude pushes Straw-chick away. "Let's see, Rosie. What do you have?"

Good stuff. Shinies. Blinkies. And a cloth with many colors and more holes than your fingers and toes. Straw-chick likes it. She coos and giggles. Scar-dude will fuck well tonight.

You get your chow. It's tough. It's bland. It's chewy. But it's warm and has whole chunks of meat. And Straw-chick shoves an apple in your palm. The cloth fits well around her neck when she struts her skinny ass around the camp.

Eat, now. Nothing else matters. There's no Scar-dude, no Straw-chick, no Redbeard-dude. All gone. Only chow and gulps of water that doesn't stink. Tummy happy. Rosie happy.

"Pass the booze."

Another voice. Another Dude. Dudes come and go. But this is *chow*.

"Pass the booze, Jackson!"

You look. Oh, why did you look? Fingers almost drop the bowl. Couple breathless gulps and chow's gone. Tummy doesn't ache. Heart does.

That's the One. Missus Scar insists. Not with itch. Missus Scar screams hot pinpricks of pain. He could be the One. You thought...thought he'd know you. He doesn't. Won't look at you. No one does.

Get up. He has the eye patch, doesn't he? And the scars. Don't your fingers know the scars they left? Don't they itch to dig them open? Focus, Rosie. Please. How many nights did your tummy ache? Your heart? How much spit on your face? How many shoves? More than all *their* fingers and *their* toes. So much more. So move your ass now, woman!

Mouse your way closer. Offer him the blinkie, still warm from granny tits. Now he looks at old, crazy Rosie. He's old too. Balding head. White beard. Another old fart. An old fart with a sharp knife. But Rosie has blinkies. And Mister Stick and Missus Scar. They'll do. *Here, One-dude. Take it. See if it fits.* It sounds simple in your head. Your tongue thinks not. Only spit and growls come out.

He wrinkles his nose. "Who's that? Why is she giving me that?" He leans closer. "Fuck, this looks like an implant chip."

"That's our Rosie," Scar-dude says, his nose deep in a mug. "She finds things. She'll trade you for a couple of apples."

One-dude snatches the blinkie. "It *could* be a sniper eye chip. Or a night vision chip. Looks like one. Right size. Well-preserved. But I had mine implanted before the war. They made the enhancements DNA-specific back then." He looks at you as if you're shit. "I don't know what poor soldier's corpse this old cunt robbed, but I doubt it will fit." He shoves it back.

No! Don't take it back! Smile! Make him wear it! Shove it back in his face. Move closer! Dudes hate granny smell.

Yes! There you go.

He looks at you. Then at the blinkie. Then back at you. *Nothing to look at here. Put it on. Come on. It can't hurt.*

Does he hear? Perhaps he does. Perhaps he doesn't. Dead eye under his patch. Doesn't blink. Doesn't shine. Ah, there *she* is. He has his own Missus Scar on his temple. Does it itch, like yours? Does it beg for its torn part? Yours aches. Yours weeps pus. Sometimes maggots too.

Yours screams.

His should too. His fingers know that. They take the blinkie. One click. One heartbeat. One held breath. Dead eye lights up. A new face. Deeper wrinkles. Surprise? Or terror?

"How?"

He scans your face with two eyes now. One human, one with night vision. What does he see? An old fart. Waste of spit. Waste of ammo. Waste of time.

"*How?*"

Stubborn dude. No words to say how. Now Missus Scar burns, a bundle of hot wires. Now she calls your fingers—commands them. Both blinkies must go where they belong. You knew that, all along. Did they beat you enough to forget what you have to do? But you remember now.

Blinkie, come home.

A click. Itch, gone. Ache, gone.

Complete.

Rosie, go to your corner now. Be the bundle of confused, short-wired neurons you always were. Your job is done. Please, don't weep. You did a great job. But it's my turn now.

One-dude sees another face now. And he knows. I've seen his gaze on countless faces before: the gaze of those who know they're about to die. He measures the woman standing before him from gray hair to bare, dirty feet, wondering if he can draw his weapon fast enough. They all do. None of them can. Now in frenzy, now in wrath, my neurons will fire up first and tear flesh from bones. Darlings, how I've missed you all. How I've missed *this*.

"Sarcomancer?"

How interesting, that his first word to me—*me*, not crazy old Rosie—would be the title given to my order by the common folk. To most people, *thinking* a bone back in place or dissolving a blood clot from the brain was surely magic, not a long dormant skill of inactive neurons. Such marvels were those tiny chips, that could rewire entire portions of the brain to a higher purpose.

Much good that did mankind.

"Sarcomancer?"

He repeats the word, my title and my shame, and now there's a hint of doubt lining his voice. His fingers trace the hilt of his combat knife, his mind ablaze with adrenaline, and his heart flutters against his ribs. A brush of my will against his aorta fills him with dread and his hand grips the hilt. He knows he'll die and it will hurt. Oh, yes, it will.

"Jackson, shut up and sit down," Scar-dude barks. "You're scaring the children."

The children. They are blameless in all this. One glance behind the circle of fire, to the gathering of scrawny, unwashed kids. There's Straw-chick, showing off her rag of a scarf to the others. She's a survivor, that one. Our eyes meet.

Go. Now.

Her eyes widen while I sniffle blood. Fuck, I stretched my neurons too far—my implant wasn't made to handle thought projection. I'd need a whole other set of blinkies for that—not blinkies, Rosie. *Chips*. Shut up and sit down! I don't need your crazy talk when I force my poor, drowsy neurons to rewire a second time. But I have to. No child should witness what's about to happen.

Go!

She nods and starts to gather the others, slowly, noiselessly, and herds them away.

One-Dude—no, *Jackson*—still stares, his mouth opening and closing as if to say something over and over again. Then he licks his lips and his eyes leave my face for a glance over his shoulder.

"I tell you, she's one of them!"

A burst of laughter from the others answers him.

Scar-dude heehaws. "How drunk are you? Their despicable lot were wiped out decades ago, after the War."

Oh, were they?

"Didn't you kill the last one yourself?" Redbeard-dude chips in.

"No, he didn't."

How hoarse my voice sounds. How many silent days? How many years? More than Rosie's fingers and toes. Now the silence ends. Now I speak. Now they'll scream.

"He missed one. Me. Your Rosie." I had another name, a long time ago. Once a blessing, then a curse from too much blood on my hands.

Now they look at me, at the gnarled husk of a woman they kicked and shoved for laughs. Do they see me or do they still see Rosie? Have my true colors come to surface? I cast off the purple decades ago for a simpler life. A life of rich, moist earth, animal dung, and my old guy's arms around me at night. A good life. A quiet life. The sadness of a barren womb. Until *they* came and turned that life to ashes. And then I donned another kind of robe made of sackcloth and chose another kind of purple—the bruises from brutes and bullies, when I ripped out the center of my neurons and birthed Rosie.

"This is my home. Leave now and leave with your lives." I know they won't. I'd kill them anyway. False hope can be such a delicious weapon. "Except that one." I point at Jackson.

Jackson growls and charges. Before he takes a second step, I reach out with every neuron, every synapse, every arduous day of Rosie's life, every tear Rosie shed without knowing why, and pluck his eyes out. Slowly. Painfully. Messily. Blissfully—for me—for my heart flits and chirps and laughs at the screams that scrape his throat like blunt hooks. He falls on his knees, his hands searching the dirt as if he could salvage his eyeballs even if he found them.

Will the others flee or will they charge? If my neurons had eyes, they'd collectively roll them when they go for their weapons. How predictable.

How fun. At last.

Come, my darlings. Come and cast your nets and hooks.

And they do. Oh, they do! They branch out in forgotten pathways and my brain lights up like the night sky. They remember now: how to scan patterns, how to reach out where tendons adhere to bone, where capillaries conjoin to form arteries, where muscle builds cradles for soft organs. Eyes, close now. Vision is so overrated. I don't need it. I smell the mix of blood and piss and shit and fear. Rip out intestines. Squeeze hearts until they pop. Crush kidneys and spleens. Every pain receptor, every nerve becomes a harp on which I play my battle hymn, until I stand alone in a garden of blood and guts.

Me. And Jackson.

He's still on his knees, scramping about for the blade he dropped when I plucked out his eyes. His lips a tight line—tough Dude. Old soldier tough. Murderer tough. He won't scream like the band of bastards who bullied an old woman for car parts and electronics.

Not yet.

"How?" Stubborn little worm. He still wants to know.

"You left me for dead. I wasn't."

I remember everything now. Rosie doesn't. And I wish I didn't either. I remember the strain of my neurons to mend every cut and fracture. Days, weeks it took me to crawl out from my hiding place in the woods. My man nothing but wild dogs' leftovers by then. His corpse light to carry, his grave easy to dig. But not before I tried, starved and wounded, to mend his mauled flesh, each failure a stab through my heart.

Oh, how the memory of his name still hurt! How I wish I could disassemble every last nerve that holds his memory so the pain would stop! But I dare not. I will not.

Not yet.

"All I did was my job. My duty. You know of duty, don't you?" There's a hint of defiance in his voice. How cute, to think he can talk his way out of *this*.

"Was it your duty to kill farmers? Or was it to smother farmers' wives in their beds?"

"We were told…We had intel…" He stumbles on words that have little meaning, about the Purge after the War, about the head-hunters of those who'd been cast in the role of scapegoats in yet another of humankind's tragedies. He presents himself as a mere player, one of the chorus, who only followed orders.

Right. They gave expensive, sophisticated night vision implants to mere soldiers? How unlikely. How trite. How boring. When his torrent of excuses makes Missus Scar itchy again, I break every bone in his hands, one by one.

He screams. Between cries and curses, he fixes his empty sockets at me. "Where was it? I looked for it, after…"

Of course he did. Blood calls to blood and rewired neurons need their implants. My scar ached for hers. His should, too, and he'd be drawn back to the place he lost it, sooner or later. I knew—I hoped—he would and I made Rosie wait for him. And despite the beatings and the abuse, Rosie did.

Poor Rosie.

"Oh, wouldn't you like to know?" He'd caught me asleep, my neurons starved of glucose in the small hours of the night, and then unfocused by the lack of oxygen when he shoved the pillow onto my face. During the struggle, I reached for his eyes and clawed out his chip with both hands and neurons. He smashed my jaw in pained rage and pried my clenched fists open to get it back. Then, he threw me down and ripped the bed apart. But he didn't find it. With my last conscious thought I carved a cradle for the chip within my palm. There it nested until I placed it in that little pouch.

Until today.

His jaw tightens. He knows he's about to die. But he's tough. He'll take it like the tough man he is.

Or so he thinks, the poor, deluded fool.

I miss my purples; they mattered once, my sigils and regalia, until the war robbed all dignity from my order. I slipped away into the shadows when my title became a burden, a cry to terrify both those deserving pain and those who didn't. And now, at this late hour, the words of the rituals rise in my throat and tickle the tip of my tongue to call my neurons back to service.

Back to torture.

And Jackson screams. I reach out to every nerve in his body, every pain receptor, and light them up. He screams, as if giving birth to countless monstrous children all at once. His innards shred and twist. He howls, all his toes shattered, as if stabbed against granite slabs, the toenails torn out one by one. He whimpers, begging for his kidneys to stop burning, countless sharp stones building up in his ureters, cutting through his bladder to be released. Every pain my tired mind can think of blooms in his body.

When he's hurt enough, I shall pull his throat out. But not before. How many hours of pain is a life worth? My old guy's life? The life I left behind when I tore apart countless neural pathways to become Rosie, harmless old Rosie? More than my fingers and more than my toes. More than all his blood cells that roll out of his eyes and nose and mouth to water my once-garden.

It's over now. My neurons beg to stop. They, too, are old and tired and want to go to bed now. Death is easy — always was. Just a nudge at a heart that's been long ready, at a brain that darkened hours ago.

Silence now. All dead. It is over.

Silence, and gnarled hands covered in blood, my sackcloth dress crimson instead of once-purple, and trembling knees that want to rest. Too many deaths, too much pain and torture and the burden of a life that should have been a blessing but became a curse. None of us should have had our neurons awakened to such power. We didn't have the hearts to match it. And now, it's time for the last of the sarcomancers to retire into oblivion.

It's time for Rosie to return. For good. Harmless, senile Rosie.

Brave Rosie.

Wake up, Rosie, and stop sniffling. You know what to do now. Missus Scar awaits. Rip it apart, as you did once before. It will hurt less this time, I promise. Your neurons won't scream as they fall back to simpler patterns.

Toss your chip in the fire. While you still know why.

There. All better now.

There you go. Settle by the fire that still burns, by the pot of chow that's still simmering. Straighten the cloth over your knees, like proper ladies do, in the presence of Dudes — even glass-eyed, gutted Dudes.

It's nice here. Smells funny, but nice. And quiet. And there's warmth. And chow. Them Dudes left their chow and fell down? They left *good* chow? Well. Shame to waste good chow. Happy tummy.

Happy Rosie.

ABOUT THE AUTHORS

KEN ALTABEF's historical fantasy novels are noted for vivid characters and powerful emotion. He is best known for the ALAANA'S WAY series which takes place in a unique fantasy world based on Inuit mythology. His critically acclaimed LADY CHANGELING TRILOGY features shapeshifting faeries, action, intrigue, and romance. Visit his website at www.KenAltabef.com.

MARIE DESJARDIN writes both humorous and dramatic science fiction, fantasy, and alternative history. Published works range from short stories to novels and screenplays. She is a *Story Quest* award winner and a finalist in the 2017 AnLab Readers' Choice Awards for *Analog* magazine. Marie delights in animals and the outdoors, learning new things, and traveling our wonderful world (nearly thirty countries so far). She resides in Colorado, where she hikes in the mountains when they're not on fire. Visit www.mariedesjardin.com or @mariedesjardin.

Born in New York City in 1957, **CELIA S. FRIEDMAN** discovered science fiction at age 12, and has been obsessed with it ever since. Her first novel, *In Conquest Born*, was published by DAW Books in 1986, and in 1996 she quit her job as a costume designer to write full time in Northern Virginia. To date she has published thirteen novels (including her acclaimed "Coldfire" Trilogy), various short fiction, and a White Wolf gaming resource. She is currently working on *This Virtual Night*, a follow-up work to her science fiction novel, *This Alien Shore*. You can find her on Quora and check out her web page at www.csfriedman.com. Her glasswork can be found at https://www.etsy.com/shop/glassfantasies.

ALEX GIDEON writes Dark Fantasy and generally horrific Science Fiction. His writing style can best be summed up by the phrase "and many people died". He enjoys exorcising, taking long walks on extraterrestrial beaches, relaxing demon hunting trips, and fishing for Old Ones. Read his questionably helpful posts on TheMillionWords.net, and follow him on Twitter @ AlexanderGideon.

FAITH HUNTER is the New York Times and USAToday bestselling author of the Jane Yellowrock series, the Soulwood series, and the Rogue Mage series, as well as the author of 16 thrillers under pen the names Gary Hunter and Gwen Hunter. She has 40+ books in print. Faith collects orchids and animal skulls, loves thunder storms, and writes. She likes to cook soup, bake homemade bread, garden, and run Class III whitewater rivers. She edits the occasional anthology and drinks a lot of tea. Some days she's a lady. Some days she ain't. For more, see www.faithhunter.net Facebook fan page: https://www.facebook.com/official.faith.hunter

D.B. JACKSON is the author of TIME'S CHILDREN and TIME'S DEMON, books I and II in the Islevale Cycle, as well as the novels and short stories of the Thieftaker Chronicles, a historical fantasy set in pre-Revolutionary Boston. As David B. Coe he has written epic fantasy, urban fantasy, and media tie-ins. He is best known for the Crawford Award-winning LonTobyn Chronicle. David has a Ph.D. in U.S. history from Stanford University. His books have been translated into a dozen languages. Find him at: http://www.DavidBCoe.com; http://www.dbjackson-author.com; http://twitter.com/davidbcoe; http://twitter.com/dbjacksonauthor.

GINI KOCH writes the fast, fresh and funny Alien/Katherine "Kitty" Katt series for DAW Books, the Necropolis Enforcement Files, and the Martian Alliance Chronicles. She also has a humor collection, Random Musings from the Funny Girl. As G.J. Koch she writes the Alexander Outland series, and she's made the most of multiple personality disorder by writing under a variety of other pen names as well, including Anita Ensal, Jemma Chase, A.E. Stanton, and J.C. Koch. She has stories featured in a variety of excellent anthologies, available now and upcoming, writing as all her various personalities. Reach her via: www.ginikoch.com.

STEPHEN LEIGH has professionally published thirty novels and over fifty short stories, both under his own name and the pen name S.L. Farrell. His most recent novel is A RISING MOON, a sequel to A FADING SUN (DAW Books/Penguin, November 2018). He also has a science fiction book in progress under contract to DAW Books. Steve's work has been nominated for and won awards within the sf/fantasy genre. He is also a frequent contributor to George RR Martin's WILD CARDS series.
Web site: http://www.stephenleigh.com
FaceBook: https://www.facebook.com/sleighwriter
Instagram: https://www.instagram.com/s.leigh.writer/
Dreamwidth: https://sleigh.dreamwidth.org

CHRISTINE LUCAS lives in Greece with her husband and a horde of spoiled animals. A retired Air Force officer and mostly self-taught in English, has had her work appear in several print and online magazines, including Daily Science Fiction, Cast of Wonders, Pseudopod/Artemis Rising 4 and Nature: Futures. She was a finalist for the 2017 WSFA award and is currently working on her first novel. Visit her at: http://werecat99.wordpress.com/ ; https://www.facebook.com/Werecat99.

MISTY MASSEY is the author of *Mad Kestrel*, a rollicking adventure of magic on the high seas, and the long-awaited sequel, *Kestrel's Dance*. She is co-editor of *The Weird Wild West* and *Lawless Lands: Tales of the Weird Frontier*, and she's working on a series of Shadow Council novellas for Falstaff Press featuring the famous gunslinger Doc Holliday. When she's not writing, Misty studies and performs Middle Eastern dance. She's a sucker for good sushi, African coffee, and the darkest rum she can find. You can keep up with Misty at mistymassey.com, on Facebook and Twitter.

R.K. NICKEL works as a screenwriter in Los Angeles. His first feature film, *Bear with Us*, is available on Amazon Prime and DVD, and his second, "Stellar People" is slated to be released sometime soon. He dove into his prose journey in 2017 and since then has subjected unsuspecting readers to a fair number of his stories. When he's not writing, he's probably playing an escape room or some Magic the Gathering. Or drinking coffee. Mmm… coffee. For more, check out @russnickel on Twitter or go to www.rknickel.com.

EMILY RANDALL is a software developer who specializes in user-centered design and accessibility. They currently work for Google on one of the many Search teams, which is both exciting and rather nerve-wracking, but they can't imagine doing anything else. In their free time, they enjoy reading, running, hiking, and generally exploring the outdoors. They're also an avid larper and get much of their inspiration for writing from the stories that they play out in the games.

RHONDI SALSITZ rarely writes under her own name, claiming it's too difficult to pronounce, spell or remember, but this time is an exception. A long-time DAW author, she's used a number of pen names in several genres such as suspense thriller, fantasy, urban fantasy, science fiction, and romance, for audiences from ten to ninety. She writes regardless of various cat antics and family, travels whenever she can, and reads from dawn to midnight. Nothing is better than a good book, and she considers them to be her dragon hoard. She is thrilled to be writing in the Zombies Need Brains anthologies.

EDMUND R. SCHUBERT is the author of the novel, *Dreaming Creek*, and two short story collections, *The Trouble with Eating Clouds* and *This Giant Leap*. Schubert also contributed to and edited the non-fiction book, *How To Write Magical Words*. In addition to writing, Schubert served for ten years as editor of the online magazine, *InterGalactic Medicine Show*, (including publishing three IGMS anthologies and winning two WSFA Small Press Awards). Schubert insists, however, that his greatest accomplishment came during college, when his self-published underground newspaper made him the subject of a professor's lecture in abnormal psychology. He is expected to graduate with his MFA from Converse College in Spartanburg, SC in June 2019. He can be found at <u>edmundrschubert.com</u>.

ABOUT THE EDITORS

DAVID B. COE is the author of more than twenty novels and as many short stories. He has written epic fantasy – including the Crawford Award-winning LonTobyn Chronicle – contemporary urban fantasy, and media tie-ins.

As D.B. Jackson, he writes the Islevale Cycle (*Time's Children*, *Time's Demon*, *Time's Assassin*), a time travel/epic fantasy series from Angry Robot. He also writes the Thieftaker Chronicles, a historical urban fantasy set in pre-Revolutionary Boston.

David has a Ph.D. in U.S. history from Stanford University. His books have been translated into a dozen languages. *Temporally Deactivated* is his first foray into editing.

Find him at:
http://www.DavidBCoe.com
http://www.dbjackson-author.com
http://twitter.com/davidbcoe
http://twitter.com/dbjacksonauthor

* * *

JOSHUA PALMATIER is a fantasy author with a PhD in mathematics. He currently teaches at SUNY Oneonta in upstate New York, while writing in his "spare" time, editing anthologies, and running the anthology-producing small press Zombies Need Brains LLC. His most recent fantasy novel, *Reaping the Aurora,* concludes the fantasy series begun in *Shattering the Ley* and *Threading the Needle*, although you can also find his "Throne of Amenkor" series and the "Well of Sorrows" series still on the shelves. He is currently hard at work writing his next novel and designing the kickstarter for the next Zombies Need Brains anthology project. You can find out more at www.joshuapalmatier. com or at the small press' site www.zombiesneedbrains.com. Or follow him on Twitter as @bentateauthor or @ZNBLLC.

ACKNOWLEDGMENTS

This anthology would not have been possible without the tremendous support of those who pledged during the Kickstarter. Everyone who contributed not only helped create this anthology, they also helped solidify the foundation of the small press Zombies Need Brains LLC, which I hope will be bringing SF&F themed anthologies to the reading public for years to come . . . as well as perhaps some select novels by leading authors, eventually. I want to thank each and every one of them for helping to bring this small dream into reality. Thank you, my zombie horde.

The Zombie Horde: Colleen Champagne, Robert Coleman, Elena Beghetto, Mark Simon Phillips, Corey T, Sarah Cornell, Jenny Barber, Larisa LaBrant, Emma L, Jim Gotaas, Arturo, Lavinia Ceccarelli, Karen Thomas, Carol J. Guess, Meg Leader, Ian Harvey, Joseph Hoopman, John Green, Cyn Armistead, Jason S. Clary, John T. Sapienza, Jr., Carolyn C, Jen1701D, A.A. Jankiewicz, Santiago Akira Kitashima, windypenguin, Dr. Kai Herbertz, Michael Kohne, Pat Hayes, Joanne Burrows, Alan Smale, Sheryl R. Hayes,

Michael A. Burstein, Todd V. Ehrenfels, Kaiqua, Anonymous Reader, David Holden, Neil Clarke, Jaq Greenspon, Michael D'Auben, Eagle Archambeault, Kristi Chadwick, H Lynnea Johnson, John Winkelman, Studio 9 Games, Joe Hauser, Misty and Todd Lambert, Michele Fry, Shaun Kilgore, Regis M. Donovan, Steven Halter, Roger Simmons, Penny, Gabe Krabbe, Simon Dick, Chris Gerrib, Justin P. Miller, James Williams, Sachin Suchak, Mark Carter, Kelly Melnyk, Tory Shade, Harvey Brinda, Howard J. Bampton, Ivan Donati, Cheryl Preyer, Michael Halverson, Sean Collins, Kiya Nicoll, GMarkC, Michael Fedrowitz, Sharon Wood, David Zurek, Stephanie Lucas, Glori Medina, Jakub Narębski, Jörg Tremmel, Andrew Hatchell, Stephanie Cranford, Susan Oke, Sidney Whitaker, Engel Dreizehn, Andrea Terdik, John Markley, Amber Bryant, Meagan Pledger, Ian Chung, Pam Blome, Sebastian Müller, Cody Black, James Moriarty, Judith Mortimore, Karina Kolb, Ronda Sanders, Chrysta Stuckless, Mark Kiraly, Michelle Palmer, Craig Hackl, Beth Kampa, David Perkins, Brendan Burke, Carl Wiseman, Andrija Popovic, Anna Rudholm, Beth Lobdell, Cat Wyatt, Chad Bowden, Kevin Kibelstis, Patricia Gates, Scarlett Eisenhauer, Molly J., Robert Gilson, Grant Canterbury, Tina and Byron Connell, Rob Fowler, Michelle T., Darrell Z. Grizzle, L.C., Gabriel Cruz, Vicki Greer, Russell Martens, Samantha T., Ron Oakes, Ben Nash, Miranda Floyd, Wolf SilverOak, Tommy Acuff, John Senn, Kevin Winter, Cat Girczyc, Pat Knuth, Betsy, Claire Sims, Jeremy Audet, Whitney Gutierrez, Christine Hale, James Conason, Andy Pfrimmer, Wendy Cornwall, Barde Press, Mark Slauter, Jo Good, Tina Nichols, Myca Arcangel, Chloe Nagle, Tasha Turner, Sheelagh Semper, B. Keith Dunn, Jude, Jennifer Berk, Hoose Family, Nirven, Terry Williams, Leah Webber, Katherine Matthews, ChillieBrick, Jennifer Robinson, Jaymie Larkey Maham, Ian M. Fowler, Martina W., Brenda Rezk, Céline Malgen, Jennifer Priester, Cory Williams, Brendan Lonehawk, Tina Noe Good, Katherine Malloy, Margaret Bumby, Cheryl Losinger, andrew ahn and sin soracco, Pierre Gauthier, Susan Simko, Kate Barela, Colette Reap, Danan Bradley, Steve Lord, Götz Weinreich, Scott Raun, William Leisner, Scott Drummond,

Julie Kovac, Kristine Smith, Michael Stearns, Veronica Kavanagh, Tim Jordan, Debbie Matsuura, Rick McKnight, Nick W, Josie Ryan, Cathy Green, A.Chatain, Toni Lichtenstein Bogolub, Brad Roberts, Stephen Ballentine, Melanie McCoy, Jamieson Cobleigh, Anne Burner, Lutz F. Krebs, Francesca, Jillian and Doug Zeigler, Peggy J, eric priehs, Christine Ethier, Patti Short, Colbey, R.J.H, Mary Alice Wuerz, Helen, Robert Claney, Gina Freed, K. Hodghead, Clariben Huntington, Ginger Field, Katrina Coll, Leila Qışın, Amanda Nixon, Tom Powers, Charles Budworth, RKBookman, Jenni P., Leonie Duane, Brian D Lambert, Dagmar Baumann, Gavran, Michele Hall, Graeme, C. L. Werner, Andrew J Clark IV, jjmcgaffey, Anne M. Rindfliesch, Gary Phillips, Stacey Kaye Manuel, Andrea Watson, Abby Kieser, Aysha Rehm, Angie Hogencamp, Elizabeth Klandrud, Annalise M., Taryn, Peter Thew, Mark Newman, Tim Jones, Donna Gaudet, Michael Kahan, Craig "Stevo" Stephenson, T.D. England, Mark Hirschman, Niall Gordon, Jerrie the filkferengi, Sheryl Ehrlich, Edward Ellis, A. Eddy, Elektra Hammond, Uncle Batman, Sean and Catherine Kane, Gail Morse, Sarah Klapper-Lehman, Erik T Johnson, Bonnie Stewart, Eleanor Russell, Amanda Hudson, Kerry aka Trouble, Stephanie Slavin, Kristin Coley, Rebecca M, Koen Andrews, Matthew Aronoff, Rachel Shell Vance, Evergreen Lee, Margaret St. John, Jonathan S. Chance, Mark Lukens, Jenn Whitworth, Yankton Robins, Carl Dershem, Erin Himrod, L. E. Doggett, Andrew Foxx, Ruth Duggan, Jonathan, Greg Vose, Danny Dyer, Beckey and Steve Sanchez, Shirley, Jesse N. Klein, Meg Fielding, Guy W. Thomas, Chantelle Wilson, Linda Pierce, Alexander Smith, Jason Tongier, Brenda Moon, Nathan Turner, Anthony R. Cardno, Catherine Gross-Colten, SusanB, compiledwrong, SwordFire, Amelia Smith, Chris Brant, David Rowe, Michael Bernardi, Kayla Sinclair, Joe Stech, Ronald H. Miller, James Lucas, Barbara Matzner-Volfing, Natascha McGilvray, Louise Lowenspets, Mark Featherston, Deanna Harrison, Phillip Spencer, Susan Carlson, Liz Tuckwell, rissatoo, Brent Johnson, Duncan's Books and More, Chris Matosky, Matt Hope, Mervi Mustonen, Kerry Ebanks, Michelle Brenner, Karen the Griffmom, Sarina McKown-Goh, K.

R. Smith, Gretchen Persbacker, Camille Lofters, Andrew and Kate Barton, Q Fortier, Sally Qwill Janin, Paul Alex Gray, Kitty Likes, Chris, Carol Mammano, Lisa Howard, Rolf Laun, H. Rasmussen, Sharan Volin, Lace, Elisabeth Bender, Frank Nissen, Steven Mentzel, William Hall, R. Hunter, Deirdre Murphy, Simba, Lisa Rich, Kathryn Haines, Mary Hargrove, Charissa Weaks, Marty Poling Tool, Dan R. Herrick, Chris McLaren, Curtis Frye, Nancy M. Tice, Elizabeth, Carla Hollar, Olivia Montoya, Paul McErlean, Sarah Eyermann, Amy Rogers, Deborah Torrance, Mark Manning, Barbara Silcox, C. Joshua Villines, NewGuyDave, Kevin Niemczyk, Max Kaehn, OgreM, Kixie K. Nowell, Ichino, Chloe Turner, Robby Thrasher, Yosen Lin, Tanya K., Daniel O., Caitlin Mininger, A.J. Abrao, Louisa Swann, Fred and Mimi Bailey, John H. Bookwalter Jr., Kevin Looney, Alex Shvartsman, Mom, Alyssa Hillary, Isaac 'Will It Work' Dansicker, Steven Howell Wilson, James McIntosh, Axisor, Olav Rokne, Michael M. Jones, Jason Palmatier, Belkis Marcillo, Elaine Costa, Jennifer Dunne, Mud Mymudes, Jules Jones, Melissa Shumake, laura robbins, Julie Holderman, Lizard L., Cliff Winnig, Rhiannon Raphael, Cherie Livingston, Amanda S., Tom B., D-Rock, Y. H. Lee, Kristin Evenson Hirst, Tibs, Linda, Keith E. Hartman, R Kirkpatrick, Yaron Davidson, H. Kriesel, Mike M, Elaine Tindill-Rohr, Kathryn Allen, Cat Rambo, Walter Prawak, Kayliealien, Crystal Sarakas, Elizabeth Gray, Lynn Kramer, Michelle Botwinick, Sharon Sayegh, Becky Allyn Johnson, Tom Berrisford, Erin Penn, Taylor Alcantar, Shawn Blackhawk, Missy Katano

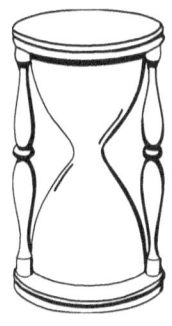

Also Available from ZNB!

Temporally Out of Order

It's frustrating when a gadget stops working. But what if the gadget is working fine, it's just "temporally" out of order? What would you do if you discovered your cell phone linked you to a different time? Or that your camera took pictures of the past?
In this collection, seventeen leading science fiction authors share their take on what happens when gadgets run temporally amok. From past to future, humor to horror, there's something for everyone.

Join Seanan McGuire, Elektra Hammond, David B. Coe, Chuck Rothman, Faith Hunter, Edmund R. Schubert, Steve Ruskin, Sofie Bird, Laura Resnick, Amy Griswold, Laura Anne Gilman, Susan Jett, Gini Koch, Christopher Barili, Stephen Leigh, Juliet E. McKenna, and Jeremy Sim as they investigate how ordinary objects behaving temporally out of order can change our everyday lives.

Also Available from ZNB!

Alien Artifacts

What might we run into as we expand beyond Earth and into the stars? As we explore our own solar system and beyond, it seems inevitable that we'll run into aliens … and what they've left behind. Alien artifacts: what might they reveal about us as we try to unlock their secrets? What might they reveal about the universe?

In this anthology, nineteen of today's leading science fiction and fantasy authors explore how discovering long lost relics of alien civilizations might change humanity. Join Walter H. Hunt, Julie Novakova, David Farland, Angela Penrose, S.C. Butler, Gail Z. Martin & Larry N. Martin, Juliet E. McKenna, Sharon Lee & Steve Miller, Andrija Popovic, Jacey Bedford, Sofie Bird, James Van Pelt, Gini Koch, Anthony Lowe, Jennifer Dunne, Coral Moore, Daniel J. Davis, C.S. Friedman, and Seanan McGuire as they discover the stars and the secrets they may hold—both dark and deadly and awe-inspiring.

Also Available from ZNB!

Were-

Werewolves rule the night in urban fantasy, but everyone knows there are other were-creatures out there just as dangerous and deadly, if not as common, each with their own issues as they struggle to fit into—or prey upon—society. What about the were-goats?
The were-crows and were-wasps?

Here are seventeen stories of urban fantasy by today's leading science fiction and fantasy authors that introduce you to some of those other were-creatures, the ones hiding in the dark background shadows, waiting to bite. Join Seanan McGuire, Ashley McConnell, Susan Jett, Eliora Smith, David B. Coe, April Steenburgh, Gini Koch, Mike Barretta, Elizabeth Kite, Danielle Ackley-McPhail, Jean Marie Ward, Katharine Kerr, Sarah Brand, Anneliese Belmond, Faith Hunter, Patricia Bray, and Phyllis Ames as they take you into the hidden corners of our world to see some lesser known were-creatures. You may want to bring along some silver … just in case.

Also Available from ZNB!

All Hail Our Robot Conquerors!

RRRAWRRR!!! ZZZZZZTTTTT!!! ZZZZAAAAPPPPP!!!

The robots of the 50s and 60s science fiction movies and novels captured our hearts and our imaginations. Their clunky, bulbous bodies with their clear domed heads, whirling antennae, and randomly flashing lights staggered ponderously across the screen and page and into our souls—whether as a constant companion or as the invading army threatening to exterminate our world. We can never return to that innocent time, where the robot overlords could be identified by their burning red eyes or our trusty robot sidekick would warn us instantly of danger—

Or can we?

With a touch of nostalgia and a little tongue-in-cheek humor, here are fifteen stories from today's leading science fiction and fantasy authors that take us back to the time of evil robot overlords, invading armies, and not-quite-trustworthy mechanical companions. Join Julie E. Czerneda, Brandon Daubs, Tanya Huff, Brian Trent, L.E. Modesitt, Jr., Jason Palmatier, Jez Patterson, Gini Koch, Lauren Fox, Sharon Lee & Steve Miller,
Philip Brian Hall, Rosemary Edghill, R. Overwater, Helen French, and Seanan McGuire as we step into the future with a nod to the past. Hold on to those stun guns. You may need them!

Also Available from ZNB!

The Death of All Things

Lie.
Cheat.
Bargain.
Fight.
Accept.
Bribe.
Conquer.
Evade.

No matter what humanity tries, Death always wins. Or does it?

Discover the answer in The Death of All Things, where twenty-two writers take their shot at the Grim Reaper with explorations of the mythical, fantastical, and futuristic bonds between life and death. Learn the cost of mortality, the perils—and joys—of the afterlife, and the potential pitfalls of immortality …

Featuring stories from: K. M. Laney, Andrea Mullen, Faith Hunter, Kendra Leigh Speedling, Jason M. Hough, Julie Pitzel, Shaun Avery, Christie Golden, Leah Cutter, Aliette de Bodard, Andrew Dunlop, Juliet E. McKenna, A. Merc Rustad, Ville Meriläinen, Amanda Kespohl, Mack Moyer, Fran Wilde, Kathryn McBride, Andrija Popovic, Jim C. Hines, Stephen Blackmoore, and Kiya Nicoll.

Also Available from ZNB!

Submerged

Everyone has their eyes set on the black depths of space ... but what about the deep abysses of the ocean? What dark monsters swim unseen beneath the waves? What ancient wonders lie hidden, waiting to be discovered? What sirens call, either here on Earth or in the icy waters of a far off planet ... or even at the bottom of a wine glass? So much remains to be explored below the surface, where light fades and the pressure kills.

Here are seventeen stories from today's leading science fiction and fantasy authors that take us into those depths, whether we want to or not. Join Seanan McGuire, Michael Robertson, Esther Friesner, F. Brett Cox, Wendy Nikel, Marsheila Rockwell & Jeffrey J. Mariotte, Jody Lynn Nye, Bill Kte'pi, Jenna Rhodes, Susan Jett, James Van Pelt, J.C. Koch, Misty Massey, A. Merc Rustad, David Farland, Sara M. Harvey, and Nicky Drayden as they explore unfathomable trenches, underwater volcanoes, and abyssal plains. Take the plunge ... into the Deep End!

Also Available from ZNB!

The Razor's Edge

One man's insurgent is another man's freedom fighter…

From The Moon is a Harsh Mistress to The Hunger Games, everyone enjoys a good rebellion. There is something compelling about a group (or individual) who throws caution to the wind and rises up in armed defiance against oppression, tyranny, religion, the government—you name it. No matter the cause, or how small the chance, it's the courage to fight against overwhelming odds that grabs our hearts and has us pumping our fists in the air.

Win or lose, it's the righteous struggle we cherish, and those who take up arms for a cause must walk The Razor's Edge between liberator and extremist. With stories by Blake Jessop, William C. Dietz, D.B. Jackson, Gerald Brandt, Sharon P. Goza, Walter H. Hunt, Sharon Lee & Steve Miller, Kay Kenyon, Steve Perry, Seanan McGuire, Christopher Allenby, Chris Kennedy, L.E. Modesitt, Jr., Alex Gideon, Brian Hugenbruch, and Y.M. Pang.